# HOW THE LIGHT GETS IN

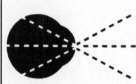

This Large Print Book carries the
Seal of Approval of N.A.V.H.

# HOW THE LIGHT GETS IN

## JOLINA PETERSHEIM

**THORNDIKE PRESS**
A part of Gale, a Cengage Company

Farmington Hills, Mich • San Francisco • New York • Waterville, Maine
Meriden, Conn • Mason, Ohio • Chicago

Thorndike Press® Large Print Christian Romance.
The text of this Large Print edition is unabridged.
Other aspects of the book may vary from the original edition.
Set in 16 pt. Plantin.

LIBRARY OF CONGRESS CIP DATA ON FILE.
CATALOGUING IN PUBLICATION FOR THIS BOOK
IS AVAILABLE FROM THE LIBRARY OF CONGRESS

ISBN-13: 978-1-4328-6628-0 (hardcover alk. paper)

Published in 2019 by arrangement with Tyndale House Publishers, Inc.

Printed in Mexico
1 2 3 4 5 6 7 23 22 21 20 19

*To my three daughters —*
*Miss A, Miss M, and Miss E.*
*May you always see how the light gets in.*

# ACKNOWLEDGMENTS

*How the Light Gets In,* like all my novels, has been years in the making. Thoughts drop into my mind like rainwater into a bucket, until that bucket finally tips and the words pour out. Many people have helped fill that metaphorical bucket. First, I want to thank Uncle Ralph Petersheim for sharing that newspaper article about the Wisconsin cranberry farmer who used old-fashioned equipment. That snippet laid the foundation for Elam's livelihood and life.

I also want to thank the resilient, hardworking women of Wisconsin who taught me so much in the time I was there: Aunt Sheila Petersheim, Aunt Stacy Petersheim, Heather Petersheim, Justine Petersheim, Elisa Shaw, Hannah Petersheim, Marissa Kendhammer, Tamara Rutten, Jessica Rogers, and the late Kelly Baird. From inviting us for meals to taking walks and talking about faith, each of you has a special place in my heart.

I would like to thank Dale and Candy Toltzman for supporting our family while we lived in Wisconsin. I will never forget when you, Dale, came to the hospital and sat there for hours until Randy came out of surgery, or how you visited our farmhouse after he came home. In a short time, you transitioned from pastor to friend, and I will forever be grateful for the key part you played in my faith journey.

I am grateful for my Tyndale team, who shows this slow writer unending patience: Karen Watson, Stephanie Broene, and Kathy Olson. Thank you for pushing me to create fiction based on Truth.

Thank you, Wes Yoder, for your support and friendship. Hard to believe six years have passed since we stood in a lobby talking about Root's Market and shoofly pie.

Thank you to Misty Adams for encouraging me to read this story aloud while sitting in a coffee shop. You are always my listener. I love you for that.

I am grateful for my parents, Beverly and Merle Miller, and my in-laws, Betty and Richard Petersheim. I value and love you more the longer I am alive.

Thank you to my daughters — Miss A, Miss M, and Miss E — for teaching me about the beauty of unconditional love, and that making memories is more important than having a clean house.

Thank you to my husband for his strength, loyalty, and love. We could never have anticipated our life story while we stood beneath that gazebo, saying our custom vows, on that Indian summer day. But I'm so glad we did it. There's no one I would rather go through "for better or for worse, for richer or for poorer, in sickness and in health" with than you. I love you more now than I did back then, and I know a lot of that is because we have walked through so much together. You are my best friend and the love of my life.

Finally, but not finally, I want to thank Jesus for revealing his love to me more during this year than any other. For showing himself faithful, for healing the broken places within me, for teaching me how to love with a more perfect love. Everything I am is because of you. I love you more now than I did when we first met, and I know a lot of that is because we have also walked through so much together. Thank you for never leaving my side.

# PART 1

# PART 1

# CHAPTER 1

The caskets were closed, of course. No flowers adorned them. No flowers were even in the church, but cool morning light fell through the windows, warming the hardwood floor and pews. The Physicians International staff member who had called to break the news to Ruth had promised there'd been no suffering. From this, Ruth inferred there'd not been much of her husband's body left to collect.

Later news articles confirmed the bombing the hospital had endured. Women and children had died; her husband and father-in-law were among the staff members killed. Ruth spent days afterward googling the bombing until her mother deemed she was obsessing over something that couldn't be changed. It infuriated Ruth at the time, but now she saw the wisdom of her mother's decision to turn off the Wi-Fi for ten hours each day, though the doling out of "wisdom" could have been accomplished with more tact.

Presently, seven weeks later, two-year-old Vivienne had no clue her father's cremated remains were scattered in a plain pine box at the front of the church. She had no clue he had even died. But her six-year-old sister, Sofie, was old enough to understand. When Ruth sat on the packed sand beside her and told her the news, Sofie hadn't cried, or even acted like she'd heard, but took a small piece of driftwood and threw it into the ocean, which the dog, Zeus, had run into the surf to fetch. However, since then, Sofie hadn't laughed, played, or spoken in more than toneless monosyllables, and those were all to basic questions — "Are you hungry? Thirsty? Do you need a nap?" — that Ruth had asked and to which Sofie had begrudgingly replied.

Because of this, Ruth wasn't about to let Sofie just sit there, stripping her cuticles off with her teeth while her brown eyes studied everything, as if trying to understand why her father's death so closely resembled her Irish grandpa's: everyone wearing black in a strange church where few congregants cried but most looked like they wanted to. Ruth, trying to distract her, dug into the tote she'd packed with the pretzels, cookies, and snack mixes they'd accumulated during yesterday's endless flights. She'd also packed Pull-Ups and wipes, a coloring book and crayons, and a change of clothes in case the upheaval of the past few days (not to mention weeks and months) caused toddler Vi to forget she was potty-trained.

Ruth could never have anticipated needing a diaper bag at her husband's funeral, and yet there were many things about her thirty years she could never have anticipated.

Ruth opened the zipper compartment and pulled out her iPhone. Switching it to silent, she pressed the YouTube app so Sofie could watch *Paw Patrol.* But then she remembered: her phone was not picking up a signal. Cell phone service was spotty in this Mennonite community in Wisconsin. There was barely running water. Late last night, after the girls finally settled enough to sleep, Ruth had stood under the farmhouse's lime-encrusted showerhead, eager for another cathartic cry — the shower was the only place she felt safe enough to let herself feel — and discovered that the water came out as a lukewarm drizzle. It could never muffle her sobs, so she held them in until her chest hurt.

Ruth pressed the photos app and passed

the phone to Sofie, allowing her to scroll through the pictures until the funeral wrapped up. Mabel glanced over as her granddaughter's tiny index finger expertly slid over the pictures and tapped the play button to watch the short video clips interspersed throughout. Ruth wasn't sure if her mother-in-law approved, but Ruth didn't really care if she did. Ruth did not want to bury her husband in Wisconsin. Therefore, she already resented the land and the extended family, who were so plentiful she didn't feel her single voice carried any weight. She wanted Chandler buried in Ireland, where she and her girls could visit him each day. And yet, was her parents' old stone house truly her home?

The surprisingly young bishop read from the Psalms: *"Der Herr ist meine Stärke und mein Schild; auf ihn hofft mein Herz, und mir ist geholfen."*

The funeral service was being conducted in both German and English. Ruth suspected that the latter translation was mainly for her benefit, since she was among the few non-Mennonites in attendance. But there was no need. The only way Ruth was going to survive the next few hours — and days, for that matter — was by blocking it all out. Otherwise, her shield of self-preservation would crack, and she doubted she could get herself back together if it did.

Ruth glanced down at her Fitbit and saw two hours had passed since she'd come into the church with her children. Her tights itched, and her eyelids felt heavy, which filled her with guilt.

How could she be fighting sleep at her husband's funeral? But she knew this fight stemmed from acute exhaustion, and from the fact there'd been few times over the past six months she'd allowed herself to sit still, because stillness meant something wasn't getting done, and focusing on getting something done kept her from having too much time to think.

And then, piercing the droning quiet, Ruth heard her dead husband's voice: an audible apparition. "Hey there, girly girls," he said. "I hope you're being good for your mama. It's a hot day —" Ruth was so stunned, she was unable to correlate that Chandler's voice was not in her head but coming from her phone. Mouth dry, she glanced at her daughter's lap. The screen framed Chandler's familiar face. Ruth reached for it, and Sofie looked up — eyes flashing — and wrenched the phone back. All the while, the simple, now otherworldly, message continued to play: "I'm looking

17

forward to seeing you again. It won't be long now."

Ruth finally got the phone away and Sofie screamed, *"No!"*

The sound reverberated off the church's whitewashed walls, echoing just as the a cappella hymn "The City of Light" had earlier as she and her daughters filed past the caskets.

Ruth's cheeks burned with humiliation and grief.

In the center of her lap, just as it had been in her daughter's, was Chandler's face: his dark beard, his dark skin, his dark eyes, so that he blended in with both the Colombian and Afghani cultures. His coloring was clearly passed down through Mabel, who looked more Native American than Mennonite, most of whom, Ruth knew, were German or Swiss.

*I miss you,* Ruth thought, and the realization surprised her as much as hearing her dead husband's voice coming from her phone.

How could she miss a man who'd been parted from her for so long? For, yes, absence did make the heart grow fonder, but then, after a while, that shield of self-preservation grew thicker, and the heart forsook fondness for survival and all-

18

consuming love for getting by. Ruth felt that she hadn't truly missed her dead husband in four of their five years of marriage. And sometimes, when she'd missed Chandler the most, he'd been sitting in the same room.

*Six Years Earlier*
*June 7, 2012*

Dear Chandler,

I received your letter today and immediately wanted to hop on a plane and adopt Sofie myself, but my parents are adamant that I am neither mature enough nor financially stable enough to consider it. Have you ever moved back in with your parents after living on your own (or at least in a dorm) for many years? It is not easy, and since I am their only child — granted, like Abraham and Sarah, when they least expected it — I find they are even more protective of me.

I have rebelled against this protection all my life, which is partly why, after college, I was so drawn to Children's Haven. Bogotá's crime rate alone about made my parents drop dead from fright. They jointly declared, "Ruth! Don't be so obtuse. You'll be kidnapped within a fortnight!" (And, yes, my English profes-

19

sor parents still use words like obtuse and fortnight.)

But then, to my surprise, I found that Colombia was beautiful: the mountains' temperate coolness; the clean lines of uniformed children — the ribbons in the girls' hair, the stark-white kneesocks beneath their pleated skirts — as they crossed the sunlit courtyard to the classrooms; the sense of well-being I felt as I understood I was making a difference in orphans' lives.

I will never forget the day the staff took a trip to Guatavita, and how I suddenly had the impulse to purchase the red silk shawl I'd seen at one of the vendors' booths. The rest of you were loading up in the bus, but I turned and quickly cut back through the crowd with pesos jangling in the knit bag banging against my hip, and little did I know that you took off after me.

What a sight we must've made, as you wove through the chaos, looking so much like them, while I, obviously, did not. I was purchasing the shawl from the woman with the wrinkled, apple-doll face when I looked up and saw you, standing there with your hands on your knees as you tried to catch your breath.

I do apologize for taking off like that, but it was worth it, at least on my end. I have loved that red silk shawl ever since.

Fondly yours,<br>Ruth

Elam awoke before the sun and walked out of his house into the fields. The smell of peat from the cranberry bog rose around him. He thought about all the leaves that had fallen off the ring of silver birches and sifted down through the bog's layers of sand. The sedimentary nature reminded him of the funeral last week, and that he only had half his life left to leave his mark before he too fell like a leaf to the ground. But Elam wasn't melancholy today. In fact, he was far from it. He loved the beginning of harvest season, when his usually predictable — and, if truth be told, rather mundane — existence transformed into an adrenaline-fueled race against the clock.

The fog rolled in across the land like an opaque carpet. This subtle transition was Elam's favorite part of morning, when everything was quiet and there was nothing for him to say or do. Elam walked along the edge of the bog, checking on the ripe red fruit hidden like treasure beneath the plants. He knelt and cupped a few in his hand.

Moisture from the dew beaded on his maimed finger. Cranberries, such tiny things, had taken up the better part of his thirty-nine years.

He would need to wait at least another month if he were dry harvesting it all like he had last year — walking the picker through the fields and laboriously gathering the pounds of fruit to sell to local grocery stores and markets. But Driftless Valley Farm's new contract with Ocean Spray allowed for wet harvesting. The cranberries didn't have to be perfect because they were going to be turned into juice, jelly, and sauce. In two days, Elam would pump water from the lakes and channels into the fields until the water rose a foot. His father had crafted the bogs to absorb the flood without being ruined, but each harvest Elam marveled that the delicate plants survived.

Elam and Tim were supposed to meet at the pumphouse at eight. Elam glanced at the flat band of horizon and gauged he had an hour until it was truly light. Elam walked back across the field, his prematurely silver hair brushing his shirt collar. A light shone through the kitchen windows. He moved toward it, his empty coffee mug dangling from his hand. He went up the front steps and saw Ruth sitting at the table, staring out at the predawn dark.

Elam paused, his right boot on the porch step's third riser, unsure if he should just stay outside until either Mabel awoke or it was time to meet Tim. But the kerosene light magnified the weary slant of Ruth's shoulders, as the shadows magnified the shadows beneath her eyes.

Just as Elam couldn't stay silent, even though he hated what it took for him to speak, he also could not stand outside while a family member appeared so forlorn.

Elam's heart pounded and mouth went dry as he entered his own house. He felt so out of place, having someone else invading his privacy, and yet he told himself Ruth must feel even worse. She didn't look up. He stood at the entrance, gripping the coffee cup, and suddenly looked down at the floor, remembering how Ruth had cleaned it on her hands and knees after supper last night. Setting the mug on the buffet table, he knelt to untie his boots.

The sound of the ceramic striking the tin covering the cabinet — where Elam's dead mother, Marta, had once rolled out her pies — seemed to rouse Ruth.

"Good morning," she said. Her voice sounded hoarse.

Elam nodded. "Good morning."

23

He peeled off his boots, picked up his mug, and padded in socked feet across the kitchen. Marta was probably turning in her grave to see Ruth's huge white dog snoring beneath her table. But Ruth's six-year-old, Sofie, wouldn't enter the house unless the dog entered too and, for hours, had kept her arm wrapped around the dog's shaggy mane and glared at Elam beneath her bangs, as if challenging him to take away her living, breathing security blanket.

So he obviously had not suggested the dog should stay in the barn.

Refilling his coffee, Elam glanced at the stove and saw a plate of fried potatoes and eggs. The brown eggshells were cracked and piled beside the cast-iron skillet. The tin salt and pepper shakers were still out; some of the granules had spilled across the butcher-block countertop.

Ruth said, "Sorry. I was in the middle of cleaning up, but . . . I got a call."

"No problem," Elam said gently. "I . . . I'm glad you're making yourself at home."

"There's enough for you, too, if you want it."

Elam paused. "What about your girls?"

She smiled slightly. "They don't like eggs."

He looked back at her. There was nothing on the table except for her phone. Ruth's head leaned forward, her wavy hair parted over her shoulders, so he could easily see the round nodules of her spine. She was too thin. "Have you eaten?" he asked.

Ruth shook her head. "You go ahead."

It didn't seem right, though, for Elam to sit across from such a sad person while eating the food she had prepared. He took two plates out of the cupboard and set them on the counter. He used the flipper to scoop the eggs and potatoes and set a portion on each plate. He carried the plates over to the table, and as he did, he debated on where to sit. To sit across from Ruth seemed too intimate. To sit at the far end of the table seemed too withdrawn. Most people wouldn't think twice about where to sit, but most people were not Elam Albrecht, who overthought everything when it came to social interaction. After a moment, he chose to sit on the opposite side of the table, but one chair over so Ruth wouldn't have to look at him with those disconcerting eyes. His foot brushed the dog. Moving his chair back, he slid one of the plates over to her.

Ruth looked up at him, as if surprised. "Thanks," she said.

He didn't say anything, just briefly bowed his head for grace and began shoveling in the food. He'd forgotten his coffee on the countertop but wasn't about to retrieve it because he didn't want to repeat the awkward squeezing of his large-boned body between the table and the wall. He'd never sat on this side of the table and so had never noticed there was not much space.

The dog snored. The faucet dripped. Elam's heart pounded. He'd sat at this table his entire life but had no idea what to do with his hands. He gripped the fork. "You . . . you . . ."

Ruth glanced over, and then away in deference when she noticed Elam's face growing red as he waited for the words to come. It wasn't a stutter that affected him. Sometimes Elam thought it'd be easier if it were. That way, the person listening would know more words were on the way and could patiently wait while he got them out. But his words seemed to get hung up somewhere between his brain and his mouth. When he was a boy, Miss Romaine — the middle-aged librarian who became his clandestine piano teacher — had said his voice box was merely locked, and music would be the key to get the words out. But Elam hadn't been out to the cabin for a long time, and he'd nearly forgotten how to speak through those smooth, black-and-white keys.

"You had a call?" There. He'd said it. Effortless.

But Ruth's mouth tightened, and he feared he'd overstepped his bounds. A few seconds passed. She shook her head and said, "Yes. I had a call. My mother called." She stared down at the plate of untouched food and exhaled heavily. "She has a buyer for Greystones."

Elam finished chewing. He poised his fork over another bite. When Ruth did not continue, he swallowed and asked, "What's Greystones?"

"My parents named their house after the city where I grew up, Greystones, because it's made of gray stone. Real creative, right?" She stabbed her fork in the egg. "My mom didn't even tell me she was putting it up for sale. I should've known, though," she said. "She was boxing up my father's things soon after he died."

"Where will your mother . . . ?"

"Live? I'm not sure. She'll probably buy a small house in town. I know it makes sense. She's seventy-five, and Greystones takes work. But I always thought I could go home again."

Elam looked across at her. Sometimes he dreamed about leaving his "family home." There were benefits to familiarity, he knew,

27

and yet he often found he was discontent with having neither experienced life nor taken risks, as his cousin had done. He didn't want to die in the same place he was born. "Could you and your girls move in with her?"

Ruth laughed. There was no humor in it. "My mom's not the grandma type. My girls are too much for her. We lived with her for six months before coming here. It did not go well."

"But you still want to move back?"

Ruth stared at her freckled hands. She twirled the loose wedding band on her finger, and the emerald reflected square prisms on the wall. "I don't know what I'm going to do, honestly. My home is no longer in Ireland, and my home's never been here."

She appeared so fragile, sitting there at his table with the first light — streaming through the yellowed curtain — patterning her face. Looking at her, Elam hated that she and her children should go through the grief he knew too well. Last Christmas, he'd sat at this same kitchen table while eating his staple supper of steak and eggs, and stared at the family picture Chandler had inserted into his annual support letter. He'd envied his first cousin for having a beautiful wife and daughters while he had almost no one. Now Chandler was dead; his wife and daughters were abandoned and nearly destitute, if it was true what Mabel had confided to him.

Elam didn't consider himself fluent in many ways, especially when it came to conveying matters of the heart, but he wished he could say more. He *yearned* for the ability to say more, such as that Chandler had loved Ruth deeply. But she must know that Elam and Chandler hadn't spoken very often in these ensuing years, and he didn't want to give her platitudes when she must've been receiving them in abundance from well-meaning people who didn't know how to handle grief. But he knew how to handle grief. Grief was best borne in silence.

Elam got up, worked his body around the table, chairs, and wall, and fetched a mug from the cupboard. The coffeepot was still warm. He brought a mug over to Ruth and went to the kerosene-powered fridge to retrieve a small container of French vanilla half-and-half. He sniffed it to make sure it was okay. His sister, Laurie, had purchased the creamer for him some time back. Horrified by the "masculine state" of his pantry and fridge, she had hired a driver to take her to town to supply him with what she considered necessities of life. Personally, he never cared for doctored coffee. He set the cream beside Ruth and then fetched the small pottery container of sugar with a wooden spoon. He worried he was turning into Laurie: trying to assuage life's woes with hot drinks and food. But then Ruth looked up — tears polishing her eyes — and smiled. "Thank you, Elam," she said. "You're kind."

*June 22, 2012*

Dear Ruth,

I am sorry for my slow reply. Children's Haven did another outreach on the mountain, where we discovered three more abandoned infants just as dehydrated and malnourished as Sofie was. Though their lungs were not as badly affected by the wood smoke and poor ventilation, I have literally been working around the clock to ensure that they are thriving. They are, I am relieved to say, and so here I sit in my scrubs, drinking quintessential Colombian coffee and writing to you. (Would my using 'quintessential' impress your professor parents? You should let them know, just in case.)

30

I can't help but smile while remembering that day in Guatavita. Janice had told me there were rumors of guerrilla activity, and I could so clearly picture you being snatched up for your pale skin and red hair. I am sure you would've been fine, in any case, and I am glad you purchased the shawl. I saw you wear it to graduation, and it was worth the risk.

As for living with parents: I haven't lived with mine since I too left for college when I was eighteen years old. After ten years, I can't imagine returning home. My parents, Chandler Senior and Mabel, are New Order Mennonite. I am not sure how familiar you are with the Anabaptist denomination, since there aren't as many communities in Ireland like there are in the States, but my parents are not the Old Order, horse-and-buggy type. They are car drivers, with electricity in their house, but my mom still wears a cape dress and prayer covering. I am the only one in my family who does not adhere to the Mennonite faith, but I do respect it.

My dad and I are especially close. He's been a doctor with Physicians International all my life, and he's the reason I decided to come here after medical school. I hope one day we can serve side by side. But that's down the road. For now, I can hear the teachers calling the children into the courtyard. Janice recently shared another rumor with me — which is only slightly less hazardous than guerrilla activity — and that is that we're having marshmallow and cabbage salad again with lunch. I noticed that every time this was served, you would look down at the end of the table until I had to come take your plate and eat what you couldn't. I am sure Chef José appreciated your thoughtfulness.

Your friend,
Chandler

Ruth needed to run. She'd been forced to give up running when the girls were little and it became too dangerous to be on the streets of Bogotá on her own. She remembered, though, the Saturday morning runs she used to take with her father: her rhythmic breaths mimicking the sea's inhalations; the mounting pain followed by the euphoria of pushing past her breaking point, tapping into that unseen strength, when her aching lungs and joints gave way to some primal force whose sole purpose was to send her body hurtling forward as fast as it could go.

Lately, she experienced that same primal urge to flee when she was standing still.

Ruth looked over at Sofie, asleep in the twin bed. Sweat curled her black hair, and she'd kicked the covers off, even though the drafty farmhouse had to be sixty degrees upstairs. Vi was asleep in the crib Elam had set up for them. Children could sleep anywhere.

Ruth wished she could be as oblivious of her surroundings.

She swung her feet over the side of the bed and almost stepped on Zeus, the clumsy Great Pyrenees who'd nonsensically claimed Ruth as master in the wake of her father's death. Moving around him, she went to her suitcase. Mabel had said she should make herself at home, but keeping her clothes in a suitcase was as normal to Ruth as keeping them in a drawer. She pulled on a fleece and a pair of nylon shorts over the Cuddl Duds she'd worn to bed. She found her tennis shoes and laced them up. Her hair still in a topknot, she walked down the hall toward Mabel's room. She knocked lightly and heard a muffled grunt. She paused, unsure if this was an invitation or a subtle hint to go away. Ruth was about to turn when the door opened. Mabel stood behind it. Her thick black hair — not a strand of silver visible — hung down over her night-gown, but the middle part was firmly fixed from so many years of being trained into a bun.

Mabel modestly bunched her nightgown around her throat, though it was as revealing as a potato sack. "Everything all right?" she asked. Dreams had thickened her tongue.

"Oh, yeah," Ruth said. "Sorry. Thought you'd be up."

Mabel waved a hand. "No trouble. I've just been having a hard time getting to sleep."

"I've been having a hard time too." Ruth paused. "Would you mind if I went for a quick run? The girls should stay sleeping for another hour."

"Sure, I don't mind at all." But then Mabel's dark eyes — so much like Chandler's — scanned Ruth's ensemble. "Is this what you wear?"

Ruth looked down at her leggings. "It's not appropriate?"

Mabel thought. *"Jah,"* she said, finally. "But what do you want to *run* for?"

Ruth's mouth tipped. "Stress relief."

"It's stressful for you to be here?"

Ruth looked down. "I'd be stressed any-where."

34

"I'm glad, though, that you're not alone."

Ruth looked up, and their tired eyes held. Each woman glimpsed the woman who'd been linked to her by law and love, and yet for as little as they knew about the other, they might as well be strangers. "I'm glad too," Ruth said. She didn't bother explaining that she still felt alone, even while she was here.

# CHAPTER 2

Ruth pressed her hands flat to the ground — the grass spiky and glittering with frost — and sensed this new world revolving around her. She pulled her right foot up toward her spine and leaned forward, stretching out her quad. She repeated this with the left. She stretched out her arms, rolled her neck as tension fled her body. The windmill creaked. Morning birds called to each other in the woods. It was easier to breathe, and to think, out here.

It seemed she hadn't breathed deeply since her father died.

Ruth knew she should walk, to ease her unpracticed muscles into a run, but her spirit demanded more exertion. She started off at a jog. The cool September wind, rushing past her ears, held the first scent of fall and of something more, earthen and damp. The moon was high and round, even as the eastern sky peeled back the edge of dawn. A cat slunk out of the barn. Ruth squinted and saw a newborn kitten dangling from its mouth. The mother cat's coat was lusterless, her sides concave from malnutrition. And yet she was using energy she couldn't spare to move her offspring to a safer place. To protect them. Ruth understood how she felt.

Ruth didn't know how she was going to financially support herself and her daughters. She had double-majored in English and art instead of pursuing the dependable teaching degree her parents wanted. She had thrived in both departments and knew — even while discussing neoclassical literature and expressionism with her peers over a questionable cafeteria lunch — that those years were some of the best of her life. And yet what did she have to show for them? She neither painted nor wrote. Carving out time for herself felt impossible, even negligent, when she considered her daughters' incessant needs. The girls were possibly even needier because Ruth was often forced to fill the roles of both parents.

She continued running, past the dark channels that were built up next to the numerous cranberry fields. The stars faded as the horizon lightened. Still running, she skimmed the fleece off over her head and tied it around her waist. When she came to the lake, she paused, standing before it, and saw a glow in the distance, next to what looked like a small house.

Ruth checked her Fitbit. She had half an hour before the girls were likely to wake up. She walked toward the glow and saw one of Elam's Clydesdales tied to the lower branch of a tree. Ruth stopped, not wanting to relinquish her solitude, but she feared Elam had seen her and would wonder why she'd turned around.

She found him inside the pump house, leaning over a rusted piece of equipment. "Good morning," she said.

Elam jumped so visibly, Ruth had to smile. "Oh, good morning," he said. "Didn't hear you come up." He didn't quite look at her but continued concentrating on his task. Ruth wondered if this was because of her apparel or because of his shyness. Chandler had never prepped her on the many nuances of Mennonite culture, because he'd never seen the need to return to his Old Order relatives living in Wisconsin, where the differences would be felt the most. But now that Ruth was here, she feared she was always doing something to offend.

"I was just out for a run and saw your light. Everything okay?"

"It will be," he said. "I'm just trying to get the pump fixed before we begin harvesting."

"What do you use it for? To flood the bog?"

He nodded. "I'm not much of a mechanic, but I'm not about to hire someone just to tighten a few bolts." He set his wrench down and walked over to her. "You're a runner?"

Ruth pulled on her fleece. She was beginning to feel a chill now her sweat had cooled. "I'm probably as much of a runner as you are a mechanic. Chandler used to run with me, in Colombia, when we were dating. It drove him crazy that I would run the streets on my own."

Elam cocked his head. "I didn't know Chandler was athletic."

"He's not." Ruth laughed, remembering when Chandler first came downstairs in Bethel House wearing mesh shorts, a T-shirt, and tennis shoes, all of which appeared curiously new. Her heart warmed with the memory, but she knew if she recalled it too long — if she understood she thought and spoke of her husband in the present tense — it would have the opposite effect. "I'm not sure I would call him athletic either. I think it was a bit of a ploy to get close to me."

"Ah," Elam said. "Makes sense."

Elam and Ruth smiled at each other. She turned to go. "Hey," he said. She looked back. "There're some potatoes and eggs in the oven, if you want them."

Nodding, she waved her thanks and headed home, the rising sun lighting her journey.

*July 15, 2012*

Dear Chandler,

It's strange to me that we spent nearly two years at Bethel House as fellow staff members, who'd sometimes pass each other on the stairs or share whatever hodgepodge was in the fridge, but then, once I left — well, let's just say I would love if you could come visit me on your break. However, I must warn you (I wanted to warn you last night, but the best reception's in the kitchen, and my mother seemed quite preoccupied with organizing her silverware drawer while I was talking with you): after you arrive, for the first three days or so, my mother will act like you are a horrible inconvenience. She will grumble about having to set the table for another person; about how much electricity you are using (even if you don't flip a switch the entire time you are here); the extra loads of laundry she's having to wash and fold (even if you wear the same clothes for a week); that you forgot to open the window in the bathroom and now the entire up-stairs is going to be crawling with black mold. Please, do not take this person-ally.

My mother treated me the same when I moved back home, which — suffice to say — caused me to immediately look for a rental property in town. But as you know, volunteer work cannot pay the bills, and I have student loans to repay. Therefore, I have surrendered to the fact that I am going to live here, at home, until I can find a better means of em-ployment than a waitress at Father Tom's. The upside is that I get to be near my father, who ensured that my child-hood was a happy one. He is retired now (as is my mother) and can often be found puttering in the garden, or sitting down on one of the concrete benches near the shore, smoking his pipe and watching the sea with his Great Pyr, Zeus, by his side. He is the antithesis of my mother, and yet they get along. I like to believe that life has merely whittled away at the pieces that once made them

npatible, now rendering them an
perfect fit.

They still love each other, though. I
saw it last night, before I talked to you.
My mother (Cathleen) yelled out the
window that he (Kiffin) needed to stop
wasting time playing fetch with the dog,
and make a salad to go with supper. He
did. He came in with a basket brimming
with butterhead lettuce, carrots the size
of my pinky fingers, and radishes. He'd
washed everything off at the spigot
outside, so he set the basket down on
the table. She was just about to complain
about the tablecloth getting wet when
he pulled his other hand from behind
his back and presented my mother with
a bouquet of purple asters he'd gathered
from near the gate.

"For you, m'lady," he said in his thick
brogue.

My mother wears neither makeup nor
jewelry, keeps her curly hair cropped
short, and sticks to a uniform of khakis
and collared shirts. So his calling her a
"lady" would've seemed incongruous to
most. And yet, I could see her cheeks
redden and eyes sparkle as she took the
flowers, planted a brisk kiss on his cheek,
and said, "Get out of here, you ol' coot."

So, if forewarned is forearmed, I hope you'll put this knowledge in your arsenal. But I promise to make my mother's harping up to you by taking you hiking along the road to Bray, where we can see the heather bending in the wind, the wild horses grazing on the pinnacle of the trail, and the seals bobbing in the Irish Sea as the frothing water appears like a spool of lace unfurled around their dark heads. And then, when we arrive at Bray (roughly ten miles later), we can replenish the calories we burned by getting some mint chocolate chip gelato from the little shop down along the boardwalk and take our time eating it while the town's multicolored flags snap in the salted wind. So, come, Chandler; I would love to have you here.

Yours,
Ruth

Ruth did not mind being alone in her grief; actually, she preferred it. Especially if the company was someone she did not know well. But Elam's sister, Laurie, was a good-hearted force to be reckoned with. In the brief time she had known her, Ruth realized Laurie took it upon herself to see that no one in her orbit should ever feel lonely. This must be why she now bounded up the steps — Tim Junior perched on her pregnant belly — and burst through the door. *"Guten Morgen!"* she sang, seeing Mabel and Ruth at the table. "Can't stay long — the kids are probably tearing the house apart — but I wanted to tell you that some of the ladies and I are making apple pies. We're starting at ten and then having lunch."

Mabel looked at Ruth. "You should go," she said. "I'll keep the girls."

The last thing in the world Ruth wanted was to interact with a group of curious strangers. For the past two months, she'd noticed — or at least felt — that people were always watching her, as if trying to judge her emotional state. Since Cathleen Galway raised Ruth, Ruth tended to conceal her emotions the same as her stoic mother had always done. Sometimes, Ruth tended to conceal these emotions even from herself, so that the only way she could understand her own thoughts was to take the time to write them down. No, the last thing in the world Ruth wanted was to be a case study for a gaggle of women who had husbands to keep their beds warm at night. But Laurie's wide-eyed, hopeful expression prevented Ruth from saying what she felt.

"Can I bring anything?" she asked.

44

"Of course not." Laurie's smile widened. "I'm just glad you're going to come."

One hour later, Ruth's rental car took a left at the intersection where another gravel road bisected the long farm lane that wound past the barns and the lake. Laurie and Tim's house looked like a miniature version of the farmhouse Elam owned. Ruth parked along the side of the road so she could make an easy exit — and a hasty one, too, if needed. The yard appeared filled with as many horses and buggies as had been at the funeral. Ruth wondered if the house could contain all the women who were surely inside, since the church had been overflowing that day. Strange, how her mind chose to remember such irrelevant details but couldn't recall the faces of the people who'd come up to her after the service to share a boyhood memory of Chandler — playing kick the can with his Mennonite peers; standing in cow pies to keep his bare feet warm one winter; building elaborate tunnels in the hayloft with Elam; telling one farmer there was a wild animal in his barn when a cow had just gotten her head stuck in the slats of a trough. All these memories, which Ruth had never heard, made her feel further removed from her husband, for it

45

seemed he'd lived an entire lifetime before they wed.

Ruth stood in the middle of Laurie's yard and considered leaving, but what would she tell Mabel? Beside her, the water pumping rod moved up and down above the cement base as, overhead, the windmill's rusted fans creaked. Chickens pecked and scratched at the overlapping gullies the wagon wheels had made. An old farm dog — a beagle of some kind — sprawled in the sunshine in front of the barn. The panorama was so iconic that Ruth momentarily forgot her insecurity and could picture the setting in black-and-white.

When no one answered her knock, Ruth entered the breezeway. The floor was littered with a hastily corralled menagerie of children's shoes and coats. There were also women's shoes, all black and close to uniform, causing Ruth's calf-high brown leather boots to stand out. She hoped this was not a sign of how she would also stand out from the women who wore them.

Ruth entered Laurie's kitchen and breathed the autumnal scent of cooking apples, cinnamon, and smoke. A long table took up most of the space. The floor was refinished pine, with a runner of scuffs marking the area that received the most traf-

46

fic. Along the back wall, between two windows, steam curled as lids danced atop massive kettles sitting on the woodstove. An assembly line of Plain women chattered while washing Golden Delicious and Red Delicious apples at the sink, slicing and coring the apples, and if necessary, cutting away rotten or wormy parts. More women dumped these apples into pots and stirred them with metal spoons. Laurie — the only one Ruth recognized, though the others had attended the funeral — stood at the table, rolling out crust.

Laurie looked up as Ruth approached, and her freckled face opened in a grin. Wiping her floured hands on her apron, she crossed the room and embraced Ruth, as if she hadn't just seen her. Still touching Ruth's arm, Laurie asked, "So, where would you like to help?"

But the din had quietened. Ruth glanced around at the women, who quickly resumed their chatter and work like a culinary battalion with apron strings crisscrossing their backs.

Laurie murmured, "Why don't you just stay here with me, then?" She took an apron off the hook beside the sink and passed it to Ruth. Over the past few months, Ruth had lost so much weight, she could wrap the ties twice around her waist and knot them in front.

Ruth washed her hands in the closet-sized bathroom and then came back to stare at the contents of the bowl. Laurie hadn't given Ruth instructions and so clearly assumed Ruth knew how to make pie crust. She didn't. Scones were the most complicated item Cathleen had taught her to bake. So Ruth watched Laurie cut the cold butter into the flour mixture and begin working the dough into balls with her fingers. Ruth replicated this and found the domestic action soothing. She wondered how long it'd been since she'd done much of anything in the kitchen besides breakfast. When you lost someone, it seemed everyone wanted to make sure you stayed fed.

Laurie asked, breaking into Ruth's thoughts, "Has Elam said two words to you yet?"

Ruth glanced over at Laurie, who had sprinkled flour across the table and begun flattening the dough, so Ruth sprinkled flour across the table and began flattening hers. "We talked a little the other morning. Why?" She stared back down at the bowl. "Doesn't he usually?"

"Usually?" Laurie laughed. "No. My big brother's about the shyest guy you'll ever meet. But —" Laurie paused to straighten the rolling pin — "I don't think I'm just being partial when I say he's also one of the kindest. Almost the entire community's employed by the Driftless Valley Farm, to the point the community's now named after it. Nobody thinks to call us River Bend Mennonites anymore. But I rarely see the responsibility stress him. Then again, Elam's not the easiest to read."

Ruth didn't know Elam or Laurie well enough to reply to this admission, so she focused on using her own rolling pin to evenly flatten the dough.

"What are your plans after . . ." But Laurie didn't finish. Ruth looked and saw Laurie's face had flared bright red. "Forgive me," she whispered. "Sometimes I forget why you are here."

Ruth said, "It's okay." And though the question was, the situation wasn't.

In truth, Ruth had no idea what she was going to do now that she wasn't living for free in Bethel House or receiving $2,000 a month from Children's Haven or Physicians International, depending which nonprofit organization currently employed her husband. Chandler's public service had qualified for student loan forgiveness, saving them half a million dollars in medical school debt. But regardless of how conservatively they lived, $24,000 a year had left little room for savings. Whatever they *had* saved was long gone.

"I'm sure you can stay for as long as you like," Laurie said, quietly, perhaps conscious of the other women whose work had again stilled so they might overhear.

"I couldn't impose on Elam's hospitality."

Laurie made a dismissive sound. "Nonsense. You'd be doing him a favor. He's always shorthanded when harvest season rolls around; I'm sure he could hire you for a few weeks."

"I — I don't think I'm staying that long." But Ruth's voice wasn't filled with conviction like when she'd told Mabel this after the funeral. She blinked back tears. Now was no time to cry. She quickly looked down at the crust, buttered one of the pie pans in the stack, and draped the dough over it, trimming off the excess with a knife the way Laurie had done. Where was Ruth's place in the world? Who were her people? For so long, she'd felt like a single mother, and yet she'd had no idea the vulnerability of walking this journey alone.

The insurance agent on the phone had the audacity to sound bored. "I understand your husband gave his life for our country, Mrs. Neufeld, but this policy does not include acts of war."

"He was going to Afghanistan," Ruth said, pressing a heel of one hand against her eye until, even with it closed, her vision swam in stars. "He wouldn't have taken that risk."

After a while, the insurance agent asked, "Should I fax the contract to you?"

Ruth cleared her throat. She focused on the creak of the windmill and on the distant, rhythmic clop of a horse leaving Laurie's house, rather than on the fact that her husband's life insurance policy was now null and void. "There are no fax machines where I am," she said.

"Then could I email it to you?"

Ruth held out her phone to see how much battery it had left. She was tired of having to charge it in the rental car each night, but what other choice did she have?

"No internet here either." She turned her head from the receiver and took a deep breath. Weeks spent untangling red tape, and Ruth had never spoken to the same agent twice. But she still didn't want to give him the satisfaction of picturing a heart-broken widow on the other side.

The insurance agent paused. Ruth knew that pause; knew he was trying to think of something appropriate to say. "I — I am sorry for —" he began.

She cut him off. "I've got to go."

Which wasn't a lie. Ruth *did* need to go. She just didn't know where.

*August 20, 2012*

Dear Ruth,

My last letter began with an apology, and it seems this letter's following suit. I am sorry that I proposed. Or, if I am not entirely sorry, I am at least sorry that it shocked you. If it makes you feel any better, it also shocked me. You were just standing there, with the sun on your hair, and I was standing next to you, fully aware that we were soon going to be continents apart. You asked me, afterward, how I could love you when I barely know you, but sometimes you can love someone without even knowing who they are.

It happened, for me, even before you almost got kidnapped at Guatavita; it happened the first week you came to Bethel House.

I came back from the clinic around midnight. I unlocked the door and saw the basket lamp above the kitchen table was on, throwing a crisscross pattern on the walls. I didn't see you until I came closer. Your back was to me, your hair twisted into a messy bun stabbed with a ballpoint pen. The table was covered with papers and a yellow sleeve of candy, but you were just sitting there, your profile turned toward the window.

I asked, "What's wrong?" and you jumped about a foot.

You turned, hand to your chest, and saw me at the door. We'd already been introduced, but we'd not really had the chance to talk. You said, "I can't stand not being able to go outside."

Now, having seen where you were raised, I understand why those low ceilings and darkened streets made you claustrophobic.

I said, "I might have a solution. But first, I've got to eat." I paused. "Have you eaten?"

You shook your head and grinned. "Just chocolate."

So I finished warming up a pot of leftover rice and beans and divided a ripe avocado between the two bowls. I asked you to follow me, and though you looked wary, you did so without question. You must've really been desperate.

Balancing our supper, I led you up the dark cement stairs, past the women's section, and then the men's. We were sneaking around like teenagers, and maybe that illicit feeling was partly why we enjoyed it. We were weary of juggling the responsibilities of adults. I led you to the trapdoor leading to the roof, and I passed you the steaming plates until I had propped the door and worked my lanky body outside. You came out, then, and we sat on the blanket one of the other staff members had forgotten. We ate our humble meal with our fingers because I'd forgotten to bring forks. You told me you wanted to become a writer, and I told you I wanted to become a doctor, and you laughed because I was still in my doctor scrubs. But then I grew serious and admitted that sometimes I became overwhelmed by the number of my patients, those sick, orphaned babies who were all in my care. I admitted that reality was proving far more complicated than the dream, and though I loved being a doctor, I didn't know if I was making the kind of difference I had envisioned when I was young. You touched my hand, then held it, and I looked at you as, somewhere in the city, a confused rooster crowed.

I barely knew you, Ruth, but I knew I was beginning to fall for you. So I hope you can see that, though my proposal may seem sudden, my love for you is sincere.

Yours,
Chandler

# CHAPTER 3

The barn doors were slid open because the lantern was not giving off enough light for Elam to work. Elam usually didn't notice when it became bad for things to remain the same — to the point his sister, Laurie, had to notify him when it was time to buy new clothes or boots — but using outdated equipment was another story. Decades of successful crops had allowed Driftless Valley Farm to grow, but the farm's demands had grown with this success. Therefore, Elam managed two hundred acres with the same equipment his grandfather had used to manage fifty. To say this was an inconvenience was an understatement. So far, Elam and his men had been able to get by, but each year, and with each additional bed, the challenge became more intense.

"Elam?"

At the sound of his name, Elam looked up and viewed Ruth's silhouette framed by the moonlit fields behind her. His chest hitched. He steadied himself by gripping one of the harvester's rusted tines. He was unsettled each time he saw her, and though he was often unsettled when he had to talk to someone who wasn't immediate family, he knew this was different. Sometimes, he could talk to Ruth with an ease he hadn't experienced with anyone but his sister, and yet that ease dissipated when she caught him off guard, like now.

"Ru . . . uth?" He set down his oiled rag and moved the lantern to the worktable.

"Sorry to bother you," she said.

"You . . . you're no bother."

Ruth rubbed her arms like she was cold. "Laurie told me you might need a few extra hands for the harvest." She paused. "Is that true?"

Picking up the rag, Elam resumed oiling the tines. Was that true? Laurie knew he had long ago settled the details of the cranberry harvest, and yet he sensed it took a lot out of Ruth to ask. Plus, how could he turn away his cousin's widow? He would just make it work.

"Ye . . . yes," he said. "We're shorthanded this year. Do you think you can help?"

Ruth said, "Only if you'll deduct room and board from my wages."

When Aunt Mabel had asked if she and her daughter-in-law and two young grandchildren could stay at his house after the funeral, Elam's only misgiving was that he was not the hosting type. Laurie had convinced him it would be fine and had deep-cleaned his house and purchased a few items to spruce up the place, which hadn't received a woman's touch since their mother died.

Though this had helped, Laurie was not the one who lived here. When it came down to it, Elam was the one who had to make his guests feel welcome. And now that guest wanted to repay him for his poor hospitality. Up in heaven, his mother must be shaking her head.

"Ruth, you are . . . are family," he said. "My home is your home."

Ruth looked down, her hair falling forward, so he could see the curls were tighter at the nape of her neck. "Thank you for that," she said.

"You're welcome." He focused on oiling the same tine. "The harvest starts tomorrow and lasts for about . . . three days. I'll see if I can find a pair of waders to fit you."

"Great. I'm looking forward to it."

He smiled in reply to hers and pushed up the brim of his straw hat to watch her walk out of the barn. She turned at the door, and he was embarrassed until he realized she couldn't see him in the dark.

"I'm grateful, Elam," she said. "For all you've done."

He nodded. "You're welcome, Ruth."

This time, the words flowed.

*August 27, 2012*

Dearest Chandler,

There is no need to apologize. You have done nothing wrong. I guess I just always envisioned my life progressing in a certain manner, and here we're discussing marriage without even knowing if we're in love. I know you think you're in love, but I am afraid you might be in love with the idea of me, rather than who I really am.

I can be mean, Chandler, and selfish.

I am an only child, and though I was not spoiled with material possessions — or even attention — I am not accustomed to sharing my space or time. This will probably sound like I'm trying to push you away, but I am not. I just do not take marriage lightly.

Marriage is not a decision you make on impulse or because that person looks good or makes you feel good at the time. Marriage joins two souls on an ever-changing journey. I thought — when I was growing up and knew better than the adults in my life — that my parents should just get divorced. But I didn't understand that they were committed to loving each other, and that commitment included loving their best and their worst selves. We are all chameleons, Chandler; changing — for good or for bad — as our environments change, and I don't want you to be disappointed when life happens around us, and I evolve to accommodate it.

If you read this and still want me, I will come back to Children's Haven . . . and to you; if you read this, and you want nothing else to do with me, I will understand.

Fondly,
Ruth

Elam only knew of one person who might have a pair of waders that were Ruth's size, but that person was his sister, Laurie, who would — no doubt — ask more questions than he was comfortable answering. But he'd already promised Ruth she could work in the bog, so he swallowed his discomfort and knocked on Laurie's door.

She called from inside, "You know you don't have to knock!"

He entered the kitchen and saw Laurie with his two-year-old niece, Sarah, clinging to her apron, a teakettle singing on the stove, and the baby, Tim Junior, in the high chair, double-fisting Cheerios into his drooling mouth. Elam bent to unlace his boots.

"Don't bother," Laurie said. "Look at my floor!"

Elam *did* look at his sister's floor and saw the detritus of a happy childhood: a chewed piece of toast, stray Cheerios from Tim Junior's tray, wooden alphabet blocks, and a toy truck: the closest his nephews and nieces would come to having a vehicle unless they left the Old Order Mennonite church. The thought trapped Elam. He didn't know how to begin.

"Do . . . do you have any waders I can borrow?"

Resting one hand on her belly, Laurie pulled the teakettle off the stove and bent to toss a few blocks into the crate. "Don't think you and I are the same size."

"They're not for me."

"Then who . . . ?" She paused, freckled nose wrinkling as she smiled. "E-lam," she sang. "That's so good of you to offer Ruth

61

work. Really, it is."

Elam shifted from foot to foot. Kneeling, he picked up his niece, who gave his scruffy cheek a kiss and then stared at him with Laurie's dark-gray eyes.

Elam said, "Seems Ruth got the idea from you."

Laurie splayed fingers across her chest, a dramatist in a burgundy cape dress. *"Moi?"*

Elam gave her the look he'd been giving her most of her life. "Don't act so surprised. You know I've never had a woman on my wet harvesting crew since you married Tim."

"Yeah, well. Tim still likes to see me in waders."

Elam blushed. Laurie stepped closer and touched her brother's arm. They were not an affectionate pair of siblings; not because Laurie was unaffectionate, but because Elam often gave off an aura that demanded ample personal space. It was something Laurie tried to respect, unless she needed to make a point. And Laurie *always* needed to make a point. "Elam." Her high-pitched, exclamation mark–clad voice had lowered three octaves, which meant a serious matter was being addressed. "You have nothing to be ashamed of."

"I . . . I don't know what you're talking about," he said, but he knew she could see

62

right through him. Laurie was one of the few people in the world who did.

Elam's niece tugged on one of his suspenders. He looked down and gently tugged on one of her lopsided pigtail braids. They grinned. Elam had always wanted children — had dreamed more about becoming a father than he had about becoming a husband — because children love more for actions than for words. And yet fatherhood had to be preceded by marriage, which was impossible since no woman wanted a man who had so little to say. Closing his eyes in frustration, Elam rested his chin on his niece's head. Sarah burrowed against him.

Laurie asked, "Will you promise me something?"

Sighing, Elam looked over at his sister and suddenly saw the little girl who'd always endeavored to bring happiness into their home: a responsibility she shouldn't have had to carry, considering she had been a child, and Elam a teenager, when their mother was diagnosed.

He smiled indulgently and nodded, knowing Laurie meant well even if her good intentions often felt like interference. She continued, "Will you let yourself get to know Ruth?"

Elam paused, unsure of how honest he

wanted to be. "I *am* getting to know her," he said and remembered similar conversations: Laurie trying to talk him into going to another hymn sing or auction or wedding he did not want to attend. He didn't know if she did this because she wanted him to marry, or because family had become her safety net and she wanted to expand and strengthen it through a sister-in-law and the children their union could provide.

Laurie stepped back, allocating him his space. "I just don't think you need to keep your walls up when you're around her, like you normally do."

Elam cleared his throat to remove the hint of irritation. "If anything makes me want to put walls up," he said, "it's when someone makes me feel cornered."

"I'm not trying to corner you. I just want to see you happy."

"I *am,*" he insisted, and then rested a hand over Sarah's ear, as if a two-year-old could understand what he sometimes didn't. "Besides, where's your loyalty to Chandler?"

"I *loved* Chandler," Laurie said. "We all did. But —" she smiled up at him again, and he knew there was no going back once her stance was made — "I am more loyal to you."

Elam's brother-in-law, Tim, opened the second pump, which sent water gushing from the reservoir into the irrigation system. A ditch channeled this water through the vertical pipes that were rudimentarily regulated by wooden slats either inserted or removed, depending on the water's desired height. Today, only a few wooden slats were in place; tomorrow, they would *all* be in place and the flooding would begin. Elam stood on the bank beside his brother-in-law, watching as the bog's water slowly rose.

"Well," Tim said, "looks like the pump's fixed."

In the distance, on the lane, Elam could see Ruth with Zeus loping at her side. The sound of her pounding feet sent a muskrat scrambling for the water, which made Zeus take off like a shot. Ruth stopped running and whistled for the dog, but the muskrat had escaped.

"That's good," Elam replied to Tim.

He was thinking not only of the fixed water pump and the harvest, but also of the sun warming his face, his lungs filling with air, his eyes viewing his cousin's young widow as she threw a stick into the channel for her dog. Elam looked away from Ruth and watched the water until a few of the first cranberries bobbed to the surface. But even though he tried to think of everything else, his mind continued echoing with Laurie's words.

*September 3, 2012*

Ruth, dearest,

I love you not because you look good or because you make me feel good (though both are true), but because I can't imagine experiencing this ever-changing, grand adventure with anyone but you. Please come back. I want you, flaws and all. The Lord knows I have my own, and we can push each other to become the best versions of ourselves, and yet love each other unconditionally when we're not.

Yours always,
Chandler

Mabel Neufeld bustled around the kitchen in her sensible shoes and sturdy apron, whisking batter for the Dutch babies she hadn't made in years. After the initial shock wore off, part of Mabel's grief had evolved from the fact she believed she was no longer needed. How could a woman who'd served other people since she was old enough to set the table or wash a dish now discover the two people she'd spent most of her life serving were gone? It was inconceivable, and yet it was a truth that crashed in on her each morning she opened her eyes.

But this morning was different. Once again, Mabel had people — *her* people — to serve.

She carefully poured the pancake-like batter into the greased muffin pan. As she did, she recalled those first two weeks after the bombing but before she flew out to Wisconsin at her niece's request. Her husband's and son's simultaneous deaths had set her adrift, and as if to compensate, Mabel had marooned herself in the bed she'd once shared with her husband.

Night after night, she ate stewed crackers for supper and tried to escape reality through the cozy mysteries she'd borrowed from the Re-Use-It shop where she volunteered. But this lonely existence, to which she was accustomed, had become lonelier because, this time, Chandler Senior was not coming home. That next week, the third and hardest week, Mabel's niece, Laurie, wrote and asked if she would like to come to

Wisconsin until the worst of the grief had passed.

*Forgive me if this is intrusive,* Laurie wrote, *but you could even bury Uncle Chandler and Chandler Junior here, beside Mamm, and know they are forever surrounded by family and love.*

An act of terrorism continued to terrorize even after death, and the overseas investigation kept the bodies from being released for burial, so Mabel hadn't even considered where the funeral should be held. She'd assumed Ruth would bury Chandler Junior in Ireland, but Pennsylvania — without Chandler Senior — no longer felt like home. It was as if, overnight, her vision had dimmed and the landscape had changed, the combination rendering her incapable of finding her way across terrain she'd once known intimately. This caused Mabel to yearn for her home state's open land and low bluffs, where bald eagles soared above shorn cornfields and windmills stood guard beside the derelict homesteads of yesteryear. It didn't take Mabel long to pack after she — a Mennonite woman in her sixties — decided to fly for the first time in her life.

Chandler Senior was the one who'd lived the adventures. She had always been content waiting for him to come home and show

68

what he'd seen through photos taken on a Pocket Instamatic, then disposable cameras, and most recently his iPhone — technologically advancing as their lives passed. But now Mabel Neufeld had to make a choice: remain in their house because it was familiar or cut ties and begin again.

Elam was waiting for Mabel at the gate when she disembarked from the plane. With a shaky hand, she smoothed the seam of her skirt. Mabel wore a prayer covering, but not a dark cape dress like the ones she'd grown up in, since — when she married Chandler — she shifted from Old Order Mennonite to Black Bumper Mennonite, which allowed them to have electricity in their home, a car in the garage (the car's chrome bumpers painted black, hence the nickname for their religious sect), and a TV they moved to the closet whenever the bishop came for lunch.

Mabel had visited her family in Wisconsin after she married, but Chandler Senior had always been with her, and later Chandler Junior, and their presence helped offset the self-consciousness she would've felt concerning the "liberal" lifestyle she now led. But she felt self-conscious as Elam reached to take her carpet-style valise. Her deceased sister's only son had never been affectionate, so she was taken aback when he wrapped his free arm around her sweatered back and pulled her into a hug. Many people had hugged her in the days since she received the news, but none of those had been men. And even if they *had* been, none of them could've possibly reminded Mabel of her Chandlers. But Elam reminded her of them.

Elam and Chandler Junior had been opposites from birth: quiet, loud; introverted, extroverted; withdrawn, affectionate; fair, dark. But Elam reminded her of all the times she'd seen the two cousins together, and whatever small mooring she'd established for herself in the past three weeks was gone. Something connected Elam and Mabel that day the two stood still as the passengers from the small plane continued to disembark. Grief joined them, but perhaps their unspoken loneliness joined them as well. Whatever it was, that bond could not be easily torn.

Elam and Mabel talked about everything but death as the driver escorted them back to Tomah. Elam told her about the harvest and the acreage they'd purchased since she left.

She asked, "You still living at your dad's old place?"

The man of few words nodded. "I have more room than Laurie does," he said. "If you don't mind living with a crusty old bachelor."

Mabel laughed, the first time in weeks. "If you're old, what does that make me?"

"Well preserved," he said, and smiled.

The memory also made Mabel smile as she opened the oven to check on her Dutch babies. They were golden-brown, buttery, and puffing up around the muffin pan, like they were supposed to. She went into the pantry and retrieved a glass pint of maple syrup, which Elam and Tim had harvested in early spring from the ancient maple trees shading the farm.

Mabel had just finished setting the table when the pitter-patter of little feet descended the stairs. Her son's children — a continuation of him, as much as if both girls shared his flesh and blood — were a tangible promise, a visible depiction that, despite death, all was not lost.

The girls toddled into the kitchen in their matching footie pajamas. Even Sofie had that soft, rosy-cheeked glow of children who have awoken from blissful dreams to a life that is nearly as idyllic. It soothed Mabel to see her looking like every child should.

"Come here, my lambs," she said, and

knelt in her sensible shoes and sturdy apron. Her granddaughters ran across the hardwood, squealing. In the doorway, Ruth stood, wearing a sweatshirt and jeans. The waders, which Laurie had lent, draped the staircase rail. Ruth leaned one hip against the doorjamb and watched Sofie and Vi being wrapped in such love, like gifts. Mabel's grateful, teary eyes met hers, and the two grief-stricken widows smiled as though acknowledging the two of them were joined by far more than law.

# CHAPTER 4

*December 10, 2012*

Dear Mom and Dad,

I am writing to let you know that Chandler and I married last week. This may seem fast, but Chandler and I have rarely been apart during the past three months I have been at Children's Haven. The marriage took place so quickly because rumors began circulating that one of the other orphanage employees (who didn't seem entirely stable) was also considering adopting Sofie, the little girl I mentioned adopting a while back.

In light of this, Chandler and I agreed a lengthy engagement was a luxury we could not afford. Janice, the director of Children's Haven, was kind enough to decorate the chapel and have Chef José bake us a cake. All things considered, it was a lovely ceremony, and I would have written sooner, but Chandler and I were determined to go through with our plans and feared that if we contacted family, you might compel us to stop.

I want you to know that Chandler and I do love each other. I believe the two of us would've made the same decision, even though it might not have taken place so quickly. I apologize for any shock this may cause you, but do rest assured I am enjoying my duties as a mother and wife. Sofie (nine months old now) is a precious little thing. You will adore your first grandchild.

With love,
Ruth

The morning sun bounced off the water and reflected into Ruth's eyes, forcing her to shield them with one hand as she watched Elam guide his Clydesdales down the bank. Twin streams of breath poured from the horses' damp black nostrils, mimicking the steam rising from the gleaming surface of the bog. Elam's straw hat and suspenders, combined with the horse-drawn equipment, made him seem like a relic from another time. Ruth, more observer than participant, wondered if the community's otherworldliness was what made it easier to breathe.

Here, she didn't check her phone compulsively to see if there were any more developments regarding the bombing. Here, she didn't have to respond to her friends' well-intentioned but intrusive Facebook messages, declaring that they were so sorry for her loss and that if she needed anything — anything at *all!* — that they were here for her.

Which was convenient since most were thousands of miles away.

Yes, a certain freedom was found in being unreachable. After the phone call with her mother, followed by the phone call with Chandler's life insurance rep, Ruth decided to just let her phone go dead. She'd returned the rental car yesterday, so she had nowhere to charge it. Besides, if somebody wanted to get ahold of her badly enough, they could call Elam's business phone, in the barn. Ruth knew the odds of anyone getting through were slim.

This pleased her.

Elam turned in the wagon seat and waved Ruth down into the water. She only now noticed that the other men had already entered with their waders and were using their rakes to corral whatever cranberries had risen to the surface from the harvester.

Ruth stood there a moment, watching the

men work, and thought of what a picture the scene would make: the steam; the horses' muscles straining beneath their saturated coats; the workers' matching straw hats and pale collared shirts. The contrast between the water and the berries made Elam's harvester appear to be a textile machine unspooling skeins of dyed red silk.

Ruth yearned to capture this moment through any medium she could — through words or through a paintbrush. It had been so long since she had noticed or imagined or stood still long enough to desire to create. But now was not the time. Picking up her rake, Ruth entered the bog. The water's frigid temperature penetrated through the waders' thick material. She sucked air through her teeth as she watched the harvester's rusted yellow tines churning the water, pulling up the cranberry bushes and shaking the berries loose.

Two of the four men used their rakes to guide the floating cranberries into the corner of the bed. The two other men unwound a large yellow boom, which floated on the water's surface like a snake and would keep the floating cranberries from escaping. And then there was Ruth. Nobody offered instructions. Nobody even looked her way. She wasn't sure if this was because she was *Englisch* or because she was wearing pants. What *was* clear was she had no purpose. Her face grew hot as she understood Elam had agreed to let her help because of charity and not because of need. Well, Elam didn't know her mother, who'd taught her that to succeed in a man's revolving-door world, you had to be tougher than a man.

The first bed took four hours, and there were nine beds to go. Ruth's legs were numb, her hands blistered from gripping the rake, but she continued walking behind the harvester, determined not to show any weakness, even though her head throbbed with fatigue.

Finally, Ruth heard the triangle bell ringing at the farmhouse. She lifted her head, peeled a piece of wet hair clinging to her cheek, and looked at Elam. He turned on the seat of the harvester and called something to the workers. Ruth couldn't hear, so she sloughed closer.

"You all go ahead and eat," he said. "I just have a few more tracts to do, and then we can move to the next bed after lunch."

The other men, even Tim, were already heading out of the bog or climbing the embankment. They tossed their wet rakes down on the grass and pulled off their waders. Ruth watched the men go, their strides stiff as they made their way toward the house.

"Aren't *you* going to go?" Elam smiled beneath his straw hat, and Ruth watched the lines deepen like quotation marks around his full mouth. "They might not leave much for you."

"It's all right," Ruth said. "I'll stay. I don't like leaving when there's work to be done."

Elam stared at her. As seconds passed, Ruth was no longer sure if pride alone drove her to remain in the bog, for there was something about Elam that made it impossible to leave.

He cleared his throat. "I guess that's . . . okay. I just don't want you . . . going without."

"I'm not," she said.

Their gazes held as the sun skipped across water, the afternoon light now reflecting in his eyes. He turned away and clicked his tongue at the horses. They pulled forward, and Ruth moved behind the wagon, using the rake to guide the berries toward the corner of the bog.

*December 7, 2013*

Dear Husband,
  I have dropped the ball. I have no gift
to offer. I'm not even sure what kind of
gift I am supposed to give for this, our
first anniversary. Is it paper, wood, or
wool? I hope it's paper because all I have
is this piece of notebook paper folded in
half and cut into a heart, like I'm not a
twenty-six-year-old wife and mother, but
a kindergartner proud of the project I
made at school. But I am proud, you see.
I am proud of us for surviving. The one
memory that seems to sum this year up
the most is when Sofie cried for hours
and hours. You remember that night,
don't you? We tried rocking, jiggling,
swaddling, gripe water, warm baths . . .
and nothing helped. You told me I should
just put her down, that she would have
to cry it out. And — delirious with
exhaustion — I screamed that you were
an unfit parent, as if you were telling me
to abandon her for good. So you took
your pillow and a blanket and went
downstairs. I watched you go through
burning eyes and remained on the edge
of our bed, holding that red-faced,
clench-fisted cherub with her legs pulled

up tight. I stayed up there for another hour before I knew that I, too, had to leave. I sobbed as I kissed her and laid her down in her bassinet, for I believed that she would feel abandoned twice in her life: first by her birth parents, and now by me. But I left her and went downstairs. I saw you stretched out on the couch — a blue glow in the room from the silent TV. You looked like you were asleep, but when I curled up on the other end of the couch, you passed me your pillow and blanket.

"I'm okay," I said. "I don't need it."

"Yes," you insisted, "you do."

My eyes stung. "Don't be nice to me after what I said. It's not fair."

I heard you smile in that blue dark. "Sweetheart, we left fair at the altar."

So I took your pillow and blanket. Upstairs, we could hear our baby crying, and I knew the Corrigans must be hearing her too. But then Sofie stopped. She stopped crying so abruptly, I convinced myself she must have stopped breathing. I moved to get up, and you put a hand on my socked foot. "I'll go check." But I knew I could not sleep unless I saw her too, so we walked up those cement steps together. We walked into our bedroom, and we leaned over the bassinet.

Sofie was sound asleep, her tiny arms — with those little pink mitts I had put on before I left her, so she wouldn't scratch her face as she flailed — stretched up as if in surrender, and we looked at each other and smiled.

The funny thing is that this horrible night is now one of my fondest memories. Still, a part of me longs to just curl up on the couch with you when you get home from work, order pizza, and watch a pointless movie (A movie! How did we ever have so much time?!), but I am grateful we have given up that mythical newlywed bliss in exchange for this fierce, colicky, beautiful little girl. So I guess what I'm trying to say is that I would choose you — and this ever-changing, grand adventure (all-night cry sessions, Sofie's and mine, and all) — again and again.

But most of all, thank you for choosing me.

Your wifey,<br>Ruth

After Mabel finished drying the lunch dishes, she took three tin pails down from the pantry shelf and led her granddaughters down the lane — the three holding hands, the grandma in the middle, their uneven shadows stretched across the gravel like a paper-doll chain — and into one of the fields Elam and his crew would dry-pick for local markets, which would then sell the berries as fresh fruit. The girls, at first, had no idea what to do. Their other grandma hadn't wanted help in the garden, but had stood out there for long spells each night, standing still as a statue, amid the weeds. But this grandma, Grandma Mabel, beckoned them forth.

"There. Right there, my lambs," she said. "God's candy."

Any mention of candy enthralled the children until Vi crouched beside a leaf, plucked a promising red berry, and popped it into her mouth. Her entire face clenched. Her too-long blonde bangs became pinned between her nose and eyes. Vi declared, "God's no good at making canty."

Back at the farmhouse, Sofie sat in the front yard — coltish legs crisscross-applesauce — and tossed cranberries to Zeus. One of the workers had tied him to a tree because he kept barking at the harvester and spooking the horses. Though this bothered Sofie, she was glad to see he didn't seem to mind. Inside, the soapstone sink brimmed with fruit. Mabel carried a sleepy, sweaty Vi upstairs and settled herself in the same rocking chair her sister, Marta, had used.

Mabel watched the dandelion-fine curtain puff in and out with the unseasonably warm breeze and could still picture her sister here, tucking summer-bleached laundry into the dresser and then coming over to the crib to lift Elam out, his chubby arm stretched toward the window, his gray eyes wide with delight. Marta would be proud of the man her little boy had become. And yet, Mabel also knew she would've wanted him to have his own babies in that ancient crib and a wife by his side. *What's the point of all this?* Mabel wondered, pressing a kiss to Vi's straggled bangs. A nephew who'd never found love; a son who could never return to the love he'd found. Mabel looked down at the toddler, going limp in her arms — a dirty thumb hooked in a cranberry-stained mouth — and thought of the toddler's widowed mother, currently working with Elam in the field, and wondered if God had a plan for their severed family after all.

When Elam and Ruth came inside the farmhouse after working all day in the bog, they discovered that the downstairs had been transformed. Cranberry branches garlanded the wooden banister. Candlelight softened the dining room's slightly worn appearance, and a fire crackled in the living room hearth. Zeus — no longer tied in the front yard — snored happily in front of the fire with one of the domesticated barn cats curled up tight against his furred white belly.

Elam left his boots in the foyer and walked into the kitchen. Where was Aunt Mabel? Where were the girls? Curious, he stepped closer to the table. It was set with his mother's wedding china. It was set for two. Elam entered the kitchen like he was entering a crime scene. He glanced at the sink and then over at the stove. The butcher-block countertop was crowded with six loaves of cranberry bread and two pans of cranberry crisp, the glass 9×13s still warm.

Finally, under the sourdough crock, Elam found the note: *Laurie invited me and the girls for supper. A casserole's in the oven. Applesauce in the fridge. Love, Aunt Mabel*

Elam pulled open the oven and saw the bubbling chicken potpie, the crust edged with marks and the top punctured with vent holes from the fork Mabel had used. Elam's face burned, and he was tongue-tied more than normal, though he had no one to talk to and nothing to say.

For nine hours, he and Ruth had worked in effortless, albeit silent, comradery, which would no doubt vanish because of his aunt's thinly disguised attempt to . . . what?

Mabel would never be so tactless as to set her widowed daughter-in-law up with someone less than two months after her own son's death. And yet Elam knew her. The only thing Mabel's soft heart loved more than love itself was to help two other people find it.

Ruth walked in behind him. Elam stood and slammed the oven door, as if he had something to hide. "Where is everyone?" she asked.

Elam passed her the note.

After a moment, Ruth said, "How kind of Mabel to make us supper." But an ominous current pulled at the timbre of her voice. Ruth continued staring at the note and half-turned to look at the table: two plates, two sets of utensils, two glasses of water, two cloth napkins pulled through two wooden rings. She slapped the note on the counter. "I'm going to clean up."

Elam watched her go, her usual elegant gait rendered awkward from soreness. Elam had no idea if "cleaning up" meant she wanted him to wait for her so they could eat together, or if he should just go ahead. Laurie, the only person he could ask, was the same person who had probably conspired with Mabel. He balled his aunt's note up and threw it in the trash. He paced the kitchen for a while, until the dog got up and started following his every step.

Anxious, Elam went outside and gasped the cool autumn air.

Complications fell away beneath this twilit sky, plain navy except for an embellishment of stars. To his right, in the distance, he could just make out the barn and his younger sister's house. Elam could picture them all sitting down to supper. He could picture, too, the surreptitious glances being exchanged between Mabel and Laurie.

Were all women this way, or only the women in his life?

Elam absently rubbed Zeus's ears, who leaned against him in gratitude, like a horse. There was only one bathroom in the house, occupied by Ruth, and so — just in case she *did* want to eat together — he couldn't possibly show up at dinner looking completely unkempt.

It'd been fifteen minutes, at least, since Ruth left to take a shower. How much longer did Elam have before she came back? He didn't know, because he'd never had to share his modern bathroom with a woman until Aunt Mabel came to stay, and he had never paid attention to how long her showers took. The aforesaid "modern bathroom" came about because Young Bishop Gish, now forty, had pushed for kerosene-powered appliances and water heaters in the community's homes soon after he pulled his name from the *Ausbund.* The change went through, but afterward, the seasoned deacons and regional bishops had added "Young" to Bishop Gish, as though the moniker would forever remind him youthful enthusiasm could compensate for neither experience nor age. No major changes had been made to the community in the past ten years.

To be safe, Elam ran inside, down the hall to his room, retrieved a fresh button-down shirt, and ran back out to the well pump. Unbuttoning his shirt, he stripped to the waist — his suspenders dangling — and doused his head and splashed water over his armpits and chest. The water was so cold, the cold was almost all he could think about. But Elam hadn't been using his cognitive abilities before the cold water because he'd forgotten to fetch a towel. He glanced behind him, at the clothesline, but Mabel's new zest for life included a zest for household chores. There were no clothes on the line.

Elam knew he probably didn't smell much better than he had before he baptized himself beneath the pump, but at least most of the day's dirt and sweat was gone. Using his dirty shirt to towel off, he glanced at the house and saw the candles made his own windows stand out against the backdrop of night. Despite everything, seeing that touched him, knowing someone lovely and kind was inside. He began buttoning his new shirt, fingers shaking, as he understood what bothered him the most about this impromptu setup from his sister and his aunt: that getting to know Ruth in a deeper way was quickly becoming a subject at the forefront of his mind.

# CHAPTER 5

Ruth stood at the window and watched Elam as he doused himself by the well pump. She no longer believed people were good for the sake of being good. They were good because they had ulterior motives: the hippie Peace Corps volunteer who just wanted to defer his student loans; the college-age "missions team" who flew down over spring break to repaint the girls' floor of the orphanage and instead acted like they were indeed on spring break: pairing off with each other, smoking in the alley behind Bethel House, blasting music at all hours, so that the baby, Vi, cried. Only half the floor got painted before they had to leave, and the old and new paint combination was such an eyesore, Chandler offered to paint the rest, so that Pepto-Bismol pink seemed wedged beneath his nails for years. And then there was the youngish doctor who wanted to patch lives back together overseas because that was easier than to watch his own life unraveling. Yes, Ruth had been skeptical about humanity long before she found herself a penniless widow with two small children underfoot.

When she came here, to Driftless Valley Community, two weeks ago, she was too shell-shocked to maintain her guard. Now, though, she wondered if her mother-in-law had been adamant about having the funeral in Wisconsin because she had her own ulterior motives.

Ruth seethed. How could her mother-in-law be so insensitive? And yet Ruth had to admit that Elam had nothing to do with Mabel's plan. That had been apparent when she came into the kitchen and saw him standing there: his large limbs ungainly and cumbersome, as if they had grown in the past hour, and he no longer knew how to maintain his own space. His soft eyes had cut up to hers after she read the note for herself. She saw his face redden, so his already ruddy complexion became accentuated with two darker-red strips. A man who blushed.

For some reason, his innocence infuriated her. Elam was almost ten years her senior, whereas there had only been seven years between her and Chandler, but Elam seemed a decade younger, at least. She knew he had lost his mom as a teenager and seemed rather lonely; however, these were the only glitches on his life's plodding timeline.

But maybe the plodding timeline itself was an additional glitch.

Chandler would've believed that, at any rate.

Chandler had never been content just living a normal life. He wanted *adventure,* which he said in such a way that Ruth knew it was meant to be italicized. But after they adopted Sofie, and Ruth got pregnant, her appetite for adventure waned. Chandler's appetite, if anything, only grew as domesticity clamped down, and at times she wondered if he would show up at Bethel House with a moped and an earring: an early midlife crisis because he'd found — with more than a little disappointment — that, italicized or not, any grand adventure became routine over time.

Ruth pulled the curtain back a little more. The light from the downstairs window played across Elam's torso as he toweled off while facing the yard. He was built so differently from her husband: broad shoulders, muscular back and arms, whereas Chandler was lean as a runner. This comparison made

Ruth feel guilty, as if she were being unfaithful in her mind, but then she remembered her vows to Chandler lasted until "death do you part."

With his death, she was freed from such constraints. The realization didn't bring the comfort she would've anticipated when she and Chandler were at their worst, and the only way she thought she could escape from such a lifeless marriage was to have one of them die.

How had the two of them transformed from lovers to rivals, who — even in bed — stayed on opposite sides? How had they lost each other, and themselves, in just a few years while their parents had been married for forty-plus years before their spouses died? Ruth didn't pretend to have the answers, and considering how things had ended between her and Chandler, she probably would never learn. Ruth let the curtain drop. She didn't even know she was crying until she touched the dampness on her cheeks. Wiping her face on her shirt, she went downstairs.

Elam walked in the front door, catching the screen so it wouldn't slam behind him.

As if he didn't want to disturb her.

"Hi," she said.

He looked at her. His silver hair curled

over his shoulders, longer since it was wet. "Hi." His smile appeared self-conscious, but then Ruth really didn't know him well enough to decipher what kind of smile that was. "Should we . . . eat?" he asked.

Ruth nodded and walked in front of him into the kitchen. Most of the candles had burned down to warm puddles of wax pooled around the fake gold stands. Elam went over to the oven and grabbed a mitt from the right-hand drawer. He slid it on and opened the oven door. Ruth was surprised to see the pie wasn't burned to a crisp, considering the time it had taken her to clean up, but Elam must've had the forethought to turn the oven off.

"Smells delicious," Ruth said.

Elam nodded. "It's going to be . . . hard, going back to eggs . . . once Mabel leaves."

Ruth appreciated the safer topic. "Oh?" Her eyebrows rose. "Is that going to be soon?"

Elam walked back across the kitchen to fetch the china plates. It made his breath catch, to see his mother's English tea rose design, though he had no idea that's what kind of rose it was. He just knew the plates were pretty and delicate, like she had been. The china set hadn't been taken from the cupboard since her death. Their family wasn't fine china–eating kind of people. It went to show how his mother had softened the edges of their stark and demanding life.

"I don't know," Elam said, scooping a steaming wedge of chicken and vegetables onto each of their plates. "Aunt Mabel hasn't . . . talked about it." Pieces of crust fell from the server and scattered across the top of the stove. He still felt clumsy in the kitchen, even after so many years on his own. For some reason, he felt even clumsier when Ruth was standing on the opposite side of the counter, arms folded, watching him juggle plates and a server and a quilted oven mitt, covered in buttercups. "That enough?" he said.

She nodded and took the plate. Together, they went back to the table. He quickly sat down, allowing Ruth to dictate her proximity. She took the end. As far away from him as possible. Shaking out a napkin, Elam draped it across his lap. He picked up a fork and started eating. He was ravenous, but, considering the fine china and candlesticks, didn't want to shovel it in like he usually did. Ruth, on the other hand, took massive bites. No doubt, after all that work, she was as ravenous as he. The guttering candle spoke into the silence. Elam didn't want to look at Ruth, in case that made her uncomfortable, but he was aware of her like he'd never been aware of anyone in his life. Damp hair framed her bare face. Her skin was luminous, her lashes nearly white without the mascara she typically used.

"Thank you for . . . all you did . . . today," he managed.

Ruth looked up from her plate and a wave of hair slid over one eye. Brushing it away, she smiled. "No problem. It was enjoyable, actually. Good for me to stay occupied."

"You'll have another . . . opportunity. We're starting the dry beds . . . tomorrow," he said.

"Which do you prefer?"

"Dry." He took a sip of water. "But wet harvest is . . . faster. If the berries are used for sauce and juice, which most . . . are, wet makes more sense. The dry berries are perfect for the . . . the local markets." He paused and used his fork to gesture to the cranberry bread and cranberry crisp on the counter. "I see Aunt Mabel's already making use of . . . the harvest."

"Do you like it?"

"Cranberry bread?"

She smiled. "No, your job."

He took another bite of pie. "For the most part. There are good days and . . . bad, like any occupation." He glanced up. "You

95

caught me on a bad day, when I was fixing the . . . pump."

"I would've never known you were having a bad day."

Elam poked at a green bean. "I'm not very good at showing . . . emotion."

"I'm not either," she admitted. "The people around here probably wonder why I'm helping you with the cranberry harvest when my husband just died."

"I don't think they . . . wonder that," he said. "Besides —" he paused, smiling — "Germans are known more for their . . . work ethic than for their demonstrative behavior."

"Well," Ruth said, "we Irish *are* known for our 'demonstrative behavior,' as you call it. But it seems to have skipped my genes." She looked down, frowning slightly, and broke off a piece of crust. "Actually, that's not really true. I used to be very demonstrative, if that's the right word. My mom often complained that I wore my heart on my sleeve. But I guess, as I grew older, I learned how to hide it."

"Are you glad you . . . did?"

Ruth looked at Elam and he wondered what she was thinking. "Honestly, I'm not sure I really like who I am at the moment."

Elam looked back down at his plate. "For what it's . . . worth," he said, "I do."

*June 2, 2016*

Chandler,

I know you didn't hear me tonight, when I told you how empty I am, or you would not be sleeping. I could feel you dismissing me even as I stood before you, holding the shampoo bottle, with the front of my pajama shirt damp with the milk my body had let down as the baby cried and you and I screamed. Is screamed the right word? I'm never sure what to call it when we fight.

I am the one who raises my voice, and you always remind me not to yell in the same imperious tone you use with Sofie. You are no longer a safe place, Chandler — a vessel I can pour my thoughts into — "I am not even thirty, Chandler, and I'm as used up, as empty as this!" — so I am writing them down here because I don't want you to read them, and you would never dream of reading my journal. I would like to believe this is because you respect my privacy, but it's really because you're not interested enough in my thoughts to take the time to read them.

How have I become so cynical? So needy? How have we so quickly grown apart? Did it start in the earliest days of our marriage as we struggled to become an instant family of three? There were times when I felt this wall building between us: each sharp word, a brick; each time we did not take the time to connect, the mortar that held those bricks together. Days would pass like that, but I would wait them out, knowing that eventually a breakthrough would come. But now the breakthroughs are fewer and farther apart, and that wall between us is growing higher — word by word, brick by brick.

If I had been kinder to you — if I had hugged you more, from behind, as you brushed your teeth at the sink, my face against your warm back, my eyes still swollen with sleep — would it have made a difference? If I had cooked more meals, so you would've come home from the clinic and seen me there — in my apron and pearls with your children all fresh-scrubbed and smiling, Sofie sitting at the table with folded hands — would you want to come home more? Would your home be more of a solace than that sterile clinic full of children whose needs also can never be met? If I had never turned you away, would you now return to me? I don't know, and so here I sit in our bed, wishing I could do things over, but too angry to begin.

I want us back, Chandler. I want the us back, who we were back then, but a part of me realizes we cannot go back. To go back would be to give up our girls and the life we've made together. So I suppose I wish I could go back to what we were while maintaining what we have.

And what we have is great — I know this, deep down. I just miss you. I miss you, and I miss the love that we shared in the beginning. I miss you, and you're sleeping right here.

Your Ruth

Ruth was sitting on the front porch when Mabel and the kids came home in the horse-drawn buggy. Ruth had been outside, waiting for over an hour, because the kitchen was suddenly too intimate once they'd finished the meal and Elam said he'd do the washing up. So Ruth had donned one of the thick wool sweaters she'd purchased from a vendor in Bogotá years ago and sat on the front porch. She felt like a teenager, sitting there with her knees drawn up and her air-dried hair flared around her shoulders. It was a cold night, and getting colder with every passing day, but the damp cold and persistent wind reminded Ruth of home . . . of Ireland.

Ruth had enjoyed her time with Elam tonight. She'd enjoyed it possibly even more than she cared to admit, which was why she escaped to the porch under the pretense of waiting for her daughters. But then she saw the horse and buggy coming up the lane — the single, tired-looking mare's plodding steps, as if she could follow the path in her sleep — and a tightening took place within Ruth. A tightening she hadn't known was loosed until that unseen depth of her grew taut.

The horse and buggy pulled up in front of the house. Ruth got up from the porch and walked down the steps. Her daughters peeked out from inside the buggy and waved, appearing like they'd been trapped in a time warp since they were wearing their regular, *Englischer* clothes.

"Mommy!" Sofie squealed, and like a little parrot, Vi squealed, "Mommy!" Both girls extended their arms to her, utterly delighted with their adventure, and Ruth lifted them out.

Vi, wide-eyed and breathless, pointed at the lane. "We wide in the sleigh the whole way down the woad!" Ruth didn't correct her and just leaned down to kiss the crown of her head. It was past their bedtime. It seemed like hours past Ruth's, but she enjoyed seeing her children so happy, so exuberant, almost as if they'd forgotten what had taken place only two months before.

Mabel said, "Driving a buggy's a whole lot like riding a bike. Impossible to forget no matter how long it's been."

Ruth didn't respond.

"Were you worried?" Mabel asked. "Did you see my note?"

"I saw the note." Ruth patted Mabel's arm. "We'll talk after I tuck the girls in."

Thirty minutes later, Ruth stood at the threshold of Elam's guest room, watching her beautiful daughters sleep, and wondered what memories they would have of the year their daddy died. Would theirs be sorrowful memories, or would they only remember the big family meals, the cranberry harvest, the moonlit rides with their Mennonite grandmother holding the reins?

Downstairs, Mabel sat on the couch

centered before the fire. Zeus was stretched out beneath her feet like a stuffed polar bear rug. Mabel wore a pair of crocheted slippers, which looked like they'd fit Sofie. Mabel said, "Did you and Elam have a good night?"

Her question was innocent enough, but her dark eyes held a certain mischievous shine.

"Yes," Ruth said carefully. "That's what I want to talk to you about."

Ruth wanted to stand but instead took a seat beside Mabel. She breathed deeply while counting to ten, a tactic she'd started implementing whenever she needed to broach a difficult topic with Chandler, this woman's son. Toward the end of their marriage, however, Ruth had never reached five before words exploded like shrapnel from her mouth.

Clearing her throat, Ruth looked at her mother-in-law. "Thank you for supper," she said. "That was delicious." Even *she* could hear the crispness in her voice, which meant she was opening with a compliment, but something far less complimentary was bound to come. "However," she added, "I found it interesting you only set the table for two."

Mabel glanced over. Her small fingers

102

gripped the crochet hook. She'd known full well what she was doing. "You and Elam were the only ones left in the field," Mabel said. "I had already fed the other workers and sent them home. And then Laurie . . ." She trailed off.

"Laurie invited you and the girls for supper?" Ruth smiled slightly. "How convenient."

"I didn't mean to upset you." Mabel set the hook in her lap and stared at her hands. Unlike Ruth, she no longer wore a wedding band, but Ruth didn't remember seeing a wedding band on any of the women in the Driftless Valley Community, married or not.

Ruth said, "You know how I interpreted it, right?"

Mabel shook her head.

Ruth sighed, not wanting to spell it out. "Elam and I came in the house, and there were candles and a fire and food. It felt like a date."

"I was just trying to be kind."

"So, you had no ulterior motives?"

Trembling lips betrayed Mabel's stoic profile. "Yes. I want you and Elam to be happy."

Ruth groaned. Zeus lifted his massive head and rolled his eyes in her direction. Seeing nothing out of the ordinary, he lay back down on his paws and resumed his canine snore.

Ruth said, "My happiness should not at all be correlated with his."

"It's *not!*" Mabel insisted. "I don't know —" Her voice broke, and guilt flooded Ruth. Her mother-in-law's behavior might be offensive, but she was dealing with her grief too. Neither of them was thinking clearly. "Today, I was upstairs, rocking Vi before her nap, and I was looking around Elam's big house, with no one living in it besides him, and I thought of you and your girls with nowhere really to go, and the idea just —" her defense grew smaller as she stared down at her lap — "came to me."

Ruth softened her tone. "You thought that since Elam and I are both lonely that we should find refuge in each other?"

Nodding, Mabel looked up and whispered, "You're too young to be lonely, Ruth. My heart breaks even more to think of your life ending when it's half the length of mine."

For the second time in one night, tears sprang to Ruth's eyes. But these tears did not stem from loss, but because it so deeply touched her that her mother-in-law should care enough to put their burgeoning relationship on the line. Ruth's life was bookended by widows: her mother and her mother-in-law, and yet seeing how differently the two women reacted to grief caused Ruth to know which path she wanted to take as her exhausted, fret-filled heart pursued its own healing.

Ruth scooted over on the couch, recently draped with a set of Mabel's doilies, which were cropping up around the house like daffodils in spring. She put an arm around her rounded shoulders. Mabel smiled and patted Ruth's hand. "You're sweet," she said.

Ruth laughed quietly. "No, I'm not . . . but I do appreciate how hard you're trying to make my family feel safe and loved."

"Oh, you *are* loved!" Mabel cried. "Having you and the girls here —" Overcome, she stopped speaking and clutched a balled hand to her chest. "It's done my heart good."

"It's done all our hearts good to be here. You're a wonderful grandmother, Mabel."

Mabel rested her head on her daughter-in-law's shoulder. "And you're a wonderful *mamm.*" She paused. "I promise I'll stop trying to matchmake and just pray that God will send someone to you who can be the kind of husband and father my own son was."

105

Ruth didn't say anything, only stared silently into the fire.

Elam steered his wagon between the last row of bushes and the wall of the channel. As the wooden wheels creaked, the women lifted their *kapped* heads, straightened their backs, and began walking toward him with their portion of the dry harvest. They carried the heaped cranberries in straw baskets so identical, it appeared they must've gotten together to weave them, the same as they had gotten together to make apple pie filling and sauce.

Ruth joined the women funneling down the rows. Her lower back ached; her fingers were stiff and stained the color of blood. And yet, when was the last time Ruth's body tingled with the miraculous sensation that came from feeling the elements on her skin — the cold, the wind, the blinding glimmer of warm sun before it slipped behind a cloud and the cold returned — that was a not-so-subtle reminder that, out of all the generations who had worked this patch of ground, who had turned this oxygen into carbon dioxide, *she* was the one who was working the ground at that very moment; the one lucky enough to be alive? She couldn't remember, and yet here she was, walking tall and empowered by the fact she'd helped contribute to the harvest.

"You holding up all right?"

Turning, Ruth saw Laurie. "Takes a while," she said. "My basket's not half-full."

"I know. This part's no fun, but tonight will be."

"What's tonight?"

Laurie's gray eyes shone. "The harvest party. Elam holds it every year in his barn."

"Your brother's quite the social butterfly for claiming he's a recluse."

"Not so much." Laurie adjusted her basket. "My *mamm*'s the one who started it. She wanted to do something special, for the workers. After she died, Elam kept the tradition up."

"No doubt with a little encouragement from you."

Laurie laughed. "Just a little."

Ruth watched Elam, taking the baskets from the women and stacking them in the wagon so they lay smooth. One woman, named Amy Brunk, was curvy and dimpled with glossy black hair shining like a raven's wing beneath her *kapp.* This wasn't the first time Ruth had noticed Amy making an effort to talk to Elam, but he just took her basket and smiled the same as he did with everyone else. Ruth's relief puzzled her, and she continued studying him to understand why. The muscles moving beneath Elam's tanned forearms brought to mind the image of him bathing beneath the outdoor pump last night. Ruth's cheeks grew hot. She looked over her shoulder and saw Laurie was still watching her and smiling. But her smile was not as generic as her brother's. Ruth, feeling exposed, had to look away.

The dry harvest, like the wet harvest, was an arduous project that exhausted body and mind alike. By dusk, Ruth alone stood at the threshold of the barn. It satisfied her, seeing the cool cement floor layered with the slatted boxes, which allowed the fruit to receive necessary ventilation before the workers returned to sort the berries early the next day.

Laurie came and said, "You'd better go home and change if you're coming back for the party!"

Ruth turned. "What're you wearing tonight?"

"A little black version of this."

Ruth scanned Laurie's cape dress. After a moment, she said, "Are you serious?"

Laurie grinned. "Have you ever known me to be?"

"Well, the only dress I packed I wore to

the funeral. Vi spilled gravy on it."

"You're not wearing a funeral dress to a party. That's bad luck!"

"Mennonites don't believe in luck."

"No," Laurie admitted. "But we *do* believe in common sense. You can borrow one of my cape dresses. I have twelve more just like this one. All in the latest colors and patterns, straight from Lancaster." She paused dramatically. "One even shows my clavicles."

"Clavicles!" Ruth mock-gasped. "No wonder you and Tim have so many kids."

Laurie laughed. "What color you want? I have everything but red, yellow, and orange, and you probably shouldn't wear those colors anyway, with your hair."

Ruth wasn't sure how to respond. She didn't want to hurt Laurie's feelings — who'd made such an effort to welcome Ruth into the community — and yet she didn't want to show up tonight looking like she was trying to fit in. Or, worse, that she was trying to make fun. But then Ruth thought of the fact that coming to the gathering in one of Laurie's dresses was far better than showing up in jeans. "I'd love to borrow a dress," Ruth said. "Any color's fine."

Laurie's smile widened. Leaning forward, she pinched the baggy material of Ruth's sweatshirt. "I'll have to tack it," she said.

"But it'll work."

"Do you want me to come over to your house?"

"I'll come to you." She winked. "It'll give me a chance to escape."

Ruth followed Laurie up the farmhouse steps into the bedroom that, in another lifetime, had been Laurie's but was now occupied by Ruth and her girls.

Laurie had been ten when her mother became too ill to have visiting children underfoot. Ruth had been twelve when her own mother forbade her to have friends over after school. Laurie felt the loss of comradery all her life, which was why she was grateful to be surrounded by her children, whose messiness and noise protected her from the loneliness she'd always known. Ruth, on the other hand, didn't feel this loss at first. But by sixth grade, the girls in her classroom had stopped inviting Ruth to birthday parties and sleepovers because they believed Ruth was the one who had chosen to remain aloof and not her mother, who was secretly embarrassed that she and her husband were the age of most of the children's grandparents. However, now, Ruth and Laurie tromped upstairs, giddy women reliving the girlhood days they'd never gotten to experience.

Ruth and Laurie entered the room. Laurie laid the dresses on the bed and looked around, inspecting the dried bouquet on the bureau and the hook rug on the floor like she hadn't been up there in years. "Elam wanted to give us this house, after the babies started coming." She patted her belly. "He said it didn't make sense for us to stay in our little house while he stayed here."

"Why didn't you take him up on it?"

Laurie shuddered. "I don't know how Elam even does it. It's like, after *Mamm* died, all the good memories I have of this place were sucked into a black hole."

Looking down, Ruth fingered the hem of a dress. "I hope it's not the same for my girls."

"It won't be," Laurie said. "Chandler's death was awful, but it happened fast. My entire childhood, I knew one day my mom would be gone. And then, one day, she was." As she spoke, Laurie calmly spread out the skirts of her cape dresses so Ruth could inspect them. Despite the heaviness of their conversation, the gesture moved Ruth. Laurie was obviously proud of her creations while Ruth could barely see a variance in

111

color or fabric.

Laurie reached for the top one on the pile — a dark-blue wave splashed across the quilt — and picked it up. She held the material against Ruth's face.

"This would contrast your pretty green eyes."

Ruth had never known how to take a compliment. She asked, "Do you like clothing?"

"I love it." Laurie sighed. "I love clothing so much, it must be a sin."

Ruth laughed. But for once, Laurie's mercurial expression remained somber.

"Growing up," she continued, "sewing was my creative outlet . . . my personal rebellion. It was like, if I could get away with an inch shorter hem or buttons instead of hooks and eyes, I could take control of the world. Or at least take control of my corner of it. For *years* I dreamed of leaving Wisconsin and studying fashion somewhere like Paris or New York."

"Why didn't you?"

Laurie's smile returned. "Why do any of us forsake our dreams? I met Tim and fell in love, and suddenly the big city didn't appeal as much as building a simple life, with him."

Laurie touched Ruth's shoulder and

directed her to the closet. There were only a few in the farmhouse. Elam had added them one winter when he'd tried sating his boredom by remodeling everything that could be nailed down. Ruth entered this tiny closet — so clearly constructed by a man who'd never known an *Englisch* woman's fondness for shoes — and kept the door open so, by the lamplight on the nightstand, she could figure out how to fit the dress over her head. After a while, Ruth stepped out of the closet and self-consciously touched the wraparound skirt. "Don't think I'm supposed to be exposed like this."

Laurie looked at her and laughed, as she expertly twisted her wrist to twine the side of her hair, which she set into place with a bobby pin. "Here," she said, "let me help you out."

She stood before Ruth and helped tack in the waist and skirt. Ruth looked at Laurie's lowered profile and tried to find a resemblance to her brother. They had the same high cheekbones, straight nose, and skin tone — slightly ruddy from summers spent outdoors.

Ruth asked, "Did Elam have dreams?"

Laurie frowned slightly, her pursed mouth lined with pins. She finished tacking Ruth's dress and stood back — a hand on her belly

— to admire her work. "All you need is a *kapp*."

Ruth thought Laurie might not respond to her question, which was fine, since she was writhing from the impulsiveness of having asked it. But then Laurie said, "Elam was grown by the time I was a teenager, and he was very private, even back then. I don't really remember him being home all that much because he spent so much time in the old hunting cabin in the woods."

Ruth asked, "Did you ever go out there?"

"Yes," she said. "But Elam kept it locked."

"Midwestern man of mystery."

Laurie rolled her eyes. "Tell me about it. That mystery's why he doesn't have to flap his gums and still he's got women falling at his feet."

"Why'd he never marry one of them . . . like that pretty, dark-haired woman?"

"Amy Brunk?" Laurie laughed. "She's been after him since she was in pigtails, but Elam's never looked at her twice."

"Because he's so shy?"

"I thought it was that, at first. But then, when Amy started giving Elam such obvious clues even *he* could've figured them out, he never pursued her. It was like he was waiting for something, or *someone*."

Laurie looked at Ruth. Ruth's face flushed

114

and eyes burned with the intensity of that piercing, smoke-filled gaze. In this, Elam and Laurie were the same. "I know he's my brother," Laurie said. "But he's also one of the best men I've ever known."

Candlelight flickered, throwing as much shadow as light across the walls and up into the eaves of the old timber-framed barn closest to Elam's farmhouse. The eaves themselves were festooned with old starling nests, and a few of the dark-winged birds swooped and dived, searching for an escape and yet — in their panic — finding none. Tables, laden with food, had been set up along the left side of the barn, and the barn floor itself was circled with the benches that had been brought in from the church. A stack of worn hymnals teetered on one bench. The room smelled of cedar chips, beeswax, and bread. Ruth entered this setting and, as so often happened in the Driftless Valley Community, sensed that time was a sentient being who not only stood still, but politely stepped backward — so that she was no longer Ruth Neufeld, emptied widow and mother, but Ruth Galway, an idealistic young woman who believed in heroes and happy endings, and that the entire world could be transformed with one kind gesture, one positive thought.

Ruth's youthful idealism faltered as she received many curious looks from the Mennonite women and men, who'd mostly seen her in sweatshirts and jeans. Her clothing had set her apart over the past two days of communal labor, but what had set her apart even more was the language the community spoke — Pennsylvania Dutch — as they chattered and laughed between the rows of cranberry bushes: their comradery helping pass the time as they worked.

The women hadn't meant to exclude Ruth. They just didn't know how to *include* her, and Ruth's personality was such that she was not about to assert herself into a conversation, especially a conversation conducted in a language she did not speak.

Ruth twirled her wedding ring with her thumb, a nervous habit she'd taken up over the past five years. Laurie was not here. After helping Ruth dress, Laurie had gone back to her house to feed her brood of children before she and Tim could slip away for the party, leaving their eldest — a quiet ten-year-old named David — in charge. Why had Ruth let Laurie talk her into wearing her dress? She feared her attempt to fit in only made her stand out more. Ruth turned toward the door, seeking an escape with as much urgency as the starlings swooping overhead. But then she saw Elam, standing at the threshold in a white collared shirt and black suspenders, his thick silver hair and tan skin burnished by the oil lamps sitting on benches flanking the door. For some reason, it startled Ruth to see him, though Elam belonged here far more than she.

If a poll were taken, many in that barn would say Elam Albrecht preferred experiencing life from the sidelines of every main event: weddings, funerals, barn raisings, Ping-Pong tournaments. It didn't matter what they did — or how often they teased him good-naturedly — he never truly took part. But this did not seem the case as he strode into the barn. He scanned the room until he saw Ruth, and there his eyes stopped. Ruth's face burned, wondering if he perceived her cape dress as a slight against his heritage. But then he crossed the floor toward her. He smiled as he approached. "You look nice. Laurie put you up to it?"

"How'd you know?"

His smile widened. "I know my sister."

Not sure what to say, Ruth looked at the tables, where the women were slicing pies, cheese, bread, sweet rolls, and ham loaves slathered in pineapple gravy; digging spoons into corn casseroles, mashed potatoes, and green beans canned from the garden; unscrewing the lids on pickles, jams, relishes, chow-chows, and chutneys that opened with satisfying pops. All of it was either adorned or laced with cranberry, in conjunction with the harvest. In the corner, Ruth noticed massive turkeys, each browned and glistening with baste.

"Cranberry ice cream, right?" Ruth said, glancing toward a man in a felt hat who was sitting on one of the benches, turning the crank of an old-fashioned ice-cream maker.

Elam nodded. "You catch on quick."

Ruth smiled again and realized that — just like last night, during supper — she enjoyed just being near him, and she found herself wondering what the two of them looked like in comparison to the community. Anyone who did not know black heels, pearl earrings, and lipstick were not standard attire for a Mennonite woman might think she belonged.

They might even think she belonged here, with him.

Ruth glanced to the side, suddenly self-conscious about more than her clothes. She took one small step away. Elam didn't seem to notice as he clapped his hands. "Let's take a moment for prayer," he called, and, stunned, every man and woman grew still. Elam did not call them to prayer. Rarely did he speak. They amended their shock and bowed their heads for the silent grace as the birds swooped soundlessly overhead. Meanwhile, Ruth stayed by Elam's side, hoping Chandler couldn't see her attraction to another man and wondering why she cared.

Ruth was sitting on a church bench in the barn, picking at the food on her plate, when Amy Brunk came and sat beside her. The women shook hands and introduced themselves, though they each knew who the other was. They turned back to their plates and to the pretense of eating. Ruth was dressed identically to Amy, except Amy's cape dress was hunter green. Ruth watched her watching Elam and wondered how often Amy had caught her doing the same.

Amy suddenly turned. "Do you plan on sending your older daughter to school?"

Ruth could've never anticipated this question. "Here? To the community school?"

Amy nodded. "I'm the teacher for first through eighth grade. Is your daughter in first?"

"Sofie should be, but our life's been so unsettled, lately I've just been teaching her at home. Or . . . I guess wherever we've been living at the time." Ruth held tight to her plate. "But no, I don't plan on sending Sofie to school here. Our stay's only temporary."

"My apologies," Amy said. "I heard you were joining the church."

Ruth tried to laugh. "The dress I borrowed from Laurie must be throwing people off."

Smiling, Amy patted her shoulder and stood. "Well, if you ever change your mind, let me know. I would be honored to teach your little girl."

Ruth watched Amy go back to the women. They were circled around one of the younger ones, who was seated and holding a newborn so bundled against the night air that he (or she, who could tell?) resembled a cocoon. To Ruth, the women appeared so cheerful and unsullied, though Ruth understood the rains of the world fell on the just and the unjust, and therefore most had been exposed to the same elements as she. But the difference was these women had a community of friends who could help shelter them from the coldness of that impartial rain, even if just by pressing a hand with their warm ones and murmuring, *"I've been there too."*

■ ■ ■ ■

Ruth left the party early. She hadn't seen her girls much over the past two days, and she was surprised by how much she missed them and the identity of motherhood that helped offset the identity she'd lost. She found them in the bathroom. Sofie and Vi were in the bathtub, filling measuring cups with water. Mabel sat on the closed toilet seat with the *Eloise Wilkin Stories,* which Ruth had packed, open on her aproned lap.

Ruth stood in the doorway, listening, as Mabel read:

"Somebody else lives in this house.
He is very tall
And he walks with long steps.
He goes out to work in the morning,
And sometimes he brings Terry a present
when he comes home at night.
Guess who it is!"

Sofie stopped pouring water. "I don't like that story."

Mabel turned the page, and Ruth knew the words she found there: *It's Terry's father.*

For years, Ruth had mindlessly read classic stories to her children like *Guess Who Lives Here* and *We Help Mommy.* Many of

121

the stories the same ones her own mother had read. But now, the mindless had become a reminder. Mabel closed the book and set it on the floor. She looked down, her part cleanly dividing her scalp, her black lace-up shoes braced against the porcelain commode. Her shoulders rose and fell as her ample chest heaved.

Ruth could fully predict how this scene would play out if she did not intervene. She stepped into the narrow, chilly bathroom, knelt on the worn towel beside the bathtub, and leaned over to touch Mabel's knee. Mabel startled and then reached out to clasp her fingers.

"I'm sorry," she murmured. "I didn't think."

Ruth smiled and mouthed, *"It's okay."* Turning back to Sofie and Vi, she said, her voice effervescent with false cheer, "You girly girls ready to get out?"

But that was another thoughtless reminder. Girly girls — the nickname Chandler, their father, had coined. Sofie looked at her mother. Her black hair was slicked back; the tips of her ears pink; her fingertips, holding the three-quarters cup, pruned. "Mom?"

"Hmm?"

"Is Dad never coming back?"

Ruth dropped her eyes to the soap bubbles floating on the water's surface. She had no idea how to address this. No idea how to be clear and concise without patronizing or causing pain. Death should come with a manual. "No, sweetheart," she whispered. "He's not."

In one movement, Sofie slid down the back of the bathtub until only her nose and lips peeked out. Vi scrambled back from her sister, toward the faucet, and wrapped her arms around her bruised little knees. Ruth leaned across the bathtub and pulled Sofie up, the girl's black hair streaming. The sleeves of Ruth's borrowed cape dress were soaking wet. Ruth held Sofie's small chest between her hands and felt her heart beating like a wild, caged thing. "Sofie, Sofie," she said. "It's okay, my baby. It's okay." But it wasn't. Sofie leaned forward against her mother's hands and cried. She sobbed from deep within, and her heart beat harder.

Ruth let go of Sofie's chest and took Sofie's face in her hands. "Sof," she said. "I need you to look at me, sweetheart. I need you to breathe." Sofie didn't seem to hear her. She just shook her head as the sobs rose and rose and rose without any promise of descension. Ruth braced herself and pulled Sofie out of the bathtub, all legs and arms and splashing water. Ruth held the six-year-old on her lap like a newborn. The force of the movement and the cool air shocked Sofie enough that her eyes unclenched and she looked at her mother. Ruth kept her eyes focused on her daughter's and breathed with her, breathed with her like that Colombian nurse had breathed with her while she was laboring with Vi.

Ruth broke eye contact to check on her other child.

Vi's knees were still pulled up snug against her chest, but she looked interested, not alarmed. How much easier it would be, Ruth thought, if both girls were too young to understand.

Ruth adjusted to place Sofie's back against her chest, the girl's bare legs splayed over her own. Water covered the tile floor. Mabel remained on the toilet seat with tears pouring down her face.

For the first time in months, Ruth prayed: *Oh, God. You've got to help me salvage this.*

Ruth whispered in Sofie's ear, "Daddy's always going to be with us."

Sofie's chest rumbled with one word: "How?"

"He's a soul, Sof. Just as you are. You have a soul right in here." Ruth tapped Sofie's chest. "It never dies. It lives forever and ever, and so that part of Daddy will always be with us."

"Where do souls live?"

"In heaven," Ruth said automatically, though, in truth, her theology was strained.

"Daddy's soul's in heaven right now?"

"Yes," Ruth said. "But I also believe he's with us here, in our hearts."

Sofie reached up and pressed a hand over Ruth's hand. "I want to be a soul too."

Ruth's breath caught. She looked at Mabel and saw she'd stopped crying and was now watching them with compassion and perhaps a bit of shock. Mabel had no doubt assumed she and Chandler were raising their girls in a Christian home, where concepts like "soul" and "heaven" were part of their everyday environment. Now, Mabel knew they had been so focused on making a temporal difference in the world, the eternal world had become opaque.

Ruth said to Sofie, "It's not time for you to just be a soul. God's got a plan for you here."

Sofie turned to study her mother's face. "It's not time for you to be a soul?"

"No," Ruth said, kissing her temple. "It's not time for me, either."

Reassured, Sofie nestled in the comfort of Ruth's arms, and Ruth held her there until the cold forced them to rise and get Sofie and Vi dressed.

In their bedroom, Ruth squeezed toothpaste onto Clifford toothbrushes — red for Sofie, yellow for Vi — and dipped them in a fresh cup of water since they'd forgotten to brush their teeth downstairs. Sofie studied her mother as she lazily brushed her top baby teeth and then her bottom, thrusting her pink tongue through the gap her missing tooth had made. She'd recovered from the bathtub episode to be her normal precocious self, and Ruth's cheeks reddened as Sofie didn't avert her gaze. Ruth passed Sofie an empty cup, and she expertly spit.

Wiping her mouth on her pajama sleeve, Sofie asked, "Can we stay here forever?"

"No, *Liebe*," Ruth said, trying out the Pennsylvania Dutch endearment she'd heard Laurie use. She took Sofie's toothbrush and tucked a strand of damp hair behind her ear. "We're just staying here until we can figure out our next step."

"But I don't want to go back to Grandma's, even if she *does* have a TV."

Cathleen Galway was a far cry from Mabel Neufeld, who read books, dressed dolls, made play dough and cookies from scratch all while the girls tore the house apart. "They're only children," she'd said. "They'll have to clean up after themselves soon enough." And yet Ruth grieved that Cathleen would never get to redeem herself by mothering her granddaughters the way she'd never mothered Ruth. Ruth reached out and touched her older daughter's beautiful face. "Do you like staying here, with Oma Mabel?"

Sofie nodded. Vi, rosebud mouth foaming toothpaste, nodded too. The room glowed with lamplight that softened the threadbare quilts piled on the bed and the German Bible on the nightstand, the gilt worn off the deckle-edge pages from so much use. The scene affected Ruth like a satisfied sigh. She felt safe here, safe in a way she hadn't felt in her life.

"Oma Mabel loves us," Sofie said, one of the simplest ways children categorize acceptance.

It was true. Each day, in every gesture, Mabel declared her love so openly, it was impossible for the children's pliable hearts not to accept that love and respond in kind. Gratitude for her impetuous, and incredibly naive, mother-in-law made emotions stop up Ruth's throat. Swallowing hard, she helped the girls into bed, remembering how she and Chandler had put them to bed in

Bogotá: the long, drawn-out ordeal of baths, jammies, hair-brushing, and shallow cups of water or milk; how the girls would snuggle up with their blankies and whatever stuffed animal they'd confiscated from the toy chest downstairs, and then Ruth and Chandler would sing to them.

A custom version of "Edelweiss" was their favorite.

Chandler and Ruth's duet could've never rivaled *The Sound of Music,* and yet each of them found a pleasing harmony as the off-key notes rose and fell. Ruth's chest ached as she now began to sing her first solo in eight long months: "Blossom of snow, may you bloom and grow, bloom and grow forever. Edelweiss, Edelweiss, bless my Sofie and Vi forever." At the end, Ruth's voice cracked, and the tears flowed, dampening her hair, which she had twisted and pulled back into a bun as if she belonged here, a Mennonite. The concept was laughable, but she cried. Ruth continued to lie there, crying, until her daughters' breathing evened, and then she sat up, dried her face, and pulled out the bobby pins trying to tame her unruly hair.

Ruth left her room and went downstairs, toward the sound of someone in the kitchen. It was Mabel. Squinting against the kerosene light, Ruth asked, "What're you making?"

Mabel said, without turning, "Cookies."

"What time is it?"

"I don't know."

Ruth crossed the floor. Sugar gritted like sand beneath her feet. Flour dusted the countertop. Mabel glanced over, and Ruth saw she'd been crying as well. Mabel turned and pulled a tray out of the oven. Steam curled around her face, deepening her color and tightening the strands of her loose hair. Using a metal flipper, Mabel scraped the cookies off the tray and arranged them on a plate. She set the plate before Ruth. Ruth looked at Mabel, and Mabel looked at Ruth.

Both their eyes filled.

Mabel's voice was choked. "I think you earned some comfort food, after tonight."

Ruth nodded because that was all she could manage. The countertop pulled Ruth as her exhaustion surged. She finally succumbed to it and rested her head on her crossed arms, sobbing as fiercely as Sofie had sobbed. Mabel said nothing, just came over and stroked her hair with floured hands. "Shhh, shhh," she soothed, as if this time Ruth could let her worries all go and simply be a child. Meanwhile, the scent of cinnamon and molasses filled the room.

# CHAPTER 6

Ruth did not go up to bed after she and Mabel ate half a dozen cookies, drank a quart of milk, and Mabel retired to her room. Instead, she cleaned the kitchen with Zeus lying at her feet, his tail thwacking the floor as Ruth swept and then slowly washed and dried. But even when the pans and bowls were all returned to their cupboards, Elam had not returned. Zeus's nails tapped wood as he followed Ruth into the living room and then past the bath toward Elam's room. Ruth turned around before she reached his door and went back into the hall. Zeus whined as she opened the front door. She stroked the coarse ruff of his neck and snapped her fingers for him to lie down. He did so, reluctantly, looking up at her with sorrowful eyes. As strange as it was, Ruth felt better knowing he was here with the girls, even though Mabel was here as well.

Blades of light pierced through the barn slats as Ruth approached from the lane. She slid open the door and found the barn empty, so the earlier celebration seemed from a dream. The couples were gone, tucked side by side in their cozy marital beds. The church benches were gone, more than likely stacked in someone's wagon and hauled back to the church for the next Lord's Day. Boxes of cranberries took up the space where the food used to be. Elam stood at the end of one table. By lamplight, he inspected the berries in his hands.

"Good harvest?" Ruth asked.

He glanced at her. "Hey," he said. "Didn't hear you come in."

Ruth remained at the entrance of the barn, a few yards away.

"The harvest does look good," he said.

"Glad to hear it. You had quite the turnout today."

Elam looked directly at her for the first time. "It's tradition," he said. "Year in, year out."

Frustration clipped his voice. It was a tone Ruth recognized because she'd once heard it every time she spoke. Ruth moved closer. After a moment, she asked, "You happy, Elam?"

His eyes shifted back to the boxes. As if

by force, he lifted his head and turned toward her. Light, from the few candles that remained, wavered as wind blew through the barn. "I was," he said. "As strange as it is, as simple as my life may have been, I *was* happy."

Ruth didn't say anything for a while, just stood before him in her thin borrowed dress. She was more uncomfortable wearing it than when she'd stood before him in a fitted fleece and shorts. But the clothes themselves didn't bring discomfort. It was the realization she had been looking for Elam, and she didn't know what to do or say now that she was here.

Sugar swam through her blood from the cookies she and Mabel had consumed. Ruth wondered if this was what emboldened her to eventually ask, "Why aren't you happy now?"

Elam leaned against the table. "It . . . it's ever since Chandler died." He folded his arms, bracing himself. "I guess it made me take a good look at my life and see all the dreams I haven't fulfilled. I'm thirty-nine years old, Ruth." He looked at her. His voice was ragged as he murmured, "If I don't do them now . . . when will I?"

"We all have unfulfilled dreams."

"Really?" His eyebrows rose. "What are yours?"

Ruth wished she hadn't spoken, but it was unfair to ask Elam to bare his soul while concealing hers. "I have English and art degrees but haven't written or painted in years."

He smiled gently. "With two young children, I think it'd be rather hard to find the time."

"We can always find time for the things we love. I just haven't made it a priority."

Her mind echoed with what she hadn't said: Ruth hadn't made *herself* a priority.

But she had never once gone hungry; she had never worried about having a roof over her head; she had never once feared for her safety or her children's, so why did she feel like the past six years of her life consisted not of living but of . . . survival?

Ruth wasn't comfortable with this subject, or at least when the subject revolved around her. She asked, "What about you? What dreams haven't you fulfilled?"

Again, his eyes moved from hers.

She added, more softly, "You don't have to tell me if you don't want to."

He nodded but cleared his throat to speak. "I've always wanted . . . a family."

Elam's answer forced Ruth to take a closer

look at hers. She wanted more time for herself. More time to paint, read, and write without the unending interruptions and demands of two small children, who gave her an often tiring and yet love-filled life. But here was a man whose greatest dream was what she had and sometimes took for granted.

It was a dream Chandler had taken for granted as well.

"That's a beautiful dream," she said. "To want a family."

Elam shrugged. "It's like what you said, though. You can always find time for your priorities. I just never took . . . the time."

His loneliness was so palpable, it pained her to look at him. Ruth moved closer because she knew what it was like to have people truly see you and then turn away. "I've not been here long," she said, "but I don't think you don't have a family because you never made it a priority. I think you're so busy making sure you're providing enough work to sustain the community's families that you never found time to build your own."

"That's kind of you," Elam said. "To give me the benefit of the doubt. But for as long as I can remember, I've never been able to let people in."

Sighing, Ruth turned and leaned back against the sorting table so they stood facing the empty barn. A crumpled paper cup was abandoned on the floor. "You're not the only one," she said. "I've often wondered if going through hard things hardens us."

He glanced over. "You mean, you don't let yourself feel so you won't feel pain?"

"Something like that. I guess, when faced with hard things, we can either choose to embrace the pain or let it reinforce our defenses."

"I won't, if you won't," he said. Ruth looked over at him, and he grinned. One of the first times she'd seen him smile since the party.

She reached out a hand. "You promise?"

"Mennonites don't take oaths."

"Then it's not an oath, Elam. Just a handshake."

He looked down and then up at her. He extended his hand. The tips of his fingers were stained with the cranberries he had labored over during the past two days. Her fingertips were stained the same. Their stained fingers touched as their hands clasped. In the background, one of the lamps sputtered and then burned out. Ruth's eyes struggled to adjust to the dimmer light. When they did, he was still look-

135

ing at her. Elam put his other hand on top
of theirs and held it there.

## December 7, 2015

Dear Chandler,

Tonight, I sat on the couch and
watched you dance with our daughter.
The instrumental version of "Bittersweet
Symphony" was playing on Pandora,
and Sofie walked up to you, batted those
big brown eyes of hers, and asked you to
dance. I batted my eyes in similar fashion
the day we wed, and you — who never
dance — danced with me in front of all
your staff, the volunteers, the children,
and Director Janice. I don't remember
very much about that moment, as my
head was swirling with all that would
take place that night. And yet, I will
always remember how we rocked back
and forth: your hands locked at the base
of my waist, and the only dress shoes
you owned (scuffed, ugly things you'd
probably had since college) trampled the
hem of my white cotton dress.

These memories, three years old today,
came back to me tonight, as I saw you
kneel to better hold our daughter. Our
Charlie Brown Christmas tree sparkled

behind you; Vivienne was army-crawling across the floor, her round eyes locked on one of the ornaments dangling from the lower branches. The music swelled. Sofie's dimpled, almost-four-year-old fist clutched the blue material of your shirt, and you rocked back and forth, the same as you had the day we wed. I loved you so much then. I love you the most when I see you being a father to these two girls who adore you in a way that I, as their mother, can often not touch.

It fills my heart with gratitude to see you so adored, and yet I must wonder why — if you're so adored by every woman in your life — you remain so dissatisfied with it. Why are you seeking this adventure elsewhere? To places that will take you away from us? Why can't you just be content? But then, am I really content with where this life has taken me? I too am surrounded by people who love me without question, but my heart still longs for something more — for a fulfillment beyond my roles as mother and wife. Perhaps you and I, dear husband, are not that far removed from one another, although lately it seems like that wall exists between us.

Let's tear it down, then mend whatever needs mended. Let's go back to how the two of us felt that day we wed, when you and I didn't have a care in this broken world because we were so wholly satisfied to have our arms around each other.

Love,
Your wife

Elam sipped his morning coffee while staring out the kitchen window. He knew the rest of the household would soon awaken, and he wanted to be in the field when it did. He was running away from what he felt and from the woman who prompted those feelings. But he had no other way to cope. Elam was not a very introspective individual, and for the first half of his life, it was a predilection that had served him well. He'd always taken quiet pride in the fact he'd never gotten heart palpitations. Not heart palpitations in the sense he should lay off a second cup of coffee with that leftover slice of Aunt Mabel's shoofly pie, but heart palpitations in the sense someone outside his body had the ability to affect it.

However, from the moment Ruth arrived at the farm, he understood that the comfortable atmosphere of his life was about to change. The shift was so distinct and tenable, he'd lifted his gaze from the cranberry bog and looked up, expecting to see a mushrooming thunderhead, but the cloud of dust from Ruth's vehicle rose into an otherwise cloudless sky. Elam had told himself that Ruth was his cousin's widow, and as such, he needed to respect what they'd had by not allowing himself to see her as anything more than family. Then there were moments, like last night in the barn, or the other night, when they stood in front of the sink as he washed dishes and she took the plates from him to dry — their wet fingertips touching — that he was so consumed by Ruth's sheer presence, he could not breathe or speak, so he was grateful she believed his stammer was inborn and had nothing to do with her. But lately, *everything* had to do with her, and Elam was frustrated by his inability to govern his emotions. This frustration made him realize that perhaps he'd never been in a relationship not because the opportunity hadn't presented itself, but because he'd never wanted to lose control enough to let himself love.

Ruth surely did not reciprocate these feelings, and therefore Elam Albrecht needed to stuff them, the same as he'd been stuffing them all his life. His thoughts drifted to

139

when he was a child of about nine or ten, before his *mamm* got cancer, before he was forced to grow up when he didn't understand what "growing up" meant. He'd spent hours in the field, trying to catch a bald eagle in a trap, unaware that there were fines for such an endeavor. He would patiently lie on his stomach, on the periphery of the cornfield's shorn scalp, and wait for the eagle to come. It was a simple box trap which held a rabbit Elam had found dead on the road. He'd waited and waited for the bald eagle to arrive, but when it did, the bird so transfixed Elam, as it awkwardly crossed the ground over to the trap on its yellow talons — its sleek black-and-white wings catching the light — he couldn't find it in him to pull the string that would trap the bird. All his life, it seemed, his heart got in the way of his goals.

Loss — like anger, like love — produces reactions corresponding with personality type. When Laurie and Elam's mother died, Laurie had made a subconscious goal to have so many people to love, she would never be lonely. Elam had made a goal to keep his heart closed, so it wouldn't hurt if that person got taken away.

Perhaps because of this, Elam had dreaded Ruth's arrival with her children, but now

140

that they were here — now that he couldn't imagine the house without the soundtrack of little feet coming downstairs, or lying in bed in his small room off the kitchen, listening to Ruth's flat voice singing the girls to sleep — he found himself delirious with joy that he was no longer alone or lonely. How could he bear it if they were to go; how could he bear it if they were to stay?

Elam heard someone on the stairs, and it was no pitter-patter of little feet. He knocked his coffee back, scalding his tongue. He was striding toward the door when Mabel called out, "Hold on there, Elam." He stopped in his tracks, like a child caught stealing whoopie pies for breakfast. His aunt came around the corner in her nightgown, her black braid unraveled from sleep. Though Mabel and his mother hadn't looked alike, seeing his aunt now made him wonder how the sands of time would've changed his mother, if she were alive.

"How was the party?" she asked.

He couldn't meet her eyes. "Good."

"I heard there was ice cream." Mabel smiled. "That alone deserves more than 'good.' "

Elam lifted his shoulders in a shrug, jaw throbbing. He remembered Ruth sitting on one of the church benches in the barn, her back ramrod straight, a plate balanced in her hands. He could tell she was uncomfortable there, surrounded by another culture and couples whose very unity proved their lives hadn't been as difficult as hers. Elam had wanted to hold her: that was the thought that made his face burn now. Even while she picked at her food, made small talk with the women, and smiled bravely — silently — while the rest of them sang, he had wanted to hold her, smooth back her hair, erase the darkness from beneath her eyes.

This wanting was a betrayal to his cousin and to Ruth.

Elam concluded, "We had a nice . . . time."

He might've imagined the coy tilt of Mabel's head. "And did *Ruth* have a nice time?"

He looked at his feet. His boots were by the door, a habit he'd picked up because the women of the house kept everything so clean. Nodding, he said, "Seemed like it."

Mabel touched his arm. "Something wrong?"

He shook his head.

"Elam," she said. "If nothing's ailing your body, then what's ailing your mind?"

He looked over at her, so plagued with guilt that he wanted to confess, even though her son was the man he felt he'd been disloyal to. Elam said, "I think you already know."

She leaned closer. "Ruth?"

He looked back at his feet and nodded.

"Oh, Elam." Mabel clasped her hands. "I've prayed for so long that you would find a special someone." Leaning toward him again, she glanced toward the stairs and whispered, "Does *she* know?"

"No," he said. "And I won't tell her." Meaning he didn't want Aunt Mabel to tell her either. "She's already been through so much. It'd do no good to lay it all on her now."

Mabel's sleep-swollen eyes shone with tears. She reached out again, and Elam was becoming so accustomed to his aunt's tactile nature, it no longer caught him off guard. "Don't you think," she said, "the love of a good-hearted man might be just what she needs?"

Elam escaped to the barn as soon as he could. He knew, if Ruth descended those stairs, everything he and Mabel had discussed would be written across his face, and the openness of that horrified him. Would he have become as infatuated with any woman, give or take ten years, who lived in such close proximity? Was this the kind of attraction that happened when you spent thirty-nine years living like a monk? Elam groaned and stepped into the barn. He kept the door open to allow the morning light to sweep through the gap. He needed to be working, but he was having a difficult time concentrating, since every time he stood in the barn, he could envision Ruth's face as she told him about her unfulfilled dreams. No, he thought, what he felt for her was not the result of some chemical backup in his blood. He didn't understand it; he had a feeling he *couldn't* understand it, but he knew he was beginning to deeply care for this woman. In truth, though, that was putting it mildly. If "caring" for someone had a spectrum, he was further from the beginning and closer to the end. He cared for her, plain and simple. He cared for her, and for her young children, in a way he'd never cared for anyone.

But what could he do about this? Nothing. There was nothing he could do.

Elam started stacking the wooden crates of cranberries on the sorting tables. He strode out to the well and worked the handle on the water pump. He filled four buckets and carried them back two at a time, finding satisfaction in the sense of be-

144

ing balanced, when it seemed it'd been a long time since he'd been anything of the sort. He distributed this water in low tubs — one at each table. Once all of this was completed, he stood back and surveyed it.

The same angst that had distracted him, once focused, had provided a preternatural energy, allowing Elam to complete the task in half the time it usually took. He glanced over his shoulder toward the house, but nobody was standing on the porch. It was just becoming habit, the same as yesterday, when he would be working in the field and glance over to see where Ruth was. He had even told his brother-in-law, Tim, to make sure she took enough breaks, for he'd done plenty of dry picking himself, and he could remember how — by the end of the day — pain darted into his lower back. But Ruth hadn't complained.

Elam all but exhaled in relief when he noticed Tim walking up the lane.

"Hey," Tim called. He paused and studied Elam. "You feeling all right?"

This was the second time in an hour his physical appearance made others think he was ill. Maybe lovesickness was an ailment one could catch, like the common cold. He glanced at Tim.

"I think I might take the day off. You got

145

this?" Elam gestured to the sorting tables. "Everything's set up."

"Sure thing," Tim said. He looked confused. Elam never took time off. He also never spoke in groups, like he did last night. But unlike Mabel or Laurie, Tim wasn't about to pry. Sometimes, Elam appreciated the more taciturn nature of his gender. "Take all the time you need."

"I'll only need today," Elam said. His tone came out more gruffly than he intended. "There's something I need to do."

Elam's heart rate slowed in the few steps he took away from the barn. He walked past the wet-harvest bogs. The boards damming up the water had been removed, allowing the current to flow back down the canal toward the lake. A blue-winged heron took flight as Elam passed. Its wings nearly skimmed the water until it rose and flapped, heading off to a more secluded location. Elam understood the crane's need for solitude. His own need had driven him here. The fallow field's wide-open plane was only broken by the distant trio of silos at the neighboring dairy farm, which appeared like white-capped nesting dolls, displayed from greatest to least. The cold was setting in. Elam could always tell as his kneecaps tightened, the cartilage ground down to bone on bone from jumping in and out of the harvester for the past thirty-some years. Although he was unusually warm natured, he would've donned a coat if he hadn't forgotten it. He'd been so eager to escape that house, he'd barely remembered to put on his boots.

A fish jumped in the lake, circles ringing the spot where the body had disappeared as smoothly as a silver coin dropped in water. Elam supposed that some men in his position would like to fish or hunt coyotes or rabbits — small prizes that temporarily satiated hunters' appetites until deer season opened and their clotheslines were strung with bright-orange garb. But Elam never took pleasure in killing. He never even took pleasure in trapping, as was proven by his letting that bald eagle eat a rabbit on that Indian summer day.

No, Elam took pleasure in music.

Elam climbed up the porch into the cabin, which didn't resemble a cabin as much as a shack, but he continued to call it a cabin because that was what it had always been called. The cabin was here when Elam's family first moved — with four other families — from Pennsylvania to the Driftless Region of Wisconsin, known for its fertile soil and rolling, unglaciered hills. Even thirty-five years ago, the cabin was such an eyesore that Elam's father considered knocking it down and turning the surrounding woods into more farmland. But Elam's father was also an avid hunter, and therefore it didn't take Elam long to convince him to keep the woods as a preserve for whitetail buck; therefore, Elam's cabin was salvaged.

Elam didn't have many friends growing up, because how could you develop friendships if you couldn't speak? He had a friend when his cousin, Chandler, visited from Pennsylvania. But Chandler talked enough for the both of them, and when Elam inevitably struggled to get the words out — or not get them out as much as set them free — Chandler ran through his gamut of words until he randomly found the one Elam wanted. This drove Elam crazy because he could tell Chandler wasn't trying to help so much as turn Elam's impairment into a game.

This was why the cabin — and the solitude it represented — became his haven. His family only used the cabin for hunting season, so it was a place where Elam could hide out. Be himself. A place to daydream and read the book of poetry he'd picked up from the "Free to a Good Home" box outside the library. Elam's parents weren't overly concerned by his stammer. They were too busy trying to get Driftless Valley Farm up and running, which was what kept Elam busy too, when he wasn't going to school at the one-room building a mile down the road, or hiding in the cabin, reading poetry by lamplight. Elam lived like this until, one day, the librarian, Miss Romaine, caught him taking more books from the free box and laughed when he jumped.

"Boy," she'd said, "you could be sneaking far worse things than Lord Byron. C'mon —" she waved a hand toward the door — "I'll show you the rest of the Romantics."

Miss Bridgette Romaine was an unusual woman, especially for such a rural area. She was black in a predominantly white town, neither married nor had a desire to marry, and possessed a fondness — some might say obsession — for opera music, cats, paper earrings, and knitting sweaters so thick, they didn't look like sweaters but raw fleeces dyed flamboyant hues. Elam would bike from the farm to the library in Tomah, seven miles away. Country boys did not often check out books of poetry, and Miss Romaine had said it was the first time in her twenty-five years as a librarian that the poetry was selected by a Mennonite boy in a straw hat and suspenders, split front teeth adorning his grin. This combination apparently piqued Miss Romaine's interest, so that she tried to make small talk while asking for the information needed to obtain his peach-colored card with the small silver chip. But Elam couldn't tell her, or when he tried to tell her, the words got trapped in his throat. He blinked and worked until tears came to his eyes. Finally, the syllables broke loose, and he said, "E-lam."

Miss Romaine was not fazed. Reaching across the desk, she shook Elam's hand and said it was an honor to meet such a well-read young man. Once a week, for over two years, Elam visited the library regularly to return and check out books. Each time, Miss Romaine made an effort to draw him out by offering suggestions or asking what he'd read. Each time, Elam found he could speak to her a little more. Finally, over her lunch breaks, Miss Romaine began teaching Elam how to speak by encouraging him to read aloud from what he'd selected.

Elam could do this because he could focus on the pages rather than on her face. In this simple way, Miss Romaine became Elam's speech therapist; later, she became his music therapist, for opera had given her a voice during a time in history when it was otherwise silenced. Since Elam couldn't hold a note, she taught him to play piano. Elam soon — as Miss Romaine had predicted — loved playing piano as much as he loved to read.

Each medium opened a world to him not confined by his tongue.

Elam now opened the thin, rectangular drawer of the desk he had made from reclaimed barn wood. From inside, he pulled out a matchbox. Sulfur stung his nose as he lit the wick and set the globe back on top. The space was no longer cold and damp as it had been. Even as a boy, he began remodeling until the cabin was as weathertight as his own house. The air still smelled stale except at the height of summer, when Elam wrenched up the two single-pane windows, which allowed some fresh farm air to cycle through. But it didn't matter. His 1903 Steinway piano (which Miss Romaine had bequeathed to him in her will), desk, and books were visual balms. The cabin was more his home than the home others claimed was his. It was spare, rustic, and considered inhospitable. Perhaps this was why Elam felt such kinship; the miserly structure reminded him of himself.

Elam sat on the piano bench and lifted the lid. The piano belonged to the cabin as much as the cabin belonged to it. Elam stroked the black-and-white keys and warmed his fingers up by doing scales. The small cabin reverberated with the sound, and it thrilled him as it had from the moment Miss Romaine first played. Because Elam's Old Order Mennonite heritage forbade instruments, he had always created his music in solitude, and his parents — who'd died before he received the piano — never knew of his gift. The melody was a forbidden, haunting language which spoke of his longing in a way he could not. After the accident that took his finger at seventeen, Elam didn't play for a year: the year his mother died. He knew it was foolish, and highly unrealistic for a farmer's son — not to mention a *Mennonite* farmer's son — but Elam dreamed of studying music.

By seventeen, Elam still had a mild speech impediment but no longer feared speaking like he had in early adolescence, and yet he couldn't imagine a better fit for him than a school where language was communicated through keys and strings instead of words. But then that dream was taken when the ring finger on his left hand got caught in the power take-off — a powerful implement that nearly scalped the neighbor girl, Esther, when her pigtail got caught.

The same power take-off just as easily, and unsentimentally, removed Elam's finger, and though he knew he should be grateful it hadn't taken his whole hand — or, worse, his life — the removal of that single digit almost seemed like God was pointing a finger at Elam, declaring that his years of subterfuge had finally received their comeuppance.

Elam played and played in the cabin. Since he'd never learned how to read music, he played the melody by heart. He closed his eyes and leaned into the song. After all this time, his maimed hand could find the keys just as effortlessly as his whole one. He finished and tilted back, unsure if the sun or the moon would be shining through the window when he opened his eyes, and almost relishing if it would be darkness, since the darkness would feel sacred, hushed.

But when he opened his eyes, the clouds must've shifted, for sunlight poured through the windows, revealing the haphazard piles of hardback books on the floor. He was rested, rejuvenated, his head buzzing with endorphins, and he absently wondered if this was how Ruth felt when she completed her runs. He smiled at the image of her: Ruth's right leg kicking out slightly farther than her left; her strawberry-blonde ponytail swishing back and forth with her uneven strides. He looked around the cabin and wondered if she'd ever had a place as magical and as secluded as this was to him, and he could suddenly see her here — not with him, perhaps, but on her own, pursuing her gift, even if no one else ever knew she possessed it.

Standing from the bench, Elam closed the piano lid and strode across the room to blow out the lamp, which now seemed lit more for ambience than illumination. His head cleared and purpose renewed, he left his cabin and walked past the lake.

He knew what he was going to do, and the thought of it pleased him.

All day, Ruth kept looking between the house and the barn, wondering where Elam was but not wanting to ask. Her head pounded as she sorted cranberries — discarding any that were soft or malformed — and washed them in the basin. The repetition seemed the only thing that kept her on task. She'd barely slept last night, but just stared at the ceiling while replaying everything Elam had said.

Ten years ago, she would've looked down on a man whose highest aspiration was to have a family. Ten years ago, at the ripe age of twenty, she would've sneered because, in her own mind, her aspirations were so much higher than that. She planned to change the world as soon as she graduated college, and though it was unclear how she would accomplish such a feat, she knew a headful of dreams would take her a long way. Twenty-year-old Ruth did not know how marriage and children would factor into such dreams, but she *did* know she would not settle for anyone who did not believe as she did: that children produced by their union were brought along on the adventure; the adventure did not stop for them.

But now, at thirty, Ruth had a different view. The adventure *did* indeed stop — or at least change — after children, and to try to deny that was like trying to deny the sun rising, or the days growing shorter in the fall. Children initiating change was an undeniable factor of parenthood.

Ruth had learned to accept this concept, because she knew it was the only way she could endure. Chandler, on the other hand, continued to live as if his family was a fixed point on the spinning compass of his life. Therefore, hearing Elam's commonplace dream had filled her with a desire she hadn't felt in years. Even now, it made her flush, recalling how she'd wanted to kiss him in that cranberry barn, and the utter travesty of this: a recently widowed woman finding herself attracted to another man. A man who was related to her husband, no less. So when Elam hadn't appeared at breakfast, and then later hadn't appeared at lunch, she began to worry. She didn't worry that something had happened to him; she worried that something had happened to *them,* and that last night, Elam could read that fevered expression in her eyes.

"You feeling okay?" Laurie asked.

Ruth glanced over. "Yes. Why?"

"I don't know," she said. "You've been . . . quiet."

Ruth thought about saying she was *always* quiet — Laurie was often the one who spoke — but she didn't want Laurie prying further, so she just nodded and continued sorting.

Three hours later, the workers were taking a lunch break when Ruth spied Elam striding across the field. She was sitting on an overturned crate and eating a slice of apple and cranberry pie Laurie said hadn't looked pretty enough to take to the party. When Ruth saw him, it was as if a trapdoor opened and every conceivable thought fell through the gap. She looked down at the

156

bite of crust balanced on her fork and saw her fingers were trembling.

Ruth glanced at the farmhouse. Mabel was pushing Vi on the tire swing Elam had hung from an arm of the tree last week. Sofie was throwing leaves on Zeus, so only his head and wagging tail protruded from the pile. She wanted to go to them. She wanted to gather them up and hide behind motherhood because that was safer than embracing her place as a woman.

Ruth swallowed her last bite of pie. "Okay if I check out for the day?"

"Oh, sure," Laurie said. "We're almost done here."

Ruth stood and crossed the field. Elam stopped walking. He looked at her for a long, silent moment and then quickly looked away. "How's the . . . sorting coming?" he asked.

"Fine. We're almost done."

"Good." Elam nodded methodically. "That's good."

Ruth shielded her eyes with one hand. "What were you up to today?"

"I was in the . . . woods."

"Oh." That single syllable conveyed all her disappointment. What was she thinking? Elam was already making attempts to avoid her: a widow on the prowl. "I — I think I'll

157

get a taxi to take us back to Chicago soon," she said. "And then maybe we'll catch a flight from there."

"You're leaving?" Elam squinted at her, crinkles folding the skin around his eyes. "Why?"

"It's just time." Ruth gestured over to the barn, to the women and men getting up from their lunch perches to resume their work. "Especially now the harvest's wrapping up."

"There's more work here for you, if you . . . need it."

Ruth smiled tightly. She heard in his voice not the desperation he was trying to hide, but his indomitable goodwill. Widowed or not, Ruth and her daughters would never be someone's charity project. "That's okay," she said. "I am sure I can find work in Greystones, too." Her words were like signing a check with nothing in the bank. She wanted to keep Elam from realizing how needy she was, but she could never go through with such plans.

He nodded, looked down, and kicked at a flat stone near his boot, sending it end over end across the rich earth. "If that's what you . . . want," he said.

Tears pricked Ruth's eyes. She looked away. "We've put you out long enough."

He stared at her until their eyes met. She watched the ruddiness gather in his face. The cranberry workers were heading into the barn. Elam turned toward her. He kneaded the muscles on the back of his neck.

"Do you mind taking a walk . . . with me?"

Ruth murmured, "I'd love to," and they began moving over the field toward the wood's unfurled edge. Their afternoon shadows touched as they stretched across the land.

Elam's mother, Marta, had been an artist, or as much of an artist as the demands of the farm and house allowed. She adhered to the wisdom of drawing inspiration from what she knew: bucolic images of the Driftless Region, the gold-and-green contoured hills covered in early-morning fog; pencil sketches of young Elam, his summer-tan bare feet crossed behind him and his cheek pinched in his teeth as he concentrated on his marble chaser as much as his mother concentrated on her artistry.

As Elam grew, he noticed few mothers in the community took an hour or two every afternoon to transform a rusty saw — culled from the barn — into a wintry depiction of their farm at dusk. Or that few mothers used pieces of barn board to stencil their children's silhouettes.

Elam hadn't appreciated any of these things until his mother's absence made him realize she was the one who'd painted all the color in their lives. Without her, the houseplants wilted and died; the windows smudged; the watercolors she'd been working on — before the cancer claimed her faculties — were slanted against the wall in her sewing room, where they would remain, the white canvas ocher-tinted by the years, until Aunt Mabel asked if her daughter-in-law and grandchildren could stay in Elam's house.

Elam contemplated all of this as he and Ruth strolled past the lake toward the cabin. They didn't say much, but the quiet wasn't uncomfortable. At least it wasn't for him, though quiet was his default, so how did he know what was comfortable? Should he say something? He glanced over, but Ruth was looking straight ahead, her profile covered in sunlight, so the freckles on her nose and cheeks stood out against her pale skin. She was beautiful to him. He supposed he should feel guilty for that as well as for the feelings this beauty evoked. But he didn't. Elam found beauty in the berries floating in the flooded bog; in the blue heron, earlier, skimming the water with its wings; in the fish jumping into the air before slipping back beneath.

So why could he not also appreciate the beauty that was so apparent in her?

Elam gestured toward the cabin, partially hidden by the trees. The entire area was a lavish palette of oranges, reds, and browns. "This," he said, "is my home."

Ruth's expression shifted in surprise but she said nothing. He let her walk up the steps first, and then moved around her to open the door. Elam heard her inhalation and knew this was the moment she took it all in. Elam, since he was a child, had collected items he saw as treasures: antler sheds, birds' nests, pieces of glass he had wound with copper wire and suspended in front of the window so he could see the sun's reflection as he played his music or read.

"Do you play?" Ruth glanced up at Elam while running a finger along the piano top.

He shrugged. "A little."

Ruth laughed. "I'm sorry," she said, holding up a hand. "I'm just so shocked."

"Why?"

Her face grew somber, and he could see the lines around her mouth. Laugh lines, he thought, drawn on her skin during an earlier, happier time. "I don't know," she said. "I guess I assumed —" She stopped speaking, perhaps afraid of offending him.

"You assumed someone who works with his hands can't appreciate the finer things too?"

Ruth looked down. "I'm sorry."

He drew closer, wanting to alleviate her distress, even though it had been self-inflicted. "It's all right," he said. His heart hammered as he took Ruth's hand, reaching for her as someone would reach for another in the dark. She flinched, and then her posture eased. Her fingers did not return his grasp, but she did not pull away. "I want you to use this space," he said. "For your studio."

"My — my studio?"

Her skin was so soft. Elam had never taken a woman's hand before, not like this. Middle-aged and he'd never experienced a touch that could evoke such emotion. "Yes, your . . . studio," he said. "Didn't Virginia Woolf say every woman needs a room of her own?"

Again Ruth's eyes widened. "Elam Albrecht," she said, "you are a marvel."

Elam smiled. A wave of sunlight broke through the window and poured into the room, washing away the neglect. "I'm a simple man," he said, "who appreciates . . . simple things."

Ruth's hand moved. Elam steeled himself for her to pull away, but instead her fingers tightened around his. She stepped toward him as he'd just stepped toward her, the ancient floorboards creaking despite their carpet of dust. She looked up into his eyes, and he saw the tears gathered in the corners of her own. "You appreciate," she said. "That's what matters."

■ ■ ■ ■ ■

# PART 2

■ ■ ■ ■

# CHAPTER 7

The day Chandler Neufeld's funeral service was held in Wisconsin was the same day he realized he was still very much alive. Chandler was sleeping in the hospital's safe room when the first bomb struck. A steady percussion followed that didn't stop for thirty minutes, although Physicians International had circulated their GPS coordinates to every side engaged in the fighting. Window glass exploded into shrapnel. Drywall crumbled to dust. Intensive care patients burned in their beds. Pandemonium mounted as the bombing did not stop. Outside, in the early-morning darkness, the white, rectangular hospital appeared to be studded not with windows, but with a series of square, amber stones reflecting the writhing lives trapped within.

The first bomb landed in the operating theater. Chandler Neufeld Senior, two years from retirement, was instantly killed, as was his assistant and the severely maimed soldier whose odds of survival were, ironically, just beginning to rise.

His son, Chandler Neufeld Junior, should've been in the operating theater beside his father, for the pair worked better together than apart. But Chandler Senior had pulled rare paternal rank and required that Chandler Junior get a few hours of sleep before he reentered the theater. Chandler knew his exhaustion posed a threat to his patients even more than a threat to his own deteriorating health, and for this reason alone, he changed out of his bloodstained scrubs, set his cell phone alarm for 4 a.m., giving him three hours of sleep in the past two days. He awoke after the first bombing, as did everyone inside the hospital who was not killed on impact. His confused thought process took precious seconds he did not have to spare. His first thought was of his father. His second was of his wife, Ruth, and their daughters, Sofie and Vi.

These thoughts created an internal war that mimicked the external one erupting around the facility: if Chandler attempted to save his father, his fellow staff, and their patients, he would more than likely lose his life. This loss would most keenly be felt by

Ruth, Vi, Sofie, and his mother, Mabel. And yet Chandler Junior was there for the same purpose as Chandler Senior: to make a difference in as many lives as he could. Adrenaline coursed through him as he rose from the cot and opened the door, running toward the operating theater in his bare feet.

The cement floor was hot and gritty with ash and debris. Putrid smoke stung Chandler's nostrils as he passed the corpses of former patients, seared to their beds. Flames cavorted around him as luckier patients ran in the opposite direction, out of the fray. Above Kunduz, cruising in the clouds, an AC-130 gunship dropped another load. This sixth bomb, the same as the others, fell through the August sky like an early, innocuous Christmas parcel until it slipped through the roof gap the second and third bomb had made.

The bomb did not drop at Chandler's bleeding feet, or this story would have played out differently. Instead, it fell four rooms over. The detonation was the loudest sound Chandler had ever heard, and as if it were greedy to retain its place, he didn't hear anything after it. He was thrown — just as the other patients and staff members were thrown — twelve feet to the left. He could've landed on an exposed beam or a cracked metal bed frame, the latter of which would have acted like a spear, and this story would have played out differently. But he didn't. Instead, by a miracle if you're a person of faith, or by happenstance if you're not, he did not land on the broken metal bed frame but on the hospital mattress. It was barely enough to cushion the blow, but it was something. Chandler would have gotten up from that mattress with a mild concussion if the seventh bomb had not fallen. This bomb did not have the same impact as the previous, but the percussion caused a burning piece of roof to collapse, which pinned Chandler to the bed.

At that moment, Mabel Neufeld was sitting in her recliner in Morgantown, Pennsylvania, reading a mystery novel, and her daughter-in-law, Ruth Neufeld, was softly singing "Too-ra-loo-ra-loo-ra" while putting the girls to bed in her parents' house in Greystones, Ireland. In the strange inconsistency of life, Mabel yawned and turned a page, and Ruth leaned over the bed, and then the crib, to give her daughters each a kiss. Neither woman's heart stopped or skipped. No lights flickered. There was absolutely nothing to indicate that the older woman was a widow and the younger was on the verge of becoming one. Mercifully,

Chandler Junior also did not know this, or at least his body did not know this. His soul was more than aware of the changes taking place, but the soul does not fear death like the body does, and so he was in a place of peace, regardless of the outcome.

The volunteers found him in the rubble when the literal smoke cleared. They sent the surviving patients to a neighboring hospital and evacuated the surviving national and international staff members. Chandler, when the bomb fell, was not in possession of his scrubs, his passport, his cell phone, or anything else that might identify him as an international staff member. Instead, he was garbed in a khaki tunic and pants, an outfit he'd purchased at an open-air market and which, unfortunately, placed him as a civilian. His dark eyes and skin — inherited from his mother — would also have placed him as a civilian if his features could have been distinguished from his burns. The fact that he was found barefoot near a hospital bed seemed to point in the direction of a patient. Chandler would have told the staff differently if he had known, but his face was so deeply burned, he could not talk. He could not think. All he could do was float in a haze of unconsciousness, tethered by the fact that he'd promised his wife and children he would return.

Some say such promises make no difference. But Chandler's spirit and flesh knew differently. His promise was what was keeping him alive. He would go back to his wife and to his daughters. He would find them, even if it was easier to surrender to the excruciating pain. This promise saved his life, but it also changed everything.

Mabel suspected something had happened between Elam and Ruth because of how they acted during supper. They were quiet, for one, which was nothing new as far as her nephew was concerned, but Ruth often carried the conversation, playing a game with the girls that she called "favorite day" — asking them about their favorite moments from the day and sharing the minutia of hers — perhaps in an attempt to help them forget who was missing at the table. But tonight, Ruth was silent. She and Elam sat at opposite ends, and Mabel noticed they didn't make eye contact. Mabel saw this because she was so intensely watching them that Sofie's dark eyes flashed her a haughty, admonishing look. "You shouldn't stare," she said.

Mabel lowered her eyebrows. She considered telling Sofie she also shouldn't correct her elders, but she'd long ago decided that, if Chandler ever settled down long enough to produce some offspring, she wouldn't be the kind of grandma who divvied out punishment like her own grandmother had done, so that Mabel, at sixty-five, still couldn't use a wooden spoon without mentally calling it a "spanking stick." No, she wanted to be a soft, cuddly grandmother who was remembered for spine-aligning hugs and a perpetual supply of molasses cookies dispensing condensation under a glass dome next to the stove. For the past few weeks, she'd finally been able to put these dreams into action. She loved having her grandchildren near. All their smiles, sticky hugs, and sassy ways were balms that soothed the ache in her grief-stricken heart.

Mabel knew her daughter-in-law would not stay on the farm unless she had a reason to remain, and now maybe that reason was here. Mabel didn't want to contemplate her motivations too long, for fear she was being selfish by silently rejoicing in her seat. Was it normal to want to encourage a union between your nephew and your widowed daughter-in-law? Mabel suspected it wasn't, and yet whoever defined *normal* didn't have black-eyed and blue-eyed grandbabies sitting at the table, who had been merely names she daily prayed for but who had no real-life connection until death stepped in and intersected their lives. Now, Mabel would do anything to keep them near.

Anything, apparently, included wanting Elam and Ruth to wed.

Mabel took a bite of mashed potatoes. No doubt they were delicious, for everything she made swam in butter, but tonight, Mabel could barely taste her food. She was too jittery with excitement, which made her heart thump hard, as it had when she received the news about her husband and son, killed when the roof caved in, as if she were living out a modern adaptation of Job. But this was a good thump. She looked between Elam and Ruth, and then from Ruth to Elam. *Yes, definitely,* she thought. Elam's and Ruth's eyes had just met, and Ruth blushed so hard, the red seeped into the roots of her hair. The funny thing was that Elam was a blusher too. Mabel remembered how this had upset him as a boy. He'd liked to portray himself a stoic, that his emotions were all buttoned up, but he could never quite pull it off with that telltale skin.

Mabel cleared her throat. "Did you have a nice day off?" She directed this question at Elam, but right away, Mabel could tell she

174

should've prefaced the question with his name, since the poor man being addressed hunched over his steaming plate of pork and sauerkraut, head down, as if being served a home-cooked meal was some strange form of punishment.

Ruth said gently, "Elam, your aunt asked you a question."

*Now* his head popped up. Mind you, his ears might not be tuned to Mabel's voice, but they were sure tuned to Ruth's. "Wha . . . what?" he asked.

"Mabel asked if you had a nice day off."

He nodded vigorously and looked at Mabel. "It was . . . nice," he said. His color deepened, and his spine curved back over his plate.

Mabel, feeling a little ornery, turned to Ruth. "And how was your day?"

Her daughter-in-law was in the middle of taking a sip of water. This bought her a little time, but not nearly the amount of time she was taking. "It was . . . great," she said.

Mabel smiled and took another bite of potatoes.

Sofie whined, "Nobody asked me about *my* day!"

Vi smacked the table with her patty-cake hands. "Me day too!"

Ruth looked at her daughters. "I'm sorry,

girls," she said. "I'm just a little . . . distracted."

Sofie's face collapsed. Her bottom lip protruded from the rubble like a spoon. Two perfect tears rolled down two perfectly round cheeks. She whimpered, "I want to go home."

Even Vi went quiet. Pushing back her chair, Ruth moved around the table, lifted her older daughter from the chair, and sat her on her lap. She cradled Sofie there, though the child's lanky legs dangled over hers. Sofie, at first, struggled to get down, but Ruth continued holding her until Sofie surrendered to the steady pressure and became nearly boneless in her mother's arms. "Which home do you miss?" Ruth asked, and Mabel understood what she really wanted to know: *What home could you miss? We have no home. We haven't had a home in a long time.*

Sofie burrowed her head against the warm, familiar slope between Ruth's chin and shoulder. It had been Sofie's favorite spot as a baby — one of the few spots where she stopped crying, a slobbery fist twined in Ruth's long, wavy hair. "The home where Daddy was," she whispered, and this time Vi did not need to parrot her sister's sentence for the entire table to hear it. The fully grown grief in those childish words sank like a knife in Mabel's overworked heart.

*May 14, 2017*

Dear Chandler,

Believe it or not, I do try. I do the laundry and dishes, pick up the house, make sure supper is ready before you return from the clinic, though I've reverted to Crock-Pots since it's nearly impossible to predict when you'll get home. I set out puzzles and books, even Play-Doh if I'm feeling particularly adventurous. I try to keep the girls occupied so that, when you come in the door, you're not entirely overwhelmed. But then the rice burns, filling Bethel House with the scent of stale popcorn; our angelic daughters begin wrestling over a toy until someone cries.

Displaying impeccable timing, this is often when you enter, and I am scraping charred grains of rice into the trash can. Every one of my efforts gone up in smoke.

"How was your day?" I ask, trying on a smile for the first time since you left.

"Good," you say. Would it gut you to reply beyond one-word answers? Do you know what it's like to not speak to another adult all day? But no, I think, you wouldn't know that because you have a "career." You wear green scrubs that garner respect and people call you Doctor. All I hear is "Mom!" in every possible form. Mom. Mama. Mother. Moooom. The last usually followed by "Come wipe me."

If only you could be so lucky as to have a job like mine.

But I am lucky. Remember the first time Sofie called me Mom?

She was two before she spoke, and she called you Da-da first. I ached to have some sort of compensation for the life I was pouring into her. And then, finally, I heard it. Mom. She wanted something — probably a piece of whatever I was eating — but I remember how I cried and cried and held her against me, until her little round body wiggled to get away.

But now, now, I cringe every time I hear that name, remembering when I was once called Ruth — or even better, love, by you.

So, you came home, after I'd been busy keeping your children alive all day, and said, "Good." Do you know what it would've meant to hear you say, "Good, love. How was yours?"

And then to have you listen as I shared about our daughters' squabbles, Vi's constipation, the exquisite yet monotonous moments that have composed my days for the past four years? But you didn't. You brushed past me without a kiss. When did we stop that, Chandler? Brushing lips, touching hands? When did we become two ships passing in the night, and sometimes I don't feel like we pass each other. I feel, instead, that we're existing in separate harbors, and I'm not sure I know how to get to you, or that I even want to try.

You went into the living room, stepped over your children, and pulled your laptop from your bag. I am sure you had to write up some report that would be turned in to Janice, who would then turn it in to the government, proof that the orphanage is doing right by the abandoned children the government had left on the streets, like dogs.

I am sure this is what it was.

But my jaw clamped tight to see you stepping over your daughters like they were misplaced toys. You sat down on the sagging sofa and powered on your laptop.

Sofie heard you, then. She lifted her head and let Vi escape, the doll Vi wanted held like a trophy in her small hand. Vi is accustomed to your behavior, for she's only known the restless version of you, which has magnified itself over the past two years. But Sofie remembers a different you — the hands-on dad, who took his role as a husband and father seriously.

She remembered this tonight, and she ran. Instead of opening your arms, or closing that blasted laptop, you instead turned your legs to the side to avoid her collision. You guarded your laptop with your arm, as if it were your greatest treasure, and that was the moment something inside of me just . . . snapped.

"I am with them all day," I shouted. "Would it kill you to play with them for the first ten minutes that you're home?"

You lifted your eyes to the ceiling, making a pointed reminder that we have neighbors, the Pickerings, who are filled with the same hopeful enthusiasm I had when I first came here. I couldn't have cared less about shielding their ears from our domestic plight. "Please don't yell," you said in your rational doctor voice

180

you use when dealing with irrational patients.

"I am not yelling!" I said, my voice rising even then, and I hated feeling like I was losing control. "I just think if you poured half — no, a quarter — of the energy that you use on your patients into your family, you wouldn't be able to recognize your own life."

You looked at me, your long fingers poised over worn keys; the gold wedding band, which I'd slid on your hand four years ago, flashing like a decoy.

"What's happened to you?" you asked.

I slammed the empty rice pot down on the counter. I turned to you, to this restless version of you that I can barely recognize. "I could ask you the same thing."

Chandler had no idea the remains belonging to an Afghan soldier named Shahid Khan were buried in Wisconsin, and that Chandler John Neufeld Senior and Junior were legally declared dead. He had no idea he was in an intensive care unit in Kabul, Afghanistan, or that he'd made the four-hour trip by ambulance, which was like riding on a rickety buckboard. Instead, his mind drifted as morphine moved like blood

181

through the parched tributaries of his veins. Chandler was back in the airport in Bogotá, where he'd last seen his wife and daughters. It was early morning, and the flower vendors were setting up their roadside stands. Chandler parked the battered van he'd borrowed from the director, Janice, and helped Ruth and the girls inside.

Dew clung to the vendors' tissue-wrapped blossoms, and the cloying scent of roses filled the air. Chandler looked at one bouquet as he passed, remembering how he used to buy from another vendor near the orphanage when he and Ruth were dating. But when Ruth noticed him reaching for his wallet, she said, "Don't. My hands are already full."

His hand dropped. Ruth scraped Sofie's hair into a ponytail. Fine curls were cropping up around the child's face from the light rain that had christened them on their way inside. Chandler helped roll the suitcases up to the check-in station, and then stood back with the girls while Ruth printed off their boarding passes. The airport was crowded for four in the morning: an elderly man, dapper in a pressed suit, held the hand of a little girl in a frothy dress the same green as the bouquets' tissue paper. A teenager openly cried while hugging an older woman with waist-length hair. Two hikers in tired, earth-toned clothes carried backpacks they would surely try to cram into overhead bins.

Everyone did indeed revolve around the still point of his family.

Staring down at his beautiful daughters, and then over at his beautiful wife, he questioned his choice to remain in Colombia while they went to Ireland on their own. Maybe he could fly over in a few days, once he got things settled at the orphanage and his luggage packed for Afghanistan, but then Ruth returned with the three boarding passes. She looked at him, and her eyes were blank of emotion, which revealed the depth of emotion taking place within.

"Say good-bye to your daddy," she said, swinging Vi up on her hip. "We need to go."

Tension radiated between them, but Chandler didn't know how to address what needed addressing, and Ruth seemed beyond conversation as it was. Instead, they hovered around each other, each of them rooted to a child, who clung to their legs.

Chandler touched Ruth's back. "Let me know when you get there," he said.

She nodded and looked at the gate. Vi reached for him. He took her from Ruth and hugged her tight. She clasped his neck with her hot, dimpled hands. Chandler's eyes welled. Clearing his throat, he kissed Vi and passed her back to Ruth.

Sofie immediately pressed herself against his legs. "Come with, Dada," she said.

"Baby, you know I can't."

She looked up at him then — big brown eyes brimming — and he felt like the worst father in the world. How could he be out of his children's lives for six months? How could he leave his wife to deal with all that was ahead of her? Ruth, no doubt, was asking herself these same questions, and he hated that she felt abandoned by him while he was still standing right here. And yet, she knew his dreams before she married him; she even encouraged him to obtain them.

But all of that changed once they had children.

Afterward, *Ruth* changed. Her need for adventure was replaced with her need for a nest; her need for spontaneity replaced with her need for stability. Chandler perfectly matched her former self, but the motherhood version did not so easily match him, and he felt this; she felt this; Chandler was sure the children felt this too, for even if Ruth and Chandler did not openly fight, the strain between them was palpable, even to a five-year-old and a toddler.

Chandler had already hugged and kissed his daughters, and therefore the last person he had to say good-bye to was her. Ruth. He looked at his wife and suddenly had a vision of the first time he saw her at the orphanage. He was crossing the stone courtyard when he heard children's voices, harmonizing with the bells marking the half hour. It was a song he'd never heard, sung in a language he could not understand. He walked toward the room and saw Ruth, standing at the front of the classroom while waving a piece of chalk like a conductor's wand. She had long, wavy hair and freckled skin. She wore a peasant top with a shin-length blue skirt and ballet flats. Chandler was not the type to notice a woman's appearance, much less her clothes, but he found this woman intriguing. She noticed him standing in the doorway and smiled.

It was a warm smile that forced the recipient to smile in return. He was no exception. A few of the children noticed him there as well and stopped singing to look. But he was a fixed junction on the unsteady track of their lives, and therefore he was beneath the rapt attention they paid the new teacher. Still, Chandler didn't want to disturb the class more than he had, so he stepped backward, out of the cool classroom doorway, and before he'd finished crossing the courtyard to his office, he chided himself for not checking to see if there was a ring on her hand.

Chandler compared that woman to the one standing before him in the airport. Five years of sleep deprivation, for Sofie still had night terrors, showed in the pallor of Ruth's skin and in the dark circles ringing her eyes. He wanted to tell her he was sorry he wasn't the man she needed him to be, and that life seemed difficult for her of late. But he didn't want her to view this confession as a final effort for intimacy, and he wasn't sure how it would be received. Therefore, he just leaned forward and kissed her. The kiss was perfunctory and landed near her mouth rather than on it. It seemed they'd been kissing each other like this for years. Where was the passion of yesterday? The few weeks after they were married, but before they adopted Sofie, that they could send each other walking swiftly back to Bethel House with just one look?

"I love you, Ruth," he said, his voice a whisper near her ear.

She turned her head away from him, and he could see the sheen of tears in her eyes. "Love you, too," she said. "Just come back to us, okay?"

Lying now in the hospital bed in Kabul, he wondered if this request was for more than just his physical return to their family, but for his emotional return as well. He knew Ruth was not the only one who'd changed with the years. He told himself he was an excellent father to his girls, and he was, when he could be there, but he was no longer an excellent husband. They had drifted apart, and he could not pinpoint exactly why or when that drifting had happened. All he knew was that his first glimpse of Ruth in the classroom, teaching orphaned children a Gaelic nursery rhyme, was one of the images he was going to conjure forth to help him recover. And then he was going to return to his children and his wife.

Splashes and squeals nearly drowned the sound of Mabel reading the now-censored *Eloise Wilkin Stories* to the girls as they played in the bathtub. In the kitchen, Ruth cleared the table. Elam plugged the sink, squirted dish soap into the rising water, and used one large paddle hand to work up some suds. Ruth came over with a stack of plates, set them on the counter on his left-hand side. He didn't say anything; he didn't even quietly hum like he usually did when he was cleaning in the wake of Mabel's latest kitchen upheaval. Ruth didn't say anything either.

Four hours ago, he'd touched her hand.

Next, Ruth brought over the tray crowded with mason jars of varying levels of water. Elam couldn't stand it anymore. He turned to her, lifted out his foamy hands to take the tray. She stared at the center of his chest. There was about a foot between them. Chandler had been the same height. Elam wondered if Ruth thought of this when she stood next to him. Or in front of him, like now. But it wasn't fair to any of them to think this way.

"Are you okay?" Elam asked.

To Elam's surprise, and perhaps Ruth's, her fierce determination not to cry wasn't enough. "No," she said, wiping her eyes. "I'm not okay. I don't know how to help my daughter."

Elam took the jars and upended them in the sink, where they were sucked down into the warm, soapy pool. He looked at Ruth and saw the sorrow rewriting the laugh lines around her mouth. He wanted to make her laugh again, but he wasn't sure that was his place, or that Ruth would let him close enough to try. It was a miracle she'd allowed him close that once.

So, instead of making her laugh, Elam

pulled open the drawer beneath the sink. He took out a clean dishtowel and handed it to Ruth. She smiled and dabbed beneath her eyes. "You're such a good man, Elam," she said. "Really. It's just that I — I don't know what I'm doing."

Elam smiled gently, took back the dishcloth she was holding out. He folded it and folded it until the soft cotton became a hard little square. "You don't need to know," he said. "I just want to get to know you. To be your . . . friend."

Ruth looked up at him. "I could sure use a friend these days," she said.

# CHAPTER 8

The intensity of Chandler's burns required sedation to take the edge off his pain, but it took the edge off his memory as well — making it difficult to recall the kind of details he should've never been able to forget: the color of Ruth's eyes, for example, or the dates when his daughters were born. Ruth had loved making a grand production out of their daughters' birthdays. She'd baked cakes from scratch, hung pink and purple streamers and balloons from the basket light in the dining room, and let the girls pick the menu for supper. In short, she tried to make their birthdays as magical as possible, maybe because Ruth's childhood birthdays had been far from it.

Chandler might not be able to remember the color of Ruth's eyes (hazel or blue?), but he could clearly remember Vi's second birthday — the last one they celebrated before their family moved to separate continents. The night before, Chandler came home from the clinic and found Ruth in the living room. Sparkles, multicolored tissue paper squares, and splattered acrylic paint covered an old floral sheet. Ruth wore a college T-shirt over a pair of his sweatpants, and her curly hair was a topknot that had, somehow, not escaped the paint. He stood silently in the doorway, like he had many times before. Ruth was so absorbed in her project, he knew it was more of a creative outlet than a task. She was transforming a cardboard box into a castle.

Even with the limited art supplies she'd borrowed from the orphanage, the piñata had a tiered roof, cupolas, and a drawbridge where Ruth would later stuff candy.

Setting down his laptop bag, he crossed the room and touched the tip of her nose.

She dabbed it with the back of her wrist. "What? My nose has paint on it too?"

He shook his head. "You look so happy. You should do this kind of stuff more often."

"When would I find the time?"

Chandler rested his hands on Ruth's shoulders, and she leaned back against his legs while still holding the foam brush. "I could watch the girls one evening a week for you," he said.

Laughter vibrated through her chest. "You

don't have to make that offer twice."

Now, in his hospital bed, nearly every inch of his body a regenerating graft of stolen cells, Chandler remembers this conversation with a pang of regret. He didn't watch their daughters after that conversation, to give Ruth a break like he planned. He never even made it to the birthday party because one of the babies from the mountain became so severely dehydrated from chronic diarrhea, he didn't feel comfortable leaving his side. Chandler believed, at the time, he was making the right choice by remaining with that child, who had no parent to care for him, while his daughters were being cared for by such a loving mom. But when he came home and saw the crumpled piñata on the dining room table, along with a piece of chocolate cake covered with a princess napkin, his chest hurt as he understood what he had missed.

He went upstairs — the same set of stairs he and Ruth had climbed when they ate supper on the roof — and stood in the bedroom his little girls shared. He walked in and looked at Sofie, asleep with her thumb in her mouth, and then he looked at Vi, already two years old.

She'd be twenty in a blink.

He heard a noise, turned, and saw Ruth

standing in the lit hallway, her arms fc
tight over her robe. She said nothing, ,
watched him until he came out. They stood
there, in Bethel House, with their daughters'
framed artwork on the walls.

"You said you'd be here."

"I know," Chandler said. "I'm sorry. A
little boy, he —"

Ruth held her hand up, flat. "Don't. I
don't want to hear it." She stopped and
looked to the side. Her eyes glittered. "You
know what kills me most?"

He didn't answer. He knew *better* than to
answer.

"Vi didn't cry for you. She didn't even realize you were gone. She's so used to you
trying to save the world, she doesn't understand your first responsibility should be to
us, your family."

*Green,* Chandler thinks, before the morphine claims him. *My wife's eyes are green.*

Elam obviously wasn't fluent in verbal communication, and yet he understood any
conversation prefaced with "I thought you
should know" was probably not a good one.
However, he was still surprised to find
himself and Ruth the subjects of the gossip.

In truth, it wasn't gossip so much as it
was talk.

And the talk probably started long before there was anything to talk about. A man and woman living under the same roof, who were neither blood related nor octogenarians, were considered prime suspects for romance, and one had to doubt if being eighty or ninety years old could protect from the Driftless Valley Community's wagging tongues.

The talk was not malicious, or at least none of the malicious talk had reached Laurie's ears. Women are naturally more inclined to see a match where there isn't necessarily one, and so the community women began noticing how Ruth stayed around to help Elam with the wet harvest, and then Elam stayed around to help Ruth with the dry harvest. And that night, after the party, Amy Brunk went back to Elam's barn — claiming she'd forgotten her great-grandmother's relish tray — and discovered Ruth and Elam talking in that oil lamp–lit dark, the two of them standing so close, Amy said there couldn't have been a hair-breadth between them.

But it wasn't until Elam and Ruth walked off toward the woods while the rest of the workers were busy sorting berries, that their suspicions were confirmed: the community's most eligible bachelor had set his straw hat for a woman — a widowed *Englisch* woman, no less.

Now, Elam looked so distraught by this news, Laurie set Tim Junior down on the floor and got up to cut her big brother a slice of bread. She slathered this with butter and cranberry preserves and put it on a plate. Elam looked at the bread like he was looking at his last meal, so Laurie got up and refreshed his coffee. "It's really not so bad as all that," she said and spooned some cream into his mug. "I just thought maybe it's time to reconsider your living options."

Elam thanked his sister for the bread and coffee, but he didn't bring either to his mouth. He just continued staring at the table, his jawbone throbbing against the weathered tan. "Ruth and the girls are finally settled," he said. "I can't make them leave."

Laurie reached across the table for Elam's calloused hand. "No one's asking you to."

He lifted his eyes. "Then what do I do?"

She smiled. "Move out or marry her, I guess."

Chandler had to use whatever time he had until they sedated him again to communicate who he was and why he needed to get home. He must come across as merely

195

agitated, and the tube in his throat, to extricate the smoke from his lungs, made it impossible to speak. He tried, though. Over and over, he tried. Finally, two nurses came. The first leaned over the bed and used a flashlight pen to check his pupils. Chandler stared back at her, unblinking, from the mask of gauze. Her eyes were dark; her skin the color of sand. She reminded him of his wife, but then Chandler knew this was ridiculous. Ruth was fair and freckled. Her eyes changed like weather.

The second nurse studied the clear bag hanging from his IV stand, calculating how much morphine was needed to navigate his distress. The nurses believed he was a civilian from Kunduz who'd been severely injured during the hospital bombing and was then transferred here. Chandler was thunderstruck by their inability to see who he was beneath the bandages — to see the ache in his chest from missing his family, to see his brain listing beneath the weight of facts that, try as he might, he could not sort out. But then he understood this was how the civilians and soldiers felt in *his* care: nothing but a pulsing group of cells Chandler struggled to restore.

Morphine entered the vein. Chandler's eyes closed beneath the bandages. His hands grew still, his mouth slack. His burned body sank deeper into the hospital bed. His mind pulled the curtain across scarier images and instead chose to replay a classic: the wedding-day reel.

After six years of marriage, it was strange to think of Ruth as his bride, and he wondered how long it'd been since he'd called her that, his bride; how long it'd been since he'd called her beautiful. All he knew was that Ruth *had* been beautiful, that day in the courtyard, when she wore a full-length cotton dress the volunteer seamstress had made in the week she had to prepare. Chandler couldn't remember if there'd been flowers, and this time it wasn't just the morphine. He'd been so focused on Ruth, and on not stuttering during the vows, that everything went out of his head except for her. The ceremony had no frills (Chandler's request) but took twice as long because the interpreter translated the English into Spanish for the hundred orphans who were gathered for the wedding (Ruth's request). Each of the children sat primly in white plastic chairs: legs crossed; chapel clothes pressed; donated shoes polished to a shine.

Afterward, Chandler remembered the taste of Chef José's *tres leches* cake: three milks, smooth as cream, with a cornucopia of fresh fruit. He remembered, mostly, because he fed a bite to Ruth, and a dab of icing lingered like a beauty mark above her mouth. Even with the kids watching, he leaned forward and kissed that sweetness. The kids broke into a dissonant chorus of squeals and catcalls, the response divided by age. Ruth swatted Chandler's chest, the icing on her own hands staining the only white dress shirt he owned, and which he'd taken such care ironing that morning. But then he caught that hand and pulled her close. Her mirth-filled eyes changed then — grew somber and deeper — and this time *she* was the one who leaned forward for a kiss.

Chandler's scarred face creased into a smile no one could see beneath his bandages.

He remembered leaving the orphanage that night, the two of them giddy with relief as the other Children's Haven volunteers whooped and beat on the roof and the "Just Married!" and "We're Hitched!"–covered windows of the old, rickety borrowed car. Chandler leaned on the horn until the volunteers dispersed and then peeled rubber outside the orphanage's gates. Ruth laughed out loud. They intermittently kissed and teased each other as he drove them down the twisting dark streets until they traded the crowded city for the distant country and crowded Bethel House for an orange-roofed mountain cottage, built entirely from stone.

The dwelling had recently been aired, but even from outside, you could feel the cold and smell the damp embedded in its crevices. It was enchanting, though, a storybook chalet constructed by the host — an architect — who lived in another, more practical, home in town. As Chandler carried his bride over the threshold, he felt guilty that the director had rented it for them for two whole nights, using money that surely could've fed the orphans in their care.

But then Chandler set Ruth down in the darkness, and she took off her sandals and crossed the floor to a large round table with a single silver candelabra on top. Chandler heard a hiss and watched as, one by one, Ruth lit the wicks. The candles threw shadows on the stone walls, the shadows writhing upward, like flames. Centered above the table was a circular skylight. Chandler took off his dress shoes, set the candelabra aside, and climbed onto the table.

"What're you doing?!" Ruth laughed, and her pearled teeth gleamed.

Chandler turned and, with a flick of his arm, extended his hand to Ruth. Clearing his throat three short times, as if to make a grand announcement, he said, "Dancing with my bride."

She rolled her eyes but let him take her hand. He pulled her up beside him, and the two of them — barefoot but still in their simple wedding finery — began to sway on that circular table beneath a circular piece of sky. Chandler gently twirled Ruth's wrist and she spun, her red-gold hair catching the firelight, her new emerald ring casting prisms on the stone tunnel, so the two of them felt they were contained at the bottom of a magical well. They danced there, and held each other there, and kissed in a way that proved that, this time, no children were watching.

Meanwhile, above them, the moon and stars turned their gazes to the clear black sky.

Miss Romaine had understood that diversion can be one of the best teaching tactics, and therefore she gave her young pupil, Elam, piano lessons to help loosen his tongue. Sofie did not need help loosening her tongue, but she *did* need help learning how to process her grief.

So Elam asked Ruth if he could possibly give Sofie piano lessons.

"Sofie?" Ruth asked. "She's only six."

Elam said, "Does she know her numbers . . . alphabet?"

Ruth nodded. "She taught herself to read last year."

"Then I'll teach her the tab method. She'll do fine."

But when Ruth broached the subject, Sofie hotly declared, "I don't like him!"

Ruth placed a warning hand on Sofie's head as she brushed her hair. "Lower your voice."

But Sofie, though not biologically connected, took after her mother. *"No!"* The scream echoed as Sofie jerked. The brush caught and hung from tangled strands. Vi, meanwhile, sat on the rug beside the bed, thumb corked in her mouth, looking between her mother and her sister through a screen of overlong blonde bangs. It was naptime.

Ruth snatched the brush from Sofie's hair. "You will *not* talk to me like that."

Sofie yelled, "I wish *you'd* got dead!"

Ruth recoiled and struck Sofie's bottom with the brush, hard. They both gasped in shock. Sofie looked up at her mother, eyes accusing, and ran out of the room and down

201

the stairs. The front door slammed. Vivienne grunted. Ruth glanced over, vision blurred, and saw her two-year-old tugging on the quilt, trying to heave her bottom half onto the bed.

Whiplashed by her anger, Ruth set the brush on the nightstand and hooked a finger through the belt loop of Vi's tiny jeans. She hauled Vivienne up and lay down beside her on the narrow bed. Ruth pulled Vi against her chest and stared at her snub nose and elfin chin. Vi snuggled in, content, and Ruth tried to remember when she'd last held Sofie like this.

When was the last time Sofie had let her? Chandler had understood his daughter more than Ruth had, or so it seemed because Sofie always preferred him to her: Ruth was the one who doled out rules, whereas Chandler was the one who often, unthinkingly, negated them.

The past months, and years, blended into an inseparable amalgam of colds and fevers, wiping bottoms, toilets, and chins, and yet there were beautiful moments tucked in there too. Ruth knew there were; she had recorded some of them, had she not? In Bogotá, she'd started keeping a journal because there was no one with whom she could speak such thoughts aloud. But she'd lost that time, recorded or not. Amid the sleep deprivation and the survival, she couldn't remember those beautiful moments tucked amid the mundane, and that was time she could never get back. Months Sofie had become a little more girl than toddler, and Vivienne a little more toddler than baby. She had to do better for them — and for herself — than just surviving, but she didn't quite know how.

Ruth stood, changed Vi into a diaper, and put her in the crib so she wouldn't follow her downstairs. Ruth saw, with relief, that Sofie hadn't gone far. Three minutes had passed since the incident, but it felt like an eternity, each second time-warped by guilt.

Sophie sat on the porch, her pink-and-purple-sneakered feet (the same kind of sneakers Vi had because they were a buy-one-get-one deal) dangling limply over the edge. Zeus lay beside her, tail still, his huge white head lightly resting on the child's knees. Ruth closed the front door and walked out to kneel beside her daughter. Her guilt multiplied when she viewed Sofie's tears.

Ruth put an arm around her back. At first, Sofie remained rigid, and Ruth knew she'd inadvertently nurtured that unyielding nature in her as well. "I'm so sorry," Ruth said and wiped Sofie's cheeks with her thumbs. "Mommy made a mistake. I should've never hit you like that."

Sofie didn't say anything. Ruth continued, "Do you know that mommies don't always know how to be mommies? That sometimes we're still learning too?"

Sofie's head stayed forward. "That wasn't nice." She swiped a fist across her nose.

"I know it wasn't." Ruth smoothed back one of Sofie's curls. "I know. But you weren't very nice either. Let's try to be nice to each other, okay?"

Being nice seemed so simple, so little to ask of a child, and yet it had been more than Chandler and Ruth could manage as adults, trapped in a union that was no longer unified.

Sofie looked up, and her bottomless eyes were filled with such loss that Ruth wondered if she was clairvoyant and had somehow anticipated what was going to happen to Chandler while the rest of them had remained unaware. Sofie leaned toward Ruth, rested her tear-soaked temple against her shoulder. "I don't want you dead."

"I know you don't," Ruth murmured and hugged Sofie tight.

Sofie worried a bloodied cuticle with her teeth. Ruth gently took that hand and cupped it between hers. She had forgotten how Sofie used to do that. Or how she'd thrust her tongue between her teeth until it grew too sore to eat, made clicking sounds, and never interacted with a stranger unless she was being held by Chandler or Ruth. Parenting Sofie felt like an endless game of whack-a-mole; you surmounted one obstacle, one nervous tic, only to find that another had taken its place.

"Sometimes," Sofie said, "I wish Daddy was here."

Ruth kissed the top of Sofie's head and hugged her even tighter, remembering the first time Director Janice had placed Sofie in her arms and declared her a mother. Ruth never wanted to let Sofie go, never wanted to loosen her grip. It was as if she'd hoped her encircled arms could protect her daughter from all the horrors of the world and never once thought that, sometimes, those protective arms could keep a child from experiencing the world at all. "I wish he was here too," Ruth said, and she was surprised to find that she meant it, for her daughters' sakes, if not for her own.

Fourteen weeks after Chandler almost died in the bombing, his lungs cleared from the smoke. It startled him, this sudden ability to breathe, so he didn't realize how bad off he'd been until the nurse reversed the intubation and that ability returned. His voice box felt wrapped in sandpaper, each swallow like shards of glass nicking his throat. But he was grateful. Each small step to full recovery meant he was moving closer to communicating who he was and how the hospital could return him to his family, where he belonged.

Chandler had passed the weeks since his morphine tapered off enough to make him aware of his surroundings — and of his boredom — by mentally composing a letter to his wife. He'd mentally composed and discarded so many drafts, he had every jot and tittle of the entire composition memorized.

Dear Ruth, *it began.*

I keep thinking about how, when we were first dating, I waited to tell you I loved you until after you moved home to Ireland and we were continents apart. And now here I am, lying in a hospital bed with nothing on my mind but you, and we are, once again, continents apart. What blinds me to the value of what I hold until I've almost lost it? I miss you, Ruth. You'd think I would miss the big

moments — our first kiss, our engagement — but instead I miss the small
ones: the girls coming to our bed on
Sunday mornings with their blankies
and stuffed animals; having to move all
their mermaid Barbies to the back of the
bathtub so I can take a shower; you
somehow destroying the kitchen by making macaroni and cheese; eating dinner
together as a family and talking about
our "favorite day." I never really played
along, did I? In the favorite-day thing.
The girls would say they loved drawing
on the walls or playing with rocks, and I
would just mumble the first thing that
came to my head because I didn't see
much in my life to be grateful about.
Well, I am grateful now.

When I look back on these years, I
have to wonder if our marriage would've
been easier if we hadn't become parents
right when we became husband and
wife. But God must've planned it like
this, knowing that, out of all the volunteers, you and I would find little Sofie
on the mountain that night, and he
would give us the grace to love this
child, even when she acts like she finds
it next to impossible to love us back. I
imagine — no, I know — that you have

sacrificed so much more than I have to mother Sofie and Vi.

Day in and day out, you are surrounded by two little people who need you like air. Meanwhile, until this point, my life has kept on much as before: an endless cycle of work, eat, sleep; work, eat, sleep, and somehow, I fit you and the girls around the edges of my days. I didn't understand, until it was perhaps too late, the value of what I held. Forgive me, Ruth. I promise, if I get to return, I will hold you and the girls close, forever.

All my love,
Chandler

# CHAPTER 9

Elam Albrecht didn't have many needs. Even in winter, he could live in this cabin without running water and be content. However, the idea of leaving Ruth and the girls in his farmhouse while he remained out here seemed wrong. As strange as it was, they felt more like family than the extended family he'd always known, and to leave them would be to leave an essential and vibrant element of his life, which he hadn't known was leached of color until it returned.

He didn't think he could do it. But not to leave meant Laurie's other suggestion, and he didn't think he could do that either. Not because Elam didn't want to marry Ruth and be a father to her daughters, but because he feared she wouldn't want him. That her heart was still Chandler's and would be until the wounds, inflicted by her grief, healed.

Was it any wonder he wasn't getting anything done? Was it any wonder he knew his entire life hinged on this decision?

Elam left the cabin and looked across the field toward the house. Mabel or Ruth had turned on the kerosene lamp, and sheets of light unspooled from the windows onto the grass. Sighing, he knifed fingers through his hair and walked between the channel and the lane. Zeus gamboled along beside him, and Elam looked down at the dog. He hadn't been a fan of Zeus when he first arrived, his canine breath fogging up the passenger window of Ruth's rental car while Vi, who — unlike the person she was greeting — never met a stranger, leaned around him to wave at Elam. But now the dog had become an extension of Ruth's family. Elam couldn't imagine them without him.

"You think I'm a fool, huh?" Elam asked. "For even thinking it's a possibility?"

Zeus looked up at him and cocked his massive head, as if afraid to tell the truth.

Sighing again, Elam climbed up onto the porch. "That's what I thought."

When Elam and Zeus entered the house, Vi squealed and ran for the door. Elam realized the child was eager to see her dog, not him. But the little girl still bestowed Elam with a smile, even if she partially shielded her eyes with her left hand. Zeus's floppy ear was clutched in her right, so the long-suffering dog couldn't move his head. Elam knelt and covered his eyes too. Giggling, Vi spread her fingers so she could peek back at him. He leaned forward and gently poked her belly. She leaped back — thankfully releasing the dog — and squealed again. Elam stood and saw Ruth sitting on the bottom step, looking up at them. "How was your day?" she asked.

He swallowed. "Long but . . . good," he said. "And yours?"

Ruth stood, glancing over her shoulder toward the kitchen, and then down at Vi, who was too busy grooming Zeus with her brush to pay them any mind. Lowering her voice, Ruth confided, "Actually, it was awful. Sofie had a meltdown earlier." She exhaled. "I guess I did too. I haven't disciplined her since Chandler died. Not because she hasn't needed it . . . but because I wanted to make sure I wasn't emotional when I *did* punish her, and here . . . I completely lost it. I hit her, Elam. In anger." Ruth hung her head. "It was one of the worst moments of my life."

Elam moved toward Ruth. The dim light from the kitchen shone on their backs as the man who rarely spoke prepared to speak because Ruth needed him to reassure her more than he needed his insecurities. "I'm so sorry," he said. "But you need to know one thing right now, Ruth, and that's that you're an amazing mother. Those girls are blessed to have you in their lives, and even if they're not aware right now, one day they will be."

In the foyer's protected darkness, Ruth leaned forward and rested her head against his chest. Elam's heart thumped so hard, he was sure she could hear it. He let his arms come up around her and held her against him. She rested there — the two of them outlined by the frame of the door — and he knew, as she surely did, that what they had here was not merely friendship.

"Ruth," he said and took her hands, rubbing them between his cold ones, and he marveled that touching her was becoming as natural as touching his own skin. "Ruth, I . . . I . . ." He stopped talking, not knowing how he could continue, and yet not knowing how *they* could continue — living like this — if he didn't at least try to explain what he felt.

But then Ruth put a finger to his lips. Taking his hand, she placed it at the base of her throat. His palm spanned her breastbone. A fingertip brushed each clavicle. He could feel her heart beating there . . . beating just as hard as his.

*November 5, 2017*

Dear Chandler,

Sometimes I wonder what it would've been like if you and I had been husband and wife for a few years before becoming parents. Would we have gone to restaurants? Or backpacking? Would we have somehow slipped away from the orphanage long enough to plan a trip overseas? And not the kind of trip that required us to pour into others, but the kind of trip that would have allowed us to pour back into ourselves . . . pour back into each other?

Instead of waking up early to give Sofie her bottle, would you have woken up early just to look at me? Would I have woken up early to bring you coffee and cream in your favorite mug? Would we have read newspapers side by side in our matching pajamas and gone out for brunch?

We never had the chance to experience any of these things, since Sofie needed us so desperately in the beginning, as desperately as she needs us now. Reactive attachment disorder. I didn't even know what that was back then until Director Janice told us. I just knew that whatever I had was not enough, and I could not mother Sofie the way she needed.

You knew her, though; somehow you did. I would be exhausted, one hand dangling over the bassinet next to our bed, so that I could still touch her in her sleep, and you would come in, and you would scoop her up against your chest.

You would whisper sweet nothings into her ear and rock her back and forth in front of the barred window — the moonlight passing through it divided into parts. I loved you then, and I hated you. I was so young, I guess, which explains some of my immaturity. And yet, I was still your bride, your newlywed, but I felt like neither. I instead felt like you and Sofie were trapped in this bubble, and I was the one on the outside, desperately trying to fight my way in. I wondered, in those ugly, exhausted moments, if you truly loved me, or if you only married me because you loved Sofie and knew you could not take care of her and take care of the other orphans too.

To this day, all these years later, I see you with our girls — your dark eyes gleaming with tears behind your glasses — and I wonder, deep down, if you love me the way you love them. I know this is my own insecurity rising to the surface, but I cannot help comparing myself to Sofie when she first became ours: reactive attachment disorder. It doesn't matter how much you hold me, I can never allow my heart to open wide enough to accept — or give — love.

"I am an American doctor."

This was Chandler's first audible sentence, after his throat healed from the smoke damage and weeks of intubation. The nurse didn't understand him, not because he didn't speak English, but because Chandler could still only whisper. After he *did* understand what Chandler was communicating, it didn't make much difference.

Chandler had no identification, and many civilians around Kabul would've claimed they were the kings of England if it meant getting out of the country alive.

Chandler rasped, "I need to speak with someone from the American embassy."

The nurse shook his head. "You can't."

Chandler tried to sit up, but even that

215

small, ordinary movement set his skin on fire.

"What do you mean, I can't?"

"There *is* no American embassy."

"No American embassy?"

Again the nurse shook his head. "The ambassadors evacuated a month ago."

Chandler didn't know if he should believe him, or if this was the response he gave to all the civilians who believed they had a special case. After the nurse left, Chandler tried to get up again, tried to block his mind from the pain so he could focus on what he wanted most: getting home. He swung his legs over the bed. Weeks of bed rest, with little to no therapy, had atrophied his muscles beyond recognition, and he knew his legs were the least affected by the burns. What would Ruth think when she saw him? The wave of pain following this thought was so intense, Chandler's mind switched off to endure it. He did not feel his body colliding with the floor, or the nurse calling for backup, or the morphine, once more, entering his vein.

Ruth couldn't sleep. She lay in bed with Sofie asleep beside her, Vi asleep in the crib, and Zeus sprawled out on the floor, his heavy breathing as patterned as a white noise machine. She imagined Elam downstairs, in the small room off the kitchen, struggling the same.

From the beginning of life after Chandler, Ruth's greatest goal had been to keep a semblance of normalcy for her girls. She feared she'd betrayed that goal tonight by allowing herself to remember how it felt to be touched by a man. Like so many aspects of life, Ruth understood she had one shot at this. Motherhood. Child-rearing. Turning babies to girls and girls to women who could also survive if faced with the unthinkable. While stumbling through the maze of her grief, Ruth could not lose sight of the fact she had to help her daughters find the way through theirs.

After the unthinkable happened, and Ruth came back to herself enough to understand that she had to explain what had happened to her girls, she got around Cathleen Galway's "no internet from 9–7" rule by staying up late googling "How to tell your children about death." She could only read the content on *KidsHealth* by first fortifying herself with a glass of wine:

1. When talking about death, use simple, clear words.
2. Listen and comfort.

3. Put emotions into words.
4. Tell your child what to expect.
5. Talk about funerals and rituals.
6. Give your child a role.
7. Help your child remember the person.

It had only been a week since Ruth received the call from the Physicians International staff member, and yet she had failed at the majority of this list. Her eyes burned from the laptop's blue glow. Her babies were already sleeping in her old bed upstairs, cuddled together beneath the fringed canopy, because Ruth couldn't bear to sleep without a hand touching them, as if to reassure herself — even while she dreamed — that her children weren't gone too.

Closing the laptop, Ruth swilled the rest of her wine. She prepared to go to bed when she noticed her mother in the kitchen, tossing half the contents of her spice drawer into the bin.

Ruth asked, "Mom? You okay?"

They each mourned the loss of their spouses, but — the same as in everything else — they went about it in different ways: Ruth Google-searched; Cathleen organized.

Cathleen said, "Some of these spices expired when you were in high school."

Ruth noticed her mother hadn't answered her question. Ruth walked into the kitchen and stood with the counter against her back. Cathleen had curly salt-and-pepper hair she kept cropped no-nonsense short. She'd once favored blazers and dress slacks, which accentuated her sharp features, but now she preferred khakis and her dead husband Kiffin's hand-knit fisherman sweaters, which still retained the scent of stale pipe smoke.

Cathleen and Kiffin were opposites in all the ways that mattered and in all the ways that didn't. For the most part, they had complemented each other, rounding and chipping until their lives became a mosaic, if not quite a cohesive whole.

But standing in the kitchen, listening to the faucet drip, Ruth saw that her mother didn't know how to live without her husband, and so she did what she *did* know how to do. By this point, Kiffin had been dead for three months, and every nook and cranny of the house had already been culled: his magazines and books, loafers and corduroys given to the thrift shop in town; his dog, Zeus, sent to sleep in the garage rather than at the foot of his master's bed, like he'd done for the past five years and his canine predecessors had done before him. It was as if Cathleen were trying to remove all proof of her husband's existence and, with it, proof of her pain as well.

But it hadn't left. Ruth could see that as she observed her mother rigidly lining up the few spices that remained, parallel to one another; little soldiers confined to a drawer. Ruth had never done well being confined, and they had butted heads most of her life.

"Everyone keeps asking me that," Cathleen said. "If I'm okay."

"I'm sorry, Mom," Ruth whispered. "I just want —"

"I know what you want." Cathleen tossed another spice. "Closure. Healing. Acceptance. But I can't do that right now, Ruth. I can't dig up all the hurt and sift through it, trying to make it all better again. That's not how it works for me."

Ruth nodded. They never talked about how either of them was faring again.

Far removed from that Greystones kitchen, Ruth turned over in the bed she shared with Sofie. The Wisconsin moon was bright against the blinds and split through them, as if to peer at those sleeping inside. Careful not to disturb her daughter, Ruth got to her feet and looked out. In the distance, the lake shone like a polished plate. The channels were thin strips framing the drained cranberry bog's shadowed bowl.

It was magic, this simple place, and for the first time since Elam took her hand, she let herself imagine how it would be to make this farm her home.

If she weren't a mother, would the decision to let Elam love her be so hard? She honestly didn't know. For six long — occasionally blissful — years, Ruth had sacrificed to take care of others, and if it weren't for Sofie and Vi, who so desperately needed her, she wasn't sure she could enter an arrangement where her independence would be sacrificed again. And yet, she remembered Elam's gift. Her art studio. A room of her own when she didn't have a roof to her name. This thoughtfulness touched her in a way few gifts had, and she knew it was more than a gift to her. It was proof Elam wanted more than the fulfillment of his dream for a family, but that he also wanted to make her own dreams come true.

Ruth, aware she was not going to sleep, walked downstairs in her yoga pants and sweatshirt. The flagstone sidewalk was cold beneath her bare feet. Her breath twisted up into the night sky. The seasons were changing. After having lived for so long in Colombia, the air-conditioned capital of the world, she anticipated the shift and wondered if this was a sign that her life season was about to change as well. The thought thrilled her, and then guilt set in that she could rejoice in a new season when the old meant her children still had a father.

Ruth glimpsed light in her peripheral vision. She turned and saw Mabel walking toward her. She carried a lamp, and a woolen shawl draped her shoulders. Her black hair was down. It was thinner at the part and the temples from the decades it'd been pulled back in a bun.

Mabel asked in her soft voice, "Are you all right?"

"Yes," Ruth replied, and, for the first time in a long time, she realized she was.

"You didn't eat much supper."

"No." Ruth looked at the ground. Her feet were becoming numb.

"Are you and Elam . . . ?" The question hung between them like breath.

Ruth lifted her head. She wasn't sure how to convey such news to her mother-in-law; wasn't sure if Mabel would be happy or sad, or if she would feel as Ruth did, a mixture of both. "Nothing's been said, no promises made. But Elam and I care about each other very much."

Mabel inhaled. "Oh, Ruth," she said. "This is such good news." She held Ruth against her, and though she meant every word, both women who stood under that watchful yellow moon had tears of bittersweet remembrance in their eyes.

Ruth went running in the morning. Nothing in her wanted to run, but she knew the endorphins would serve her later when she was trying to care for the girls despite having gotten so little sleep. To her surprise, Laurie came out of her house when Ruth ran past it.

Ruth slowed her steps.

"Morning." Laurie smiled. "Mind if I come along?"

Ruth *did* mind, in fact. She needed to clear her head before talking to Elam, but she couldn't very well tell this to his sister. "Not at all," she said. "Should I walk?"

Waving dismissively, Laurie said, "Nah, running's fine." She tugged on the waist of her cape dress. "I bounce back quicker if I stay active during pregnancy." She gave Ruth a sidelong glance. "What's your secret? Looks like you haven't gained an ounce since Vi."

Ruth smiled tightly. "Grief's a good diet plan."

"Oh," Laurie said. "Of course."

Ruth regretted her curt reply. It wasn't Laurie's fault she wasn't in the mood for chitchat. Trying to soften this, Ruth explained, "My dad died three months before Chandler, and I didn't have much of an appetite for months before then." Ruth paused. "He had cancer."

Laurie tucked some hair under her *kapp* and began to jog. "My *mamm* died of cancer."

"I'm sorry," Ruth replied. "Elam told me you were young."

Laurie glanced over, eyebrows raised. "He told you about that?"

She nodded.

Laurie was quiet for a while, or at least it was a while according to Laurie. Then she said, "I'm glad to see you and my brother getting along."

Ruth's body stiffened, tightening the tendons connected to her left collarbone. She reached up and massaged them, knowing they would ache later if she didn't. She didn't say anything, and their breathing became ragged. Ruth was running harder than she'd run in years, and to her surprise, Laurie kept up — her stride long and loose even as Ruth was straining to do everything she could to maintain the pace. She wanted to quit, and she sensed Laurie wanted to quit too. Both women kept pushing themselves. "Elam seems like the strong and silent type," Laurie rasped, "but that's really just a cover. He's got a heart larger than anyone's."

Ruth stared straight ahead, breathing hard through her nose. She sensed this was a warning. She was the one who'd just lost her father and husband. She was the one who could barely close her eyes without imaging Chandler's last horrific moments after the deadly bombs fell. She often wondered how quickly he had died and if his last thoughts were of his daughters or of her. And then Ruth understood that this was exactly why Laurie felt compelled to offer such caution. She feared Ruth cared for Elam because he was her solace in this time of distress. It made Ruth wonder if this was indeed the case. But should grief discount love, if love is what this was? Ruth wasn't sure. She wasn't sure if her attraction to Elam was valid, or only the repercussion of finding security in his presence, where otherwise, there was none. But wasn't this partly why she'd also ended up with Chandler? Weren't security and love intertwined?

Winded, Ruth stopped running. Laurie continued a few yards more before she stopped and looked back, running a hand over her stomach. Ruth looked at her too.

She rested her hands on her waist and forced herself not to gulp for air. "I won't hurt your brother."

Laurie smiled sadly. "You shouldn't make promises you can't keep. We're only human," she said. "We can't love someone without also bringing them pain."

Ruth saw Elam walking by the lake when she returned from her run. He didn't look her way as she passed, but she sensed he knew she was there. That he had, perhaps, positioned himself so she could approach him if she wanted but wouldn't feel cornered if she didn't. She honestly wasn't sure what she wanted either. Laurie's thinly veiled warning had alarmed her, causing her to second-guess a decision she hadn't known she had made.

Ruth rubbed her left shoulder as she walked toward him. Elam's back was to her, but she could tell from the hard lines of his body that he could hear her drawing near.

"Good morning," she said.

He turned, smiled. "Saw you and Laurie running. Could she keep up?"

"Keep up?" Ruth made a deprecating sound. "She gave me a side stitch."

Elam laughed, his eyes polished by the early light. He was a handsome man, she thought. Not handsome in the sense you noticed right away, like she had with Chandler, but handsome in a way that grew on you, part by part. Ruth stepped closer. She reached out and took Elam's hand. She was still wearing her wedding band — gold and emerald, because the gemstone was so affordable in Colombia, and Chandler had thought the green would remind her of home.

She could take it off now. She was ready for a new season, ready to move on.

Elam looked down at their conjoined fingers and ran a thumb across the top of her hand. "I thought about you last night," he murmured. "I could barely sleep."

"I know," Ruth said. "I couldn't either."

He glanced up at her face. "Does this mean you feel the way I do?"

Ruth's smile widened. A breeze cooled her neck. All her worries, insecurities, and questions had quieted in his presence, and she just felt peace. "Yes, Elam. I do."

Elam leaned down and hugged her then, sweat and all, and the lake reflected their embrace before the blue heron rose, splintering their union as its wings lifted into the sky.

# CHAPTER 10

*Two Months Later*

Elam awoke and looked at the four walls of his one-room cabin, which had served as his home since Ruth agreed to be his bride. Laurie had offered to let him stay at her house until the wedding, but Elam wasn't the type who enjoyed inconveniencing other people, though he doubted there were many types who did. He would rather sleep on the cold, hard ground than send his little nephews and nieces out of their beds. Besides, sharing a bathroom with an eight-member family was all the incentive he needed to haul water from the channel and heat it over the hearth, taking care of his needs the same as his ancestors had done.

Folding his arms behind his head, Elam smiled up at the exposed rafters of his cabin. He couldn't remember such contentment. For so long, he had longed for a family, and now that family was here. Though

228

Sofie and Vivienne weren't his own, the love he felt for them wasn't anything less than what he would feel for his own flesh and blood.

Elam heard a knock on the door of the cabin. He rose from the old army cot beside the piano and buttoned his shirt. Ruth, his fiancée — how that foreign word still danced on his clumsy tongue! — stood on the porch. Light-colored ringlets had sprung up in the moisture induced by her run. He could've stood on that threshold until dusk and just looked at her.

He supposed, from what he heard, that years of familiarity would solve such mystery and attraction. But he wondered if these unions were between couples who had gotten married when they were young, and not old enough, like him, to know finding someone to love you wholly was one of the greatest mysteries of all.

Ruth said, "Good morning," and rose on tiptoe to kiss his cheek.

Stepping back, he rubbed a hand across his jaw. "Sorry," he said. "I'm not shaved."

She grinned. "I don't mind. I like you with a bit of scruff."

"Want to come in?"

"Is that allowed?"

"Don't think the rules of courtship are

the same for adults."

He pulled the door open wider as he spoke. She took a seat on the piano bench, as if it seemed the least intimate perch in the room. "I came to talk to you about something."

"What?" Elam paused, his heart beating hard. "Are you having . . . second thoughts?"

"No." Ruth gripped the piano bench. "I was just thinking that you might not know what you're getting yourself into, becoming an instant father to two little girls."

He smiled. "I have enough nephews and nieces to know what I'm getting into."

"You're right." Ruth slapped her thighs and moved as if to stand. Instead, she remained seated. She looked up at Elam. "Will I have to wear a *kapp*?"

Elam laughed. "Only if you want to."

"But —" she pulled on the thumb holes of her fleece — "I won't have to join the church?"

"I love my community," Elam said. "I love being near my sister, but you might want to move somewhere that would be a fresh start for us. And I'm okay with that."

Her voice rose as she asked, "You are?"

"Absolutely. Being Mennonite doesn't matter all that much to me. What matters to me is that we live our lives for God."

Ruth stared at her hands. "And how do we do that?"

"By loving him and loving those he puts in our lives."

"You make it sound so simple."

Elam looked at her in confusion. "Is it not?"

She sighed. "I don't know."

Elam walked away from the threshold. "Here," he said. "That's the most uncomfortable spot in the room." He removed a pile of books from a rocker with a hand-caned seat. Ruth stood from the piano bench, but she didn't sit. Instead, she remained standing in front of him. Elam stared down at her and placed his hands on her shoulders. "Do you know how much God loves you?"

Ruth glanced up at him, then away. Tears shone in her eyes. "No," she said. "I don't."

"He wants every part of you, Ruth. There's nothing in you that isn't beautiful to him."

Ruth's shoulders hardened. "You only say that because you haven't seen my ugly side."

"Even in your anger, your pain, he loves you. Even then he finds you worthy of love."

The tears moved down her face as her shoulders melted beneath his hands. She looked up at him. "Why do you say such things?"

"I'm not just saying it, Ruth. I *know* it. Because, like him, I only see you through love."

Ruth had grown accustomed to living without a husband long before she became a widow. Nevertheless, there was something oddly disconcerting about seeing her fiancé standing by the door with his bag, conjuring forth the anxiety that had always accompanied Chandler's trips. The driver who was taking Elam to the Madison airport would be here any minute. Ruth then remembered, and understood, what made her heart pound as she tried to work up the nerve to tell Elam good-bye. The last time she told Chandler good-bye was the last time she saw him alive. She knew it wasn't wise to compare the unions, and yet she wasn't naive enough to believe that she wouldn't carry the scars from one marriage into the next.

"Hurry back," she said and rose on tiptoe to give Elam a kiss.

He glanced over her shoulder, toward the kitchen, where Mabel was doing dishes with a little girl on a chair standing on either side. And then he leaned down and kissed Ruth harder. They pulled apart, thirty and thirty-nine years old and yet as flushed and self-conscious as teenagers. "I will," he said, squeezing her hand. "I wish I didn't have to leave you and the girls."

Ruth laughed. "It's a three-day cranberry convention, not a cross-country trip."

The van pulled up in the drive. Seeing it, for the first time Ruth wondered about the complications of being married to someone who didn't own a car. But, she reminded herself, Elam wasn't going to force his beliefs on her; therefore, she could drive them around. Right?

Elam waved as the van pulled away. Ruth stood, staring out the window for a long time, praying that, this time, the man she cared for would return.

Zeus started barking after nightfall, when they had just sat down for supper. This wouldn't have been unusual if he weren't in the house. But he paced back and forth in front of the windows, and Ruth feared he was going to damage the front door by continually scratching at the wood in his effort to get out. Finally, she opened it and watched as the darkness swallowed his lumbering body whole. Ruth returned to the table. The girls were watching her with wide, concerned eyes, and she realized they looked scared for the first time in months.

"It's fine." She smiled. "He's probably chasing off some deer."

But Zeus didn't stop barking, even after the dishes were washed and put away and Ruth was upstairs, getting Sofie and Vi ready for bed. Sofie's impossibly large eyes connected with Ruth's. "You don't think something's gonna hurt Zeus, do you?" Sofie was too young to take life so seriously, and yet what six-year-old had been through what she had?

"No, no, honey," Ruth reassured. "I'll go check on him right after this. Promise."

Sofie nestled beneath the quilt. Vi — in snowman footie pajamas that matched her sister's — stood in her crib, her blonde pigtails sprouting like dandelion fuzz above her slightly protruding ears. She sucked her thumb, cheeks working, as she looked toward the window. Such protective love flooded Ruth, her chest physically hurt like it had when she needed to cry and couldn't. As strange and as premature as it was, Elam's presence in her children's lives offered stability in a way Ruth — despite all her striving — could not. She believed this was why they were so unsettled while listening to Zeus bark. The oversize galoot offered them protection as well. Ruth tucked the girls in with the faded pink blankets she had wrapped them in since infancy, brushed their bangs back from their foreheads, and sang "Edelweiss" the same as she had been singing for years. Ruth then crept from the room, leaving the door ajar.

She needed to fulfill her promise to Sofie.

Early-winter clouds had rolled in, muting the moon, even though it had been so bright two evenings before, Ruth could've read the lines on the palm of her hand. She shivered as she walked through old snow toward the barn, where Zeus was barking. In Elam's absence, Laurie's husband, Tim, was going to tend the farm. Even after three months, Ruth had trouble navigating the many outbuildings during daytime, to say nothing about the natural discombobulation that came with the dark. Ruth wasn't surprised when she found Zeus standing outside the chicken coop.

He had never disturbed the birds before, but maybe he also felt strange in Elam's absence and believed he could get away with more while the master was gone.

"Zeus! Come here!"

He ignored her.

The white scruff on the back of Zeus's neck stood up. All four legs were firmly planted on the gravel-strewn ground outside the coop. Zeus didn't deign to turn his head in her direction. He just continued to bark, over and over: deep, guttural sounds that reverberated around the barnyard. For the first time, she was intimidated by her own pet and understood that Great Pyrenees were working dogs and not just the easy-going throw rug Zeus often was with her children.

Ruth stepped closer, wishing she had brought the oil lamp that was sitting on the kitchen table. In another lifetime, she would've had her phone.

"What is it, boy?" Some instinct of her own told her not to touch him. Zeus turned his head and whined, and then he scraped at the coop door like he'd scraped at the door in the house.

She opened it and smelled chicken dung and feathers. The birds were oddly still, despite the ruckus Zeus was making outside. Then she heard it, a muffled squawk. But it wasn't a squawk as much as it was the sound of something struggling for breath, dying. Ruth pushed the door open wider, wishing the clouds would move so the moonlight would allow her to see inside.

She could perceive the hunkered red-and-white shapes of the chickens, all perched on the boards that ran the length of the coop, and then Ruth heard a sharp hissing sound that sure wasn't coming from a chicken. She backed up and slammed the door, her heart concussing in her ears. Zeus was salivating, whining, barking . . . coming unglued. Ruth knew something was in the coop with the chickens, but she couldn't make out what.

Ruth walked into the barnyard, but Zeus stayed by the coop. She looked up at the farmhouse. Everything was dark. Mabel was sleeping. Before she left, Ruth had put on a sweater, but she hadn't put on a coat. So she started to run — partly to warm up and partly because she didn't want her fiancé coming home to a slew of dead chickens. A light shone in Laurie's kitchen. Encouraged, Ruth walked up to the door and knocked. The light moved closer, and Laurie opened the door. She wore a floor-length flannel gown that strained against her eight-months-pregnant belly. Her eyes and lips stood out against a green mud mask.

She asked, "What's wrong?"

Ruth fought to keep a straight face. "I think something's eating the chickens."

"Really?" Laurie looked over her shoulder toward the stairs. "Tim's just gone up to bed." She ushered Ruth inside and disappeared into another room with the lamp. When she came back, a .22 rifle was balanced over one arm. She passed the oil lamp to Ruth. "Let's go," she said.

Ruth decided if Laurie wasn't going to mention the mud mask, neither would she.

Zeus was still barking when they approached the coop.

Ruth whispered, "What do you think it is?"

Laurie whispered back, "Probably a fox or coon."

Ruth held the lamp while Laurie pulled the coop's wooden latch to the side. The door swung open. Laurie pushed her head inside, her face mask incongruous with the rifle, pregnant belly, and flannel gown. It took all of Ruth's strength to hold Zeus's collar, since every ounce of his body was trying to bust into the coop.

Laurie asked, "Can you move in here with the lamp?"

Ruth said, "Why are we whispering?"

Laurie whispered back, "I don't know."

Ruth quickly let go of Zeus, darted into the coop, and re-latched the door to keep him out. The lamp immediately illuminated a snout-nosed opossum. Beady black eyes glared at them in the light. Disturbed from his nocturnal snack, he hissed and sputtered with feathers ringing his pointed mouth. The hen he had killed was splayed on the ground by his feet.

Ruth believed she had so far lived an adventurous life, but the creature's scaled pink tail and prickly gray body was about the ugliest sight she had ever seen. Almost as an afterthought, Ruth screamed, but — in her defense — she did not drop the lamp.

The scream ricocheted off the interior of the coop. The opossum backed away from the light and the sound, hissing madly, but this couldn't be heard over Ruth.

"Hold it still!" Laurie called, as if she were in battle, commanding, *Hold the line!*"

Ruth snapped out of her hysteria as quickly as she had entered and calmly resumed holding the lamp. Without the light swinging wildly, Laurie moved deeper into the coop, driving the opossum into a corner so he was far enough away from the chickens not to cause them harm. She raised the gun, aimed, and pulled the trigger. This time, the sound not only reverberated off the walls, it reverberated inside the walls themselves and inside the chests and heads of the women, so it seemed even their bone marrow and teeth rattled with the percussion.

"Got 'im," Laurie said. She turned and grinned at Ruth.

Ruth just stared at her future sister-in-law: Laurie's pea-green face mask, her wide pink mouth, her bright, white-rimmed eyes, all captured by an old-fashioned oil lamp. Yes, so far Ruth had lived an adventurous life, but she had never lived an adventure like this. Suddenly — as suddenly as Ruth had emitted her scream — she began to laugh. She laughed so hard, she had to hold the lamp steady in one hand and her stomach in the other. Seeing her, Laurie looked confused, and then she began to laugh as well. The two very different women laughed and laughed as the smell of gunpowder and chicken dung filtered through the cool November air. It was the first time in a long time Ruth had felt anything overtake her like this, other than sorrow, and she embraced the release of it until tears of happiness and relief trickled from her eyes.

Every day, more bombs fell on the city of Kabul, decimating block after block until it sounded like a giant, mythical beast were slowly encroaching on the hospital, causing Chandler to fear he would die in a bombing identical to the one he had survived. So he left. The hospital was overrun with patients, and the nurse didn't even blink when Chandler said he was checking himself out. For there was no "checkout" procedure. There were no computers to update or forms to fill out. He merely put on the clothes and shoes, which had belonged to another patient.

Chandler didn't allow himself to think how the hospital had obtained them; he was only grateful the nurse didn't make him leave in the dirty hospital gown he'd been wearing all week. Plus, the clothes were clean, and the shoes only a half size too small, which didn't bother him as much as not having socks. Chandler put on this outfit and walked through the doors of the spare cinder-block hospital. Though his olfactory system yearned for fresh air after four months breathing in the odor of waste and decay, he found the scent was not the hospital's alone.

Chandler had to fight the urge to turn around as he stepped off the broken sidewalk. He had flown into Kabul with his father, his passport, his credit card, his cell phone, and a carefully packed suitcase. Now, he was scarred, weak, and stepping into a war zone with nothing but a dead man's clothes on his back. His build and dark features helped him blend in. He wasn't sure if this was a blessing or a curse. A blessing, he supposed, as he walked the street, since anyone overtly foreign would be singled out, and yet it was his nationality that could save him, if he could only reach a city that wasn't as devastated as the one he was in.

Therefore, Chandler began to walk. He walked east, toward the rising sun, because that felt safer than forcing himself to walk into the darkness. *The sun and the moon,* he thought, *are the same.* No matter where he was in the world, no matter how long it would take to get home to his family, the sun that shone on his family was the same sun that shone on him. He just had to follow it; to remain focused, regardless of the pain that accompanied each step.

Chandler Neufeld wondered if this separation was what he deserved.

Far too often, he had escaped to the clinic, where he was confident in his abilities. At home, he got the sense he was doing it all wrong. He gave the girls baths but forgot to rinse the conditioner from their hair so the girls' bangs looked greasier than before he began; he folded towels, but they weren't folded in the way the narrow shelves required. He put the food away after Ruth cooked, but he just set the plastic containers in the fridge, not bothering to cover them with the coordinating lids, or even tinfoil, which Ruth said allowed the food to dry out and absorb the smells. Yes, Chandler was incompetent at home, and so he escaped. It was easier to make a difference when the people you were ministering to didn't see you fail. So when the opportunity to leave Colombia for Afghanistan came, Chandler contacted his dad and asked if he'd like to go with. He knew Ruth believed that Chandler Senior had contacted him first, and it was a subterfuge he didn't mind perpetuating, since this way his father took more flak.

He and Ruth weren't at a good place; they hadn't been for a long time, and he thought the distance would be healthy for them — would allow them to take an objective viewpoint of their marriage and family and see where they were headed with both. He would never leave her, Sofie, and Vivienne, or at least that's what he told himself as his plane left Bogotá. But sometimes there were easier ways of leaving, and the escape route he'd chosen was humanitarian aid. Yes, this was his punishment, as he plodded in a dead man's shoes in the ruins of a dying city, the buildings against the rising sun looking like they were, once more, going up in flame.

In September, Elam had offered his cabin to Ruth as her private art studio, and for two months, it had become her haven as well as his. But she'd never had the courage to use it without him there, like she was doing now. Ruth walked up the porch to the cabin, found the key in the planter — where he'd said it would be — and unlocked the door. The hinge groaned as the scent of musty books and dust rose to greet her. The spines of his jewel-toned classics had softened with frequent use and age, and silverfish glittered like bookmarks between the pages as they unfurled, like living things, in Ruth's hands. But Ruth loved entering this portal into the inner workings of Elam's heart and mind, shelved with all those things he held dear.

A notebook, scrawled with illegible lyrics, rested on the piano top. Next to it, a series of candles had melted, gluing the four into one waxen tray. An indigo-blue pottery jar displayed a clutch of dried wildflowers. Elam's cabin was an ode to natural beauty and wonder, and she loved imagining him — large-boned, capable Elam — out in the woods or in the cranberry fields, gathering these small treasures and tucking them into his pockets, to keep them safe.

Ruth couldn't recall when she'd last taken delight in the natural world before coming here. The morning they flew to the States,

Ruth had woken the girls and led them from the lonely house in Greystones down to the beach to say good-bye. But even while anchored by her daughters' warm hands, the waves hadn't reminded her of the countless, salt-sprayed mornings she and her father had searched the packed shoreline for shells; instead, they had reminded her of her own impotence. Every day, people lived and died, and yet the waves continued to crest and recede — pulled by the moon but impervious to the sun's rotations.

Ruth walked over to the desk and the chair in front of it, both repurposed from barn wood. The pastels she found there crumbled at her touch; the sketch paper was yellowed; the horsehair brushes frayed. Ruth didn't check, but she imagined the oil paints were in the same condition. However, Elam had set up an easel in the corner, near the window, and spread a drop sheet beneath, the sheet more than likely pulled from his own cot bed. Ruth rose from the desk and lit another candle. She moved it closer to the easel, and that is when she saw it. A letter: to her, from Elam, balanced on the tray. She smiled as she opened the page and read:

Dear Ruth,

If you're reading this, I am delighted, because this means you've taken my suggestion and come out here while I'm gone. I pray this cabin serves as a refuge for you — a place where you can create and dream and be. This cabin has been my refuge for years, and that is why I want to share it with you, my future bride. I still haven't quite wrapped my mind around that concept, not because it scares me (well, okay, maybe a little), but because it's so difficult for me to finally understand that, in a few short weeks, a long-held dream will come true.

I already hate leaving you, and I can't imagine how much more difficult it's going to be to leave our little family once we're truly one. Thank you for coming into my life. Knowing you and your daughters has caused me to believe that all things truly work together for good — even the hard, painful things. I know you still struggle to see that God loves you, so I pray you will not only discover yourself while you're out here, but also discover and encounter his love. Take all the time you need, and please make yourself at home. All I have is already yours.

Love,
Elam

Ruth traced the words. The scrawl was nearly as illegible as the lyrics on the piano top, and yet the letter itself was beautiful. The last time she'd received a letter like this, she and Chandler were living continents apart. She didn't understand how she could deserve a second chance with a man like Elam, and if she wasn't going to repeat the same mistakes, she needed to find healing for her heart. Setting the letter aside, Ruth picked up a pastel that was the color of the Wisconsin sky. She pressed it to the yellowed paper and began to sketch an image of the farm. A place that had been foreign to her so recently, and yet already felt like home.

When it was finished, she sat down at the desk, looked out the window, and recalled every step in her journey that had brought her here. It seemed she was submersing herself in water, how tangible was the sense she should hold her breath. But then she exhaled, pressed the pencil to paper, and wrote: *The caskets were closed, of course. No flowers adorned them.*

# CHAPTER 11

The afternoon Elam returned, Vivienne ran out the door in her stocking feet and clutched his legs. But even when she stood on tiptoe — her arms stretched toward him, clearly wanting to be held — she didn't come to his knees. Elam couldn't deny her. He scooped her up and tossed her into the air, so that her fine hair fluttered and her gleeful laughter rippled around them like the tail of a kite. Sofie had run toward the door as well. But when she saw who'd arrived, she stayed behind it: a grubby hand pressed to the door's left jamb while she chewed on a strand of dark hair. It was as though she were inwardly debating if it was okay to take part.

Chandler had spent the majority of Vivienne's young life either at the orphanage's clinic or in Afghanistan. Therefore, she had no qualms about opening her heart to Elam. Her sister was another story. Sofie might

248

not have the words — or the self-awareness — to express how she felt, but her every behavior conveyed that to embrace Elam was to be disloyal to her father. Because of this, Ruth hadn't worked up the nerve to talk to Sofie about her marriage to Elam. Elam had offered to be there for the conversation, to offer support, but Ruth feared how Sofie would react, since six-year-olds aren't prone to having the same filter as adults.

Sophie asked, "Why'd he come back?"

The question startled Ruth. She thought her older daughter didn't know she was being observed. Rising from the bottom step, Ruth walked over to the door and stroked Sofie's hair, simultaneously tugging the wet curl from her mouth. Ruth said, "Because this is his home."

Turning, Sofie looked up at her mother. "Is this our home now too?"

Ruth's legs trembled as she knelt. It was difficult, trying to navigate this unexplored world. "Yes," she said. "This is going to be our home. With Elam, Grandma Mabel, and Vi."

Sofie's pupils were swallowed by the black holes of her irises. "Will *you* be here?"

Ruth's body deflated with relief. Maybe telling her wouldn't be as hard as she feared.

"Of course, my darling," she said. "Mommy's never going anywhere."

But just like that, Sofie withdrew and stared out the window again to watch Elam tickle Vi beneath her chin. The easygoing child threw back her head and giggled. "You can't say that," Sofie said, and her young voice held no hint of anger. She was, with the preternatural clarity of a six-year-old, simply stating facts. "Daddy told me he was never going anywhere too."

Chandler feared falling asleep, but exhaustion made wakefulness no longer an option. He crossed the street and entered the gaping doorway to another bombed-out building. He hoped it looked too decimated to appear inhabitable to anyone else. The first floor was covered in a sheet of plaster dust, the particles of which floated in the air, though the bombing must've happened weeks ago. The scent of decay overlaid everything, so Chandler climbed the cement steps to the second floor, hoping to escape it. Three days had passed since he'd eaten, and he wasn't sure if his weakness was due to chronic hunger or his body still struggling to recuperate from the severity of his burns. The bombing was strange in how it could flatten entire blocks, and yet leave a table set for dinner, along with a glass vase of synthetic flowers, each petal and leaf encapsulated in fine dust. Chandler prayed everyone in the household had been rescued, but he knew from the months he'd spent performing emergency surgery that, even if a vase of flowers could remain intact, the same was often not true for the human body, which could withstand many things but succumbed so easily to man-made destruction.

He walked reverently around the table, his fingertips trailing lines in the powder. There were four chairs. One had a booster similar to the one Vi used at home. The only piece of cutlery at this place setting was a rubber-handled spoon. At that moment, he missed his family so much, the pain in his heart far surpassed the pain in his body. What would the father say if he could be here? Would he berate Chandler, as he deserved, for leaving his family? Would he tell him how important it was to be with your loved ones until the end, not to abandon them when they needed you most? Would he rebuke Chandler's selfishness, disguised as altruism? For wasn't it easier to be someone's knight in shining armor, halfway around the world, than to participate in the unsung day-to-day efforts required of child-rearing and marriage?

Chandler felt sick in a way that had nothing to do with his recuperation. He walked through the kitchen and saw pots on the stove, the lids on top, but the outside wall was gone, allowing cold, fresh air to rush through the space. Chandler sank down in front of the stove, and the towel, draped over the handle, brushed the top of his head. He thought of his wife, and of his little girls, and the choices he had made, which had culminated in him leaving them. And not for the first time, sorrow and remorse overcame Chandler so that he began to weep, yearning for a glimpse of his loved ones' faces, and yet finding himself sitting on the floor of a still-life tomb.

Elam and Ruth took a walk after the children were in bed. As they walked, Ruth wondered how different her relationship with Elam would be if he'd been the man she'd married six years ago. She imagined they'd be like they were now — holding hands in companionable silence as they each stared out at the field. Chandler, in some ways, had been a good husband; she saw that now he was no longer here. He was not the type to bring home flowers, run her a bubble bath, or rub her feet — all things that would've made her swoon with shock.

But there was that one time when Chandler came home, after being at work for twenty-four hours, and found Ruth sitting on the couch with Sofie and Vi.

The girls' cheeks were flushed and eyes polished by an internal heat. It might've been his proclivity as a doctor, or maybe his proclivity as a father, but whatever it was, Chandler went from pure exhaustion to full-time nursemaid in minutes. He checked their temperatures, changed their diapers, made Sofie a homemade version of Pedialyte in the kitchen, and warmed a bottle for Vi from the breast milk stored in the freezer. Ruth knew she must've smelled of her children's vomit. Her hair was a rat's nest, and she hadn't had time to brush her teeth or change out of the pajamas she'd been wearing when Sofie first got sick. But Chandler didn't seem to see any of this. Instead, he came out of the kitchen with a cup of tea and a piece of toast.

"Have you eaten?" he asked, setting the plate and mug on the coffee table. Ruth shook her head, not even realizing she hadn't until now, since the scent of sickness kept her appetite at bay. He sat next to her on the couch. He took Vivienne, giving her the bottle, and Sofie climbed onto Ruth's lap. Ruth stroked her daughter's sweaty black hair and took a bite of toast.

Chandler reached for Ruth's hand, but then let go to wipe Vi's chin with a corner of her blanket. "We'll get through it," he said.

Ruth looked over at him and smiled wearily. "We will."

And they did.

Vi's case of the flu wasn't nearly as severe as Sofie's, probably due to the antibodies in Ruth's breast milk, but Sofie's fever soared so that the staggered doses of ibuprofen and Tylenol could barely touch it. When the thermometer stopped beeping at 103.7, they stripped her down, laid her on a towel, and wiped her with a damp washcloth, waiting to see if her temperature would drop. At two in the morning, too anxious to let Sofie sleep on her own, Chandler and Ruth lay on either side of her on the narrow twin. The nightlight on the windowsill flickered pink, purple, blue, and green. Ruth looked across Sofie's radiating body up at Chandler and felt such love for her husband, it seemed impossible she could have ever felt anything else.

Elam squeezed Ruth's hand, drawing her back from that dingy apartment in Colombia to a prosperous cranberry farm in

Wisconsin. Everything Elam did was gentle, an alluring contradiction since his hands were calloused in a way Chandler's had never been.

Elam asked, "What were you thinking of?"

Ruth didn't want to tell him. Unending comparison was no way to begin a marriage. But at this point, she didn't know how to stop. "I'm thinking that I'm glad you're back."

He smiled at her, but then stopped walking. "I got something for you," he said. "While I was gone." Elam looked at his booted feet, and she looked down too, as if it were there. "I wasn't sure when to . . . give it." He rubbed his neck. "I wasn't sure you'd even want . . . it." Swallowing, he reached into his pocket and pulled out a small leather pouch.

Ruth took it from him and glanced up. "You crazy man. What have you done?"

Elam shrugged and pocketed his fists, as shy as a schoolboy. She loosened the pouch's thin string and fished inside for what she knew was there. Her heart thumped hard. She kept her eyes on the pouch. Ruth had been engaged twice in her life, and neither engagement was typical. Therefore, she didn't think it strange she didn't have a ring. Elam was Mennonite, after all. He wore no wristwatch, and nobody else in the community wore any jewelry, unless they were hiding it somewhere Ruth couldn't see. Ruth pulled it out and ran her finger over the facade, reading the details like braille. It was a Claddagh — hands holding a heart — a piece of jewelry native to Ireland. A heart. Before coming here, Ruth had wondered if she had one.

"I saw it," Elam said. "In Boston. It reminded me of you."

Ruth looked up at him through tears. "I love it."

"I'm glad." Despite the darkness, Ruth could see how his eyes squinted at the corners, and Ruth reveled in the fact that Elam was happy, and that this happiness stemmed from her.

She slipped the ring onto her left ring finger. So little time had passed since she'd removed Chandler's wedding band that a white patch of lighter skin still encircled that finger. She wasn't sure of the significance, but she could feel it in her spirit as Elam's Claddagh covered that pale spot. The heart facing out so that everyone she met would know she was already his.

Sofie was the first to notice Zeus was missing, but Ruth initially didn't think too much of it. The Great Pyrenees was becoming increasingly independent and often ventured to the far reaches of the farm, as if he could not be content until he had marked every shrub growing on the two-hundred-acre property. At lunchtime, Ruth stood on the porch, calling for the dog and clapping her hands. She half expected him to come gamboling past her with burdock matting his coat, so Ruth would have to brush him down with the currycomb Elam used for his horses. And yet, Zeus did not return. Ruth bundled her daughters and led them out of the house, each girl holding her hand. The sky was lead gray and oppressive, as if burdened by the beginning of winter.

Ruth found Elam in the barn, looking over a ledger book — the kind she hadn't seen since she was a child visiting her professor father's office. Elam did everything the slow way, by hand.

She asked, "You seen Zeus anywhere?"

Sofie watched Elam from beneath the brim of her red hat lined with faux fur. Her eyes shone out at him with mild distrust, but Vi let go of Ruth's hand to climb onto Elam's knee. Closing the ledger, he bounced her and let her fiddle with the zipper of his coat.

"No," he said, meeting Ruth's eyes.

257

"When did you see him last?"

"This morning," Ruth said. She shrugged. "I'm sure he'll turn up."

"Maybe he found a lady friend." Elam's face flamed as soon as he said this. Ruth had been married for five years and endured all the exposure surrounding a hospital birth. There were few things that could make her blush anymore, so she rather enjoyed Elam's discomfort.

She said, "He's already fixed."

But Ruth became worried when Zeus still had not returned after dark. He always came home after dark, at least for a few hours, and Ruth wasn't sure if that's when he became too hungry to continue roaming or if his sense of responsibility beckoned him home. The girls had a hard time going to sleep unless he was there.

Mabel offered to stay with the children while Elam and Ruth carried a lantern out into the field to look. They called his name and walked, called his name and walked. They passed the barns, the lake, the bogs, and the channels. Finally, they gave up and returned to the house. Mabel was tucking Sofie and Vivienne into bed when they came upstairs. Elam stood in the doorway while Ruth went inside the room. She sat on the bed and reached out to stroke her girls' hair.

They were night and day in both their personalities and looks, and Ruth's mouth went dry as she considered the impossible task of trying to raise them.

Sofie asked, "Did you find Zeus?"

Smiling, Ruth touched her daughter's cheek. "No, *Liebe,* but he'll turn up."

Sofie's lips quivered as she tried not to cry. Elam must've seen this in the lantern light, even from the doorway, for he cleared his throat and said, "I'll go back out and look."

Ruth turned to him. "Really. You don't have to."

He smiled. "I want to. Besides, it's a good night for a walk."

When he left, Sofie asked, "Is Elam a nice man?"

"Yes," Ruth said, pulling her closer. She looked out the window, toward the darkness, and saw Elam's lantern bobbing across the expanse of the field. Elam was out searching for a dog because he knew it was the only way her older child would sleep, but also because it was the only way he could win that child's heart. "He is a very nice man."

Ruth awoke to someone tapping her shoulder. She looked up at Elam, standing by the

259

side of her bed. She had no idea what time it was, but the context had returned. Fear cramped her stomach. She checked to make sure the girls were sleeping and re-covered them with quilts.

They walked out of the room together, and Elam said, "Zeus got hit."

Ruth knew, by his expression, just what he was trying to convey. "Is he dead?"

Elam glanced at the door, as if to ensure the girls would not overhear.

"No." He winced. "Not yet anyway."

Ruth nodded, but tears rose in her eyes. Her daughters. That was all she could think of — not Zeus's condition, not how bad off he must be. All she could think of was them. But Sofie especially, who did not seem strong enough to lose another thread in the unraveled tapestry of her life. Ruth went downstairs, and Elam followed, his hand on her back. They walked out of the house. Elam's horse and wagon were tied to the porch post in the yard.

Elam led Ruth toward the back of the wagon. He'd placed a blanket down, and Zeus lay on top of it. It was hard to see in the dark, but Ruth could hear the animal's labored breathing.

"Oh, baby," she said and climbed up into the wagon, lifting the dog's massive, leonine head onto her lap. His muzzle was wet with blood. Ruth wiped a hand across her tear-dampened face. "How'd you find him?"

Elam climbed up on the wagon's other side. "I rode my horse out on the road, to make sure." He stroked the dog's flank. "I came back for the wagon once I found him."

Ruth's crying became audible. "He'll have to be put down, won't he?"

Elam said, "It's up to you, but he's suffering pretty bad."

"Can we call the vet?"

"I already tried, from the barn. Nobody answered."

"Could we drive Zeus there?"

"The vet's an hour away, and he could already be out on another call."

Ruth began crying harder. Elam moved around Zeus and ran a hand over Ruth's hair. "I could do it," he said. "It'd be very quick."

Ruth looked up at him, and then she understood. "You would shoot a dog?"

"I know. It's awful, but I don't want him to have to wait until we can get ahold of the vet. Do you?"

Ruth shook her head and leaned forward, sobbing against Elam's chest.

Elam continued stroking her hair, the same as she'd stroked her children's a few

261

hours ago. "It's all right," he soothed. "It's all right." And she felt he wasn't just speaking to the heartbreaking situation before her, but all the heartbreak which had preceded it.

"Go ahead," she said. "Are you sure you know how?"

Elam nodded. He held her, wiping her tears with his thumb. "Laurie had a pony when she was little, named Socksie. She got into the grain bin one night and foundered."

Ruth's stomach twisted.

"There was nothing to be done." He paused. "My family didn't have money for a vet, and my *daed* was taking care of *Mamm,* so I did it. For Laurie."

Ruth looked up at him. "Oh, Elam. How old were you?"

"Sixteen. I remember it like yesterday. It was quick, though, Ruth, and I'll make sure it's quick now, too."

Ruth looked down at Zeus. The poor animal was whimpering, his fight for life becoming more intense. She stroked Zeus's muzzle, swallowed a sob, and stood. Resting a hand on Elam's shoulder, she climbed down from the wagon and entered the house.

She sat on a rocking chair in front of the cold fireplace and wrapped her arms around

262

herself. She couldn't get warm, even after she got up and pulled a blanket from the cupboard and draped it around her shoulders. Five minutes must've passed before she heard it, the shot, distantly, as though Elam had driven the wagon into another field. Ruth began sobbing in earnest then, the sound of it ripping her apart. She got up from the rocking chair and stretched across the couch and cried, grieving the pain her children were bound to experience in the morning, and the pain their young, innocent lives had already endured.

Ruth expected Elam to return to the farmhouse after burying the dog. She knew she should participate in the burial itself, but she was suddenly too spent and remained on the couch as if some unseen force tied her there. But Elam did not come. Hours passed, and Ruth's emotional exhaustion induced a catatonic-like state. She didn't fall asleep so much as she tumbled headlong — dreaming of bombs and blood and her beautiful daughters crying over a grave, crying in a way they hadn't over their father's. Ruth loved Zeus; that was not a question, but she did not mourn him because of him. She mourned him for her girls.

What Ruth feared the most, as she was lying, shivering, on the couch, was that the loss of Zeus would reawaken the loss of their father. Sofie was the greatest concern, since she had barely spoken when they took that long, silent flight from London to New York. What if she regressed to the point Ruth lost her? What if, this time, she never got her back?

Ruth awoke before dawn, when the headlights from a car swept over the front of the house. Ruth sat up on the couch, bleary-eyed and confused that she had fallen asleep there. Then she remembered. She stood and wiped her dry mouth on her sleeve. She needed water, but she was too curious to see who was here to take the time to get a drink. She was walking toward the front door when it opened, and Elam stepped in. He was wearing the clothing he'd been wearing last night. His shirt was stained; Ruth didn't care to think about how that stain had gotten there. "I need you to come see something," he said.

Ruth stepped closer. Elam's bloodshot eyes told her he hadn't slept since everything happened. "What is it?" she said.

But Elam did not say. He simply put his hand on the small of her back, like he had earlier, reminding her she was safe. "It's okay if you want me to return him. I just thought —" he riffled a hand through his hair — "I guess I thought it was a good idea, but now I'm not sure."

Ruth looked up at him and then walked down the porch toward the van. The driver — a man Ruth hadn't met — waved, and she waved halfheartedly back.

Elam moved in front of her and pulled open the van door. The interior light came on, and Ruth saw it there, the snow-white pup, pressed down into the floorboard like that proximity could keep him safe.

"Oh, Elam," she said. And even *she* wasn't sure what she thought. Could loss be so easily replaced? Could her daughters go to bed with one pet and wake up with another? Ruth felt a sinking sensation in her gut as she knelt beside the van and stroked the puppy's head. His hair was like down. Zeus's had been coarse, especially around his ruff. Was she attempting to replace her children's father with another man? Did she really think it was that easy? Because it was not. She had never experienced loss to this extent, and yet she knew that, even if they had a stepfather who adored them, a part of their spirits would always be longing for their dad.

Elam said, "There's a family who sells Pyrenees and Samoyeds over in Cashton. I remembered it after I put Zeus down. He's a little boy. The last of the litter."

The driver couldn't continue sitting in the driveway, idling, but Ruth didn't know what she should do. Should she make Elam take the puppy back? Should she thank him? Tears stung her eyes again, and she wiped them discreetly with the palm of her hand.

"I really *can* take him back," Elam said. "I explained the situation, and they were very kind. She said she'd even waive the home inspection."

Ruth sensed the smile in his voice, but she wasn't sure she could return it. Instead, she scooped the puppy up from the floorboard and carried him toward the house. She could hear Elam speaking to the driver. The van left. She sat on the porch steps. She found herself cradling the puppy, her hand supporting the warm globe of his belly, her other hand nestled in his fur. Elam came and sat beside her. After a while, he asked, "Did I make a mistake?"

Ruth wondered if Elam had made the same poor correlation she had: comparing their hasty union to the replacement of a dog. She shook her head and squeezed his arm. The two of them hadn't talked about love, but she knew — sitting there on the porch of the farmhouse where they would live as a family — that she *did* love this man, who was so unbelievably kind, it caught her off guard. "You didn't. I think the girls are going to love him."

The dog whined, and she adjusted him in her lap. The couple sat there, then, on the front porch of their Wisconsin farmhouse, as the morning sky shifted from navy to mauve.

"I love you," Ruth said. She had not been planning to say this, but as soon as the words were uttered, she was so glad she did.

Elam looked down and then over at her. For a long time, he didn't speak, but he didn't need to. The look in his eyes conveyed everything. "Oh . . . Ruth," he finally said, pressing a kiss to the side of her hair. "I love you so much. You have no idea how happy I am."

Ruth wanted Elam to be the one to present the puppy to Sofie and Vi. This seemed like the least she could do, considering how hard he'd worked to contact the driver and the seller of the dogs. It warmed her to see Elam's excitement as the two of them sat at the kitchen table with their plates of eggs and steaming mugs of coffee, their ears tuned for any stirrings from the girls.

The puppy dozed at their socked feet, which touched slightly. *This is how it'll be,*

267

Ruth thought. She could see it all so clearly — their simple, fulfilling life here on the cranberry farm. They would wake early, just to have time to drink their coffee and talk about their day's plans as husband and wife rather than as father and mother who were flung into the ceaseless demands of parenthood from the moment their young children opened their eyes. Elam's work allowed him to remain on the farm, and so Ruth imagined him coming in for lunch and again for supper — their family a solid unit rather than a shifting composition.

Elam's thoughts must've been in the same vein as Ruth's, for he smiled at her across the table. Now they'd spoken of love — of what they'd each long since known — it was as if a wall between them had fallen, and their marriage wasn't just a concept, but an awakening dream.

They heard it, then — the sleepy "Mama?" coming from the top of the stairs.

Ruth and Elam didn't merely stand; they bolted from the table, as if this were Christmas morning and the roles were reversed. She loved Elam for taking something she'd dreaded and turning it into a gift. Elam picked the puppy up from beneath the table and carried him under his arm, like a football, but his other hand rested on the pup's gray-tipped ears.

Sofie stood next to the staircase railing, her blankie in hand, her black curls springing free around her face, and her little tummy protruding against the zipper of her pajamas.

"I have a . . . present for you," Elam said.

"A present?" She looked from Elam to her mom, trying to understand.

"The puppy," Ruth explained. "Elam brought it back home for you."

Sofie left her blankie on the steps and walked down them. Only at the base did she reach for the animal. "Is it yours?" she asked, looking up at Elam.

His smile widened. His happiness hid the fact he had not slept. "It's *ours*," he said.

Sofie nodded and reached out, stroking the puppy's head. "A boy or a girl?"

"A boy."

"Zeus likes him?"

Ruth met Elam's gaze. She knelt and put her arms around Sofie, pressing one hand to her chest. This was a second chance to use simple, clear words; to listen and to comfort; to tell Sofie what to expect. "Zeus died, sweetie." Her daughter's heart thrummed beneath her hand.

Sofie looked at Ruth and then she looked down at the puppy. "Where?" she asked, not *how,* and Ruth wished that none of this had happened. That her daughter's sensitive spirit had time to fully recuperate before she received a blow like this again.

"On the road," Ruth said.

"By a car?"

Ruth leaned forward. She closed her eyes and breathed in the scent of her daughter's shampooed hair. She nodded, and Sofie began to sob. She sobbed hard, as hard as her mother had — almost as if the loss of the dog had given her permission to mourn the loss of her father, too — but then she sat on her mother's lap, with Elam beside her, and stroked the puppy's head. Once her crying had quieted, Sofie looked up at Elam. "Can I name him?"

Elam smiled and murmured, "Yes, Sofie. Anything you want."

"Everest," she said, tears still glistening on her round cheeks. "From *Paw Patrol.*"

As Ruth's eyes filled, she thought, *This is a start.*

# CHAPTER 12

Elam and Ruth were married in the barn. Young Bishop Gish oversaw the ceremony, and he was as somber conducting the wedding as he had been conducting the funeral. Ruth wondered how hard it was for Elam to talk the bishop into officiating the service. The past ten years had served to decelerate his forward thinking, and therefore he probably frowned on the fact Ruth did not intend to join the Mennonite church. Still, Young Bishop Gish got the job done. Ruth carried no flowers but wore a creamy satin dress with a chapel-length train. Laurie had sewn it and accented the cinched bodice with a fleur-de-lis pattern, each swirl outlined with delicate crystal beads. So much time and effort had clearly been invested in that dress, Ruth suspected Laurie had created it from the vision of the one she'd never been allowed to wear.

Laurie stood beside Ruth, and Tim stood

beside Elam. For the children's sake, and hers, Ruth had requested that the ceremony be immediate family only. Sofie and Vi were wearing matching dresses Laurie had made from the material left over from Ruth's.

Mabel sat between her granddaughters and kept one soft, warm arm on either side of their shoulders, so it was impossible to tell if Mabel was receiving comfort or giving it.

Ruth met Mabel's eye before Bishop Gish declared her and Elam husband and wife. The entire ceremony had been conducted in English, out of deference to the *Englisch* bride, but the bishop read 1 Corinthians 13 from his German Bible. Ruth mentally translated as he read, recalling the day she'd married Chandler, and how they'd gripped each other's hands as they'd said their vows: *for better, for worse, for richer, for poorer, in sickness and in health . . . till death do us part.* Death had finally parted them, but looking back, it seemed this parting had been inessential.

Each time Chandler chose to care for orphans over his family; each time Ruth snapped at him the second he came in the door; each time they got the girls to bed and reached for their smartphones instead of each other; each time they failed each other and were, in turn, failed, caused a division neither attempted to bridge. Tears stung Ruth's eyes as she looked at Mabel, her mother-in-law, who would soon be her mother-in-law no more but her husband's aunt.

Mabel mustered up a smile, which Ruth bravely returned. They would forever be joined by their loss and their love. This knowledge brought Ruth immeasurable comfort.

Ruth looked at Elam again. She sensed he'd been watching her the entire time, during which her mind had been lost in the forest of memory. She smiled, contrite, and squeezed his large, square hand. As Elam began saying the vows she'd first said six years ago, Ruth found herself recalling the letter she'd written her deceased husband the previous night:

Dear Chandler,

I'm sorry. I'm sorry I failed you, and you failed me, and we didn't take time for each other. I'm sorry we lost each other in parenthood and in the monotony of life, a monotony which was found even on the mission field. I would do better, if I could do it all again. I would be more patient, more kind; I would understand your needs and pray that, through that understanding, you would then try to understand mine. We failed each other; we did. But I don't want to fail now. I don't want to fail this beautiful, good man, who is willing to love our broken family, even though not every part of us is entirely on the mend.

Young Bishop Gish did not tell them to kiss when they became husband and wife; no one in the audience clapped or cheered and no music played. But Elam held Ruth's hand as they walked out of the barn, and Ruth could see the sunlight beyond it etching the lines of the old plank wood. She remembered her high school art teacher's favorite quote. It was from a Leonard Cohen song, "Anthem." *There is a crack, a crack in everything. That's how the light gets in.*

Elam sat stiffly in the passenger seat and picked at the left cuff of his shirt. In thirty miles, he'd made no move to touch his wife; in thirty miles, he'd not even made an effort to talk. Ruth's Claddagh ring, on the steering wheel, flashed as she turned on the radio to fill up the silence. She sorted through the station controls with her thumb, surprised to find they were playing the same songs they'd been playing when she drove another budget rental from Illinois to Wisconsin. A lifetime ago. She glanced over at Elam. Did the radio offend him? How had they never discussed this? She punched it off, just to be safe.

This honeymoon felt nothing like the one Ruth had taken with Chandler. With Chandler, she was still wearing her wedding dress when they left the orphanage in the battered two-door they'd borrowed. Ruth had rested her aching feet on the dashboard so that, in the morning, they could see the print of her ten bare toes against the windshield's bug-splattered glass. Chandler had driven with his left hand while keeping his right on her upper thigh. The young couple was filled with the kind of naive anticipation that time all too quickly cures. It was as though their entire adventurous life was unfurled before them, bordered by twin headlights.

The silence, now, had less to do with anticipation and more to do with fear. Ruth's hands began to sweat on the steering wheel. She looked over at Elam. Had she imagined the moments they'd shared? Had she imaged the desire in his eyes or the comfort of his foot touching hers while the rest of the family obliviously consumed a home-cooked meal around the table?

Well, first things first. She cleared her throat. "Mind if I play some music?"

Elam smiled. "Not at all."

She pushed the radio back on and settled on a classical station, which seemed like the one Elam would most enjoy, considering his love for the piano. How had she married someone whose musical preferences were a mystery to her? Panic clamped her throat.

"Door County should be quiet this time of year," Elam said, and then added, with uncommon redundancy for a man who said so few words, "There shouldn't be any crowds."

Ruth said, "Thank you for arranging everything."

"My honor," he replied. "I just hope . . . you like it."

She heard the small hitch in his voice and understood what she should have already known: This was Elam's first honeymoon, but it wasn't hers. This was his first wedding, but it wasn't hers. This would be a first for him in so many ways, and no doubt he was experiencing more anxiety than eagerness as she drove but he tried to navigate how to please her.

Ruth relaxed her grip on the steering

276

wheel and surreptitiously wiped her right hand on her jeans before reaching for his left. "I'm looking forward to having time together."

He clasped her fingers. "I am . . . too." They didn't say anything for a while. Just when she was about to pull her hand away, Elam said, "I want you to know that I am seeing this trip as our chance to get to know each other better. Nothing more . . . nothing less."

Ruth nodded. "I guess we haven't gotten to know each other very well yet, have we?"

"Well, in the context of a husband and wife leaving on their . . . honeymoon? No."

"Were we crazy to do this? To get married so soon?"

Elam laughed. A short, relieved sound. "Probably," he said. "But I'm glad we did."

A denouement of snow began to fall, suspended in the high beams. The atmosphere in the car began to change as well. "I'm glad we did too," Ruth said. "Life's too short otherwise."

Elam kissed the inside of her wrist. "I just hope we've got all the time in the world."

It was after midnight when they drove up to the cottage, nestled between pine trees and an apple orchard on the far side of an old farm. Ruth got out of the car and stretched, staring up at the sky. The snow had stopped as abruptly as it had started, and the heavens were jet black and scattered with stars. Lake Michigan bordered the acreage, and yet the January wind — sweeping across the water — seemed to carry with it the scent of brine. The air was colder than Ruth expected. She hunkered inside the wool sweater she had packed, at the last minute, for the trip. The car's automatic headlights were still on, and Ruth could see the cottage was composed of dark-gray shake siding, trimmed in white. Flower boxes and a wraparound porch adorned the front. The narrow window beside the main door was stained glass. The door was painted teal and had a tarnished brass knocker in the shape of a butterfly. Ruth walked toward this door, taking in the numerous bird feeders in the front yard, dangling from shepherd hooks, and the remnants of perennials that would not resurrect themselves until spring.

Behind her, Elam opened the trunk of the car and took out their bags. Ruth had packed the carry-on she had brought with her on the flight from London to New York and then Chicago. Watching Elam carry it up to the house now, along with a small duffel, made her marvel at the unpredictable nature of life. When she was riding in that small red car with Chandler, she could've never anticipated that, six years later, he'd be dead, and she'd be about to embark on another honeymoon with his first cousin — a man who was a stranger to her half a year ago, and who was, in many ways, a stranger to her still.

And yet, wasn't the unpredictable nature of life what made her cherish it? Without that unpredictability, would she have taken the risk of marrying Elam? Without it, would she hug her daughters so fiercely throughout the day, as if holding them could prevent them from being able to leave the sphere of the earth as their father had? Ruth didn't know. The older she became, the more she realized how little she *did* know.

But as she walked up to Elam, he looked over and smiled, and the swirling thoughts pervading her mind grew calm. She was safe here, with him. She was, perhaps, not as safe as she could have been if she'd protected herself from pain by refusing to embrace love. But a life well lived wasn't meant for safety; a life well lived meant flinging your heart into the void.

"Ready?" Elam asked. Ruth looked up at him and nodded. Rather than carrying her across the threshold, as Chandler had done in their stone house in the mountains of Colombia, Elam simply set their bags down by the door, unlocked it, and reached for her hand.

Ruth entered the cottage in front of Elam. He stepped in behind her, but neither of them turned on the lights. The ceiling was low, the space small, so the bedroom was visible even from the front door. Ruth walked across the living room and ran her hand over the top of the mantel, constructed from a barn beam, so she could feel the notches and the stippled worm holes the years had honed. The owners of the cottage had laid wood for a fire. Elam stepped up beside Ruth to find the matchbox. The fire helped, providing Elam and Ruth with a focal point that wasn't each other. They stood before it for some time, listening to the kindling slowly crackle and burn. Otherwise, the cottage was silent. No children fussed. No puppy whined. No dishes clanged as Mabel made supper. Their ears were tuned to the soundtrack of their breathing. Finally, Elam turned to Ruth. She sensed rather than saw this, and she turned to him as well. He placed his hands on her shoulders and ran them down her arms. "My wife," he said.

Ruth shivered, a reflex of body temperature or a premonition, she did not know which. "I am," she said, trying to match his smile. Elam moved his hands back up and rested them on her neck. Her voice was steady, controlled, but the pulse at her throat would give her away.

"I won't . . . hurt you," he said.

"I know that," Ruth admitted. She reached up and wrapped her hands around his. "I'm more afraid of hurting you."

Elam smiled and wiped a thumb against her wet cheek. "Vulnerability's always a risk," he said. "But I'd rather . . . take it, wouldn't you?"

She nodded, and he pulled the sweater from her shoulders. It fell to the floor as Elam's fingers whispered against her collarbone. Ruth's body replied, though she spoke not a word. Elam leaned his head down and kissed her, long and deep, before scooping his bride into his arms and carrying her across the cool cottage floor to their bed.

Dear Ruth,

I found a notebook and a pen in the bombed apartment complex where I've been staying. That wasn't all I found. There were cans of food buried in the

281

rubble, which I opened with a knife I discovered in the drawer next to the stove. But even though I was starving, that notebook and pen excited me more than the food. Or at least they were just as exciting. Because I wanted to do this: sit here, in the middle of such madness, and write to you. I miss the sound of your voice. The "We need to talk" voice, which means I'm in trouble; the higher-pitched voice you use when being goofy with the girls. You have another voice you use for them too, which reminds me of a growl, and whenever I hear this, I know it's high time to kick into gear and help you. But the voice I miss most is the one you save for the two of us, when it's late at night, the kids are asleep, and we are in bed — the streetlights coming through the window the only light in the room.

Many times, I would look over and watch you as you talked about the children or about your day. I knew you were lonely. I could hear that, too, in your voice as you talked, but I didn't know how to fix it, and because I didn't know how to fix it, I often didn't let myself truly hear you, because hearing you and not being able to fix what was broken meant I had failed.

I regret this so much. I want you to know this. If I could do it all over, which I pray I have the chance to do, whenever you and I are next lying beside each other (such a dream to me, and to think how I used to collapse, unthinkingly, into bed!), I will not nod off — my back to you — while you are sharing your heart. Rather, I want to stay awake all night long, just listening to the rhythm of your voice, but this time, I will really listen to your words, and I will hear them, and I won't try to fix anything but simply let you talk to me. I would do so many things differently if I had the chance, Ruth. I hope it's a chance I get. I hope it's not too late. That I won't die here in a place that was once my refuge from monotony and has now become my living hell, and instead I will get to live with you and our darling girls, and I really think I will never want to go anywhere ever again. So speak to me, my darling Ruth. Help me find my way back home.

I love you,
Chandler

Elam opened his eyes to a strange ceiling

above him. It neither sloped like his room beside the kitchen, nor was it exposed like the ceiling in his cabin in the woods. Rather, it was composed of thick pine board, stained with a cream wash, so that most of the circular knots still showed through. As Elam stared, the memories came back, of what he was doing in this cottage, and who was here with him. He turned his eyes from the ceiling and glanced over in the bed. He saw Ruth there: the strap of her slip had fallen down onto one shoulder. Her hair — more red than gold in this light — tumbled down her freckled back. Elam felt shy this morning, though he'd felt far from it last night. His face burned to recall how he had touched her, as if her body were an extension of his. But he guessed, in a way, it was.

Elam pulled on his pants, built a fire, and then opened the front door to a transformed world. A foot of snow had fallen overnight, the top inch layered with the same ice that coated each bare branch of the straggled apple trees surrounding the cottage. The newlyweds had been so intent on each other, they hadn't noticed the shift taking place outside. Wisconsin's midwinter snowfalls had always been Elam's favorite. As a child, he'd liked to imagine the unglaciered land protected by that pristine blanket until the ground thawed and spring came again.

Elam was older now and understood that sometimes the bout of ice and cold extinguished life rather than protected it. But standing on that porch with his boots untied and his winter coat unbuttoned over his bare chest, he was filled with the same excitement as when he was a young boy with an entire day before him of sledding, hot chocolate, and endless rounds of Dutch Blitz. Elam tromped out into the snow and pulled the crate of dry goods from the back of the car. If not for Mabel, who knows what Elam and Ruth would have eaten during their first morning as husband and wife. Elam carried the food back inside and heard the shower running.

He turned when he heard Ruth sing. The bathroom door was open and steam poured through the gap. He wasn't sure how long it'd take him to become accustomed to the fact he could indeed look at his bride, but then he thought it was better *not* to become accustomed, but to constantly view their union as some miraculous occurrence that didn't happen twice.

Elam was making pancakes when Ruth came out from her shower, wearing a robe he hadn't seen. He wasn't sure how he should approach her, wasn't sure if the intimacy they'd experienced last night also existed this morning. Maybe she needed space? Elam smiled at Ruth but didn't say anything. She walked over and wrapped her arms around his waist, burrowing her face into the curve of his back. Elam's family was not the demonstrative type. This was partly due to their heritage, and partly because Elam's mom was unsure if the same affection should be bestowed to boys as well as girls. So this sudden physical touch surprised and pleased him.

"Good morning."

Elam felt Ruth's simple greeting, which they'd exchanged so many times, reverberate through his spine. He loved this woman. He loved this woman so much, it made him fearful, because he knew how it felt to love someone and then lose them to events beyond your control. But he would rather live with risk than live without her.

Elam turned with the flipper in hand and opened his arms to Ruth. She stepped closer and nestled against him. "Did you sleep all right?" he asked.

"Better than I've slept in months."

Her body was warm and fragrant against his. He could see the widow's peak of her damp hair, spiraled up in the towel. "I don't think I'm ever going to get over it," he said.

Ruth looked up. "Over what?"

"Over the fact you married me."

She winked. "Maybe it's better if you don't."

He stared down at her and set the flipper on the island behind them. "I won't," he said. Then he leaned down and kissed her again. It was a kiss that lingered and grew until the burning pancakes on the griddle set off the cottage's smoke alarms.

Chandler John Neufeld Junior reread the letter to his wife, put his head in his hands, and began to weep. He was cracking, and he knew it. He should've never left the hospital. Even if it'd gotten bombed, even if he had died there in the bed, it was better than slowly starving to death while moving around the lifeless city like a ghost. His isolation came down to fear. He'd had minimal human contact in the past few weeks, but he was beginning to understand he was never going to make it unless he took the risk of letting others know who he was. So it was either die from starvation or die at the hands of an unknown terrorist who could use his videoed death to evoke fear in American hearts. But whatever he was doing now was not going to work. Determined to get home, Chandler stood, folded the letter to Ruth, and slid it into his pocket.

He descended the building's crumbled steps and walked out into the city. He'd attempted to travel at night, where he could skulk in the shadows, mostly unseen. But his debilitating hunger had driven him out, seeking food over safety. After so many days of traveling in darkness, the stark sunlight burned his eyes. Everything was the same — white and ruined — everywhere he looked, so sleeping in one apartment complex was the same as sleeping in one twenty miles away. Chandler walked, his throat thick with dust, until he came to a series of structures that didn't look as destroyed as the rest. He had no map, and even if he did, the blasts had destroyed most of the street signs and turned landmarks into dead ends. So he walked. He walked until the stranger's ill-fitting shoes formed blisters on his heels.

A dog barked somewhere, a man yelled, the sound of gunfire rebounded in the distance.

Chandler looked up, which had become habit for those who were unfortunate enough to get rained on from bombs in the sky. Nothing was there. The color was a disarming clear blue. Chandler's inability to think clearly prevented him from seeing the man coming around the corner with an

AK-47 across his chest. He yelled at Chandler in Arabic. Chandler instinctively raised his hands and backed up. The man yelled some more, his great bull chest heaving inside his black T-shirt. It appeared to Chandler like the blackest shirt he had ever seen, since everything around the man was an impressionistic depiction of gray and brown, the buildings that remained splashed with graffiti the color of blood.

"Sorry!" Chandler said. "I'm sorry!" though he knew not what he was apologizing for.

Now this man would know he was American. But the man didn't seem to care. He just pointed at Chandler, pointed at the road, and then struck the butt of the gun with his ringed hand. The sound clanged inside Chandler's head like a bell. The nonverbal communication did the trick. Chandler knew what the man wanted — and what he *didn't*. Chandler backed up farther, his hands still raised, and didn't dare turn around until the man — satisfied he was leaving — stepped back into the ruins.

Only once Chandler was safe in an alleyway, wishing for darkness, did he begin to wonder how he could've become this person who searched for food amid rubble and wore a dead man's clothes. Chandler no longer had any idea where he was going; the destroyed streets were a maze with no destination, and yet he would continue walking until he could walk no more, envisioning his family at the end, though he was beginning to doubt his return.

Elam and Ruth didn't eat their pancake breakfast until noon. Instead, for those hours, they remained tangled up in bed, listening as the sun warmed the earth enough to cause slabs of snow to slide from the tin roof. Elam rested one hand on Ruth's stomach. Her body enamored him, and not just because he'd never been with a woman before. She was soft and yet strong — a combination which reflected her soul as well. Ruth was marvelously unselfconscious, laughing as he studied every inch of her skin, as if she were not just an artist, but her own work of art.

"What happened here?" he asked, tracing a thin white scar on her shin.

"The neighbor boy threw a rock at me and told me to go away. I was six."

"He probably liked you."

"He sure had a funny way of showing it."

"And here?" He ran his thumb over her knee.

"Rollerblading with a friend from high school. I wiped out on the hill."

"What about this?" Elam picked up her ankle, examining the tiny vertical scar.

"Nicked it shaving," she said. "There was a piece of skin in the razor."

Elam winced. "My mother and sister never shaved."

"Not that *you* know," Ruth said. "The other week, I caught Laurie wearing a mud mask."

"A mud mask?"

Ruth couldn't stop laughing. Trying to explain the mysteries of the female life put them into perspective. "It's this green mud that you put on your face to make yourself beautiful."

Elam still cupped her ankle. "And you do this?"

"Not often," she said. "But yes. I have."

The fire had gone out by the time the newlyweds cleaned up the kitchen and got dressed.

The cottage was cozy but would feel cramped if they didn't get some fresh air soon. Ruth put on the thermal hiking gear she had bought in preparation for the trip, but Elam just wore pants, a long-sleeved collared shirt, suspenders, and his coat.

"Aren't you cold?" she asked.

He shrugged. "I don't get cold."

"Must be nice," she said, "living in Wisconsin."

They trudged out into the snow, and it seemed strange to Ruth to be on a walk without Zeus loping at her side or one of the girls tugging at her hand, dragging a blankie or a doll.

"Do you miss them?" he asked.

"My girls?"

He nodded.

"Yes," she said, "I do. This is the first time I've been away from them."

Elam didn't say anything. She felt him looking at her. "You and Chandler never went away?"

Ruth shook her head. "An orphanage requires a lot of babysitters, so there was really no one left to watch the girls. Plus, Chandler had a hard time leaving the clinic."

"I'm sorry," he said. Elam reached for her gloved hand with his bare one, and the two of them walked along the lane, past the apple trees someone had planted a long time ago. Half of each trunk and half of each branch were etched with snow, showing which way the wind had blown. Ruth glanced over at their shadows, traced across the untouched white. She clutched his hand and pointed. "Look," she said. "That's us."

the untouched wine. She clutched his hand and pointed, "I only," he said. The t-shirt

# CHAPTER 13

Chandler fought off emotion as he walked toward the structure, charred and pock-marked with bullets like so many others, but one of the most majestic images he'd ever seen: the American embassy in Kabul. He pulled himself forward, each step a battle between collapse and will. Impassive soldiers stood before the gates with M16s strapped across their chests. The one man looked at Chandler without turning his head. The other didn't spare him a glance, as if he'd seen grown men cry one too many times. The second soldier patted him down and let him in. Chandler was grateful he'd discarded the knife he'd found at the ruined apartment complex.

More guards were inside the building, as silent and still as the ones outside. A woman stood behind the desk. Her red lipstick and coiled black hair made Chandler feel he was looking at an avatar from some other time.

She addressed him as she saw him, in Farsi.

Chandler shook his head. "I am American," he said, and with those words, he knew — for good or for ill — there was no going back.

For four glorious days, Ruth and Elam enjoyed the newness of their life together. The TV sat in the corner like a dull gray eye because they never turned it on. They didn't go to restaurants, to the movies, or to the many art galleries in town. Instead, they stayed where they were — tucked in their cottage with the stained-glass windows and gray tin roof. They kept the fireplace roaring and prepared and ate meals by candlelight. They bathed together in the narrow clawfoot tub, with Elam's knees jutting over the lip and water sloshing onto the floor. Hand in hand, they walked to the candy cane–striped lighthouses placed like chess pieces over the island, and Ruth filled her coat pockets with the shoreline's smooth, egg-shaped stones.

She and Mabel had agreed that Mabel would call every two days from the phone in the barn, leaving Ruth a message so she would know the girls were all right. Otherwise, Ruth's phone would remain off. The first message had been a cheerful update saying the girls were eating and sleeping well, though Sofie had complained her knees hurt the previous night. The second one, yesterday, had been an update saying the girls had helped make spritz cookies and then cut snowflakes from construction paper and hung them all around the house.

Meanwhile, real snow fell and then thawed, and then fell again, quilting the ground so it would've been impossible for Ruth and Elam to drive away from their cottage if they wanted to. But neither of them wanted to. At night, before they fell asleep, Ruth fantasized about living there forever. She could create art and sell it at one of the galleries in town, which catered to summer and fall tourists. Elam could farm cranberries here, or apples, or cherries, or any of the hardier crops that kept the farmers surviving, if not thriving, all year round. The two of them could live, love, and die while existing as each other's axis upon which their worlds spun.

But then Ruth thought of her daughters in Mabel's care, and her fierce love for them realigned all rational thinking. She couldn't stay here, as much as she wanted to, because Sofie's growing pains were a sign she missed her mother. Two-year-old Sofie started having growing pains in earnest once she understood Ruth would drop everything and sit on the couch and rub her kneecaps with lotion until Sofie either fell asleep or her bottomless love tank filled. Growing pains were Sofie's orphaned heart crying for attention, and if Ruth did not return soon, she knew the ground she and Sofie had gained would begin to slip away.

Two days after arriving at the embassy, Chandler stood under a hot shower, marveling at the commonplace miracle until the water grew cold. The first day at the embassy, he'd spent being interrogated; the second, filling out paperwork. He knew from a few secondhand accounts — mostly inexperienced tourists who'd been pickpocketed overseas — that losing one's identification papers was more than just a hassle, but he could've never anticipated the amount of red tape that'd have to be cut to return someone to the States.

Chandler couldn't understand what the holdup was. Ruth had often informed him he leaned toward some rather naive thinking, but he thought one call to Physicians International, and he'd have his one-way plane ticket home. It was not working out that way, and as he rinsed the lather from his scarred body, he refused to contemplate why.

An hour later, Chandler was dressed and seated across from a suited man who looked at Chandler like he was a terrorist. "You claim you are Chandler John Neufeld Junior," he said, his Southern accent lengthening the vowels, "and you work for Physicians International."

"Yes," Chandler replied. "Yes, that is right."

The man looked down at a paper. Chandler hated that the other side of the table was too far away to read what it said. The man's face hardened, his pencil mustache an accent mark above his flat mouth. Chandler didn't know what else to say, so he looked at his hands, fingers interlocked. "Well, Mr. Neufeld," the man said, "we've been in contact with the director of Physicians International, and he says that Chandler John Neufeld Junior died during a July bombing raid in Kunduz, Afghanistan."

Chandler's throat tightened. "That — that can't be right," he said. "I was in the hospital for months. I was very badly burned, you see, and maybe — maybe they didn't know I was alive."

The man shook his head, made a tsking

sound Chandler knew should invoke his silence. "No," he said. "Chandler Neufeld's death certificate was processed on July 17, 2018." The man studied Chandler. Chandler forced himself to hold his gaze, to look neither surprised nor devastated, though he was both. Did Ruth believe herself a widow? Did his girls believe they were fatherless? His heart sank as pain sprang to his eyes. The man continued, his stone face unsoftened by a dead man's tears, "If Chandler Neufeld is dead, sir, then who are you?"

The stone-faced man allowed Chandler to make one long-distance phone call, as if he were in prison. He called Ruth, of course, to explain the unexplainable: that her deceased husband was still alive. His pulse beat in his throat as he dialed her number. *By heart,* he thought. *What a strange term for numbers in your mind.* It went straight to voice mail. Her message was condensed now, nothing like the rambling one she'd had when they first started talking. Back then, it'd made him smile to listen to her voice; sometimes, when he'd called her in Ireland, he hoped she wouldn't pick up so he could hear that indefatigable cheer of hers, that breathless "You've reached Ruth

Galway's cell phone! Sorry I missed you! Please leave your name and number, and I'll be sure to call you back. Have a great day!"

Now, the message simply said, "You've reached Ruth Neufeld. Please leave your name and number, and I'll call you back." It wasn't just that her voice had deepened as she'd gotten older, which it had; it was the timbre of the voice itself — weariness and resignation had replaced the exclamation points and cheer. When was the last time Chandler had listened to her voice? *Truly* listened? He couldn't even remember the last time he'd left a voice mail. Their last few months together, their communication had been reduced to texts, devoid of pronouns, punctuation, and emojis: *Home late, Get milk, Supper at 6.*

Chandler cleared his throat, aware he was being watched by the stone-faced man, who didn't seem to believe his story. He stared at Chandler as if he might begin talking in code.

"Hey, Ruth," he said. His voice broke, splintered, and the tears he'd been holding back leaked through the cracks. Only then did the man have the decency to look away.

"It's me," he said. "Chandler. I'm alive, love. I'm sorry it's taken me all this time to

300

reach you." He couldn't speak anymore. He hung up, for his quiet crying had turned into sobs, as if Ruth had been the one presumed dead and not him. But his resolve to speak had been derailed by that phrase, *"I'm sorry it's taken me all this time to reach you."* Because that was what had happened. It had taken being stranded in a city built of ghosts to realize how much he needed his wife and daughters. He would not take them for granted again.

Ruth powered her cell on in the morning to check for Mabel's final message about the girls. The honeymoon's bliss was countered by Ruth's concern for Sofie that grew each day she was gone. She walked out on the porch and sat on the swing, wrapped in the tartan blanket she and Elam had slept on in front of the fire — the two of them spooned together on the rug, Elam's arms around her all through the night, the way Ruth had always imagined married couples slept when she was a teenager awakening to such ideas and yet had never experienced before now. Ruth's anxiety eased, thinking of this, of her new husband who was inside, making oatmeal and coffee while humming a melody Ruth recognized from the classical station they'd listened to on their way here.

The white apple flashed on the black screen, and Ruth's phone made a dinging sound. Ruth looked at it and saw she had two voice mails. She didn't recognize the first number but saw it was from *Kabul, AF.* Assuming it had something to do with the bombing, Ruth decided to listen to Mabel's message instead.

Ruth smiled. Her mother-in-law's accent was stronger over the phone, but perhaps the same could be said of Ruth's. The girls were happy, Mabel said. They'd generously saved two of the spritz cookies for Ruth and Elam and had taken Everest, the new puppy, out for a walk. No doubt, Mabel would be exhausted when the couple returned, and Ruth was grateful Laurie had watched the girls in the afternoons to give Mabel a little break. Ruth pressed Play on the second voice mail. She held the phone to her ear, absently staring out at the snow.

There was so much static in the message that at first, she wasn't sure what — or whom — she was listening to. But then the man started crying. She could hear that clearly. Ruth sat up straighter on the swing, and her heart began to pound before her mind could think, as if some soul-deep part of her understood before the rest of her did.

*Chandler.*

It was Chandler, her husband, crying on the other side of the line. Ruth dropped the phone. It skidded across the porch and landed in the bank of snow pillowed over the straw-like perennials she had admired when they first drove in. The sound zapped her awake. She scrambled off the porch and grabbed the phone, which hadn't sunk into the snow as much as it had slid down the embankment. She wiped the case off on her robe and looked to see that the strange number that marked her husband's voice was still there. She walked back onto the porch and stood there, shivering, as she pressed Play. Chandler's voice again, and this time she could distinguish his words: "I'm alive, love. I'm sorry it's taken me all this time to reach you."

Ruth glanced over her shoulder toward the cottage, as if she had anything to do with her dead husband's reappearance. For this is what he was to her: a dead husband. He was no more alive, although she heard his voice, than the plants that needed pulled or cut away before fresh ones pushed up for another season. Chandler was not a part of her life now. He was not a part of the lives of his girls. He'd made that choice when he chose his "calling" over his family.

Ruth opened the front door carefully and

pulled her coat and hat down from the tree stand. Her boots were lined up beneath; Elam's beside hers. The sight of his shoes brought tears to her eyes. She stood on the porch as she pulled on her boots. She put her coat over her bathrobe and fished the green knit hat and gloves set from her pockets — the hat and gloves Mabel had made.

*Mabel.*

Ruth wanted to tell her, but she couldn't. She couldn't for so many reasons. How would it be if Ruth thought one of her daughters, heaven forbid, was dead, only to discover — months later — that she was alive? This news would devastate her and heal her at once.

Ruth had to tell Mabel in person, so she could catch her in every possible way.

Ruth walked off the porch into the tundra. She walked toward the orchard, looking to the left, where Ruth's and Elam's boots had made a pattern in the snow. The two of them in tandem, as if that were the way it should always be. Ruth walked among the frozen branches. The flat land glittered, each blade of grass encapsulated in ice, so that to stand and stare through the tip of one blade would be to magnify a thousand. Ruth took off her gloves to touch the blades and the branches. The cold felt good to her, shocked her system, and helped her think.

She was torn apart by this. Any woman who has ever loved a man and conceived his child would be callous not to be glad he was still alive. But Ruth was only glad for the children's sakes. She was not glad for her own. In Elam, Ruth had found a refuge when she hadn't realized she was in need of shelter. She thought of the way he'd rested his hands on her shoulders that first time, or how he placed his hand on the small of her back whenever they were out together, simply letting her know she was loved and he was around.

It was beautiful and priceless, their union, and Ruth began to cry — and then to sob — as she understood, with mounting clarity, that Chandler would return to this haven, which would cause her to lose this refuge, where she could rest in the security of Elam's arms.

Ruth wiped her face and her nose and looked at one of the apple trees. It was a smaller tree, perhaps a dwarf, and she could see a nest from a previous summer tucked into one of the corners where the branches formed a V. The nest was sheathed in ice, the collision of seasons so exquisite and sad that it took her breath. Ruth reached out and touched the nest. Then she wedged her fingers beneath the nest and broke it free, so that slivers of ice rained down onto the snow, studded with grass. She looked at the nest up close, seeing its unbearable perfection, and slipped it into the pocket of her coat.

She knew it would thaw and turn wet, the delicate nest wafting of decay, but she did not care. She wanted to seize beauty where she found it. She wanted to hold it close before life crashed into this crystalline world and made her surrender what she'd built.

Ruth knocked her boots on the porch step to clean off the snow and opened the door, peeling off the boots to keep the remaining ice, embedded in the treads, from melting inside.

She didn't want to tell Elam. She didn't want to destroy what they shared, even if sharing this intimacy with him meant she was taking from someone else. The only slight relief she felt had to do with their daughters, and yet she was aware Chandler's return would upset the careful equilibrium of their lives, which she had worked so hard to reclaim.

How could he do this to her? The stages of grief were marching backward. Denial, anger, bargaining, depression, and acceptance all jockeying for a position inside her heart and yet finding none. Ruth entered the cottage. Elam was seated at the kitchen table, drinking coffee.

He looked up when she closed the door. "Have a nice walk?" he asked.

She hadn't told him she was taking a walk; she hadn't told him anything, really, and she loved that he hadn't worried about her being gone. Perhaps this is what happened when people married when they were older. They were more secure in who they were and therefore didn't need the reassurance of the young. Ruth wasn't sure she could speak — if she could pull off that everything in their lives was the same — but she knew she had to try.

"Very nice walk," she said. "But cold." Ruth added a shiver to help convince him — and maybe herself — that she was being sincere.

Elam watched her, though; she could sense that. He could detect some minute change in her voice she hadn't even heard. "Yes. It is cold," he said.

Ruth came inside and sat on the couch between the kitchen and the fireplace. She cupped her hands between her knees. Her body started shaking. Her teeth rattled together the same as when she was a kid and had walked home from school while carrying a piece of ice shaped like a clear glass paperweight, which nearly froze to her bare hands by the time she came in the door.

Now, the same as then, Ruth bit down hard on her lips, trying to keep her discomfort from being obvious. But Elam was nothing if not observant, especially of his new bride, and he got up from the table and came over. He sat on the coffee table, placed his socked feet on either side of hers, and, leaning forward, rested his hands on hers.

"You're trembling," he said. "Were you out there without a coat?"

Ruth shook her head.

"What happened? Honey . . . ?" he said. "What's wrong?"

Again, Ruth shook her head. She closed her eyes to hide the tears rising behind them. She couldn't keep this from Elam, as much as she wanted to try. "I checked my voice mail," she said. "To see if Mabel had called —"

"Are the girls all right?"

She opened her eyes. Looked at Elam's pale face. She could see such paternal panic in his gaze, the welling tears spilled down. He deserved this, didn't he? He deserved a family, even if it wasn't one he had helped create. "The girls are fine," she said. "Mabel said they're fine. But I received another voice mail. It — it was from Chandler."

Elam's hands remained on hers, his feet bracketing her own. "Chandler," he said. That was all. And yet she could tell this single name had the ability to rewrite their story.

"Yes," Ruth said. Her trembling had stopped. "Yes. It was Chandler. He didn't speak much, but it appears there's been some kind of . . . mistake."

*"Mistake?"* Elam's eyes widened. "You mean . . . he's alive?"

She nodded. His hands tightened on hers as he said, "How do you know it was him, and . . . and not somebody's idea of a . . . sick joke?"

Ruth shook her head. "I don't, I guess. But the way he said my name, Elam. The way he cried. It made me think this must be real."

Elam released her hands. He shifted on the coffee table. "Did you . . . call him back?"

"No," Ruth said. "I couldn't."

He looked at her face again, studied it like he could understand more if he could just keep himself from looking away. She knew he didn't mean to — that he might not even be aware he was — but she could see a hint of accusation in that open stare.

"He's your . . . husband," Elam said.

Ruth couldn't breathe. Behind Elam, on the floor, was the nest of blankets where the two of them had spent the night — his arms around her, the firelight glistening on their skin as they spoke. "But you're my husband too."

Elam stood and moved around the coffee table. He leaned against the mantel like its sole purpose was to hold him up. He stood there for a long time. The cottage brightened as the sun filtered through low-lying clouds. The faucet dripped in the bathroom, or maybe it was the showerhead. It seemed that neither of them breathed or blinked.

How could they possibly move on from this? How could anyone?

Finally, Elam said, "I don't know . . . if I am." He swallowed. "Your husband."

Ruth got up from the couch. The belted robe came undone; her pajamas beneath felt too cold for the sudden chill enveloping her. She reached up and touched Elam's shoulder until he looked at her, his eyes wet. She cupped his face in her hands, his two-day beard rough against her fingertips. Oh, how she loved this man. The awareness poured through her with a nearly maternal tenderness. She would do anything she could to protect him. To protect *them,* even if that union seemed a betrayal to the ones who knew them well.

"You are," she said. "You are, Elam. We did nothing wrong. Do you understand me? Chandler was dead. We *buried* him. Whatever happened between us was innocent."

Elam looked down at her, his wife, his bride, who was also someone else's. He reached down and wrapped his arms around her, feeling the formidable set of her spine even through the soft robe. "I love you," he said. "I love you so . . . incredibly much."

"I love you too," she said. They'd whispered, in the protected dark, sweet nothings to each other, but these words now meant everything, and each of them knew that. "We'll get through it," she said. "No matter what happens when we return to the farm, we'll get through it."

*We'll get through it.* An echo of what Chandler had once said to her.

Elam nodded and bent forward to wipe the sadness from Ruth's face. "I couldn't bear to lose you," he said.

Ruth thought of all the times Chandler had seemed determined to leave her and the children, even if he would've never admitted it to anyone, much less himself. And now, here was a man, her husband, who was not only determined not to lose her, but who was determined to fight to keep what they had. *I love him,* she thought.

She loved Elam Albrecht so much, loving him felt like dying.

Elam and Ruth remained on Washington Island for the final day of their honeymoon, and yet their time together didn't feel the same — that this was their oasis, their retreat from the world. Rather, their togetherness felt sullied, somehow; as if this physical trip were the culmination of Ruth and Elam's emotional affair.

And yet, the beauty in their last day together was that they knew their time together could very well end. As much as she wanted to, Ruth couldn't ignore that Sofie and Vivienne's father was very much alive. It was, she knew, selfishness that propelled her yearning for seclusion; selfishness that made her want to remain in Elam's arms. So the night before they were to return to Tomah, Ruth and Elam sat on their nest of blankets in front of the fire. They'd prepared another wintry picnic supper but hadn't touched a bite. Instead, Ruth sat before Elam, and he wrapped her in his arms tightly, as though it were up to him, alone, to keep her there.

They stared at the flames, oddly comforted by their predictable, undulating glow. They didn't speak for a long time. They breathed, and they thought separate thoughts with the same underlying theme: *What is life going to look like when we get home?*

They didn't know if Chandler would be there, on the porch steps, waiting for them. They didn't know if Mabel even knew her son was alive, and this made Ruth feel a liquid-hot flash of guilt. *But that is tomorrow,* she thought. Tomorrow, everything would change, but in this moment — tonight — she was safe and secure in her husband's arms.

Chandler was not waiting on the front porch when Ruth and Elam arrived. The farm looked much the same as it had when they left, except for the cold, which had cast its spell here as well: unfurling a blanket of snow over the bogs and fields and fringing the lake and channels with ice. Elam paid the driver who'd picked them up after they returned the rental car. Then they stared up at the farmhouse, Elam's arm around her, as the bottoms of their suitcases soaked up the slush. They stared up at the farmhouse and felt like something should appear changed, but it wasn't. Ruth trembled. She trembled with fear, and she hadn't even trembled with fear on the morning she learned Chandler had died.

Elam murmured, "You all right?"

Ruth looked over at him. His face was a blank canvas, but his eyes were shaded with all that remained unknown. "I have to be," she said. He nodded and picked up their two bags in one hand. He took her hand with his other, and they walked up the porch into the house. Snow blew off the roofline and dusted them as they entered. Ruth automatically braced, expecting to get bowled over by Zeus. But he was not here. Instead, Everest, the pup, slept on an old pillow near the fire, looking no worse for the wear despite her daughters, who were probably loving him within an inch of his life. "Hello?" Ruth called.

Ruth heard the mingled singsong of her daughters' voices resonating from the bedroom they shared. Grabbing the banister, she mounted the steps two at a time. The girls squealed, "Mom-my!" as Ruth came into the room. Mabel was seated on the bed with Vivienne, who had the warm, soft glow of someone who'd recently been asleep.

Sofie's curls were a braided tangle over one shoulder, and Ruth wondered if Mabel had had the courage to brush the tender-headed, dramatic child the entire time she'd been gone. Ruth herself could barely work up the courage.

Having never been away from her children for more than a few hours, she hadn't had the opportunity to really miss them, to really *see* them as someone who had never been around them before might view her children, and the beauty of them took her breath.

"Did you miss me?" she asked, pressing a daughter against each leg. Sofie's head rested against her abdomen while Vi's rested against her knee. When had they gotten so tall? When had they morphed from babies to children, from tiny sparks in the womb's darkness to these fully fleshed girls? This awareness brought such panic, Ruth knelt and clutched them against her, as though she might never get the chance again. Tears leaked from the corners of her eyes.

Vi asked, "Did you bwing us a tweat?"

Ruth laughed, the sound like a sob caught in her throat. "Elam has your treats downstairs." The girls looked at each other, their mouths and eyes O's of joy.

Ruth waited until they had safely descended the steps, and then she turned back to Mabel, who smiled and asked, "So, how was it?" *She has no clue,* Ruth thought, and experienced this urgent, overwhelming sense to protect her the same as she had wanted to protect her girls. None of it made sense. Ruth knew she should be bursting at the chance to tell Mabel the news. She remained silent.

Ruth exhaled. "We had a lovely time. Thank you for watching the girls."

"You're welcome. They were good as gold."

"But I'm sure you're worn out."

"Well." Mabel smiled. "It's a good thing the Lord gives us children when we're young."

More silence followed. But Ruth supposed this silence came simply because everything was deafened by the sound of her heartbeat roaring in her ears. "Mabel," she said. The tone of Ruth's voice made Mabel turn toward her daughter-in-law, for this is who Ruth would always be to her. Ruth said, "First, I think you should probably sit down."

Mabel, the same as Ruth, had experienced enough heartache to assume the absolute worst when someone tells you to sit down, to essentially brace yourself for something that could otherwise knock you off your feet. So they entered Mabel's bedroom, and Mabel sat, suddenly appearing very old: her veined hands knotted in her lap, her mouth like a gray, scarred wound.

Ruth, gathering her courage, or perhaps stalling, glanced around the room. She noted Sofie's blankie on the bed, along with Vi's stuffed, bright-pink flamingo, Mango, and realized the girls had probably been sleeping on either side of their grandma the entire time she and Elam had been gone. Ruth walked toward Mabel and sat down beside her. The double mattress wasn't as new as the one in her room, and the springs protested beneath their combined weight. Ruth reached for her mother-in-law's hand. She held it tightly; she held on to it for dear life, for life and death was what this was. "He's alive, Mabel," Ruth said. "Chandler, your son, is alive."

Mabel looked over at her in disbelief, and Ruth saw mirrored in those familiar eyes the same confusion, and even fear, she had felt. "What . . . ? How?"

Ruth shook her head. "I never got to talk to him."

"Then how do you know it's true?"

Ruth kept her hand in Mabel's. She could feel how her mother-in-law shook and was glad she had insisted she sit down. "Chandler left a voice mail on my phone. When I called the number back, I found out he was at the embassy in Kabul, Afghanistan, when he called."

Mabel gripped Ruth's hand tighter, so her short nails bit into her flesh. Ruth let her hold on. The pain kept her from growing numb. "But he's not there now?" she asked.

Ruth shook her head. "They weren't at liberty to tell me anything about him, even though I told them that he — he —" She stumbled over the word now, the same as she had when she'd said it on her honeymoon with Elam, hunkered in the bathroom with the door locked and the shower running to cover her voice. "I told them that Chandler's my husband."

Mabel's face looked more stricken than relieved. "Oh, Ruth," she said. "My son's alive."

And then she began to weep, withdrawing her hand from Ruth's to cover her face, her small, rounded shoulders shaking with the swelling violence of her sobs. But in between them, Ruth could hear the question she herself had been unable to voice: "How is Elam going to bear it?"

Without much formal discussion, they

decided the children and the rest of the community — even, at this juncture, Tim and Laurie — would not be told Chandler was alive until they heard from him again. At Mabel's and Elam's insistence, Ruth kept her cell phone charged, the volume pushed up high, and carried it with her throughout the day.

Two days passed, and she heard nary a word. Ruth began to wonder if she'd imagined it all. But when she looked at her phone for the hundredth time and saw *Kabul, AF* beneath the strange number, she knew she hadn't imagined anything.

At night, after Ruth had read three books and sung two bedtime songs — always ending with "Edelweiss" — she waited until she was sure Sofie was asleep and would then perform a gymnastics-worthy roll out of bed, landing soundlessly in her socked feet on the floor.

She would creep downstairs, where Elam, her husband, was waiting for her to return to their room. The second night, Elam was sitting up in bed, reading, the glow of the lamp casting light on the whitewashed walls, the room paneled with wooden siding, interspersed with pine knots like miniature portholes, so Ruth felt she was sleeping in the hold of a ship.

Elam tucked a bookmark between the pages and closed the book, setting it on the nightstand beside the bed. "The girls fall asleep okay?" he asked.

Ruth nodded. They had agreed he would gradually become more and more a part of their lives, but for now, in the beginning, they would behave as if everything were the same as it had always been. But it wasn't, because Ruth now crossed the room toward the bed. Elam pulled the covers back for her, and she crawled beneath them while wearing one of the Cuddl Duds sets she wore under her clothes when she ran. He exuded warmth and comfort, and Ruth lay against his chest, feeling the steady rise and fall beneath her chin.

"It's nice being home, isn't it?" he said.

Ruth nodded, her limbs gradually releasing the tension she didn't know they'd been holding. Sometimes, when she was standing in the kitchen or brushing one of the girls' hair, she found she couldn't breathe, and the only thought that kept her from panicking was that, at the end of the day, she would find herself here — in their little porthole room beneath the eaves — where the love they had for each other could keep the entire world from entering in.

But it did.

Ruth's cell phone rang in the pocket of her robe, which she'd discarded on the arm of the cane-backed chair. Ruth stiffened. Elam removed his hands from her shoulders.

"You should get . . . that," he said.

Ruth didn't say anything. It rang again.

"Could be . . . him."

"I *know*," she said, tone sharp. "That's why I don't want to answer it."

But for Mabel and Elam's sake, Ruth got out of bed and crossed the room. She didn't recognize the number, but she didn't expect she would. She glanced at Elam, their eyes touching briefly, before she pressed the green button and said hello.

"Ruth?"

Ruth nodded at Elam and automatically turned her back. But she did not leave the room. Her chest grew tight. She opened her mouth to speak. No words would come.

"Ruth," Chandler said. "It's me."

"I know," she replied, and she sensed, once more, that she was conversing with the dead.

"I'm in Paris," he continued. "On a layover. Are you in Ireland?"

"No. In Wisconsin." She swallowed. "With your mom."

"Really?" His voice rose. This was not the

conversation you have with your spouse when she realizes you're alive. "That's great. Then I'll change my flight to Wisconsin."

She knew their meeting was inevitable, but that didn't mean it wasn't cruel. "How soon do you think you'll be here?" she asked, meaning, *How much time do we have left?*

"I'm not sure," Chandler said. "Getting flights has been hard. Maybe two days?" He paused, and she could hear his tear-filled smile. "Honey," he said, "I'm coming home."

Ruth closed her eyes. For years, she had wanted, and even prayed, that her husband would physically and emotionally return to her, and now that prayer had been answered. Their meeting wasn't the only thing that was cruel. A God who delayed answering prayers until the supplicant no longer wanted them answered was crueler still.

"I'll be here," Ruth said. Which is what she had always said to Chandler. *You leave. I'll be here, waiting.* Always waiting. But this time, Chandler didn't know she had moved on.

Elam, behind her, asked, "Is he . . . coming here?"

Ruth bent to slip the phone in the pocket

of her bathrobe and walked back over to the bed. She didn't get in, as she had before, but sat on the mattress edge. Her eyes burned as she placed a hand on the crisp white sheet. For the second time in the past few days, she felt guilty thinking of Elam as her husband. It angered her that the love they shared should be tainted by someone who, for years, hadn't offered her the support she needed. "Yes," Ruth said. "Chandler is coming here."

Elam couldn't look at Ruth, another man's wife who was also his. Regardless of how you viewed it, the situation was impossible. And yet one thing was clear: he wasn't going to give her up if she didn't want him to. But he was too scared to ask if she did.

He asked instead, "What do you . . . need me to do?" Because doing something — *anything* — seemed easier than just waiting here.

Leaning across the bed, Ruth grasped both of his hands. "I need *nothing,*" she said, "but for you to continue being the man I love."

Elam looked up, then, into her fevered eyes. "It's crazy," he said, "how, a few months ago, I would've given my right arm to hear my cousin was alive . . . and now . . ." He shook his head in disgust. They were not only talking about Ruth's first husband; they were also talking about the father to their children, Sofie and Vi.

They deserved to have Chandler back, even if it meant Elam lost them all.

"Now," Ruth finished for him, withdrawing her hands, "you dread his return."

"I can't live as if I'm your husband while knowing your husband's alive."

Ruth folded her arms across her robe. "What are you saying?"

Elam sighed. " 'Do unto others as you'd have them do unto you' is pretty clear. If I was Chandler, I wouldn't want you sleeping in bed with another man."

"But we've not even really been . . . together since we found out he's alive."

Elam said, "I know. I thought that would be enough. But I can't do this either, Ruth. I can't be here like this, with you." He looked across the bed at his wife, in her soft pajamas, her hair undone. She saw him swallow. Saw that this was devastating him, but it still revived that seed of rejection that had taken root long before she became Chandler's wife. It was a seed that had been planted in childhood when Ruth misinterpreted her mother's reserved, taciturn nature as a sign she was not loved.

"You're saying you don't want me."

324

Elam looked to that porthole wall. He pushed his thumbs against his closed eyes. "Oh, Ruth. I could never not want you. I could never not love you. The problem is I love God even more, and that love makes it impossible for me to compromise you like this."

Ruth stood from the bed. She glared down at Elam, and the pain of every time Chandler hadn't fulfilled a promise came flooding back. "You're just scared," she said. "You're just scared you're going to lose me, so you're pushing me away before that happens."

"Yes," he said. "I'm scared. I'm not just scared I'm going to lose you. I'm . . . I'm terrified. Everything inside of me wants to pull you into this bed and make use of the time we have left. But if I do that, Ruth, it'll change the beauty of what we have *now*. I don't want to make you that kind of woman, and I know you don't want me to be that kind of man."

Elam then picked his pillow up and walked out of his bedroom to sleep on the couch.

# CHAPTER 14

Chandler's prop plane touched down in La Crosse, and he couldn't help thinking that coming back from the dead was rather anticlimactic. He had watched enough deployment reunions on YouTube to expect the same level of pomp and circumstance. Nothing fancy, really, perhaps just a few supermarket balloons and a poster that read *Welcome Home, Daddy!* decorated with prints of his daughters' precious hands. However, when he disembarked and entered the airport — which was dusty and partitioned off with yellow caution signs due to the construction that was taking the better part of a year — he found that his wife, Ruth, was standing there alone. She watched him approach, her arms crossing her chest as if she were cold.

She wore jeans, boots, and a green parka he hadn't seen before. The hood was pulled up over her hair, and Chandler could tell she was not smiling. His eyes moved away from her to the few tarp-draped corners of the airport, trying to see if perhaps this was a joke and, at any minute, his mom and daughters would burst from the bathroom, bellowing, "Surprise!"

But nothing happened.

So Chandler approached Ruth. She called from a distance, "Did you have a nice flight?"

Chandler stopped walking and looked more closely at her, for the sentence wasn't a question as much as it was a warning. He wondered why. "Yeah," he said. "It was fine."

She did not extend her arms, but he stepped closer to her. He leaned toward her mouth, for a kiss, and she held her right cheek out toward him. Again, he paused, thinking his wife's brusqueness had to be a joke. But Ruth, he knew, was not the joking type. He kissed her cheek and noted the familiar scent of her sandalwood perfume. At least that was the same.

"Where's your luggage?" she asked.

He held up his empty hands. "I travel light."

"No doubt," she said.

"The girls didn't come?"

"No." Ruth did not meet his eyes. "I

327

wanted the chance to talk to you first."

When they exited the airport, she led him over to a plain white minivan. Chandler looked at her for an explanation, and she said, "I don't have a car, so I use the community's driver."

"You don't have a car?"

Ruth said, her voice an abyss, "How could I have afforded one, Chandler?"

"I'm sorry," he said, sensing this was not enough.

Ruth's back was to him as she strode toward the van. She pulled open the sliding door, and Chandler got in beside her. The driver turned and nodded at him. Chandler had no clue who he was. He was wondering how they could possibly talk when Ruth said, "Are you hungry? I was thinking of stopping for lunch at this little Norwegian diner. It's on the way home."

*Larsen's.* It startled Chandler to hear his wife speak about the places he'd known since boyhood. And though he was hungry — had, in fact, eaten nothing that wasn't offered on the flights — more than any necessity in the world, he needed to get back to the farm to see his daughters. But he sensed the necessity of this "lunch" as well and therefore said, "Sounds great."

Ruth leaned forward and gave the address

to the driver. He punched it into his phone and pulled out of the parking lot. A light rain began to fall. Chandler and Ruth sat side by side, but there was enough space between them for both of their children. He glanced at her profile, saw the stoic expression belied by flushed cheeks. Ruth was as striking as the day he left, if not more so, since spouses tend to envision an ill-defined version of the mate they daily see. He didn't know how to interpret her behavior, but he thought that his wife just needed time. They hadn't seen each other in ten months, and perhaps she just didn't remember how they'd been.

Chandler's own cheeks flushed as a slide-show clicked through his mind: late-night fights that dissolved into early-morning conversations Ruth communicated solely by slamming cupboards as she made their girls breakfast. Perhaps the reason she was sitting so far from him — the reason she hadn't given him the kind of reception he'd dreamed about during the recent nightmare of his life — wasn't because she didn't remember, but because she couldn't forget.

Ruth sat across from her first husband, an untouched cup of potato soup before each of them, and tried to recall how they began.

She knew their relationship started on the roof of Bethel House, when she and Chandler had shared a blanket and listened to a distant rooster crow in the darkness, a satellite blinking overhead and the sky flooded with stars. Or perhaps it was on the mountain, when the two of them discovered Sofie sleeping on a makeshift bed in her biological parents' ramshackle house, the tarps and sticks so poorly tethered, it seemed that, at any moment, the entire contraption would go sailing over the cliff.

Their eyes had met in the dim light emitted by the fire smoking in the center of the room. Sofie was crying, wailing, and each ragged inhalation revealed how very sick she was. The smell of defecation was rife in the small space, and Ruth could see the pile of soiled cloth diapers on the unmade bed. The parents — impossibly young and scared — looked at Chandler and Ruth.

Ruth took off the yellow clown wig she'd been wearing to help the children not be afraid as Chandler administered the shots. She remembered pulling Chandler aside and looking up at him. The smoke, combined with the face paint, made it difficult to see. And yet, that wasn't the reason tears streamed from her eyes. She asked, "What can we do?"

Tugging his long sleeve out from beneath his windbreaker, he carefully wiped her face. "We help," he said. "In whatever way they need."

That moment, even more than the rooftop dinner and all the moments that came after, was when Ruth and Chandler began. That was the moment she glimpsed the man he was and knew she loved that person, even if she wasn't sure she loved him in the context of wife and husband, woman and man. And now, here they were. The Midwestern downpour streaked outside the windows of the diner. The booth where they were seated was bright red, the table gray Formica flecked with glitter. A Nordic quote, encapsulated with red and teal swirls, bordered the walls. The diner was crowded, independent dairy farmers and employees from the nearby organic dairy plant crowded into booths and chairs at the counter. A rotating glass display encouraged diners to save room for sugared slices of cherry, apple, or blueberry pie — all made daily from scratch — but neither Chandler nor Ruth noticed much about their environment.

They were each too lost in their own thoughts. They were each somewhat despondent, wondering how they'd hopscotched from those magical, painful moments in Colombia to here: when they knew everything about each other and yet had nothing to say.

Ruth squeezed lemon into her tea and fished out a seed with a spoon.

Chandler looked at her. "Do the girls know I'm . . . back?"

"From the dead?" Ruth's spoon clinked onto the saucer. "No," she said. "They do not. I thought about telling them last night, when I was tucking them in, but . . ." Stopping, she gripped the handle of the cup. "A few months ago, I had to tell them their father was dead, Chandler, and now . . . now, I'm just supposed to erase all that emotional trauma by telling them you're alive." She swirled the tea. Her knuckles stood out, white, on her chapped hands.

Chandler saw Ruth no longer wore her wedding ring; in its place was another ring, a Claddagh, if he remembered right. It cut him to see that, and yet he supposed, if the roles were reversed and he'd been the one to receive news of Ruth's passing, he might've taken his wedding ring off too. He shook his head, not aware he was doing it.

Ruth said, "What?"

But he didn't ask her about the ring, or lack thereof. After everything she had gone through, after everything they had and hadn't shared, he didn't feel he had the right.

Chandler asked, "How have you been?"

He was so polite, it set her teeth on edge. Ruth took a sip of tea. "It's been hard."

"I can't imagine," he murmured. "I tried to, after they told me I'd been declared dead. I tried to imagine what it would be like to be separated from you like that, and how I would tell the girls." He reached across the table with both hands, hers still wrapped tight around the cup. "I'm sorry. I'm so sorry you had to go through this alone."

Ruth looked down. A burst of laughter from a nearby booth caused Chandler to look away, and this was when she extricated her hands from beneath his. She folded them in her lap and twirled the ring Elam had given her. Everything about this time together, about this conversation, felt like a betrayal not to Chandler, as she might have thought, but to *him,* Elam — the husband who had rejected her as well.

"Something happened when you were away," she began. "I came here without knowing anyone. Even your mom . . . we didn't really know each other." She swallowed. "Elam was here too." Chandler still said nothing, and the silence made her uncomfortable. Ruth zipped her jacket up to her neck, as if it could somehow gird her. "We arrived at the beginning of the cranberry harvest," she continued. "Elam allowed me to help him out in the fields. It was so good for me. It gave me something to focus on besides my own loss."

Chandler said, "I'm glad." He had this new way of looking at her that was disconcerting. She wasn't accustomed to being stared at so intently. Most of all, she wasn't accustomed to being stared at so intently by *him.*

"Elam and I got to know each other. We became friends. We were living in his farmhouse, with Mabel and him, and he was so good with the girls, so patient and kind . . ." Her voice trailed off. She risked another glance at Chandler and suspected, by the fact he was looking around the diner rather than at her, that he was beginning to understand. "We fell in love," Ruth said. "Elam and I. It — it happened so quickly. Neither of us expected it."

Chandler looked at her. "So I take it Elam's not glad I'm coming home?"

Ruth's nails cut into the palms of her hands. "It's hard for him, Chandler," she said. "He feels guilty, I guess. You have to understand, we all believed you were dead."

334

"But I'm not," Chandler said, with the first hint of annoyance. "I'm right here."

"It was different then," Ruth said. "We were . . . I don't know what we were, but Mabel was all for it too. So, we . . ." She looked away, couldn't bear to see the look on Chandler's face when she told him.

"You married him."

Ruth flinched. Chandler's voice turned ludicrous every redemptive thing that had happened over the past few months. She despised him, suddenly — or maybe not so suddenly — for doing that to her, for making her embarrassed for the relationship that had changed her life.

"Yes," she snapped. "We got married. Elam and I got married and were on our honeymoon when we received the call that you were alive."

Chandler stood so quickly that his plate rattled, but he was still trapped in the booth. He said, "Did you sleep with him?"

"Elam and I married each other," she repeated. "In every sense of the word."

"You must've been upset," he said, his voice low, "to discover I was alive."

Ruth said nothing. A few of the diners were looking their way and to agree with Chandler would only make the conversation worse.

■ ■ ■ ■

Ruth watched Chandler stalking up the driveway in the cold January rain. They hadn't talked for the rest of the trip, and she could see how they hadn't been together two hours when they'd fallen into the same pattern as before: she giving him the silent treatment and Chandler too stubborn to be the first to speak. She hated the immaturity that still rose within him. And her. Chandler was nearing middle age, and she was thirty, nearly thirty-one. Shouldn't they be above such pettiness? Drying her face on the collar of her fleece, Ruth decided to see their daughters before Chandler did, in case the sight of their father caused Sofie to have a panic attack. Vi, on the other hand, was so young when he left, she might not even recognize the altered man for who he was.

Ruth asked, "You mind waiting on the steps a minute?"

Chandler's smile was tight with contained anger. "Whatever you need me to do."

She nodded and walked up the porch toward the house. She entered and saw one of Elam's insulated parkas hanging from the coat tree by the door. She pulled it off, wanting to breathe it in for comfort, but instead turned and went back out.

"Here," she said, proffering an olive branch. "This'll keep you warm while you wait."

Chandler begrudgingly said, "Thank you," and pulled the jacket over his cheap sweatshirt.

They were both tall men, but Elam was broader shouldered, so the sleeves dangled over Chandler's hands. Ruth watched him, saw her first husband wearing her second husband's clothes. Turning from the sight, she opened the door and stepped from the portal of one world — one life — into the next. She could hear her young daughters — who were, she thought, once again *theirs* — giggling in the bedroom and the accented cadence as Mabel read them a book. Vivienne was about to take a nap; Sofie was about to have quiet time. A part of Ruth wanted to let their daily routines continue, undisturbed by revelation, but it was cruel to make Chandler wait. It was crueler still for Ruth to deprive her children of the man whose absence would leave a gaping hole. For the girls, for Mabel, Ruth climbed the stairs.

Mabel's hands shook as she closed *Eloise Wilkin Stories'* gold-edged pages. Ruth nod-

337

ded, nearly imperceptibly, but Mabel saw it. Tears distorted her vision as she kissed her granddaughters' heads. Rising from the bed, Mabel crossed the room and touched Ruth's shoulder. Ruth reached up and clasped Mabel's hand. Both women stood there a moment, drawing strength, as one woman prepared to welcome back her son and one woman prepared to welcome back the man who'd fathered her children but whom she no longer wanted to be married to.

Mabel walked downstairs then, one hand gripping the banister the same as Ruth had done. Bordered by the glass window, she could see Chandler on the porch. She would've been able to pick her only child out of a crowd by the back of his head alone — that dark hair, which was straight except for where it curled at the base of his neck; that slightly stooped posture he'd affected in his youth when his arms and legs appeared to sprout overnight. With each step toward him, Mabel felt the years falling off her grief-worn body and hope rise inside of her like a living, breathing thing. She opened the door, and Chandler turned, her son.

His eyes looked at her without really seeing her, so Mabel touched a hand briefly to her *kapped* hair, self-conscious about the physical changes that had taken place since she'd lost both her husband and her son overnight. But her son, she saw, was not exempt from the grief she had experienced. He, too, had lost a lot in the past few months.

"Mom," Chandler said, with a tenderness he had not displayed since his voice changed.

He stood and moved across the porch toward her, arms spread wide. Despite his gaunt frame and the faint red-and-white scars that patched his day-old beard, his face was recognizable by that same reckless grin. But it trembled at the edges now.

Mother and son held each other, sheltered, as the rain streaked by, and Mabel began to sob against him. Sob mostly from the euphoria of relief since she hadn't allowed herself to cry after her grandchildren started sleeping in the next room. Finally, Mabel stopped and pushed back from her son to dry her eyes. She was laughing and crying at once. Chandler smiled, and she smiled too. The door was open still, and she could hear Sofie, upstairs, screaming, "Daddy!" and then the surprisingly thunderous sound, for a child so slight, as she pounded down the stairs.

Sofie ran to him, her body a case study in

kinetics, dark eyes wide with the miracle of it all. Chandler picked his older daughter up and spun her around and around, the tie on her striped sweater swinging loose along with the tangled black banner of her hair.

Ruth came down with Vivienne on her hip, who smiled at Chandler like she smiled at everyone. Ruth watched her husband, twirling their firstborn daughter, but there, Ruth could also see *him:* Elam, who stood under the eaves of the barn, watching through the streaking veil of rain that separated them both. His handsome, craggy face was grave with emotion, and for a moment she just watched him as he watched them — his family, his future, and yet . . . not. She tried to smile at Elam, to let him know everything was all right. But she didn't know that, not really. And when he turned away from the sight, she knew that, deep down, neither did he.

# CHAPTER 15

Sofie wouldn't let her father out of her sight to the point she stuck her hand beneath the door whenever he dared to enter the bathroom on his own. "I can see your feet!" she'd cry. "Can you see my fingers?" It was endearing, the way she loved him, and it softened Ruth's heart to see how uninhibitedly he loved her in return. But because the children wouldn't leave Chandler's side, Ruth and Chandler had no opportunity to further discuss what they'd said at the diner.

Ruth stood in the doorway and watched Chandler napping in the living room with Sofie and Vi. He had barely closed his jetlagged eyes when Sofie ran across the living room — trailing her blankie in anticipation — and Vi followed suit. Giggling, they pinned him to the couch and sucked their thumbs as their blankies overlapped his chest like tattered flags. Earlier, Chandler had built a fire in the grate, and it now

341

crackled and popped, adding to the idyllic atmosphere as the rain fell and the sky swelled shut with clouds, making it seem later than five o'clock.

But it *was* five o'clock, and Elam had not returned.

If Chandler noticed his cousin's absence, he had made no comment. And yet, why would he? That was just another topic in their marital Pandora's box they could not discuss. Ruth watched her first husband and daughters sleep for a few more minutes, and then — feeling like a stranger around those she knew most intimately — put on her jacket and went outside. The barn was dark, empty; the space fetid with the composted scent of year-old hay. She walked toward the area where they'd sorted cranberries and where she and Elam had first stood with their bodies so close, it seemed even light could not come between them. He was not there either. Then Ruth thought and knew where he was.

Most of the snow had melted beneath the day's unending torrent, leaving a frozen brown crust along the bank that could possibly remain there until late spring. Ruth wore insulated boots, the laces loosely tied, and yet she started to run, cutting past the channels and the lake. Lamplight shone through the cabin's two small windows. Ruth's breath hitched and her mouth grew dry, knowing Elam was inside and yet not knowing what she could possibly say. He opened the door as soon as she knocked. It appeared he'd been waiting for her for quite some time.

They embraced wordlessly, the frustration dissipating that had been there when she'd left for the airport. Ruth cried with relief, as Mabel had done a few hours prior, but also with sadness, for Ruth couldn't help wondering why her life had been dealt such an unfair hand. Elam didn't cry but held her until her crying ceased. Spent, she remained shielded in the hard fold of his arms, secure in his embrace in a way she had never been in Chandler's.

"How are you?" Elam asked, and tears rose once more in her eyes. *He* was the one who was in the midst of losing, not her. But was *losing* what this was? She refused to believe it.

"I'm fine," Ruth said and then choked on her laughter, because they both knew she wasn't. "I don't even know who Chandler is anymore. We're like strangers."

Elam rubbed her shoulders in silent reply. She didn't realize how much tension was gathered there until the knots began to unwind. "How'd he take it?"

Ruth closed her eyes against his chest. "Not well, and we haven't gotten to talk since we came home. The girls won't let him out of their sight."

Elam recoiled at this — the mention of the girls — and she wondered if it hurt, the fact that their true father had returned, replacing him, the step.

"It's going to work out," Ruth said. "I promise."

"How?" He lifted a hand. "I'm sorry. It's just hard to know . . . my place."

"I understand," Ruth said. "This is an impossible situation for all of us." She looked to the side, wanted to look anywhere but up at him. "Maybe Chandler and I will get to talk more tonight. After the girls are asleep."

"I'm sleeping here," he said.

Ruth looked around at the spartan furnishings. "I wish I could sleep with you."

Elam blanched and moved to sit on the cot that was in no way a bed. "I wish you could too," he murmured. "And then a part of me wishes I would've never pursued you. That my cousin could return here, to his wife and children, without any complications."

Ruth remained standing by the door,

344

which was propped open enough to let the damp breeze in. She turned and closed it, and then crossed the room to sit beside Elam. Reaching out, she took his hand. "You're not a complication," she said. "You and I are married, remember?"

"I know we're married. But you're married to Chandler, too."

"If I could change that, I would."

He removed his hand. "We have to respect Chandler's place in your life."

"What about yours?"

Elam smiled sadly. "That's what I'm hoping to figure out."

She looked down. "When are you going to see him?"

"Chandler?" He folded his arms. "I don't . . . know."

Ruth nodded and remained close to Elam, although she could already feel him drawing away. The problem was, she wanted to remain here for the rest of her life, but she could never leave her children. They called her back to the farmhouse, back to the uncertainty surrounding her marriage to Chandler and her marriage to him. Legally, she wasn't sure her union with Elam still stood. And yet, right now, she cared about nothing but the comfort of his distant warmth, and so she stayed. She stayed until the darkness condensed, the stars came out, and a night bird's cry echoed across the water, as if calling her home.

Ruth walked up to the farmhouse and could see Mabel in the kitchen, setting the table for supper. She could hear her daughters giggling — *always* giggling — in the living room, and Chandler's deep voice as he roared, playacting either a lion or a bear. Despite everything, despite the unknown, Ruth found herself smiling at this mingling of familiar sounds she hadn't heard in so long. She'd forgotten that about Chandler; how, when present, he filled an entirely different role. She was the physical and emotional nurturer and, if necessary, the limp-wristed disciplinarian. Chandler, on the other hand, was the parent who provided fun. He would get the girls accustomed to nightly tickle fests and wrestling matches (he let them win, resembling Gulliver being attacked by Lilliputians); chocolate chip pancakes for breakfast and plastic bags of lemonade brought home for lunch. But then he would disappear, on one mission or another, and the girls' behavior spiraled downward from this abandonment, forcing Ruth to become the disciplinarian once more and to despise her husband for the cycle he'd set into motion.

She entered the house now and looked to the right, observing Chandler on the ground with Sofie wrapped around his back and Vi around his leg. He was so intent on playing dead he didn't hear Ruth come in. But Vi saw her standing there and squealed, "Mommy!"

Chandler looked up at her, smiling, and in the firelight she could see how thin he was, and the scars from the bombing that had mottled his cheeks. She wondered how extensive his burns were, if the body she knew as well as her own was changed.

"Help, Ruth," he groaned. "They're beating me up." As he said this, he gently flipped Vi over on the rug and tickled her belly. Sofie's hold tightened on his neck, and he fake gagged.

"Be gentle, Sof," Ruth said.

Chandler met her eyes, and some unknown source of anxiety tightened its grip. She walked out of the living room and entered the kitchen. Mabel was standing at the counter, slicing bread on a wooden cutting board. Ruth wiped her hands on her jeans.

"Can I help with anything?" she murmured.

"No, I'm okay." But Mabel wouldn't lift

her head.

"Did you have a good afternoon?"

Mabel said, "I've been busy."

Ruth wanted to ask, *"Busy doing what?"* For she hadn't seen her mother-in-law in the kitchen and had heard no sound from her room. But there was something in the set of Mabel's shoulders that caused Ruth to watch in silence as her mother-in-law continued slicing bread.

When she was done, Ruth stepped closer and took the cutting board over to the table and set it down. That's when she saw there were only five place settings on the table. They were missing one. "You didn't set a place for Elam?" she asked.

"No," Mabel snapped. "I didn't set a place for him. He hasn't had the decency to come here and tell his first cousin he's grateful he's alive."

Shocked, Ruth glanced over her shoulder toward the living room, but Chandler and the girls were oblivious to the conversation taking place. Ruth walked back over to her mother-in-law, who furiously wiped crumbs from the sink's soapstone lip. Mabel stopped and balled up the washcloth in her fist. She looked at Ruth, and behind her glasses, tears welled.

"Elam hasn't done anything wrong. And

neither have you. I just feel so much . . . guilt."

Ruth looked at her in disbelief. "Guilt?" she asked. "What for?"

Shaking her head, Mabel took her glasses off and wiped her eyes. "I'm the one who encouraged you," she said. "And encouraged *him*. I thought —" She took a breath. "I guess I thought it all made sense, so it must be the will of God: Elam never marrying, and you a widow with two little girls. But when I stop and look back on it, when I let myself really *think*, I know I encouraged the two of you because I was trying to keep you and the girls here, near me."

With this admission, Mabel began to cry. Ruth moved in, closer, and pressed her mother-in-law's soft body against her lean frame. "Shh," she said, "shh," and she could feel Mabel's fevered heat, the same as with her own children when they were most upset. "There is nothing wrong with wanting your daughter-in-law and grandchildren around."

Mabel looked up and whispered, "But don't you see? It wasn't about seeking God's will. It was about seeking control."

Ruth made more soothing sounds and stroked her mother-in-law's back. Chandler must've overheard his mother's crying, for

Ruth heard him ask, "Everything all right?"

She turned and saw him standing there: his deep-brown hair long and the kerosene light casting shadows, so she couldn't see his matching deep-brown eyes. But she could hear the surprise in his voice, the surprise of finding his wife and his mother — practically strangers when he left — together like that, embracing, in the kitchen.

And Ruth thought, *Oh, Chandler, if you only knew how much has changed.*

Ruth, Chandler, and their girls sang "Edelweiss" — just as they'd been singing it as part of the children's nightly routine for the past few years. It was dark in the room, except for an oil lamp that cast a honey patina on the hardwood floor and on the entrance rug leading to the bed. By its light, Chandler looked over at his wife, and she looked at him.

Ruth allowed herself to recall the journey of their lives and how that journey hadn't ended up at the destination she'd envisioned when they first fell in love. But their lives, as fallible as they were, had provided shelter for the two precious children who were nestled into their beds. Ruth and Chandler sat next to each other on the floor between Sofie's bed and Vi's crib, each holding a hand of one of their daughters. The girls snuggled their blankies, their thumbs in their mouths so the lyrics were misshapen ("Bossoms of snow may you boom and go").

And then Chandler did it. With his free hand, he reached for Ruth's. The part of her which was loyal to Elam — as short as their own fragile union was — did not want to allow him to take it; the other part, which was loyal to the history she and Chandler shared, allowed him to interlace their fingers. Ruth sat there, in that golden darkness, with her face growing damp with tears.

Like Mabel, Ruth wondered if she should've entered into a relationship with Elam so soon after her husband's death. It had all happened so quickly, nearly effortlessly, causing Ruth to assume this was the will of God. But what was God's will, anyway? She'd believed she was following God's will when she married Chandler, and see where *that* had gotten them? Or did the will of God allow her to make her own choices, as Ruth's father had once said?

Ruth's parents did not often discuss politics or religion since their lives held a certain level of formality, which exhibited itself even at home. But Ruth was so distraught after Chandler had visited and proposed, her father forfeited this unspoken rule. They were strolling along the beach that day — both of them bundled up in corduroy slacks and sweaters, the thick, cable-knit wool dyed the colors of the sea. Ruth's father kept throwing pieces of driftwood to Zeus, who would leap from the salty foam with his prize clenched in his jaws.

Her father said, "I think God winks a bit at our self-torture."

Ruth glanced over and could see the weathered skin around her father's ageless green eyes was creased with mirth. She asked, "What do you mean?"

He stopped walking, and she did too. "You act as if there's only one purpose for your life. One destination. One end goal. And you will miss it if you marry the wrong man." Sighing, he glanced at the distant, white-tipped waves curling forward before being sucked back out by a never-ending pull nobody could perceive. "The older I get, the more I see my life — as simple as it's been — has had *many* purposes: a son, friend, educator, husband . . . father." Smiling fondly, he touched Ruth's back. "All these things came together to make me who I was, who I *am*." He paused. "If I'd married someone other than your mother, would I have been happier? Probably."

Ruth's eyes widened, shocked to hear him admit what she'd always known, but the truth was softened by the smile in his voice. "But am I glad I did? Yes. I would've been bored out of my mind, married to someone who just smiled at me and said *yes* and *no.* So what's my point? My point is this." Her father held out his hand. Ruth could see the jagged scar below his thumb, which he'd sliced into while cutting an orange, and the stains on his fingers from pinching tobacco for his pipe. "God's will is like this hand. The five fingers represent the five different routes your life could take — and yet, regardless of what you choose, are you still not contained in the palm of his hand?" Ruth nodded at her father. Despite her education and life experience, his confidence in her made her shy, like she was five years old again. Chucking her chin with those tobacco-stained fingers, her father whistled for Zeus, who had gamboled up ahead.

Even now, was Ruth in God's will, though she'd inadvertently married the wrong man? And if she *had* married the wrong man, which one shouldn't she have wed? Ruth couldn't answer; she felt adrift from *everything* except for the tether of her husband's hand in hers. And for the first time in a long time, she thought of Chandler like that — her husband. And it wasn't with any romantic attachment, but with the attachment of having experienced so much heartache and joy with a single person who knew her life history and her daughters' life histories better than anyone. For better or for worse, for richer or for poorer, in sickness and in health: these counterparts unified them, as was intended, and it was difficult — if not impossible — to try to separate the love she felt for this person from the memory of his having also inflicted so much pain.

After a while, after Sofie had stopped squirming and Vi's breathing had evened with that contented snuffling sound, which was a two-year-old's version of a snore, Ruth and Chandler carefully and quietly got to their feet. Ruth's heart beat hard, and her mouth was dry — reactions similar to those she'd experienced before their wedding night — as she extinguished the lamp.

But this experience wasn't like that at all.

Ruth pulled the door closed when they'd left the room, but Chandler pushed it back open so the oil lamp in the hallway shone in. Ruth whispered, "Sofie's no longer scared of the dark."

Chandler looked at her, and though it was

hard to perceive his expression, she could tell it hurt to hear how his daughter had grown up since he'd been gone.

Ruth and Chandler walked silently down the steps. The entire house was dark except for the fire, burning in the grate. Mabel had retired shortly after supper, and Ruth now wished she hadn't. They needed someone who could act like a buffer, preventing Ruth and Chandler from discussing all that needed said.

But it was just them.

Ruth asked, "Would you like tea?"

Chandler had never been a tea drinker. He preferred coffee: hot, black, and as strong as cast iron. But he smiled and said, "Tea sounds great."

Ruth went into the kitchen. The kettle on the stove was warm from supper. Still, she took her time preparing the beverage and hoped that when she returned to the living room, the simple gestures would serve to quell her shaking hands.

"Thank you," Chandler said, taking the mug from her.

She sat down beside him on the couch but far enough away that anyone observing from the outside would think they were simply friends. Growing up, Ruth's mother had believed physical touch had to be earned, like an allowance, and therefore Ruth always found herself striving, in adulthood, to replenish what she'd lacked as a child. But then she'd had children of her own, who touched her all the time, and rather than filling that need, it made her realize what she needed was to be given focused time and attention. And how could she receive focused time when her first husband was always gone?

Chandler looked at her. He set the tea down on the worn leather trunk that served as a coffee table. "I'm sorry for how I reacted earlier," he said. "It all just came as a shock."

Chandler's anger at the diner had validated hers, but now Ruth didn't know what to do since he was approaching her in the opposite spirit. She turned away. "That's understandable," she said. "We've all had our bit of shock in the past few months."

Chandler didn't say anything. Ruth set her own tea on the trunk and folded her arms.

The silence between them hadn't been comfortable in years, but now it was nearly unbearable. Chandler cleared his throat. "What do we do now?" he asked.

Chandler had always left the hard things up to her: discipline, budgeting, meal prep, household chores. She snapped, "This situation doesn't exactly come with a manual."

"I know that, Ruth. I'm just concerned how this is going to affect the girls."

"You should've thought how this was 'going to affect the girls' before you left."

Chandler yelled, "Stop it!" Standing, he strode over to the mantel. His back to Ruth, he said in a softer voice, "Just stop, okay? I know you're hurting. I'm sorry for that. I'm hurting too. But it doesn't help either of us to try to make the other person hurt even more."

Shame burned Ruth's face as she stared at Chandler's stooped back. Why did she reflexively spew such venom? Chandler had done her wrong, but if their wrongs were tallied, she knew she would see she had the same amount as him. At the same time, she hated Chandler for rebuking her, for making it seem like she and Elam had orchestrated this. Her shame was replaced with a searing flash of anger, of defensiveness, and she knew it was because she'd remembered that Chandler was getting what he deserved. "Do you have any idea how bad it was *before* you were even declared dead? I was a single mom, Chandler. A single mom who was also trying to care for her dying father. You left me with this. You *left*. You went overseas to save the world at the expense of your own family."

He didn't look at her. He stayed at the mantel and covered his face with one hand. She heard him curse beneath his breath. He turned, and Ruth saw, by the firelight, that there were tears in his eyes. The mantel, the fire, the pain of communication was reminiscent of Ruth's recent conversation with Elam, but in this setting, the source of the pain was reversed. Chandler pinched the bridge of his nose and breathed hard.

"Do you have any idea how bad it was over there — any idea what I went through to get back to you and the girls?"

"I'm sure it was terrible. It's a miracle you're alive. I know that. But you're acting like I cheated on you, Chandler. I didn't. I *buried* you." She gestured to the blank window, in the direction of the church. "I watched your plain casket get lowered into the ground. I had to keep hold of Vi's hand because she kept trying to get close to the hole to peek."

Chandler shook his head. "I should've never left. I realized that when I was sitting in a bombed apartment, trying to write you a letter from the paper and pen I found in the rubble. I thought of you, of all you'd been through, and felt sick." Stepping closer, he said, "I'm sorry, Ruth. I'm sorry I left you and the girls. I'm sorry I wasn't there for you even before I left."

The construction of Ruth's anger collapsed into grief. She got up from the couch and rested her hand on Chandler's arm. Seeing the tears coursing down her face, Chandler leaned close and wrapped her in a hug. The unfamiliarity of his words combined with the familiarity of his body resurrected something in Ruth she hadn't known had died. She allowed her husband to hold her. Allowed herself to fall completely into the moment. She wound her arms around his neck and felt the heat of the fire against the side of her jeans. They said nothing — just stood there, embracing each other, and cried.

Neither of them heard the door open. Neither of them noticed Elam had entered until the puppy, who'd just come down the steps from the girls' room, began to bark. Ruth looked toward the door, toward the intruder, and saw Elam standing there, observing her holding another man when he was her husband too. Chandler moved back from Ruth. He looked toward the door and said, "Good to see you, Cousin." Elam said nothing as Chandler strode across the room and stood in front of him. The men were silent. Chandler's fists clenched. He stared hard at Elam and then gestured back to Ruth. "Thanks for taking care of my wife while I was gone," he said.

Chandler opened the door and walked out, not bothering to close it behind him.

"What was Chandler like?" Ruth asked. "When the two of you were young?"

Elam did not answer right away, and the firelight did little to reveal the enigma of his thoughts. The puppy twirled around his feet: a white fluff ball that, at this point, appeared more like a duster than a pet. The dog rolled over, pedaled his paws, and yipped, as if this would encourage Elam to pet him. Which Elam did. Kneeling to scratch the pup's soft belly, Elam stayed down, averting his gaze, and Ruth could see he preferred animals to people, the same as her father had, for dogs exhibit the kind of loyalty few people can boast. Watching Elam's gentleness with an animal that could offer little in return, Ruth's throat tightened. She walked over and put a hand on his arm, unconsciously mimicking how she'd touched Chandler a quarter of an hour ago. Elam looked up and smiled, but the guarded expression in his eyes stung.

"When we were young, Chandler was

brave . . . the life of the party." Elam paused. "I wanted to be like him, but I couldn't. I could barely talk."

"But look at you now," Ruth said. "You communicate far better than he ever could."

Elam stood. "There can be no life," he said, "in comparison. If you do that, Ruth, one of us will always be found wanting. One of us will never be a whole man."

Elam walked out the open door, and Ruth picked the puppy up and crossed the room to peer through the window beside it. The darkness had transformed Chandler and Elam from living, breathing, broken men into two-dimensional figures. At the moment, Ruth wondered if it would've been easier that way . . . for her. If Chandler and Elam had never existed, she could've never known them intimately, but she, in turn, would have never been known.

Elam and Chandler sat on the stoop of the farmhouse where they'd sat many times before. But they did not speak. Chandler because, after so much solitude, he was out of the habit, and Elam because silence was what he knew best. They just stared out at Driftless Valley Farm — the barn and the outbuildings, the weather vane's pointed silhouette, the mirrorlike reflection of the channels and lake, the distant pump house where Elam and Ruth had first truly talked. Each man was lost in a maze of his own thoughts; neither wanted to find his way out.

Even more than betrayal, which Chandler acutely felt, he experienced a vivid sense of loss. He was not naive enough to blame the entire situation on Elam and Ruth. He had emotionally abandoned his wife before he'd physically left her, and she had come here, to the cranberry farm in Wisconsin, to lay him to rest in more ways than one. His head hurt as he imagined his wife and daughters at his funeral. He pictured them garbed in stereotypical black: Ruth in sunglasses with her red-gold hair falling in waves around her face; Vi's hand knuckle-clenched in Ruth's as his youngest tried to peer over the hole to see why the box was being lowered into it. He pictured Sofie — with her adult eyes and child-like curls — understanding more than her younger sister, and yet not understanding enough to feel the full weight of the grief. Or maybe she *had* understood, and he was only telling himself she hadn't to make it easier.

Elam cleared his throat.

At the sound, a muscle twitched in Chandler's jaw. He couldn't look at his cousin. Even sitting this close to Elam made

Chandler think of Elam being with Ruth.

Elam said, "Would you like to see where Uncle Chandler's buried?"

Chandler Junior stared out at the darkness. "I would."

Elam stood and Chandler did as well. They walked together up the lane. In the distance, on another farm, they could hear an old dog baying against the dusk and the echo of the coyotes that had startled it. The stars were clear overhead; it was cold enough to wear hats and coats but neither man felt the need. They didn't feel anything but their own disconnect.

The wooden teeter-totter in the church playground moved up and down in the wind.

Elam said, "I'm glad . . . you're back."

Chandler made a derisive sound.

"I mean . . . it. You're my cousin. We had a lot of good memories here . . . didn't we?" Elam paused, forcing a smile. "Remember when — ?"

Chandler said, "I'm in no mood for a walk down memory lane."

Elam fell quiet.

They entered the churchyard, which never fully recuperated from the ruts made by horse hooves and wagon wheels each fellowship Sunday. The hard ground sparkled with frost. The men walked around the church, toward the back, where the small graveyard was.

Most of the graves belonged to the farmers who'd died here long before the Albrecht cranberry farm and those surrounding it became a far-flung Mennonite community. Quartets of young birch trees divided the churchyard from the adjacent field, their bark curling like shaved silver in the moonlight. Chandler's father's grave was easy to find. The ground was grassless and sunken, as was the grave beside it. Chandler stared down at this second grave, which upset him even more than the first. Chandler was almost buried here. His wife and children were almost separated from him for the rest of their temporal lives. He didn't understand why he'd been given a second chance.

He knelt and pressed his fingertips to the dirt. It was winter-hard, nothing like the soft, cocoa-like matter Chandler used to sift when he and Elam would search beneath rocks and fallen logs for worms to fish the Kickapoo River. Chandler spread his hands over the dirt anyway and wondered who had died in his stead. Another doctor? A nurse? A patient? A man with a family . . . a life?

Chandler had no idea who it was, but he vowed the man's death would not be wasted. He then began to weep. He wept like he hadn't wept since he sat in that bombed apartment complex where a family had once lived. He wept as he thought of his wife being remarried and of his baby girls having changed in even small — nearly imperceptible — ways. He wept because he was angry; he wept because he was sad. He wept because he was powerless to do anything but cry.

All the while, Elam stood beside him, and in that silence, Chandler felt comfort. They could never go back to what they'd been long before Ruth came here as a widow and, a few months later, became his bachelor cousin's bride. But the fact that they were family might keep whatever relationship they had from completely disintegrating. Chandler wiped his face with the bottom of the button-down flannel shirt he'd borrowed from Elam. Elam rested his hand on Chandler's shoulder. Chandler stiffened at first, and then he stood.

He said, "I know what happened is not your fault."

Elam said, "Thank you . . . for that."

Chandler paused and thought of his wife back at the farmhouse, wearing a sweater he'd never seen, her curly hair darker than he remembered. He wouldn't give up on

their marriage; he wouldn't give up on being the father to his children just because
his cousin had fallen in love with his wife.
He looked at Elam now, and though there
was no malice in his voice, both men could
hear the warning as Chandler said, "Don't
thank me just yet."

Elam and Ruth stood on the porch. Elam
held a pillowcase stuffed with toiletries and
a few extra sets of clothes. They were pain-
fully aware Chandler was feigning sleep on
the couch in the living room, which was
separated from the porch by a single-pane
window; the glass so thin, condensation
gathered on the sills whenever the temperature fluctuated outside.
    Ruth looked up at Elam. In one glance,
she had to convey what she felt since she
could not tell him what he meant to her,
and words, anyway, could not be enough.
    He said, "I guess I should be heading that
way."
    Ruth turned toward the woods. The cabin
would be cold when Elam entered it; the
fire out, the drafty crawl space skittering
with mice. "You sure you can't stay?" she
asked.
    "I'm sure." Smiling, he touched her face.
"Circumstances are awkward enough."

Hugging her body against the cold, Ruth remained on the porch. She watched Elam walk down the lane until she couldn't distinguish him from the trees. She didn't want to enter the house. She didn't want to pull open that door and step into the place where she'd imagined living as Elam's wife. But even without entering, Ruth couldn't see a way out, and she couldn't see a way through. It was as though she were inhabiting some kind of stasis, which prevented her from doing anything but breathing in and breathing out, surviving in the way she'd lived for so long.

Ruth would've stayed there, on the porch, until her lips turned blue and her body shivered in a poor effort to warm itself, but then a scream split the silence. Ruth knew that scream. Since Sofie's infancy, she had learned every emotional range of her older daughter's voice. She was inside and up the stairs in seconds, but Chandler had already beat her there and was cradling Sofie on the bed. Despite her daughter's sobs, Ruth found herself consumed by the tension snapped like high-tensile wire between herself and her first husband. She walked into the room anyway. *She'd* been the one to care for Sofie all these years: who'd woken when she screamed, who'd made such an effort to keep her life secure and free from nightmares, and who'd then comforted Sofie when her worst nightmare came true. Ruth wasn't about to stop mothering simply because Chandler now believed he had the right to judge her abilities as a wife.

Chandler brushed Sofie's sweat-rimmed curls back from her face. "What is it, love?"

Their daughter clung to him — to his shirt, to his hands, to whichever part of him was within her grasp. She clung and whimpered like a wounded thing, "I thought you were dead."

Chandler turned toward Ruth. Immense, immovable sadness sat like a boulder between them. This sadness had existed long before the bombs fell and the sky churned red, as if the stars themselves were burning. It had happened in tiny increments, in tiny decisions: the decision to choose someone else, or *something* else, over each other. These decisions were made with the belief that the other person would always be there. That there would be more opportunities to hold hands on the couch, to slow-dance in the kitchen, to tell her husband how capable he was, to tell his wife how beautiful he found her, even after the nights of child-induced sleep deprivation and deprivation, period, which could underscore the eyes with weariness, as well as the soul. It was not all Chandler's fault, and neither was it all Ruth's. The fault lay in the combining of imperfect selves that resulted in a vast separation of two people who were supposed to be one.

Ruth crossed the room now and sat on the other side of Sofie. She glanced over her shoulder, toward Vi, and saw that the child was sleeping, like she seemed to sleep through everything. Vi was so lighthearted and easygoing; the complete opposite of her sister, and Ruth wasn't so sure Vi took after her. Ruth stroked Sofie's hair. Her hand brushed Chandler's, and he drew it away. The sadness loomed; that boulder was immovable.

After what seemed like an hour, Sofie came back to herself enough to open her eyes. She looked up at Chandler. Ruth could see her body relaxing as her six-year-old mind understood her father's death was only a figment of some waking nightmare. Still clinging to him, she said in her guileless voice, "Can you and Mommy sleep in here, with me?"

Chandler looked at Ruth, and Ruth looked at him, stricken by the fact they were both rendered speechless. Chandler wiped the tears from Sofie's face and said, "Yes, I can sleep in here." Sofie looked over at Ruth, awaiting her mother's answer. Ruth did not want to sleep in here with Chandler. And yet, if that was what it took to make Sofie feel loved and secure, she could not say no. She nodded and Sofie sat up, wiping the tears and mucus from her face. If Ruth didn't know better, she would think this entire drama had been contrived.

So while Chandler held Sofie, Ruth went downstairs and fetched her pillow from Elam's room, and the pillow on the couch Mabel must've gotten for Chandler before she went to bed. She gathered these, a few blankets from the cracked stone crock near the fireplace, and carried everything back upstairs. Sofie's twin bed was against the wall and most of the other space was taken up by the dresser, changing table, and crib. Ruth shook out the blankets on the floor and tossed the pillows at the head. Sofie leaned over Chandler's arm to look, and smiled.

"See?" Chandler said. "We're both here, Sof. We're both going to be here all night."

Sofie nodded, satisfied, and Chandler kissed her before tucking her back in. Ruth kissed her as well and then sat on the pallet of blankets in her wool sweater and jeans.

Chandler could not sleep fully clothed, and he peeled off his T-shirt and socks and lay down beside her. She didn't look at him, *couldn't* look at him, but remained staring at the ceiling.

"Ruth," he said. "Ruth."

She glanced down and saw him. Chandler's chest, which she knew so well, was rippled from the burns. She might not like him — might not have liked him for a long time — but they were bound by law and by their children's love, and it hurt to see the pain he'd endured.

Ruth was not the only one who'd been forced to survive.

She murmured in the dark, "Yes?"

"No matter what," he said, "we're still going to be a family."

# CHAPTER 16

Ruth awoke to the farmhouse ceiling above and the hardwood floor beneath her back. In the drifting haze between dreaming and consciousness, she had difficulty pinpointing this moment in the timeline of her life. And then she turned on her side and saw Chandler. He was still asleep, and so she studied him. She looked at his eyes, moving restlessly beneath their lids, and at the ink-black stubble that had thickened overnight, nearly covering up his scars. She studied the heartbeat pulsing at the indentation beneath his throat, and wondered how long it'd been since the act of making love with this man had seemed a true expression of love.

When Ruth's eyes shifted back up to Chandler's face, she found him studying her to the same extent. They stared at each other in the pearled dawn, neither one blinking, that pulse thudding harder at the base of Chandler's throat, and Ruth knew, like she always had, that he wanted to cross that chasm, though he made no move to touch her. But then Vi woke up and started whispering to her sister, who groaned in response. Ruth was grateful for the interruption, grateful for the chance to break off the unnerving eye contact with her first husband and instead be the mother to his children, a role she began preferring after Vivienne's birth.

Sitting up from the floor, Ruth pulled on the toe of Vi's footie pajamas. Vi squealed and hung her head over the side of the crib, pale hair fluttering. "Mommy!" she cried. "Daddy!"

Ruth laughed and stood to tickle her younger daughter. As she giggled and thrashed, morning sunlight streamed through the windows, the edges of which were laced with frost. The view beyond it looked like a winter scene from a pop-up book.

From the kitchen, Mabel called, "Time for breakfast!" and the giggling girls screamed in delight. Chandler walked down the stairs, carrying Sofie, and Ruth followed, holding Vi's hand. She watched her husband's and her daughter's silhouettes, and how they changed when Sofie rested her head on his shoulder, her small hand splayed across his back as if sheer force alone could keep him there.

Mabel turned from the stove when they stepped into the kitchen. Her eyes filled with tears as she stood there in her tattered robe, a flipper — balancing a sunny-side-up egg — trembling in her hand. Then, with no words exchanged, they all sat at the farmhouse table with a centerpiece of pecan pancakes topped with butter cubes melting down the stack. Ruth cut up a pancake for each of the girls and reached for the pitcher to pour the maple syrup, which Elam had tapped and boiled. She froze a moment, staring at that pitcher, and thought of Elam out there in the cold, with no family around him, and probably with nothing warm to eat. She looked back at her two daughters, who were smiling in anticipation, and thought, *Why can't this be enough?*

"Can we pay in the snow?"

Ruth looked down at young Vivienne. Except for their brief stint in Ireland, caring for Ruth's father, her children had always lived in Bogotá. Until this winter, they had never played in the snow. They'd neither experienced a cold so fierce it takes your breath, nor the comforting thaw when you finally come inside. So after washing up the breakfast dishes, Ruth went upstairs and rooted through the girls' things, piecing together a hodgepodge of items that would win no fashion awards but would at least prevent frostbite.

Chandler helped the girls put on their layers and then sat them on the steps to work their feet into three pairs of socks. He held Vivienne's bare toddler foot for so long — its tiny arch; its five perfect, pea-shaped toes — Ruth could see he was struggling not to cry.

Chandler didn't have any warm clothes, so Ruth went into Elam's room. She didn't allow herself to breathe in his earthy scent while she picked an outfit for the father of her children. It felt wrong — a double-edged sword of betrayal — to do something as simple as this, and yet this was what she was faced with: a constant battle between fulfilling her daughters' wishes and fulfilling the desires of her heart. Those two things had become mutually exclusive, but they'd become mutually exclusive even before this time. For didn't motherhood have a way of culling away a woman's desires and returning her to duty? Wasn't this, also, what caused so many marriages to implode, as that duty — that daily fight for survival —

prevented husbands and wives from acting upon the desire which had created those children in the first place?

Ten minutes later, the snow was stained pink from the dye in Sofie's cheap gloves as she packed the dry flakes and lobbed the misshapen snowball at her father. Chandler darted and the snowball disappeared into a drift. Vivienne fell face-first into the snow and started to cry. Kneeling, Ruth scooped her up and brushed the snow from her cheeks, stretching Vi's hand up to the sky as more flakes fell. Chandler came over to check on them, and Sofie came over too.

He knelt before his younger daughter. "You okay there, girly girl?"

At the nickname, an expression of recognition rose like dawn on Vivienne's face, and when she smiled at Chandler, Ruth could see she wasn't just smiling at a kind man who doted on her and Sofie; she was — for the first time since Chandler's return — smiling at her dad.

Ruth's heart swelled with joy. She turned toward Chandler, grinning with affection, which also shone in her eyes, and he leaned across the drift and kissed her. His lips were warm; his face against hers was cold; snowflakes melted where their skin touched, appearing more like teardrops than snow. This time, she did not want to move away.

After Vivienne, for the second time, fell headfirst in a drift, and Chandler tried to teach Sofie how to do a snow angel, only her coat didn't have a hood, and the snow slid down her neck, the shock of the cold making her cry, the parents gave up and each carried a child up to the house.

Mabel had the forethought to spread old towels in the foyer for their wet shoes. Chandler helped Sofie out of her layers while Ruth helped Vi. The girls ran off, into the kitchen, and Ruth and Chandler were left to fend for themselves. Chandler must've noticed how fast Ruth was unlacing her boots, for he said, "I'm sorry about what happened . . . outside."

Ruth nodded, tugged off her damp wool socks and balled them up. She couldn't think of an appropriate response. In that kiss, in that physical token of love they'd exchanged so often out of habit, she found she was still attracted to Chandler, and yet she couldn't admit this without desecrating her relationship with Elam, which wasn't old enough to have made a habit out of anything. So she said nothing. She just looked at Chandler, standing there with his wet hair curling over Elam's jacket. He had always been a handsome man, and Ruth could recall a time in her life — *years* of her life, in fact — where she didn't want to be anywhere but with him.

However, that was back when he didn't want to be anywhere but with her too.

Thankfully, from inside the kitchen, Ruth heard Sofie crooning, "Mom-my, Dad-dy; Mom-my, Dad-dy." Ruth listened to the lyrics of that song, and then she looked over and met Chandler's eyes. Such sadness existed there, such regret, that she had to look away. She walked into the kitchen and saw their daughters seated at the kitchen table — their cheeks still circled with red from the cold. They wore matching chocolate mustaches from the hot chocolate Mabel had made. Mabel herself was standing in front of the stove, where she always seemed to be these days, as if the kitchen was the only place in the house where she felt comfortable.

Meanwhile, Vivienne joined in the song, "Mom-my, Dad-dy; Mom-my, Dad-dy," and the disparate sisters tilted back their dark and fair heads and swooped their spoons through the air, believing everything in their worlds was perfect. And into this fray of love and life and marriage and loss,

Chandler and Ruth waltzed. They stood behind their daughters' chairs, hearts full and torn, as Mabel passed them mugs of hot chocolate, and outside the world flurried with white, and at the edge of this familiar Rockwellian display, a man — who was no longer a bachelor but no longer someone's husband — sat in a cabin and waited for the next step.

Sofie whined, "How come you and Daddy can't sleep beside us like last night?"

"Because," Ruth said, "Mommy doesn't sleep as well on the floor."

"Then can I sleep between you?"

Somehow, Ruth and Chandler had managed to navigate the rest of the day and the parenting duties it entailed — supper, baths, hair and teeth brushing, books, cups of water to quench Sofie's sudden, all-consuming thirst — without looking or speaking directly to each other, reminiscent of how little they'd looked or spoken before Chandler left.

But Sofie's question forced them to look at each other now. Chandler nodded once at Ruth, and her stomach sank, understanding he wanted her to explain their new family dynamics, probably since she was the one who'd initiated the change. They couldn't keep up the subterfuge of the perfect family forever because the children needed to know the truth. And yet, to inflict pain — for information's sake alone — was unfathomable.

So Ruth sat very still, and very straight, on the end of the bed and looked at the brush marks in her daughters' wet hair; their smooth, high foreheads; Vi's sparkling, wide eyes in contrast to Sofie's narrowed ones, which appeared confused and more than a little wary, as if she'd already learned it was better to keep herself from being caught off guard.

Clearing her throat, Ruth folded her hands in her lap. "Your father and I, we love you very much." It was clichéd to say such a thing before wrecking your children's lives, but it seemed important, somehow, to establish this bedrock before tearing down everything around it, so Sofie and Vivienne could know all of this had nothing to do with them.

But was that the truth?

Chandler and Ruth's marriage had begun to implode after they found themselves shifting from newlyweds to parents nearly overnight, as Sofie's adoption went through faster than even the orphanage director had planned. Therefore, flirtatious quips were replaced with parental batons, and as reality set in, Ruth found the exchange of such batons was neither fair nor graceful. Chandler had signed on the same line as she, and yet *she* was the one who carried most of the weight. Three years later, when Vivienne was born, this weight increased but the division of responsibility remained the same. So, no, it wasn't the children's fault their marriage had imploded, but the implosion itself had everything to do with them.

Ruth tried again. "Your father and I love you very much, and we love each other too and always will —" Chandler nodded and smiled at the girls, but Ruth could see his expression was as sincere as her words. "But remember when we thought your daddy was . . ." Ruth paused, searching for a euphemism. "No longer alive?" Sofie nodded but Vi looked as carefree as always, as if that period had already been lost in the mercifully morphing maze of her toddler consciousness. "Since I thought your daddy wasn't coming back, Elam and I fell in love." Ruth wiped her hands on her jeans. "We got married. And now we're going to live here, with him."

Sofie looked between her mother and her father, and Ruth watched the moment her words registered. It was as if Sofie's mind decided to take a break until everything made more sense. This was a self-defense mechanism, a way to retreat when life became too harsh. Ruth didn't want her daughter to go to that place, to revert to the dull-eyed, taciturn girl she'd become after Chandler's pseudo-death. Ruth reached out toward Sofie to draw her back, but Sofie scrambled away from her mother. Her mouth became a large, dark slice as she screamed. Plugging her ears, Vivienne tried to get away from her older sister but remained on the bed.

"Baby, baby," Chandler crooned to Sofie. "It's okay."

Leaning forward, he wrapped his arms around his older daughter and rocked her against his chest. Sofie held tight to him and watched Ruth, and she could see the accusation in her dark gaze. Ruth didn't blame her. If she looked at it through her daughter's young eyes, she would also blame herself. It was difficult, if not impossible, to try to understand what had happened between her and Elam, so how could she possibly explain it in six-year-old terms?

Vivienne tentatively unplugged her fingers from her ears and looked at Sofie. Vi smiled, but Sofie's face remained a caricature of nothingness; an eerie reverberation from the reactive attachment disorder Ruth and Chandler had battled since her adoption.

"My da-da," Sofie said in a baby voice, and she buried her head in Chandler's chest.

Chandler rested his head on Sofie's and looked at Ruth. Unlike his daughter, there was no accusation in his gaze, and yet Ruth felt it from all sides: she was choosing a relationship with a man she'd only known for the past six months over the resurrection of her family, marriage, and home. What kind of woman — and mother — was she? But she knew: she was the kind of woman who'd found life in not only being spoken to and looked at, but also in being listened to and studied like her words held meaning, like the shape of her face was the last map of the world.

Sofie cried herself to sleep. She had cried herself to sleep before but never for the reason she cried herself to sleep tonight. Throughout it all, Ruth and Chandler remained next to her bed, trying to soothe the pain they'd dealt. Now, the parents of the two little souls tucked under quilts upstairs sat on the couch. The fire had burned down to nothing but dull orange ash. The household was quiet. The darkness wrapped around them, and yet the facade of intimacy it created only exacerbated that they had no intimacy left.

After a while, Chandler said, "That was hard, wasn't it?"

The mere mention of what had taken place caused tears to rise in Ruth's throat. When she knew her voice wouldn't break, Ruth said, "I didn't plan on any of this when I married you."

Chandler sighed. Leaning forward on the couch, he rested his head in his hands. "Of course not," he said. "Can you imagine if we could have seen what our married life would look like before we said, 'I do'? All the heartache? Neither of us would have gone through with it." He turned toward her on the couch, and Ruth watched their shadows merge on the wall. But he did not touch her, and she was grateful. "We had a lot of joy, too, though. Didn't we?"

Ruth wanted to weep. She remembered their first dance as husband and wife, signing Sofie's adoption papers, Chandler kissing her forehead — with tears in his eyes — after she gave birth to Vi. She had never had time to mourn her marriage to Chandler because she was too busy mourning his death. And now, she found herself grieving him while he was sitting beside her.

*How is it possible,* she thought, *to feel such distance from someone whose child you have borne? Whose body has lain beside yours in the bed?* And despite everything, a large, consuming part of her still loved this man. Even Ruth's body responded to his nearness. She wanted to move closer, to lean on him, to draw comfort from him after such a taxing night. But this wasn't possible. It hadn't been possible for years.

"Chandler?" she whispered. "What happened to us?"

Her husband, and the father of her children, lifted his head and looked at her, having heard the sorrow in her voice, and the grief, as if she were not speaking to him so much as his ghost. "There was this one night, when I was in Afghanistan," he said, "and I was sitting in that apartment complex I told you about. It'd been bombed to the point you couldn't tell how many rooms there were, or how many people had lived there. But the kitchen was pretty much intact. A pot of rice was on the stove and a houseplant was above the fridge. I sat there and could see smudges on the chair legs from all the hands that had touched them, and I placed my hands on those fingerprints and closed my eyes, imagining the children who'd sat there, and their parents, and all the different times they must've sat around that table — not comprehending that one of those times would be their last — and I began to cry. I missed you and the girls so badly, it felt like a weight on my chest."

Chandler reached out and took her hand, and she allowed him to hold it, because he was the first person who'd made her a wife and a mother, and for everything she'd lost, she remained both of those things. "I think —" He paused. "I think I sat at our kitchen table every day and never took time to understand that one day my girls would be grown and everything would change. I felt like time would go on forever; that life would go on the same as it always had, but that wasn't the case. I didn't know that wasn't the case until it became too late, and I lost you all."

"You haven't lost them," Ruth said, squeezing his fingers.

He looked over; she could feel his breath on her skin. "No," he said. "But I've lost you."

## CHAPTER 17

Ruth, again, couldn't sleep. Part of the problem was that she didn't know *where* to sleep. She didn't feel comfortable going into Elam's empty bedroom with Chandler asleep on the couch, and Ruth didn't want to risk disturbing Sofie by moving Vivienne back into her crib.

So Ruth crept upstairs and knocked on her mother-in-law's door. Even as she did, she felt nervous to be vulnerable with Mabel like she had before Chandler returned. But then the door opened, and Mabel was standing there, holding an oil lamp that illuminated her tired face.

Ruth, suddenly overwhelmed with affection, reached across the doorway and rested her hand against the side of the older woman's cheek. "I love your laugh lines," she said.

Mabel reached up to place a hand over Ruth's. "They were carved by tears, too."

Ruth didn't ask to come in, and Mabel didn't invite her. She merely pulled the door open, and her daughter-in-law crossed the threshold into the room. A black wrought-iron bed frame contrasted with the white walls. A crocheted doily scalloped the edge of an end table centered between the bed and the small window. On top, a dried bouquet, left over from summer, sprouted from a blue Ball jar. Looking, once more, at her mother-in-law's things, Ruth saw she had brought as little to Wisconsin as Ruth herself had.

Ruth said, "We told the girls tonight."

"About you and Elam?"

Ruth nodded.

"You mean, you and Chandler aren't going to try to reconcile?"

"How can we? There's nothing of us left."

"There's *plenty* left. You have a covenant before God, and you have the girls."

"Chandler broke that covenant when he went to Afghanistan."

Mabel stared at Ruth. "That's not how a covenant works."

Ruth's heart beat in her hands. "But I made that same covenant with Elam. If the two of us were just entering a relationship, then, yes, I would understand setting it aside to focus on rebuilding our family, but

Elam deserves as much consideration as Chandler does."

Mabel looked at her until Ruth blinked and looked away. "You really believe that?"

Ruth didn't reply, and she knew a reply wasn't expected, for the intensity of such a question had to be rhetorical in nature.

Mabel's stern expression didn't change as she abruptly turned and walked toward the bed. Ruth noted the rumpled hook rug beside it and the worn Bible open on the quilt and knew Mabel had been up here, in the darkness of her small room, praying for their family. This testament of familial and divine love should have touched Ruth. But she felt manipulated, as if it were staged. Was Mabel using God to get Ruth to do what she wanted?

Old bedsprings creaked as Mabel took one side of the bed. She patted the spot beside her. Ruth stared at that spot and then stared at Mabel's hand. Ringless, slightly swollen at the knuckles, and embroidered with veins, that hand revealed Mabel's life history better than the rest of her did. Mabel would lose just as much as her granddaughters if Ruth chose a life with Elam and forsook the one she and Chandler had made. Ruth flexed her own fingers, twirling Elam's Claddagh, and walked toward the bed. Part of the reason Ruth shied from such an invitation was because she had never received one. Not one like this, from a woman who could've been her mother. Ruth's own mother had never made such a simple invitation throughout Ruth's childhood and teenage years, when the invitation was needed most.

Mabel set the oil lamp on the table as Ruth sat down. She turned toward her daughter-in-law. "Every covenant relationship," she said, "has moments when it would be easier to throw in the towel than persevere. The hardest time for us as a couple was when Chandler was a baby and Chandler Senior was in medical school. We had no money, not even for groceries, so we had to live off whatever I'd picked from the garden or canned. I was home with Chandler Junior all day, and because I'd grown up so Plain, I'd never learned to drive. I was isolated during one of the worst winters in Pennsylvania history. So whenever my husband came home, I wanted to talk and reconnect, and he just wanted to eat and go to bed. We lived like this for over a year, and I will tell you that, by the end of it, I had no idea who I was, or what I was doing, married to a man I knew I loved but didn't like very much."

Ruth murmured, "How did you find each other again?"

Mabel smiled sadly. "It was simple but hard," she said. "I forced myself to forgive him; then I mentally drew a circle around myself and focused on fixing the person inside it. And each day, instead of counting the ways Chandler was failing me, I started praying for him. I started praying for him more than I ever prayed for anyone in my life. More than I even prayed for our son. I put him at the forefront of my prayer life, and it changed everything." Mabel paused. "I don't think anything changed with him, really, but God changed my heart. I started seeing my covenant relationship with my husband as an earthly picture of God's covenant relationship with me. His love wasn't fickle. He didn't only love me when I gave my all to him. He loved me in my brokenness. In my selfishness. If I was going to love my husband like Christ loved me, that meant I had to love him without reservation. Even when he did not deserve it. Understanding this was such a gift. I went from begrudging my husband his freedom, to come and go as he pleased while I stayed home to care for our child, to being grateful he was working so hard to provide for us and wanting to bless him for it."

"So it all came down to your perspective."

Mabel nodded. "It did. I focused on God's love for me, and this awareness caused my heart to expand and my tongue to lose its edge. I became a kinder, gentler person who put my spouse's needs before my own. Chandler Senior didn't know what had happened to me, because I didn't tell him, but he could see the difference in each area of our lives. We went from being partners to being friends again, and by becoming friends again, we became lovers." Mabel laughed, and then grew serious. "I know this has to be the hardest season you and Chandler have walked through, but I also know there are two little girls, sleeping one wall away, who are worth fighting for, even if you think your marriage to Chandler isn't."

Ruth looked down, the sacrifice that was being asked of her burning like acid inside her chest. "I'm sorry we're putting you through this, Mom."

It was the first time Ruth had called Mabel "Mom," and each woman understood this moniker was a penance and a gift. Mabel blinked to clear tears from her eyes. "I'm sorry too," she said. "But I doubt you would've pursued a relationship with Elam if I hadn't pushed you."

Ruth reached across the quilt and took Mabel's hand. "You made a suggestion," she said. "That was all. *I* am the one who made the choice to enter into a relationship with him." She paused, recalling sleeping with Elam in front of the cottage fire and the indescribable sense of peace she felt, as tangible as his arms. "It wasn't all for nothing," Ruth continued. "I have to believe that, or else I don't know how I could go on."

Mabel asked, "Do you want to sleep here tonight, Ruth?"

Ruth murmured, "That's actually why I came up."

"I'm sorry if I've given you more than what you asked."

"No, please. Don't apologize. You've given me what I didn't know I needed."

Mabel blew out the lamp. The two women crawled beneath the quilts. The older woman believed she was at the beginning of the end of her life; the younger woman believed she was at the end of the beginning of hers. But both believed falsely. They were each at the cusp of a *new* life, a new beginning, and though it didn't resemble what they'd had, or even wanted, it would be what each of them needed — a fulfillment of a promise; a future and a hope. But they couldn't foresee, and so it was a long time before either woman slept.

The sun hadn't risen when Ruth awoke, but she knew as soon as she opened her eyes that God's answer was the same. Mabel snored softly beside her, the steady rhythm threatening to put Ruth back to sleep. But she had to get up now if she was going to talk to Chandler undisturbed. She tiptoed downstairs in the same clothing she'd worn to bed. She crossed the living room and knelt before the couch much like she'd knelt before Mabel's window last night, looking out at the moonlit farm and silently asking God for another, less painful way. But there wasn't one. Now, Chandler was still sleeping. Chandler's longer hair, tumbled over his brow, made him look younger than he was. Ruth allowed herself to look at him, not as she'd looked at him before — as her husband or the father of her children — but as a man whose journey had briefly paralleled hers. With this perspective, the part of her heart that had died toward this lovely, imperfect man beat, for a moment, with perfect, unconditional love.

Ruth whispered his name. Again she said it, as loudly as she dared. This time, Chandler stirred. The quilt covering him dropped to the floor. He turned on his side, exhaled, and opened his heavy eyes. They widened when he saw her there.

Ruth's courage faltered. She considered making up some excuse for why she was there. But then she recalled her conversation with Mabel and knew part of the reason her marriage to Chandler had failed was because neither of them had understood skirting the truth was the same as dishonesty. "Chandler," she whispered, "can I talk to you a minute?"

He nodded and sat up. His appearance made it seem he wasn't fully awake, but just his body responding from muscle memory, which recalled all the times Ruth had woken him with a similar question before launching into a diatribe. But that similarity was where the cycle of their past stopped. Swallowing, Ruth said, "I never told you I'm sorry. I never saw I even had anything to be sorry for. I was so focused on everything *you* were doing wrong, I didn't see I was equally to blame. I'm sorry for that, Chandler. I'm really sorry."

Ruth's tears fell as her words fell: fast, hot, and undeterred.

Chandler leaned forward on the couch and took her hands. "Ruth," he said. He stopped there, at her name, until she looked up at him. "Please don't say you're sorry when I've made so many mistakes. That makes me feel worse."

"We *both* made mistakes," she insisted. "And often, our mistakes fed off each other: you neglected me, and I became bitter because of that neglect. But I had a choice, even then. I didn't make the right one, Chandler. I blamed you for not being enough for me, for not being *there* for me, but you're just a man, not God. You were never meant to fill up my broken places. You were never meant to fill up my cracks."

Chandler relented. He leaned back on the couch and sighed. "How different our marriage would have been if we'd known at the beginning what we know now."

She let go of his hand as she stood. "I guess that's why some people stick it out. They grow up together instead of growing apart." She paused. "I'll be back soon. I have to go see Elam."

Light vanished from Chandler's eyes. "Take your time," he said. "I'll stay with the kids."

Even in that simple sentence, Ruth could hear what he did not say: *This is our life now: taking turns and exchanging custody of our children. This is the norm. Or will become it.*

But he did not know their lives were about to change again.

Ruth sensed the temperature change as she stepped outside. Water dripped from the icicles barnacled to the roofline, and for one of the first times since she came to Wisconsin, her breath didn't rise in a cloud. She closed the door behind her, heard the definite little click. She glanced through the tempered window glass, watching as Chandler's silhouette disappeared around the corner as he, presumably, lay back down on the couch. She walked in the dark toward the cabin. Layers of frost were thawing, forcing Ruth to slough through the mud filling the lane's potholes that had been patched with ice or snow for months.

The lamp was already lit in Elam's cabin, and Ruth could hear deep, mournful music notes riding the morning air like a soundtrack to grief. He felt the same as she.

Elam stopped playing when she entered but did not rise from the bench.

"Good morning," she said.

He asked, "Do you want to sit down?"

"That would be wonderful, thank you."

Ruth feared Elam would walk over and pull out her chair, take her jacket . . . touch her in some way. But he didn't. She sat at the kitchen table and didn't know what she would do if she suddenly found herself too close to him. For as much as Chandler drew her to him because of their life history, Elam drew her to him because of the life they had yet to share.

Elam turned on the piano bench, his arms folded, knees pointed toward the wall. Ruth looked away and swallowed.

Ruth loved *each* man, albeit in different ways, so where did that leave her? It left her doing whatever she possibly could to keep her girls' lives as normal as possible, when they'd experienced so little normalcy in the past five years. It was for them she was willing to risk everything; it was for them she was willing to give everything up. "I came here," Ruth said and stopped, because — the same as when she'd told the children — she couldn't begin such a conversation without telling Elam how much he meant to her. But when she glanced up, she could see by the way he was looking at her, he knew what she had come here to say.

"I came here to let you know I'm going to try to reconcile my marriage to Chandler."

Elam hung his head. "So this means," he said, "you're going to annul ours."

Ruth straightened, and her spine grated against the back of the chair. "Yes," she said.

"I don't have any other choice."

Elam nodded but didn't look up. She watched morning light sneak its way through the crevices of the cabin. "I'm sorry," she added. "That it's come to this."

"It never should have," he said.

Ruth's throat sealed over her effort not to protest, not to declare that, *yes,* it should have happened. To deny the rightness of them was to deny their love. But was this truly love? Yes, Elam adored Ruth in a way she'd never been adored before, but over time would that have changed? As they lived day in and day out beside each other, witnessing each other's flaws and bitterest heartaches, would he eventually take her for granted, the same as his cousin had done? The same as Ruth had done? She didn't know, but she suspected as much.

Life's beauty could only be seen once the dross of the everyday had been removed; for Chandler, being separated from his family had removed the dross; for Ruth, his death had removed the dross, but the results had manifested themselves in wholly incompatible ways.

"I am not sorry it happened," she said. "I'm just sorry it has to end."

Elam looked up. Tears shone on his weathered face, his soft heart also incompatible with such a hard-looking man. "That's where we're different," he said. "I'm sorry for both."

Ruth could no longer hold back her sobbing by the time she passed the channel. She wrapped her arms around herself while the audible force of the pain ravaged her body, but she continued walking as if an inner compass directed her toward the farmhouse — which dually represented her life with Elam and the life that now existed inside it, with Chandler and their girls. Even as she succumbed to her grief, Ruth knew she had to stop. She didn't want to scare the children, who hadn't seen her cry like this even after receiving news of their father's death.

Ruth finished walking up the lane and sat on the porch steps. She stared at the acreage, the mud-brown fields interrupted by the cranberry-red barn. Despite being caught in the purgatory between seasons, the land was beautiful still. She wondered if she could stay here while trying to reconcile her marriage, at the expense of the marriage she wanted. Elam had told her she could; that *he* would leave, since he would always associate Driftless Valley Farm with their star-crossed union. But this same reason was why she didn't want to remain.

However, Ruth also wasn't sure if she and Chandler had a choice. They had no home, no money, and Mabel wouldn't have any to spare until someone bought her modest house in Pennsylvania. Besides, where would they all go?

The door opened behind Ruth. She wiped her nose on the sleeve of her jacket. The person walked across the porch and sat down. Ruth looked over and saw Chandler. Compassion filled his eyes, and the divine love she'd experienced earlier melted away. If not for him, she wouldn't need compassion. If not for him, she wouldn't need to give anything up.

"I wish this wasn't so hard," he said.

Ruth steeled herself by folding her arms. "The girls awake yet?"

"They woke up about thirty minutes ago. Mom's getting them breakfast." Chandler had changed in response to Ruth's brusqueness; the intimacy from earlier was also gone.

"Mabel helps out so much," Ruth said. "I don't know what I'd do without her."

Chandler wasn't wearing shoes, and his socks didn't match. Ruth found it strange how six years of marriage had ingrained in her the need to take care of him. "My mom only has us," he said. "That is, I guess she only has me and the girls."

Ruth looked straight ahead, her gaze transfixed on the lane, and not on the woods, leading to the cabin where Elam was surely gutted by her decision. She had to gather her courage, her fortitude, before she could tell Chandler what she'd done. Part of that, she suspected, was because it would be more difficult to go back on her word once it was spoken aloud. "Mabel has me, too," Ruth said. "Elam and I have decided to annul our marriage."

At first, Chandler didn't respond. They could hear their daughters squealing in the kitchen. Sofie and Vivienne started their days either playing or fighting, and more often than not, the first led to the second before the sleepy dirt had been rubbed from their eyes.

He murmured, finally, "Why did you do it?"

Ruth said, "I did it for them." She glanced over her shoulder, and they both turned toward the window, where Vivienne and Sofie were outlined by the frame. They were in the midst of fighting over the peanut butter lid, and it was clear Vi had won the first round, since her mouth was smeared with the contents. But the parents did not focus on that. They instead focused on the image of their children's wild bedhead hair and matching princess jammies. It was astounding how such a simple sight could slay a parent's heart with love. "I did it for our girls."

Chandler, again, said nothing. Ruth looked over and saw he was still staring at their children, but a muscle throbbed along the scarred line of his jaw. "It doesn't feel too good to be with someone who thinks she's just given up the love of her life."

Ruth thought, *Who says I am with you?* Though her heart had received healing last night, her thoughts and her tongue remained coupled with the reflex of her defenses, the predictability of them like the pull of the tide. "It didn't feel too good," she said, "to be married to someone who forgot that's what I was supposed to be to him."

Turning from the window, Chandler looked back at her. "I never forgot that you were the love of my life; I just got too busy to show you."

Ruth found herself momentarily cowed. The Chandler who chose to serve with Physicians International instead of supporting his family would never have admitted to busyness or neglect. But then he ruined it by adding, "Why'd you put Sof through that last night, saying you were staying with Elam, if you were going to change your mind first thing this morning?"

"Because I didn't *know* I was going to change it until God changed my heart."

"How do I know you won't change it again?"

"I won't, Chandler. I've had a break-through."

"Sounds like it."

The abruptly charged quiet reminded Ruth of their previous conversations, when it became so difficult to communicate without fighting, they decided it was easier not to speak. After time had passed, he asked, "So what does this 'annulment' mean? That we're going to walk back into this house and pretend we're a normal husband and wife?"

Ruth looked over at him. "Our relationship wasn't 'normal' long before this."

"I'm aware of that," he said. "I'm aware of that more than you probably think."

Ruth's stomach tightened. There were moments, throughout their years of rather unholy matrimony, when she really *did* wonder if she was the only one who seemed to understand marriage was supposed to be about more than mere survival. "How come you didn't say anything?" she asked. "How come we never talked about how unhappy we were?"

"I didn't think you *wanted* to talk. You shut me out, Ruth. Every time you looked at me, all I could see was this anger in your eyes."

Ruth knew this was true, and yet it still hurt to hear it. She'd never learned how to be strong without being angry, and every morning she woke up — before changing sodden nighttime diapers, fixing breakfast, getting the girls dressed for the day — she felt she was fighting the battle of her life. "How did we get this far away from each other?" she asked, her voice wavering.

He said, "I have no idea." Clearing his throat, Chandler glanced over and looked at her in a way that made her drop her gaze. "Did *you* have dreams?" he asked. "I mean, I know you had dreams when I first met you, but did you still have them after . . . the girls?"

Ruth hunkered forward on the steps. An icicle slipped off the roof and shattered on the ground. She nudged the pieces with her boot. "Yes," she murmured. "I had dreams. If I hadn't been so tied down by motherhood, my dreams could've been as adventurous as yours."

After a moment, he softly asked, "What were they?"

She looked at Chandler. Her green eyes narrowed. She feared he would discredit her dreams and make her world, once again, feel small. "I wanted to travel to Italy with you — not to Florence or to Rome, but to the little country villages with crumbling houses and fields of flowers, their faces all turned toward the sun. I wanted to write a book. I wanted to learn to do pottery, to paint. I never meant to lose myself in the middle of trying to keep everyone alive."

Chandler exhaled and ran a hand over his face. He was touching his scars, she realized, and she thought about the ones she'd seen on his body.

Ruth fixed her gaze on the barn. "I'm willing to co-parent with you," she said. "But I'm not willing to become your wife."

Chandler paused. "Physically, you mean."

Her cheeks grew hot.

"I can live with that," he said. "We weren't very physical before." Ruth tried to decipher if this statement was laced with allegation, but Chandler just smiled and held out his hand. "If we're not going back to husband and wife, can we at least go back to being friends?"

Ruth almost laughed, thinking it'd be

easier to go back to being brother and sister. But then she thought of Mabel's story, of how she hadn't liked Chandler Senior until she began putting him at the forefront of her prayer life, which had spurred Ruth to kneel in front of the window after Mabel was asleep and pray. So here, now, she tried again: *God, if you really want me to do this, you're going to have to help me forgive Chandler; you're going to have to help me* love *Chandler.* Which was really asking for the same thing two different ways. For how can you have forgiveness without love, and love without forgiveness?

Ruth looked at Chandler's hand, saw the gold wedding band glinting on his finger. It was a different ring than the one she'd given him at their wedding because he had misplaced his at the clinic in Colombia: a carelessness that wouldn't have hurt if he hadn't been so careless about her as well. But Ruth was different now, not as tender-skinned, and she wasn't sure if this was an asset or a flaw. However, Chandler was different too. They weren't the same bright-eyed newlyweds they'd been when they said their vows in an orphanage courtyard. They were older but in many ways not wiser. Mutual disappointment had tarnished their love. And yet, the tapestry of a shared life unfurled between them, pulling on each of their hearts with tangible threads. This was why Ruth reached out her hand and clasped Chandler's. She could feel the threads pulling her in, even more than the moment he kissed her. The attraction was still there, an attraction that had once connected them as much as the child it created. Elam's Claddagh ring cut into her hand. Ruth knew she needed to take it off. But she couldn't, not yet. Instead, she held Chandler's hand tighter, and he rose, pulling her to her feet. They stood there, on the farmhouse's front porch, and stared at each other as the winter silently thawed.

Elam packed his clothes in the canvas duffel he used the few times a year he went out of town. Ruth had made her decision, and he wanted to respect it, but he also didn't want to leave without telling Sofie and Vivienne good-bye. He'd been a father figure to the sisters for only a few months, and he suspected they meant more to him than he meant to them — especially now Chandler had returned — but Elam knew that, if he was ever going to look back on this heartache without regret, he had to walk the path to healing without compromise.

So he walked.

Unbeknownst to him, since the snow was gone, Elam's footsteps traced those Ruth had made a few hours earlier, and though his face remained dry, his heart was just as heavy as hers had been. He walked past the lake up to the house he'd lived in since childhood, and somewhere deep inside, he suspected he wasn't just saying good-bye to Ruth and her children, but he was also saying good-bye to a way of life. This thought didn't grieve him nearly as much as the other.

Elam knocked on the front door of his own house. Through the windowpane, he watched Chandler approaching. Chandler opened the door with a sheepish expression, as if he fully realized how strange it was that the two men had twice exchanged roles.

Chandler said, "Ruth's —"

Elam held up his hand. "I came to say good-bye to the girls."

At that acknowledgment, a towhead peeked out from behind Chandler's legs. Elam knelt, set his bag on the porch, and looked at Vivienne. The sight of her took his breath, but he supposed that was to be expected, since the sight of her mother did the same. "Hi, Vi," he said.

Dropping her gaze to her Hello Kitty

socks, she whispered, "Hi."

But then Everest took the opportunity to dart outside, and Vi ran after him. In unison, Elam and Chandler called, "You're not wearing shoes!" They glanced at each other. Elam stood, and Chandler gestured to Elam's bag. "You going somewhere?"

"Yeah," Elam said, but left it at that. He wasn't quite sure where he was going to go.

"I'm sorry we haven't had the chance to catch up."

Elam glanced at Chandler. "We haven't had the chance to catch up in ten years."

"I know. I'm sorry for that, too."

Into this awkward impasse, Vivienne came skipping with the pup at her heels. The two left a series of foot- and paw prints on the chipped porch steps. Everest looped circles around them, barking, as Vivienne wrapped her arms around Elam's right leg and held on tight, eyes clenched, while saying, "I give ya a li'l' *squoosh.*"

Elam was touched and reciprocated by reaching down to rest a hand on her head. But the two-year-old looked up at him, and beneath her fringe of bangs, her wide green eyes grew even wider. She glanced at Chandler and darted across the porch to hold his leg like she thought she'd been do-ing in the first place. As usual, the child was oblivious to the emotions her thoughtless gesture caused.

For Chandler, it brought immense joy to know Vi found in him security and comfort.

For Elam, it confirmed what he already knew, but the knowledge still broke his heart.

Elam's sister, Laurie, was on the floor of her kitchen, mopping up some milk leaking down through a leaf in the table. The rectangular table itself was edged, like picture-frame matting, with varying sizes of sticky white handprints, evidence of the homemade yogurt sweetened with maple syrup his nieces and nephews had eaten for breakfast. Elam stood in the entrance, his felt hat in his hands, surprised that his life had imploded while the lives orbiting it had stayed the same. Laurie looked up and smiled. But then she saw his face, and her smile disappeared.

"Elam?" she said, his name lifted with concern. *"Vas is letz?"*

Brother and sister had been avoiding each other over the past few days, but for entirely different reasons. Laurie and Tim had wanted to let Ruth and Elam get settled as a family, and Elam couldn't bear to share that he, Ruth, and the girls no longer

411

*were . . .* a family. However, now he knew word of Chandler's return had not even reached Laurie's ears. He glanced through the kitchen to the living room. Three of his nieces and nephews, too young for the Driftless Valley Community school, looked at picture books while lying on a blanket beside the woodstove. He glanced back at Laurie. "Can we talk somewhere else?"

Laurie awkwardly reached around her pregnant belly and mopped up the rest of the spill. She entered the living room and waved the soggy tea towel at Faith, who was almost five and therefore in charge. Laurie and Elam walked into the breezeway, colder than the rest of the house by at least ten degrees. Wind rattled against the small window. Beyond it, Elam could see the gray sky, bisected by Laurie's empty clothesline. Tim had cleaned and painted six gourds white and strung them on baling twine attached to the pole. Elam had a hard time imagining the purple martins who would return to these birdhouses in a few months, eating the bugs that would otherwise eat the garden. To him, it seemed the seasons had been replaced with a perpetual cold.

Laurie, to her credit, was silent for a minute before she whispered, "Has someone died?"

Elam turned from the melancholic image of that empty clothesline. In Laurie's face, he could see the child she'd been when their mother died. Even now, Laurie viewed death as the greatest obstacle of life, which also seemed to explain why she never paused between having children, as if her offspring were balusters, conceived to impede the quick sands of time. "No," he said. "No one's died."

"Then what happened?"

He looked away, gathering himself. "Chandler's returned."

"But he's . . ."

"Dead? No, it was someone else. They buried the wrong man."

Laurie was silent for so long, Elam glanced back at her. All color had drained from her face. His sister's inability to hide her emotions — and, furthermore, to display them for the world to see — had often frustrated Elam, because such openness was the opposite of him. But now he loved her for it. Her pain was a reminder he was not alone in how he felt.

"Oh, Elam," she murmured. "What does this mean for you?"

"This means my wife's going back to her first husband."

"But — but you just got married. We were

just taking care of the farm because you were on your honeymoon!"

Elam looked at his boots in shame. The mere mention of *honeymoon* evoked images tainted with the fact Ruth's husband had been alive the entire time, and Elam had known for the end of it. When they were nestled in their cottage between the apple orchard and the lake, Elam had convinced himself their togetherness was not wrong if they didn't continue to consummate their marriage. But now, he regretted having stayed there at all after he learned the truth. He wouldn't have done that if he had known Ruth would return to Chandler. But he realized Ruth hadn't even known how quickly everything would change.

Elam looked at Laurie. "Chandler contacted Ruth when we were on Washington Island. We knew he was alive, but she told me —" His voice cracked. "She told me she was going to stay married to me. But that was before we came home."

"What happened then?"

"Sofie couldn't understand why her parents weren't . . . together, like before."

A scream resounded from the living room; the children's play had increased a decibel for each minute Laurie had been gone. Holding up a finger, she walked out of the breezeway into the kitchen. She called, "Sarah, *sittsit unnah!*" albeit more gently than normal, and returned. She looked up at Elam, and her eyes slowly filled. "Oh, Brother." Laurie reached out and touched his arm. "The reason you chose Ruth — when no other woman could turn your head — is because you knew she was the kind of woman who'd give up everything to protect those she loves."

Elam spent most of the afternoon at his sister and brother-in-law's kitchen table, talking over how to sell the farm to Laurie and Tim without making it a burden on their family. No surprise that Laurie had insisted on feeding him lunch, and though Elam hadn't had an appetite in days, it soothed him to sit down and consume a meal with those who knew and loved him best.

Once the interest-free payment plan was settled, and Laurie was reassured that Elam was not going to disappear off the face of the earth, Elam went out into the barn and called their driver.

Thirty minutes later, Elam got out of the van and looked up at the Tomah Motel. Like so many mediocre landmarks, Elam had seen the structure all his life but had never taken the time to study it. The architecture was pure '60s: one flat level that somehow managed an asymmetrical design. In the summer, the outside was festooned with flowers purchased from the Mennonite greenhouse down the road. But the window boxes were empty, and the lack of color accentuated that the hotel's paint hadn't been touched up in years. Stucco peeled away from the building's bottom half, where dirty snow had accumulated all winter. But at least the inside was clean. There was a mini fridge, TV with cable, Wi-Fi, and a coffee-maker. Modern conveniences at the push of a button, which made Elam miss his cabin even more.

Elam sprawled across the bed while careful to keep his boots dangled over the carpet, so he wouldn't make the cheap coverlet dirty. He had no idea where to go from here. He'd told Laurie he needed a change, but the truth was his personality wasn't the type to handle change well. He was forty years old and routine-oriented to a fault because routine felt safe. It was predictable. Now nothing was predictable except for the fact nothing truly was.

Chandler, Ruth, and the girls sat before the living room fire. Slightly blackened popcorn kernels clustered on the bottoms of their bowls, and popcorn remnants, which had somehow escaped the puppy's notice, scattered across the rug like oddly shaped pebbles. Chandler's index finger marked the page in the first book in the Little House series, and Ruth sat against a pile of throw pillows with Vivienne on her lap, watching his face shift in accordance with the voices.

Sofie watched Chandler too. Her reflective eyes followed her daddy's mouth as he read, as if she couldn't rely on her ears alone. Everest curled in her lap, tail wagging, though he was entering that long-limbed stage foretelling he wouldn't be a puppy for long.

It was the perfect end to a perfect day. Or at least the day was perfect in the eyes of the children, and that was what mattered. Or this, at least, was what Ruth told herself. Chandler finished the chapter, showed the page's illustration to the girls, and closed the book. Sofie set the puppy down, nearly comatose from the warmth of the fire, and went to sit on her father's lap.

"I like being with you," she said. "I want to be with you all the time."

Chandler looked at Ruth. His mouth thinned as he swallowed hard. "I like being with you, too, sweetheart," he said. "I want to be with you, your sissy, and your mommy all the time."

Sofie turned in Chandler's arms. Her eyes met Ruth's. A challenge there, in that dark gaze. At six years old, the foundling child possessed an eerie knowledge of the ways of the world. Perhaps this was because she and the world had been so harshly introduced.

Sofie asked her mother, "Do you want to be with us all the time?"

Ruth's breath caught. Vi shifted in her arms, the child's blue eyes lowered as she stared sleepily at the flames. "Yes," Ruth said. "I want to be with you, your sissy, and your daddy all the time."

"Walk with me?"

Ruth looked at Chandler, smiling at her from the doorway. She remembered all the times she had asked him that same question, when they shared Bethel House with an older missionary couple whom she could trust to watch the girls while she got an hour of fresh air.

Early in their relationship, Chandler had been her bodyguard, her protector, and yet after they married, his desire to go running — or even walking — with her stopped. He'd grown busier. His workload at the orphanage's clinic increased exponentially until she could almost see his responsibilities weighing his shoulders down. But shouldn't there be some contractual agreement that you must perform the same duties which won your spouse's heart?

So, now, Ruth considered telling Chandler no, the same as he'd told her no all those years before she gave up and took walks on her own. But then she recalled Mabel's words, Mabel's suggestion that she needed to forgive her husband and embrace the man before her and not begrudge him for no longer being the man he'd been back then. Because she wasn't the same woman either. Therefore, Ruth nodded, closed the page of the slim maroon book she'd taken from Elam's library in the woods, and rose to her feet.

Chandler's grin widened. He lifted her jacket down from the coat tree by the front door and opened it. Turning her back to him, Ruth slid the jacket over her arms and zipped it up. "Thank you," she said and knew from his expression that showing gratitude was something she'd done without thinking when they were dating, but that gratitude had slowly dissipated after they married and her dissatisfaction grew. *Which came first?* she wondered. Chandler's inability to put her first, or Ruth's inability to

419

show him the same kindness she would've shown a stranger?

The married couple walked together yet apart; their proximity, or lack thereof, appearing to mirror how they'd walked beside each other for most of their married life. But this was not walking weather. Drizzle slipped through the sieve of clouds, and the land looked like a hasty abstract, smudged in gray and brown. The glimmering lake and channels alone held a reservoir of beauty.

Though their pace was slow, Chandler's breathing hitched between steps, and Ruth wondered if he'd damaged his lungs in the bombing. She had never asked about that night (or morning, she supposed, since it was 2 a.m. when the first bomb fell), and he'd never shared, as if they each knew it was best to put the past behind them.

Ruth glanced toward the cabin in the woods, then looked to see if Chandler had noticed. She wondered if he even knew the cabin was there, and if he did, if he realized its significance. She doubted it, considering how little contact the cousins had had since their teenage years. Now, no lantern light beckoned from the windows; no wood smoke signaled from the chimney. It was as though Ruth's decision had pulled a curtain across that magical world, forever removing it from view. She wondered if the same was true for Elam. He hadn't come to say goodbye.

"You will heal; it will just take time."

The sound of Chandler's voice startled Ruth. She glanced over again, nearly expecting someone else to be walking beside her. Who was this man who spoke so gently?

"What do you mean?"

But even as Ruth asked, she understood. Chandler was her husband. The father of her children. The keeper of her secrets. The man who — for good and for bad — had once known her more intimately than anyone else. Of *course* he could tell she was hurting. Of *course* he could tell she wanted Elam to be walking in his stead. She hated to think how this knowledge hurt him, and yet, at the same time, she blamed him for it too.

If Chandler had wanted to protect their love, he should've invested more time in their relationship. But he hadn't, and therefore — after she learned of his death — it was easy for Ruth to give her heart away. She wondered, her pulse keeping time with Chandler's hitched breathing, if she would've eventually fallen for someone else even if Chandler *hadn't* died. That thought thinned the magic curtain surrounding her union with Elam, so she banished it quickly.

"What I mean," Chandler said, "is that time heals everything, not just physical wounds." He paused and looked over. "But can I ask one thing?"

"Yes," Ruth said. "You can always ask."

"When did you stop loving me?"

She inhaled sharply, stunned by the bluntness of his words and the hurt she felt behind them. This wound was fresh. "But I *do* still love you," she said. "I'm afraid I always will."

Chandler shook his head. The clue was in the word *still*. Pulling off his toboggan hat, he dragged an agitated hand back through his unruly hair — one of the few physical characteristics he shared with his cousin. "Then when did you stop being *in* love with me?"

Ruth stared straight ahead. For so long, she had wanted to ask him the same thing.

What was the difference between loving someone and being *in* love? She supposed the first was born out of duty and the second out of desire. The first meant you bookended your days with each other, but the days themselves were spent contemplating other things.

The second meant you woke and slept

with that person on your mind.

How could Chandler and Ruth both have believed they were not loved or seen?

"It took time," she said, "just as it took time to fall in love with you. I guess I daily focused on your faults so I wouldn't be hurt when you failed me."

"So you're saying our marriage's failure was my fault?"

*Yes,* she thought, *that's exactly what I'm saying.*

But then she remembered how taken aback Chandler had been by her simple thank-you as he held out her jacket, and the revelation that he was not the only one in the wrong. If the construction of love required two people, equal energy must be required to tear it down.

So she said, the first step in reparation: "No, it was my fault too. You did so much for us every day, but I was blind to it because I was angry. I felt you were choosing the clinic over us."

Chandler stopped walking. Rain fell more heavily now, so he had to squint at his wife to see.

"Sometimes, I thought of it like the other woman. You would come home at night and look at me, at the girls, and it was like your mind was already focused on whatever you needed to accomplish the next day."

Chandler blinked rain from his eyes. "Why didn't you tell me?"

She looked down, saw how the water softened the tracks of some small creature that had scurried across the mud. "I thought you knew," she said. "I all but told you so many times."

He cursed beneath his breath. "All but telling me does not count as *telling* me."

"I know." She exhaled. "I'm sorry."

"You're not the only one. I guess we were just too exhausted from the day to talk."

Ruth distinctly remembered the many days he was referencing: by the time he came home and they ate supper, cleaned the kitchen, bathed the girls, and got them into bed, there was no energy left to invest in each other. He would take his laptop and sit on the couch, sometimes with a mug of tea, and she would sit on the other side of the couch with a mug of tea and a book. Some nights, Ruth wouldn't even read but would watch her husband above the page — her heart so raw and hurting, she feared he could hear it through the lapel of her robe.

As Chandler knew Ruth more intimately than anyone else, so did she know him, and yet she didn't know how to reach him. And here, all along, he'd felt the same about her. Had he spent those nights rereading the same emails? Watching her above his laptop too? Tears stung her eyes for the exhausted young parents they'd been, and that was only last year. If just one of them had extended love, the cycle would have stopped. Their relationship would've changed.

"Why didn't you tell me you missed me?" she cried. "Why didn't I tell *you*?"

Chandler looked at Ruth. "I don't know," he said. "Maybe we didn't want to be vulnerable with each other? Maybe we feared we were the only one who felt that way? But one thing I've learned through all of this is that —" he stepped closer and cupped her face; she felt the dampness on her cheeks paint his palms — "I sure miss you now."

# CHAPTER 18

Elam walked down the sidewalk while eating a stale English muffin, remnants of the continental breakfast provided by the Tomah Motel. He had no destination in mind, convenient since his legs were the only medium he had to take him there. He'd spent the morning in his room but found few things more depressing than sitting by himself in a rent-by-the-week motel while the sun fought to penetrate dusty blinds. Besides, he'd only watched fifteen minutes of television before he became disenchanted with society as a whole. Elam had been too shy during his teenage years to dabble in the outside world like a few of his Mennonite friends (hiding contraband Walkmans, cigarettes, and *Englisch* clothes in their rooms), but he'd still often wondered if he were missing out. Now he knew he hadn't been. If anything, his shyness had spared him from making poor decisions he would have later regretted. Really, when it came down to it, there was only one forbidden thing he regretted not pursuing, and that was music.

Elam swallowed the muffin, his dry throat muscling it down, wishing he'd accepted the continental breakfast host's offer of orange juice in a carton with a peel-off lid. But Elam did not enjoy being fussed over, and he felt the host's grandmotherly attention even more because he appeared to be the only resident in the motel. He continued walking: past the post office, hardware store, greenhouse and bulk food store, gas station, and then — finally — the church. Elam had never darkened any other church door in Tomah besides the community's.

He went through the foyer, and the same sunlight that had tried penetrating the dusty blinds of his motel now swirled through the stained-glass windows in a multifaceted kaleidoscope. The church was empty, and the garnet-colored carpet bore vacuum stripes. Elam self-consciously looked down at his boots but he kept them on, figuring it would be worse to be walking around a somber church in socks. His heart seized when he saw the piano tucked behind the Communion bench. His work-hardened hands scrolled across the satin backs of the pews.

He walked up three steps and around the Communion bench and the offering plates with the red padding on the bottoms that matched the carpet. He went over and sat on the bench. He glanced out through the sanctuary, seeing the sturdy, walnut beams supporting the vaulted white ceiling. Fingers trembling, as if conduits directly connected to his heart, he lifted the piano cover and touched the black-and-white keys.

To be a man of so few words and yet to have the need to produce sound was one of the harshest contradictions. But as a bird needs to fly, a fish to swim, an author to write, and an artist to paint, Elam pressed down on the keys and began to play. He poured his sorrow into the melody, his tears into the chords that rose to the ceiling. There were only a few times in his life that Elam Albrecht lost all sense of self, but creating music was one of those times. He played and he wept and he poured himself out over the keys until the keys and the bench and the air and the sunlight, swirling through glass, all seemed to be pulse points, beating inside of him.

Only then, once he was finished, the chords still echoing inside the building, did he know that, if Ruth was now forbidden to him, he would now pursue this forbidden thing.

# CHAPTER 19

*Five Months Later*

Ruth stood at the edge of the Mississippi. It
was strange to think the same river that all
winter had been a jigsaw puzzle of ice now
flowed all the way south, where the water
grew darker, moved slower, and teemed
with a kind of life that could never survive
here. But it was lovely, Ruth had to admit,
though it could never replace the ocean
beside Greystones. However, Ruth was
beginning to understand she could not trust
her memory, for time sanded off the rough
edges and made her wish for something that
had never been, and never could be.

The cold water lapped against her knees.
The warm June sun reflected off the water
onto the underside of her wide straw hat.
Ruth closed her eyes and thought: *Just be.*
She listened to her daughters' mischievous
giggles as they packed coarse brown sand
over Chandler's body, so all that was dis-

played was his dark head of hair contrasted by his wide, white grin. She looked at him, and her eyes and heart acknowledged the importance of the moment. It was as though each day Chandler awoke, he determined afresh to win her. Even last night, while they ate supper at the farm table, and Sofie said she needed more milk, Chandler and Ruth had both leaped to their feet. Sofie asked, "Daddy, why do you do everything now?"

Chandler had said, "I'm doing what I should've been doing all along."

Ruth couldn't quite pinpoint what was happening, though. A part of her mourned being her daughters' main source of support. This made no sense, since she'd so long mourned that she had to be a single mom. *Perhaps we only mourn what we cannot have.*

Chandler's voice interrupted her thoughts. "Ruuuth! Help me!" As he'd done every time the girls had covered him with sand, he acted like he couldn't pull his arms free.

Ruth walked over and leaned down. "What are you doing?"

She tried to sound stern but failed miserably.

Chandler's hand shot up and clasped her wrist, pulling her down in the sand on top of him. They lived in close proximity but

431

hadn't been physically close since the snowy day he kissed her. Chandler's warm, sandy arms wrapped around her waist, and the children squealed and put fistfuls of wet sand on her back. She'd forgotten what life was like before she and Chandler had drifted apart, for just as time dulls the sharp edges of bad memories, so time dulls the good ones as well, or at least the good ones that are too painful to recollect. But life had been good, hadn't it? The sun, the warmth, the water, the children giggling as they threw sand onto their parents reminded Ruth of this.

They were whole; they were together; they were good.

But then she felt it again, in her womb — that mysterious, subterranean flutter, which was becoming more pronounced as each week passed. There was no mistaking its origins. She looked down into Chandler's eyes, crinkled with mirth, speckles of sand caught in the salt-and-pepper strands of his beard. Before the bombing, they'd been black.

She sat up, heart pounding, mouth dry.

Chandler pulled himself free from the sand and sat beside her. "Something wrong?"

Ruth turned toward her daughters, saw

their twin expressions of unadulterated joy. Her children — brought to her by genetics and divine intervention — were her life's greatest gifts. She would do anything for them, and she had proven that by staying with their father.

But what was she willing to do now that the child she carried was not his?

Chandler said again, his warm hand splayed across her back, "You sure nothing's wrong?" Ruth imagined she could feel the metal of his wedding band branding her skin. She turned to him and met his eyes. "Yes," she said. "I'm okay."

They camped out that night, on a small island encircled by the Mississippi: just the two girls and their parents, a campfire and some stars, as Sofie had requested when they'd asked what they would like to do to celebrate the beginning of summer.

As if they were a standard, summer-vacationing kind of family.

The girls — exhausted by a day soaked in sun and water — slept soundly in the tent, and Chandler and Ruth sat next to their campfire, watching the half-moon shining through the pines.

Chandler said, "I have something for you."

Ruth looked over at him skeptically but

did not speak.

He rose from the log and disappeared into the tent. It was a five-person tent, and she was suddenly grateful for the space. If she needed to, she could go toward her own side, and he could stay on his. Turning, Ruth watched Chandler duck as he exited.

"I'm sorry it's not wrapped," he said and passed her a box. A medium-size wooden box with a gilded latch. She lifted the latch and saw, inside, a set of six sealed ink pots and a silver-tipped quill. The box also held six Moleskine notebooks. "What's this for?" she asked.

"A bottle of ink and a book for each year I should've given you time to write your story."

Ruth's throat grew tight. She swallowed her tears and murmured, "Thank you."

Chandler ran a hand over her back and then drew it away, as if sensing she might spook. "I'm sorry I haven't done things like this before. You deserved better," he said.

She looked over at him. "So did you."

They were quiet for some time. Ruth trailed her fingertips over the bottles, held the inks up to the campfire light, seeing the turquoise and garnet glow like jewels.

Ruth looked over and suddenly remembered what day it was. "I'm thirty-one?"

Chandler laughed softly, conscious of the children asleep in the tent. "Yes," he said. "You're thirty-one. Happy birthday, Ruth."

"I was twenty-three when we met. Just a kid, really, though I didn't know it back then."

"For better and for worse," Chandler said, "I'm glad to have grown up with you."

Ruth touched his hand. "For better and for worse, we've carved out a life."

And even if she didn't say, *I wouldn't want to do it with anyone other than you,* she knew it was what Chandler longed to hear. But Ruth *was* grateful Chandler was back, that their girls would know their daddy. That, Lord willing, they could continue to grow and change together as they watched their darling daughters grow from girls to women who would marry and have children of their own. But despite everything, Ruth felt that stirring in her womb — that subtle reminder everything in her life could not line up perfectly again.

"Chandler," she said. "I have to tell you something."

At forty, Elam Albrecht was going back to school.

It was a small music school located in Madison, which offered classes to nontraditional students. Even so, Elam was one of the least traditional of the nontraditional students and the least classically trained. And yet, when he entered the soundproof room and rested his hands on the piano's keys, a singular, focused intensity consumed him, which, for the first time in months, allowed him to contemplate something other than Ruth.

Elam never realized, having been a boy when he'd last studied music, how physically demanding piano playing could be. He spent hours in soundproof room 2375, so that the other students began to think of it as his — the quiet but nice "Amish" man, who'd only recently learned to drive a car and wore button-down shirts tucked into blue jeans and boots; *nice* boots, but boots just the same. His silver hair had grown longer, and he could feel it now — like a living thing — as he pressed the keys and pumped the pedals, experiencing a synergy of body, mind, and spirit he'd only before experienced during his most intimate moments with Ruth. It made him euphoric, this daily practice, even while it wore him into a mind-numbing fatigue.

When he finished practicing, he wiped down the keys and the top of the piano with a small, white towel as if he were wiping down weight equipment at the gym. Walking out of the soundproof room with his backpack over his shoulder, Elam could hear his boots clicking on the polished floor. He strode past the bust of the founder and the cupola, lit from above, so that the music notes — snippets from famous compositions — glowed in front of his steps.

Elam exited the building, feeling the tepid June air soothe his hot skin. The entire campus was dark and deserted, which was when Elam liked it best. The streetlights, white and round as a spilled string of pearls, cast an opalescent glow upon the sidewalk. He entered the apartment building within walking distance of the campus and nodded at the security guard as he went to check his mail. He sorted through the junk mail and bills, throwing everything but the latter into the trash, and then he discovered the letter.

His palms grew slick when he read his old address at the top-left corner.

He had only seen a few glimpses of Ruth's handwriting, but even without seeing her name, he somehow knew it was from her.

After months without any sort of communication, except to sign and date the annulment papers and return them to the state, Elam did not want to read in front of the security guard whatever she'd written. Sweat broke out along Elam's hairline as he pushed the brass button for the fourth floor, where he lived. The letter burned in his hand, the skin of his palm damp around it, so that he lifted the letter up to his chest and smoothed it out. He unlocked his apartment, flicked on the lights, and entered the kitchen, the only room in the modest place where he felt at home. He used a steak knife from the stand to slice open the back of the envelope and pulled out the paper.

Only one piece of paper after all this time.

Elam had to swallow his disappointment, and then realized how ludicrous it was to be disappointed Ruth had written him a short letter when she was married to another man.

Dear Elam,

I hope you are well, but I suspect that these past five months have been as difficult for you as they have been for me. I still feel that I have made the right decision — for the girls' sake, if not for mine — and for the most part, I have been grateful.

I know we agreed not to be in contact, but I believe I have stumbled upon an exception to the rule. I am writing to you, Elam, because — well, I am pregnant. I've been to the doctor, and she said I should be due in the early fall. September. The same month we met.

I wasn't sure if I should write you; I wasn't sure if this news would hurt more than heal, but I wanted you to know that, despite everything, you and I will always be connected. I honestly am at a loss on how to go from here. I would like to see you again, if possible, but I understand if it's not. Just know that I will forever cherish the short time we had together, and I will forever cherish our child, created through the union of our love.

Ruth

Elam carefully refolded the letter and slipped it back into the envelope, as if that action could keep its information contained. He slid to the floor and sat there, on the cold tile of his air-conditioned apartment, and covered his face with his hands. He, the same as Ruth, had no idea how to go from here. In her womb, his daughter or son was being created, and yet he could not be a part of the child's life without wrecking the lives of Ruth's other children.

The pain, as Elam wrote and told her he

would also like to meet, was a physical ache that made him short of breath. Once he was done — one page, a manifesto of loss — the full moon gleamed through his window. He walked toward it, the new envelope in hand, and pressed his other hand to the glass, seeing the beauty of his maimed finger and understanding that, though his life was not turning out the way he'd once imagined — the way he had once hoped — he would always have his music, and in this, he would find his life again.

Ruth and Elam met at a state park located between Tomah and Madison. Ruth pulled up beside the kind of nondescript gray car that looked like a government vehicle, but Elam had already told her it was his. She got out, holding the parcel in front of her stomach. She sensed Elam's eyes on her as they neared each other, his desperate search to identify any change of her anatomy that would prove her claims.

Elam wasn't sure how he should greet her, for his cousin's wife had also once been his, and he could tell by Ruth's reluctance to meet his gaze that she felt the same as he.

"Did you . . . have a good trip?" he asked, and then hated himself for offering something so benign, but that was all he had.

She nodded gently. "You look tired."

He attempted to smile. "Well, you look wonderful," and it was true. Ruth's skin was lustrous, red-gold hair thick, the whites of her teeth and eyes gleaming with health.

"Thank you," she said. "I want to give you this."

For the first time, Elam noted the package she was holding, wrapped in brown paper and tied with a piece of twine. A small pink rose, from the bush beside his old house, was tucked down inside it.

"I'm writing a novel," she said. "The first time in years I've written anything more than a few journal entries."

Elam took the package from her since she was holding it out. "It's for me?" he asked.

Ruth looked down. "It's the novel cover. Don't look too closely. It's just a rough draft."

The sun slowly sank behind the earthen dam, gleaming off the flat water and blanching the cattail tips ringing the lake a vibrant white. Elam looked up at the sky and then over at the pavilion in front of the lake. Cattail wisps drifted along the edges and swirled like pulled cotton across the cement floor inside. He gestured, and they walked over and sat on one of the picnic benches, beside each other but not so close that their shoulders touched.

Ruth glanced at the parcel in his hands. "Well?" she said. "Aren't you going to open it?"

"You want me to right now?"

She nodded.

Elam carefully peeled away the brown paper and saw a small canvas stretched across a wooden frame. He turned it over. The vibrant red of a flooded cranberry bog contrasted by the vibrant blue of a Wisconsin sky. A man and woman in silhouette, standing before each other, the sun shining between their bodies. But they were not touching. Much like he and Ruth now.

He cleared his throat. "It's . . . beautiful."

"I'm dedicating the novel to our daughter. I actually started writing it before I knew I'd conceived, and afterward . . . it just felt right, writing the novel as a story to her."

He looked over, his eyes raw. "You think it's a girl?"

Ruth allowed herself to take his hand. "The ultrasound shows it is."

Elam choked down a sob before he replied, "I love her already."

"I know," she murmured. "I do too. She'll always be a part of us, no matter what."

"Does Chandler know?"

"Yes. I figured it wouldn't take him long

to figure out the baby's not his, since we've not —" Ruth glanced away — "resumed all aspects of marital life."

Elam's face burned. For months, he'd tried repressing the images of Ruth with Chandler, but they were there, regardless. "Was he . . . okay with the pregnancy?"

"No. Not at first," Ruth said. "But now he realizes we have to accept what happened if we're to thrive."

Elam picked the painting up and turned it over in his hands. He studied the man and woman — that loosening spiral of sunlight between their bodies. "Maybe you should let the girls think that the child's Chandler's. Let the child think she is Chandler's, too."

"Oh, Elam," Ruth said, and her voice caught on his name. "We'll make it work. I would never expect you to give up your rights as a father."

Elam couldn't look at her, couldn't look at that mound pushing against Ruth's shirt, representing the baby he would never be able to claim as his. "I think it'd be best," he said, "for our child to be raised as if she belonged rather than always believing a part of her was different." He stared at the painting, wiped the moisture from his eyes. "You see how Sofie struggles, knowing she is different. I also know what it's like growing up different. I wouldn't wish that on anyone, especially not my child."

Ruth moved down the bench toward him. "Elam," she said, "even if I agree to your wishes — and I'm not saying I do — our child will always be yours."

"I know that," he said and put an arm around Ruth. She moved even closer on the bench until their hips met, and yet they continued looking straight ahead, at the setting sun on water. "Thank you," he said. "Thank you for making my dream come true."

Ruth looked up at him and sniffed. Tears streamed from her eyes. "What dream is that?"

"That I . . . I could have a family." Elam reached down and tentatively placed a hand on Ruth's stomach. The hard swell there, signaling the life inside it, made him weep. He held his hand there for a long time. "You've made my dream come true."

Ruth rested her head on Elam's shoulder and placed her hand on his, communicating a lifetime of words she could never say. "You're welcome," she murmured, and the cattails stirred as the wind changed.

Dear Ruth,

Thank you for the letter and picture of Aria. Words are unable to convey what I felt when I looked at that perfect, tiny face for the first time. It's like that image was a piece of my soul I hadn't known was missing. I will carry it with me always and will rest in the fact that I do have a family, even if I remain grateful that you are allowing Chandler to be her father.

I hope you've recovered well. (I almost scratched that out after I wrote it, because surely there are better things to write about than your health. But I don't know how to write about such things without betraying you or Chandler. So I won't. I will keep my letter focused on your health and the beauty of our child and my deep regret that I won't get to raise her beside you, though everything inside of me yearns to do just that.)

I'm going to compose a song in Aria's honor, a melody that is as delicate as she is. Whenever I play it, I will think of her, and I will think of you, her beauti-

ful mother, who transformed my life
without realizing it.

Sincerely yours,

Elam

# CHAPTER 20

*Twenty-Two Years Later*

Aria Cathleen Neufeld's wedding was held at Driftless Valley Farm at the beginning of the cranberry season, which seemed fitting, Elam thought, since the union that had formed Aria's life took place at the beginning of the harvest season as well. Still, it was strange to drive a rental car up the lane Ruth had first driven twenty-some years ago, with two little girls in the backseat and a big white dog, Zeus, panting against the window. Elam hadn't been back to the farm since Mabel's funeral, where she was laid to rest beside her husband. But this was a happier occasion, as weddings always were. Happy occasion or not, Elam had dreaded this day since he learned his daughter was born. He knew he would be just another extended family member, sitting in the audience, rather than the father of the bride, walking his daughter down the aisle, the

447

daughter whom — like her mother — he'd only allowed himself to love and cherish from afar.

Two young Mennonite boys in matching straw hats and smiles directed Elam to park in the left side of the field. The farm had expanded since Elam sold it, but he didn't know by how much. He really had no desire to know, since that aspect of his life felt so removed from him now, as a piano teacher at Eastern Mennonite University, where he'd started out as a transfer student after his first taste of higher education in Madison. Tim was single-handedly responsible for the farm's continued success. Chandler had helped with the harvest when he could, but for the most part, he had spent the recent decades traveling to the Mennonite and Amish communities in the Driftless Region, playing country doctor, pediatrician, midwife, or counselor, depending on what need was at hand.

Elam got out of the rental car and closed the door, pocketing the key and keeping his hand in his pocket to hide how his fingers shook. The wedding was supposed to be held by the lake, but a recent cold snap had forced the wedding party into the barn: the very same barn where Ruth and Elam had wed. Surely this held significance for Ruth as well.

Laurie spotted her brother coming toward the barn, squealed, and ran across the field to meet him. "Elam!" she cried. "I didn't know if you were going to make it!"

Laughing, Elam leaned down and gave Laurie a hug. He murmured, "I wouldn't miss it."

Something in his voice made her pull back and search his face. *"Wie gehts?"*

Laurie knew this day would be hard on Elam because she was one of the few people in the world who knew Aria was his. As always, Elam couldn't keep secrets from his sister.

"I'm fine," Elam said and smiled to reassure her. The years hadn't changed Laurie much. Perhaps she looked a little tired around her eyes, and her energy level had tapered off to that of a thirty-year-old, but Elam suspected similar changes could be seen in him.

The siblings embraced again and then Laurie squeezed his hand.

"Come," she said. "I saved a seat for you."

Elam wished he could sit toward the back, but he didn't want to call more attention to himself by refusing to sit with family. So he studied the program until he had the groomsmen's names memorized, but then Ruth came in on the arm of David, Tim and Laurie's son. Elam didn't expect to feel as much as he did, watching Ruth walk down that aisle she'd once walked to him. He'd thought the years would have dulled the ache. They hadn't. The loss was as startling as that final day in the park when Elam watched his wife walk back to her car. Elam looked down, gripping the program, until Laurie nudged him. Sofie and Vi were striding down the aisle, clutching bouquets of cranberry and baby's breath.

Both were married women now, and Sofie was expecting her first child, but in Elam's mind, they would always remain those little girls in matching pajamas, who would giggle while peering down at him and Ruth from the top of the stairs. It hurt to realize this, but he knew his heart was going to experience a whole lot more pain before the day was over. He braced himself for it, like a man getting a bone set without sedation.

There was no way, really, to be prepared.

In the back, the stringed quartet transitioned to Canon in D, and Aria strode down the aisle on Chandler's arm. Aria was everything Elam had wanted her to be. She appeared confident and strong, as if she'd always known her place. *My word. She's beautiful,* Elam thought, and he could tell Aria truly *was* beautiful, even though he looked at her through the biased eyes of a father. She resembled Ruth. A younger version of Ruth. The version Elam had never gotten to meet since Ruth had already survived a few hard blows before their lives so briefly intertwined.

But Aria also had that glow, which can only come from the naive, heartwarming belief that love can conquer all. No significant pain had ever marked her young life, and though it tortured Elam not to be a part of it, he was glad to see she had lived her twenty-two years believing she was conceived because of her father's return, not because of his absence.

Aria Neufeld was not different. She belonged. Perhaps now, after all this time, Ruth understood Elam had made the right choice by staying out of their lives, and that was why she'd sent him a handwritten note along with the wedding invitation: *Come. I want you there.*

The wedding reception was held in a hotel ballroom in La Crosse. Elam ate the catered food, drank a flute of sparkling cranberry juice, and tried not to track his daughter as she moved around the room in her wedding

451

dress, as if he might never see her again. He'd taken such little part in Aria's life, he didn't feel he had the right to encroach by talking to her. Besides, Ruth was also there, in her beaded gold dress, looking as lovely as her daughter as she thanked the guests for coming. He didn't allow himself to watch her either. He was so focused on not watching either of them, he nearly spilled the flute when he glanced up and saw Aria standing by his chair.

"Cousin Elam," Aria said, and leaned down to kiss his cheek. "So glad you could come."

It cut and healed him — the innocence of such words.

Elam gave Aria an awkward side hug and shook hands with Aria's husband, Matthew, whom he'd only seen in the small photo accompanying the invitation. And if Elam's handshake was a little firmer than it needed to be — well, that was the one right Elam felt he could take.

But then it was time for the first dance, and Matthew led Aria onto the small wooden dance floor: her train tacked in the back, and her veil removed, so Elam could see her hair was the same shade as her mother's. This was followed by the father/daughter dance. Elam continued sitting at his table near the dividing panels, which partially hid him from view.

But Ruth still saw him. She came over and leaned down toward his ear. "Can you play for them?" She gestured loosely, and her wedding ring glinted. "There's a piano in the corner."

Elam made a show of looking, but he had noticed it before.

"Please, Elam," she said and placed a hand on his shoulder. "Do it for me."

Elam sat there a moment: Ruth's hand still on his shoulder, his heart pounding in his ears. Elam couldn't look at her. He just nodded and rose from his seat. Buttoning his suit jacket, he crossed the ballroom floor over to the piano. He sat on the bench, lifted the lid, and tested the baby grand's keys. It was in tune. Chandler led Aria — his daughter, Elam's daughter — onto the dance floor, and Elam struck the minor chord of the haunting melody he had composed after Aria's birth, "Letting Go Is Not Good-bye." During the refrain, Elam allowed himself to look at Ruth. She was watching him, her eyes gemstone-green with unshed tears.

*"Thank you,"* she mouthed, and he nodded.

He would do anything for her, and so it would always remain.

# PART 3

# CHAPTER 21

*March 19, 2019*

Dear Chandler,

I don't know why I keep writing you letters I know you are never going to read. Perhaps I need to write them just like I needed to write this book: to understand the past six years and see that, if I could go back, the only thing I would change is that I would have loved you better.

The truth is, knowing what I know now, going through what I have, I would have still married you. For six years, you and I were two souls joined on an ever-changing journey. It was a journey that required us to give our best selves — in the valleys and on the mountaintops — and sometimes we did this without expecting to get the best in return; sometimes we did not give our best, but

457

for the most part, we loved each other anyway.

I write this because it's a reminder. A reminder that, even though you're gone, I don't have to end here.

Be well, my love. Be at peace. I promise I'll keep your memory alive in our daughters' hearts, but it's time I reclaimed the pieces of mine.

Ruth

Ruth folded the letter to Chandler and set it on top of her manuscript. She tied a piece of twine around it all and held the bundle against her chest. *The Book of Ruth* — conceived from grief, labored with love, born for closure — was as precious to her as a child, as precious to her as Aria would have been, if she had actually existed. Ruth looked around the one-room cabin, at the table and chair where she had written her first novel over the past six months.

Six months. How had time passed so quickly? After Elam offered his cabin to Ruth as her art studio, she knew she could not leave. But Elam, wanting to protect Ruth's reputation, also could not stay. He returned to the cabin each night to sleep but never entered it during daytime hours, allowing Ruth to use it just like he had promised.

In the meantime, they had cautiously waded in the shallows of their relationship while hopeful of the depths waiting to be explored. They had taken walks after the girls were in bed. They had stayed up late, talking and cuddling in front of the fire, so Elam had had to awaken Ruth and tell her she should head upstairs to bed. They had introduced the girls to snow, to *Little House in the Big Woods* and *Farmer Boy,* and Elam was so comfortable with them now, he never stuttered as he read. Ruth now did the marketing for Driftless Valley Farm and had enrolled Sofie at the community school, where Amy Brunk, Elam's longtime admirer, treated the little girl with such kindness, Ruth nearly felt guilty she had been the one to claim Elam's heart. But not even guilt could diminish what had been restored.

Sofie and Vi were blooming. They had never lived in a community like this, where their grandma and cousins were within walking distance of their house. They had never lived in a house where their grandma let them brush her hair fifty times each or help her make cookies, which they could sample if it wouldn't spoil their supper. The girls were so daily inundated with familial love, the culmination nearly eliminated the pain from the paternal love they'd lost. Whenever Sofie's pain did awaken — often at night, when her subconscious dictated her dreams — Ruth would get up and hold her, rocking her on the bed and singing "Edelweiss" until Sofie's body had relaxed and the tears on Ruth's face had dried.

But mostly, in the past six months, there had been healing. Ruth's shattered soul was piecing itself back together, one day at a time, and with each piece, she could see how God's hand had never left her, even in her broken state. If she had known then what she knew now, her marriage to Chandler would have been different. If she had known he was not responsible for her wholeness, because he was broken as well, she wouldn't have placed expectations on him that he could never meet. God was the only one who could provide such wholeness, the only one who could piece together the broken shards of her heart. Never again would Ruth rely on a man, a husband, to provide her sense of identity and worth. If she ever married again, she would not place such unrealistic expectations upon her husband, and he must not place such expectations upon her. With this perspective, Ruth prayed marriage would look different.

Standing, she carried her book over to the fire. She knelt and stared at the flames. If only the story had been true. If only Chandler's father had urged him to go down to the hospital's safe room to sleep that night. If only he had been there, instead of dying after the first bomb fell. If only he had come back to her and the girls, giving Ruth and Chandler a second chance to understand each other's perspectives and love each other well. But *if only* hadn't happened.

Instead, Chandler had died and Ruth had obsessed over details that couldn't be changed until she realized the only way she *could* change them — the only way she could find closure — was by giving them a different ending. And if her novel had allowed her mind to drift to a union with Elam Albrecht, to envision how he would fight for them if faced with losing her — well, perhaps that hope was healing in itself.

Now that the story was birthed, Ruth found the hardest thing was she'd thought she could claim it, but the creation of the story itself was what belonged to her: all those hours she'd wept, written, painted, and sketched her broken heart whole. Now that her story was born, now that it was cradled in her loving hands, she stared at it in wonder while aware this was like the song Elam had never written for a daughter they'd never had: "Letting Go Is Not Goodbye." Letting go of the past didn't mean Ruth would forget what she and Chandler had shared. The final, rewritten chapters of their love story were the most important parts — not the keeping of the book Ruth had created. So she set the tearstained manuscript onto the logs and watched the fire's heat riffle through the pages — turning them as if looking at the letters and sketches interspersed throughout — before, in a burst of light, devouring the tome.

Six months of work gone in seconds. Six years of marriage gone just as fast.

All of creation stood witness to the facts of birth, death, and resurrection. One day, she would see Chandler again; one day, Sofie would no longer cry out in her sleep for a dad who could never come soothe her; one day, Ruth would no longer see herself solely as a widow, and perhaps — if her novel proved prophetic — she would again be someone's bride.

Ruth waited until the fire had dwindled to ash and then left the cabin and walked out by the lake. A blue heron lifted its wings, splintering the moon floating in the water, and took to the air. The farmhouse stood on the knoll, aglow with light. Ruth heard the screen door slap. Zeus came gamboling down the steps, panting toward her, his large white body standing out in the dark. He ran and pressed his wet nose against her legs, grateful for her return. And as she rubbed the dog's ears, she could see him on the porch, Elam, waiting for her return in more ways than one. Silent and steady, Elam stood at the door, his broad shoulders appearing to support the frame.

Ruth walked toward the house, toward him, thinking, *My story is just beginning.*

# A NOTE FROM THE AUTHOR

Five years ago, I took a walk in Wisconsin with my one-year-old daughter. It was below freezing, and the wind chill made it feel colder. I remember bundling her into the stroller so snugly she could barely move. Her brown eyes blinked at me between the pink hat and the fleece blanket I'd pulled up to her chin. The yard of my husband's uncle and aunt's white farmhouse, where we were staying, was studded with giant hardwood trees. The lavender sky was a backsplash for red dairy barns, and the gravel road beneath the stroller's wheels was an icy white sheet.

Once we returned to the farmhouse, I put my daughter down for a nap and thought about a woman coming to Wisconsin after losing almost everything. That's when I knew I would write a modern retelling of Ruth set in a Mennonite community. What I did not know was that two years later, my husband and I would sell our home in Tennessee and move, with two little girls by then, to a home with grid-tie solar power seven miles from that Wisconsin farm where I had the idea for *How the Light Gets In.*

A few months after we moved, my husband's uncle shared a newspaper clipping with me regarding a local cranberry farmer who only used old-fashioned equipment. Turns out, Wisconsin is the nation's leading producer of cranberries. I could picture my modern Ruth in a flooded bog, gleaning berries, just like the biblical Ruth gleaning barley in the fields.

I will forever cherish the season we spent in Wisconsin. Sometimes I can still hear the off-kilter squeak of the windmill that stood in our front yard or the sound of windows cranking open on the first warm day of spring. But by the end of our second winter, I asked my husband if we could move home to Tennessee. We had moved to Wisconsin on a two-year "try it out" plan, and I was asking to leave even before the two years were up.

My husband had poured himself into our little homestead: remodeling the 1920s farmhouse, raising and butchering chickens, putting new boards on the old dairy barn, planting three hundred pine trees and long rows of raspberries and blueberries, sowing wildflowers, and building raised garden beds. He was living his dream in Wisconsin — the place he'd started visiting when he was a teenager and would go hunting for weeks at a time — and now I was asking him to give it up. Knowing how lonely I was for our families in Tennessee, my husband put our farm on the market, and to our great surprise, it sold two weeks later.

We moved back to Tennessee and entered the hardest season of our marriage. My husband had dreamed of homesteading in Wisconsin, and now he had sacrificed that dream to bring me home. He never verbally expressed resentment, but the tension between us was palpable. Around Christmastime, I spoke with an older woman friend about our situation. Her advice was simple, and yet it changed everything: she told me I needed to put my husband at the forefront of my prayer life. Up until that point, frustration had prevented me from really praying for him, but now I began in earnest. Early in the morning, before the girls awoke, I would walk around our land and pray for our marriage. I prayed for the ability to understand the loss of my husband's dreams. And you know what? I began to understand his perspective. I began to appreciate what he had sacrificed to bring me home.

Over a year has passed since that difficult season, and I have never loved and respected my husband more. There's something about walking through hardship together that brings those rote marriage vows to life. Furthermore, I now know my husband can never be responsible for my happiness, for my wholeness; neither can I be responsible for his. We each have to pursue an intimate relationship with Jesus to experience true, lasting intimacy with each other, and this independent pursuit has drawn us more closely together than anything. My husband and I talked about this experience today when we were in our minivan, our now three little girls all piled in the back. He said, "When I gave my dreams and the desires of my heart to Jesus, I found that he became the dream and the desire of my heart."

Friends, my dream and the desire of my heart for this novel is to offer hope to marriages, especially those enduring challenging times due to the stresses of life — children, jobs, health, ministry obligations, you name it. Many of the emotions Ruth deals with in this story were in some part drawn from my actual experiences. Please know that I did not write those scenes from a place of judgment, but from a place of empathy. I want you to know that there's a community out there, wanting to press your hand and murmur, "I've been there too." So, please, don't give up hope. Your love story is not over. It is just beginning.

# DISCUSSION QUESTIONS

1. This novel asks significant questions about marriage and commitment. How do you feel about the answers Ruth comes up with? How might your choices have differed from hers?

2. Ruth and Chandler are probably a typical couple whose jobs and children cause them to move apart emotionally, even before they are physically separated. Have you experienced a similar challenge in your marriage, or have you seen this happen to people you know? What could they have done differently to prevent this estrangement?

3. Elam set aside his dreams of marriage and family because the circumstances were never right for it. Do you have dreams that have yet to be fulfilled or that you've had to set aside for a season? How

471

did Elam keep from growing bitter at having his dream deferred? What can we learn from his example?

4. Chandler is doing good, important work in the world, and yet his family suffers for it. Have you ever been in this situation? What are some ways we can discern the right priorities for our various commitments and obligations?

5. Did you enjoy learning a little about cranberry harvesting? What was particularly interesting or surprising about it?

6. Did you enjoy reading Ruth and Chandler's letters to each other in the years before this story takes place? Did they enhance the story for you, or did you find them distracting?

7. How did you react when Ruth chose between Chandler and Elam? Was it the choice you wanted her to make? Why or why not?

8. What was your reaction to the conclusion of the story? Did you find it satisfying or

frustrating? Why do you think the author chose to tell the story this way?

9. Why do you think Ruth chooses this strategy to work out her loss? What does she gain by it? Does it seem like a realistic way to process grief?

10. Good novels often present what feel like "no-win" moral dilemmas. Can you pose another way that Ruth's novel might have played out? Another way you would have preferred? Why?

11. Which characters in the book have a "happy ending"? Is that good enough for you, or do you wish the author had resolved things differently? How do you see things unfolding for the characters in the months and years ahead?

12. The author used the biblical book of Ruth as a stepping-off point for this fictional story. What similarities did you see? What are some of the differences? How do you feel about using Bible events as the basis for fiction?

# ABOUT THE AUTHOR

**Jolina Petersheim** is the critically acclaimed author of *The Alliance, The Divide, The Midwife,* and *The Outcast,* which *Library Journal* called "outstanding . . . fresh and inspirational" in a starred review and named one of the best books of 2013. That book also became an ECPA, CBA, and Amazon bestseller and was featured in *Huffington Post*'s Fall Picks, *USA Today, Publishers Weekly,* and the *Tennessean. CBA Retailers + Resources* called her second book, *The Midwife,* "an excellent read [that] will be hard to put down," and *Booklist* selected *The Alliance* as one of their Top 10 Inspirational Fiction Titles for 2016. Jolina's nonfiction writing has been featured in *Reader's Digest, Writer's Digest,* and *Today's Christian Woman.*

She and her husband share the same unique Amish and Mennonite heritage that originated in Lancaster County, Pennsylvania, but they now live in the mountains of Tennessee with their three young daughters. Jolina blogs regularly at www.jolinapeter sheim.com.